# Reprisal

# Thomas A. Knight

**ISBN-13: 978-0986843754**
**DragonWing Publishing**
**ISBN-10: 098684375X**

Credits:

Cover Design and Illustration © 2014, Claire Stratford

Editing and Proofreading By: Claire Stratford
Structural Editor: Thomas A. Knight
DragonWing Publishing

Find the author at: http://thomasaknight.com

2014-02-05

## Other books by Thomas A. Knight

**The Time Weaver Chronicles**
The Time Weaver
Legacy
*Reprisal*

**The Spell Breaker Chronicles**
The Spell Breaker (Coming in 2015)


For the latest news and updates on Thomas A. Knight,
visit:
http://thomasaknight.com

For additional works by Thomas A. Knight, visit:
http://www.amazon.com/author/thomasaknight

To my oldest daughter, Larkin.
May the fire in your heart and soul
always burn like the sun.

# Table of Contents

# Chapter 1 - The Bridge

The bridge over the Algorn Canyon was less than an hour's travel to the west. It meant salvation for Malia Corsair and the exhausted remains of the Findoor militia. Her orders to them were simple: keep running, no matter what. The horde of undead pursuing them didn't sleep. They didn't eat. They ran, and killed, and ran some more. Nearly a thousand soldiers fell to the undead force before the militia realized what was going on. Another thousand fell in the retreat. The fallen rose again, animated by dark magic, and joined the growing undead tide.

"We are almost there," Malia shouted to her troops between breaths. "Do not stop, do not look back. When you get to the bridge, just keep running, we can hold our ground on the other side."

She didn't have to look to know her orders would be followed without question.

The hill before them sloped down toward the canyon which stretched from north to south, separating the Kingdoms of Findoor and Caldoor. The bridge spanning the canyon had stood for centuries. It was one of only a few crossings that led into Caldoor. The canyon itself was a long drop into a rocky river, created in some great earthquake thousands of years ago. It was too great a distance to jump, and a fall into the canyon was certain death.

Malia glanced to her left where her father ran beside her. He was a farmer and in good shape for his age, but the days of running had been long and she could see the strain on his face. "It is not far now, father," she said with a smile.

He nodded an acknowledgment, but couldn't speak through his labored breaths.

*We need time,* Malia thought as she slowed her pace and allowed the rest of the militia to pass her.

Five hundred men remained of the valiant Findoor militia, once one of the greatest armies Galadir had ever known. Malia watched the men and women run past, their faces exhausted, and considered her options. Many times since Grian unleashed his terrible spell, Malia had seen people fall to exhaustion, only to be slain and reanimated. Her forces dwindled as she was unable to stop and help those who fell behind.

Now her meager force ran ahead of her. She stopped at the back of the lines and turned to face the oncoming undead. A number of others stopped after her, wondering what she planned.

"We need to buy some time for the remaining forces," Malia said without turning.

"General Corsair, how do we stop such a horde as this, even for an instant?" It was the voice of Ceridan, one of her closest commanders.

"I do not know, but they are mere minutes behind us. The troops are tired, we are slowing down, and at our current pace, we will not make the bridge before they catch us."

"So we fight?" Ceridan glanced toward the fleeing Findoor troops, more of which had stopped to see why their general had paused.

"We fight, and give the others a chance. We need only one to inform the Caldoor regency of the impending danger." Malia laid her hand on the black steel sword Merek had given her and drew it from its scabbard. As loud as she could, she shouted out to the few soldiers who stood by her. "We fight for Findoor. We fight for Galadir."

Despite their fatigue, the soldiers managed a battle cry in return and drew their swords.

The undead horde flooded down the hill at them, outnumbering them at least a hundred to one. Humans, Narshuks, and other races Malia had only heard of all ran toward them with blank stares and unholy strength. Some of them carried injuries they had obtained during past battles when the men and women of Findoor had battled for their lives and lost. Some were missing limbs, some had bloody gashes, and some were almost unrecognizable as anything but shambling rotting masses. They all moved forward in deadly silence, even if they had to crawl.

Malia called on the one force she could use with ease, letting the magical power of fire fill her up and directing it into her sword. The blade came to life, bursting with flames that reflected in her eyes. "Attack! Slay all that you can."

Her first swing slashed out at a group of human warriors bearing a Findoor crest on their chest plates. She spoke the words of magic as she struck them, sending waves of fire forward. Her sword cleaved through their bodies and the power flooded out, consuming them and turning them to dust.

She paused, not realizing how much power she had poured into the spell, but before she could give it much thought, there were more undead approaching. Her sword tugged at her power, almost begging to be swung again, and so she did, lashing out at the next wave of shambling undead. The second hit required no words. The power flowed through her and into the sword, flaring out far beyond her own reach in a fan of fire that consumed the undead flesh like it was dry tinder.

"By the gods," Malia said in disbelief.

The soldiers around her took notice of the second hit, but again the undead forces surged forward, leaving them little time to contemplate the phenomenon. Malia felt the pull of the sword, its thirst for power, and its desire to unleash that power on her enemies, and so she indulged it, swinging over and over at the undead. Each time she swung, the sword blazed with power, incinerating undead by the hundreds.

She paused for a moment and turned to her soldiers. "Run to the bridge. Go now, I shall hold them off."

Ceridan shook his head. "Nay, I won't leave you behind. Your father would never forgive me. Come, we will retreat together."

Malia opened her mouth to protest but stopped short when she saw a shining light in the sky to the east. It was golden and appeared to be moving toward them with great haste. "Morganath. Ceridan, it is Cedric and Morganath. They have returned." Her excitement was staunched by the approach of more undead threatening to overwhelm her small force. She swung at them again, allowing the sword to draw magical energy through her. Fans of flame shot out with every stroke, reducing undead to ashes. Malia fought with a ferocity she had never known, but watched the eastern sky as the golden dragon drew closer and banked to the north. When he dropped from the sky toward the undead horde, she called out, "Run. Flee to the west."

Her soldiers retreated without question just in time for the great gold dragon to swoop down on them. From his mouth he spewed a great stream of liquid fire that created a wall of flames, incinerating any undead in his path and stopping the advance of the army. Malia heard Cedric's gleeful cries as they passed, but didn't stop to wave. She focused on the bridge before her and ran for her life.

The bridge drew closer by the second, but Malia held back enough to ensure that every one of her remaining soldiers made it before her. When the last one had begun to cross, she slowed, stepped onto the bridge and turned to face the army that had begun its advance again. Walking backward, she watched Morganath make several more passes over the silent army. It didn't matter how many he torched, the remaining wretches continued, some of them burning as they walked. Malia was halfway across when the first of them stepped onto it with her.

A voice behind her startled her. "What are you planning?" Ceridan asked. "You're not going to take them on by yourself."

"I will slay each and every one if I have to," Malia said, her voice tainted with anger. "They have taken everything from us, and I intend to make them pay."

Ceridan's hand grasped her shoulder. "Easy, General. It's Grian we want, not those poor wretches. Stick with the plan. We will get help from Caldoor and regain our kingdom."

The undead approached fast, but Malia turned away from them anyway to face Ceridan. "Do not speak that name in my presence. He is the Defiler, the Usurper, a vile maggot in the corpse of a once great kingdom." Ceridan backed up from her tirade, trying to direct her attention to the undead approaching behind her, but she ignored him. "He has taken our homes, our people, and our kingdom, and all we can do is run. We keep running or die and become one of them." A tear ran down her left cheek as she lost control of her emotions. "I just want them to go away," she said, and turned back to face the approaching creatures. Drawing all the magical energy she could muster, she ran through the first of the undead with her sword and screamed a single word. "Incendras."

A massive stream of fire burst from her hands and the sword, spreading out and flowing down the length of the bridge. Any undead in its path were vaporized, and still it continued as the sword took over and lapped up the energy. She felt its greed as she fed it, but didn't stop. The bridge caught fire, the ancient ironwood fueling the flames, and still she continued, ignoring the frantic voice behind her. The sword felt good in her hand, and rage fueled the spell as it extended beyond the bridge and into the horde gathering on the other side. When she could take no more, she ended the spell, raised the sword into the air with the blade pointing down, and drove it into the bridge up to the hilt.

The wood exploded, starting at the sword and spreading out before her, tearing the bridge apart. Flaming chunks flew into the air and fell into the canyon as the eastern half of the bridge crumbled. Supports split and fell, the railings gave out, and the entire structure sank as only the western half remained. The only thing holding it up was stone and chains in the ground on the other side. Malia gripped the sword and used it to keep herself from falling into the canyon, but Ceridan wasn't so lucky. He slid down the surface of the bridge and fell off the end, catching one hand on a stray piece of wood. It was all that kept him from falling into the canyon below.

"Malia, help me," he shouted, and drew her out of her emotional break.

She looked down at him and realized her mistake. "Hang on, my friend." He was too far down for her to reach and she had no rope, but her magic had not failed her yet. She attempted to call on the power of air, but the magic wouldn't come. The sword in her hand surged back at her, an angry feeling, like it didn't want the power of air. She removed her hand from the sword and balanced herself without its aid and tried again. With some difficulty, she drew the required power to her and spoke the words of the levitation spell she had performed many times with ease in the presence of Merek. "Levitas seriosa metai."

The spell formed in her mind, and the magic flowed, taking hold of Ceridan and lifting him up from his precarious position. When he was level with Malia, she held out her hand, seized his, and pulled him to safety. The bridge creaked and groaned beneath them as they looked at each other. "Thanks," Ceridan said with a sigh of relief. "Now, let's get off this bridge before it collapses."

"Indeed," Malia said, taking hold of the black steel sword and pulling it free of the charred wood.

The two of them stepped up the bridge with care so as not to stress the crumbling structure. Supports gave out beneath them, and more than once they had to stop and steady each other as the remains of it listed to one side or the other as they climbed. When they were within twenty paces of the other side, several soldiers tossed ropes to them to act as safety lines in case the bridge gave out. They made it, but with only seconds to spare. There was a great rending sound as it crumpled against the side of the canyon and fell into the river below. Stones and chains were dragged down by the weight, and pulverized the remaining wood as they landed on top of it.

It was several moments before Malia was able to bring herself to look up, and when she did, the sight startled her. The undead horde that had chased them for many hundreds of miles was retreating back into Findoor.

Morganath flew to a clearing behind her and landed. The moment he touched down, Cedric slid from his back and ran toward her. Another man beat him to her though. Her father stepped up behind her and rested a hand on her shoulder. "I thought I had lost you," he said, his rugged voice trembling.

Malia turned to him and smiled. "I am okay, Father. Is everyone else well?"

He nodded and wrapped her in a warm embrace. "Don't startle an old man like that. It'll be the death of me."

She returned the hug and whispered in his ear, "You will not lose me. I have the power of Lyecha to aid me."

Father and daughter separated just as Cedric reached her. "I didn't know you could do that," Cedric said with a smile.

"Neither did I," Malia said. "It is good to see you again, and just in time. What news do you bear from the east?"

"A new council is born, but whether it is good for Galadir or not has yet to be seen. Ducain's Keep was in utter chaos when I arrived, and was only slightly better when I left after they had sorted out their leadership. Things have happened so fast – and the wizards there have grown so accustomed to being ruled – that there were few there who could take on the role required of them. I gave as much aid as I dared before returning to you."

"Some things never change. Wizards squabbling over power rather than focusing on the task at hand," Malia said. "What about Seth? Have you heard anything?" Her hand rose to the gold pendant around her neck, the symbol of Lyecha.

Cedric turned his masked face toward the ground. "Nothing."

"He must be out there. Have there been no signs at all?"

"Well, Morganath did note one thing. The wild rifts near Findoor Castle have stopped. We would have taken a closer look, but feared what foul magics might be cast at us if we got too close."

A spark of hope lit in Malia's heart at those words. "Then he must be out there still. He will return when he is able."

Ceridan approached the pair and cleared his throat to get their attention. "My apologies for the intrusion. We have company coming from the west. It looks like a full garrison of soldiers bearing the Caldoor crest."

Malia gave him a curious look and said, "Why would a garrison of soldiers be meeting us? Perhaps one of our runners made it alive?"

"I don't know," Ceridan said. "You may be right."

"Let us not make them wait then. Stay by my side and we shall walk out to meet them." Malia sheathed her sword and turned to the west, but before she moved further, she looked back at Cedric. "You as well. You're familiar with Caldoor and their customs. We could use your knowledge."

Cedric shifted from one foot to the other and coughed. "Perhaps not. I've not had many favorable run-ins with Caldoor soldiers. I'm really the solitary sort anyway. But do keep me advised. I shall wait here for you." The nervous smile on his face was all the evidence Malia needed.

"Very well. Stay with the rest of the soldiers, some of them may need healing. I shall not be long." She returned his smile and walked away with Ceridan by her side.

Many soldiers greeted her as she walked through the crowd, thanking her for getting them to safety. Malia returned the greetings, but continued to walk with purpose to the west where a large number of Caldoor soldiers approached in full battle gear and riding warhorses.

She stood in the field and removed her helmet so that she could greet the approaching commanders properly. As they closed the gap, the front line of soldiers lifted spears or nocked arrows in bows.

"General, they mean to attack us," Ceridan said, his voice alarmed.

Malia had already dropped her helmet and raised her hands in surrender. "Follow my lead, it will be fine. They may be patrolling and have mistaken us for invaders. They will stand down when they see the condition of our forces."

"I hope you're right," Ceridan said, raising his hands like Malia.

Several soldiers bearing banners broke away from the main garrison and rode ahead toward Malia and Ceridan. Within seconds the soldiers were standing before them with spears in one hand, pointed at the pair, and flags in the other. The man in the center, hidden by his armor and helmet spoke first. "By royal order of the King of Caldoor, I hereby put you under arrest on charges of mutiny, treason, and destruction of Findoor and Caldoor property. Disarm yourselves and your troops, or we will be forced to cut you down."

A wave of shock ran through Malia as the commander of the Caldoor force listed the charges against her. She was struck speechless as a torrent of emotions ran through her and took a few moments to regain her composure before she addressed the soldier. He waited with his spear poised to strike at a second's notice. "There must be some mistake," Malia said. "We are fleeing Findoor, as the throne has been usurped by a dark defiler. We have run for days with little food or water, and now seek the aid of the Caldoor army to rid our fair kingdom of the foul creatures this defiler has created."

"Ha," the commander said, his voice mocking. "Save it for the judges. I'll see you hanged for crimes against both kingdoms. I will tell you once more, disarm yourself and your invaders, or I will be forced to cut you down."

"Crimes? Invaders?" Malia said in astonishment. "I lead no more than five hundred men and women, many who are too exhausted to walk any farther, some who are injured, and you have the nerve to accuse us of invading your kingdom?"

Ceridan placed a hand on her shoulder as she reached for the hilt of her sword. "General Corsair, I recommend we stand down. We can sort this out with the King when we get to Caldoor Castle. Our people will not be served well by seeing their General slain."

Malia looked down at her hand and realized what she was doing. With a deep breath, she calmed herself. "Very well." With one smooth motion, she unbuckled the belt around her waist and removed the sword and sheath. When she handed it up to the Caldoor commander, she lowered herself to her knees. "We surrender on the condition that we receive an audience with your fair King before we are tried for any crimes we are accused of."

"Oh, not to worry, General Malia Corsair," the commander said. "Our King is most eager to meet the woman who brought down the great Kingdom of Findoor."

# Chapter 2 - Awakening

The months following the incursion on Denton, Iowa were hectic for general Neil Mathers. There was a mess to clean and cover up, a great many witnesses to silence, and a very large amount of research to be overseen. Now that the excitement was beginning to settle down, he sat in his office reading over witness reports of what had been chalked up as a very large, very expensive publicity stunt pulled off by a movie production studio. The military had even arranged for a movie studio to produce and release a movie using some of the footage acquired during the incident. The idea of using a movie to cover up the incident had come from Toby before his untimely death.

Mathers looked out his window at the parking lot where the strange portal to the other world had been opened. Since that day, most of his resources had been devoted to reproducing what the strange man in black had done, only in a controlled environment where they could turn it on and off. After the attack of the man in black, and the death of the one soldier who had been administered the serum, the Specter project was mothballed. It turned out to be much too dangerous for humans when the soldier lost control of the power he produced and incinerated himself and four other scientists in the process. Creating a controlled portal to the other world seemed a much more promising project, if his science team could figure out how to do it.

His eyes drifted back down to the reports on his desk and he tossed them aside into a large stack of other papers he would never read. Underneath the reports was a simple beige folder with the word *CLASSIFIED* written across the front of it in big red letters. Mild curiosity caused him to flip open the cover, assuming it to be the latest batch of failed test results. What he saw took him by surprise.

Inside the folder was a list of names, places and events that had been recorded by their data mining algorithms. When the incursion happened, Mathers instructed the military geek squad to set up Internet data mining models in order to capture any information that might leak about the event. In the last few weeks, the hits had dried up, and he had assumed the system would be turned off as the cover-up was completed. Instead, they continued to monitor the system, and had a fresh batch of hits involving several scanned images that had been posted to the Internet. There was a series of strange events surrounding certain people who had come into contact with these images.

The first was a man right in Denton who raved on his social networking sites about deciphering the images and being able to make things move without touching them. Another was a woman in Australia who could create water out of thin air. Many more of these events, all involving apparent *magic* were cropping up all over the world.

*Alkirk,* Mathers thought. *I need Alkirk.*

He closed the folder, picked up his phone and dialed the extension for the lab buried deep underground. "Yeah, it's Mathers, get me Hartford." After a short pause, Mathers continued. "Hartford, I have a new project for you. Perhaps the portal project could be repurposed. I need you to find Alkirk and bring him to me. No, forget opening a portal for now, just get him here. Can you do it? Good. Let me know when you have some results." He hung up the phone, sat back in his chair and smiled to himself.

5

The day Seth gave Dave McAllistar the book with the cryptic symbols in it marked a new chapter in his life. He went from being a laid back womanizing socialite to being an obsessive hermit as he worked on deciphering the pages he had scanned. Seth's disappearance and the strange events in Denton that were being covered up were even more motivation to figure out what the symbols meant. He ignored the phone, wouldn't answer the door, and even went days without sleeping. Food and water were a necessity, but he ate and drank only when he became desperate. His body became gaunt and undernourished, but he didn't care.

"I'm almost there," he told himself as he worked out the latest round of calculations. *Almost there* was relative to Dave. He had deciphered the first page, and gained the ability to perform telekinesis, which he added to his documentation online. He showcased the entire process across social networking sites, message forums, and anywhere else Dave could post the photos. The Internet became his sole lifeline to the outside world.

A computer program Dave had written worked on the more complex math for him. The symbols, Dave discovered, were a very complex language that had many layers to it. Each layer he peeled back held new secrets, and new powers. Others had discovered this as well, and a race was now going on as to who could break the code the fastest. Dave had a head start because he scanned the pages.

"If only I had the whole book. It would make this so much easier," Dave said. A message box popped up on his screen to let him know the current calculations were complete. His eyes lit up as he finished the last of his manual calculations as well. There were words this time, and lots of them. More than there should have been for five pages, but he had seen this before. One layer of the text had revealed a portion of what appeared to be a children's story. Something about two men named Krycin and Merek. Had he been a normal person, he would have given up there, but he found a code inside the code, and dug deeper into the text. Now he was three layers deep, and new words were appearing.

He tried to read what was on his screen but stopped part of the way through. Something burned inside of him, like a fire had lit in his chest. It wasn't painful, but he could feel the warmth growing as he read. When he stopped, the fire remained, and continued to grow. *Think, Dave, think,* he thought, as a sense of panic took him. He'd heard of one other person who had been researching these pages who had written about the same thing. When his posts stopped, somebody went to investigate and found a pile of ash in and around his computer chair. Nobody could prove the ash was him, but Dave was starting to think it was true.

The fire inside him grew larger and painful. He looked around his desk, searching for something that might help him and spotted a glass of water across the room. He summoned his power of telekinesis and spoke, "Incitatas." The power pulled the glass to him and he caught it in his left hand. When he gulped down the water, it did little to settle the heat in his chest, though it did bring him to his senses. "Of course, it's at the cellular level. I have to finish reading this."

He turned back to the monitor and continued reading where he left off. The pain went away, leaving only the warmth to grow and spread throughout his entire body. As he reached the end of the text, he realized he could manipulate the warmth with a thought. He raised his hands toward his office door, and spoke the last word. "Incendras."

The warmth flowed out of his body and through his hands into a ball of fire that shot forward into the closed door and exploded in a burst of flames. It consumed the entire door in seconds along with a portion of the framing around it before going out. All that remained were scorch marks and ash.

"Jesus Christ," Dave said, and laughed. "This is incredible..."

His celebration was cut short by a loud bang on his front door. It was the first time in weeks he had heard a knock at his door, though there had been many. This one was different though. It was commanding, not passive.

It occurred to him that blue and red lights were flashing outside his window. In all his excitement over his newfound power, he hadn't noticed. "Shit, the Police. What do they want?"

He ran to his bedroom to throw on some clothes and heard the bang again, more urgent this time.

"Mr. McAllistar, open up," a man with a gruff voice yelled through his door.

Dave found a shirt and a pair of pants that he was sure was at least partially clean, put them on, and ran to the door. As he ran, he tried to remember the last time he had done laundry.

When he reached the door, he unlocked his deadbolt, and opened it to find two officers standing outside his front door. "Sorry officers, you got me out of bed. Can I help you?"

The officer closest to him – Tunny, by the name embroidered into his uniform – spoke up with a funny look on his face. "Mr. McAllistar, it's 4pm."

Dave couldn't help but snicker at this. He hadn't been watching the time and couldn't remember when he had last slept. Time meant very little to him as he researched the code in the scanned images. "Right, I'm a late riser."

"Sir, we were sent out here to locate you as your family and your employer have both reported you missing. Do you mind if we have a look around inside, just to make sure everything is okay?" There was genuine concern in the officer's voice.

"Oh, I'm fine. I'm sorry to have caused so much trouble for you. I'm just feeling under the weather and would like to get back to bed."

Officer Tunny raised an eyebrow at this. "Sir, nobody has heard from you, other than online, in weeks."

Dave heaved a sigh and fidgeted with his hands. "Look, I'm fine. I've been feeling sick lately, but I'm getting better now. Tell them all not to worry about me."

"Mr. McAllistar, we really need to take a look around. So either you cooperate, or we'll bring you in on suspicion and return with a warrant. We all know you haven't shut yourself in there because of a cold, and by the smell of things, you're doing more than resting."

Dave's heart surged as he realized they must have heard the explosion he created. He looked in the mirror just inside his door and broke out in a cold sweat. The face looking back at him was unshaven and sickly looking, with sunken in eyes and jutting cheek bones. It was the face of a meth addict, and these officers thought he was running a lab in his house. *Shit, shit, shit. What do I do?*

He looked back at Officer Tunny and took a deep breath. "Look, I have no intention of going anywhere with you. There's nothing going on here. I'm just a guy who's been very sick. Just leave me alone, and nobody will get hurt." It occurred to Dave after he said it, that it was the wrong thing to say.

Tunny lifted his hand to his gun, as did his partner, and his tone changed. "Step out of the house with your hands behind your head. I'm not going to tell you twice."

Dave lifted his hands up in front of him. "Now boys," he said, backing up a step. The same warmth welled up inside of him again, the fire in his chest that would consume him alive if he didn't release it. His eyes darted from Tunny to his partner as he took another step back. "I'm warning you," Dave said. "Stay back."

Tunny drew his gun and aimed it at Dave. "Put your hands behind your head, now."

"I don't want to hurt you," Dave said as the fire grew inside of him. The word was in his head, the one that would release the energy, but he struggled against it. "Go away, leave me alone."

The pain inside him made it hard to see past his own hands. Dave's struggle to contain the fire took all his concentration. Officer Tunny stepped over the threshold with his gun drawn and screamed at him to get on the ground. Dave backed up another step and cried out against the pain that lit up every nerve in his body. His cry turned into a word that made the pain stop and brought him relief as a ball of fire escaped his hands.

It struck the officer in the chest and vaporized him on contact, leaving a smoking pile of ash blowing back toward his partner. His gun fell to the floor with a loud thud, along with his cuffs, badge, and anything else he carried that wasn't flammable.

Dave came to his senses before Tunny's partner did and looked from the ash pile in his doorway to the dumbstruck officer. Without warning, he bolted through his house, trying to run to the back door. *Get away, Dave. Get away from this.*

He knocked over tables and chairs in his panic and slammed doors behind him. When he got to the sliding doors that led to his back patio, he fumbled with the lock. He heard footsteps echoing through his house as Tunny's partner advanced and he could hear the faint sound of sirens in the distance. *Great*, Dave thought. *Backup.*

The lock clicked, he slid the door open, and launched himself into his backyard, looking around for a way out. *Sophie. Get to Sophie's place. She'll know what to do.*

His looked up into the sky and heard the officer behind him cock his gun. A quick shift from his right foot to his left saved his life as the officer fired his gun, and the bullet grazed his right ear instead of going through his head. Pain bloomed on the side of his head and blood flowed from the wound, but he was able to maintain his concentration. *Go up. It's the only place he can't follow you.*

Dave's heart pounded as he focused and spoke the word he had only used to move small objects. "Incitatas."

An unseen force lifted him up into the sky as the officer pulled the trigger a second time. The bullet pierced Dave's right foot as the ground fell away. The pain in his foot overtook the pain in his ear, and his spell faltered. He pushed the pain out of his mind and concentrated on getting away. Wind whipped past him as he flew from his house unconcerned about what direction he was going at first. After a few minutes, when the panic had settled and he was sure he had gotten away, he came to a stop floating above Denton. He looked down and saw how far up he was. "Holy crap," he said, losing concentration for a split second causing him to plummet from the sky. It was quick thinking that saved him as he regained his focus and halted his fall. "I have to get to Sophie's place."

Blood dripped from his foot in a steady stream, though his ear had stopped. He knew he had a small window to get to her place before the blood loss would take him. With that in mind, he oriented himself in the direction of her apartment building, and willed himself to move through the air.

## Chapter 3 – Long Live the King

In the Arvok Caldera, father and son lay unconscious after closing the rifts in Findoor. Serrin was the first to wake, rubbing his eyes as they regained focus. Unkempt grassy fields surrounded the pair, and Alkirk Manor stood before him, crumbling from lack of maintenance. He scanned the area for signs of life and watched a stag bound away when it saw him move. The ruins of the lab at the center of the caldera were a harsh reminder of the events from his past.

"Has it really been that long?" he asked. A groan off to his right reminded him that Seth was there. He looked down at his son and gasped. Burns covered his body from temporal stress and magical overexertion. Serrin focused his mind and called on the healing power of water. Energy flowed through him and into Seth, healing his wounds. The red marks on his skin faded and his cuts and bruises disappeared. Despite this, his son didn't wake.

"Let's get you in the house at least." With a thought, he called on the power of air to lift Seth up and guided him toward the manor.

The front door had long ago rotted off its hinges and the inside was weathered and dusty. Serrin looked for tracks or footprints in the dust to see if the house had been used at all, but there were none. He pulled Seth along with him as he stepped inside, and looked into the parlor. The couch that once rested against the wall was now rotted and useless. He gave up on that idea and decided to check the upstairs for a bed that might be usable. "This house used to be so grand. I once dreamed of bringing you here, Seth, and your mother as well. We could have lived here, happily, as a family. I wish things could have been different between us."

There was less dust in the second floor hallway. *There's hope still,* he thought with a sigh of relief. A few steps brought him to a room that would have been Seth's, had he been born there. The room was in almost the same shape as when Serrin closed the door so many years ago. The decor was simple, with neutral colors on the walls and a wood floor that creaked as he guided Seth into the room. It had been built as a nursery with a child-sized bed, a dresser, and a small table, as well as a rocking chair that Serrin had built with his own hands as a gift for Catrina. One of the things he lost when his lab was destroyed was his shop, where he spent his spare time building small pieces of furniture like that for locals. A stale smell hung in the air, but nothing overpowering, and when he opened the window, the light breeze cleared it out right away. He found some blankets in a closet, laid them out on the floor, and moved the pillow from the bed. Serrin then pulled Seth over the blankets and lowered him down until he was resting with his head on the pillow.

"Rest now, my son. May Lyecha be with you." He walked out of the room, closing the door behind him. Now that Seth was taken care of, he set about cleaning up the house, starting with the front door. He took some old rusted tools from where he left them in the back room, removed the broken door, and used one of the interior doors to replace it. Once it was working again, he set about sweeping and dusting and making it feel a little less abandoned.

After several hours of work, Serrin heard footsteps coming down the stairs. He ran to the hallway, nearly tripping over his broom in the process, to greet his son with a smile. Seth stomped down the stairs with eyes only half open, but smiled back at Serrin as he descended toward him.

"It took me a few minutes to remember where I was," Seth said. "Did you bring me inside?"

"I did. Lucky for us, your room was nearly untouched by dust or the years of abandonment. I'm amazed actually, as the rest of the house is a disaster."

"It's been a hundred years since anyone has been here," Seth said. "It's strange to think that I was here only a day ago by my time."

"Think you're up for a bit of a walk? I'm starved, and in my time, there was a town just to the south of here. There are no supplies worthy of eating left in the house."

"Yeah, I think I can walk. I'm still tired, but a good meal will do me well. We can't waste too much time though. Findoor is still in some kind of trouble. Those things that Gladius and Tyriel fought, they looked like zombies or something."

"They were bodies that have been defiled through reanimation. But these are not like the zombies you see in Earth movies. They don't eat, they don't sleep. They are not driven by need or want. They are foul creatures, twisted remnants that serve only the wizard who raised them. If you cut their heads off, they will continue to advance, as they are driven by magic and magic alone, and must be destroyed entirely, or have the magic unmade."

"They sound delightful," Seth said with a smirk. "Let's go then."

The pair left the manor and walked south until they hit a small stream, then followed the stream for an hour before they reached a very small hamlet. There were only a few shops and a single road leading in and out of the town. It was mid-afternoon and most of the people in the town were still hard at work, but a few were in the tavern eating. Serrin smiled as he looked around. "Just as I remember it. Your mother and I used to come here, and my father before me. In fact, there are likely still people here who would remember the Alkirk name, even a hundred years later."

"Lets hope so," Seth said. "Because the last time I checked, we didn't have any money."

Serrin stopped and patted his pocket, making a jingling sound. "Do you think I would walk all this way with you for nothing? Come, we'll get a good meal here."

He led the way into the tavern where a few patrons were eating meager dinners and drinking ale that looked so watered down it might as well have been water. Nobody looked up or said a word. It smelled of old wood, long dried spirits, and food that might have satisfied a dog. Serrin approached the bar, sat down at a stool, and invited Seth to do the same. An old overweight barkeep walked up to them and asked, "What'll it be, folks?"

"Just a hot meal and a drink before we head down the road," Serrin said.

"That'll be two silver," the barkeep said.

"Two silver? Have prices really gone up that much?" Serrin asked.

"Each. An' if ya don't like it, there's another town a day's travel down the road who'll charge ya double. Food's hard to come by since trade stopped from Findoor. Been weeks since we seen anything from them, so we gotta be careful with what we got."

Serrin nodded and placed four silver coins on the counter. "I hadn't realized things had gotten so bad."

"Bad? Don't know if they're bad. Ain't heard nothin' from that direction. Anyone who gone, don't come back. Findoor's a lost cause, far as I know." The barkeep shrugged and walked to the kitchen to get their meals.

Seth leaned toward Serrin and said, "Things are worse than I thought. The kingdom should be under Malia's control, not overrun with corpses. We need to go there as soon as we can and find out what's going on."

"Agreed. We must be careful, though. If there are undead walking the fields outside Findoor Castle, then they may be under siege, which would explain the trade lines being cut off."

Seth was going to say more, but the barkeep returned with their orders. The plates he set before them were only half filled, as were the drinks. Both men looked down at the dishes, and then back up at the barkeep, who said, "What?"

"Nothing at all, my friend," Serrin said. "I thank you."

The barkeep was about to walk away when he hesitated, then turned to face them again. "Where you fellas from anyway? Ain't never seen you round here before."

Serrin looked up and spoke without thinking. "Alkirk manor, about an hour and a half north of here."

"I know where it is," the barkeep said. "As does everyone else here. Place is famous. Haunted it is. If you just got there, I recommend ya don't go back." He leaned over the counter, getting as close to Serrin and Seth as he could without landing in their food. There was a hint of alcohol on his breath, but his words weren't slurred and he walked steady enough that Serrin doubted he was drunk. With a hushed voice, the barkeep continued. "Legend says the ghost of Krycin himself haunts the place, always looking for his fair bride who was taken from him during the Lyecian war."

Seth sat bolt upright and scoffed. "That's ridiculous..."

Serrin kicked him in the shin and smiled at the barkeep. "What my friend means is, it's ridiculous that you all would remember the Lyecian war so clearly. It was so long ago. What makes you think the old manor is haunted?"

"There been kids up there, at night. An' they be sayin' that there are some eerie lights and sounds comin' from the manor an' the old lab where Krycin did his research."

"I thank you for the warning. When we finish here, we shall head off down the road and be of no further trouble to you," Serrin said, his tone pleasant and genuine.

The barkeep nodded and grunted an approval, then went back to doing nothing behind the bar while they finished their meals. They headed out of the tavern and walked down the road some before Serrin came to a halt and turned to face Seth.

"Understand this," Serrin said. "You are *not* Krycin anymore, and you never can be again. This whole time travel business, it's dangerous and unnatural. I don't know how or when you gained this power, or why you felt it wise to go back to begin with, but you've already seen the kind of damage you can cause by doing so. It can't happen again, and we can never speak of it again. You are Seth, I am Serrin, and unless there is good reason to divulge it, we are *not* Lyecian. Even a hundred years ago, Lyecians were not always met with the kind of acceptance we get from Findoor or Ducain's Keep. In this time, where Lyecians are gone from the world, we may be met with outright hostility, and we don't need any enemies. Not now."

Seth took a step back, his face holding an expression of shock. "Understood," he said, and looked down at the ground. "You sound just like I remember you when you used to scold me. I was only five, but I remember it now, as clear as if it were yesterday. Let's get to Findoor, and like you said, be cautious about it. When I left, we had won the war against Gladius's simulacrum, but I don't know what happened after that."

"We'll travel another hour down this road just to be sure we aren't being watched, and then teleport the rest of the way."

When they felt they were a safe distance from the town, they stopped again and looked at each other. "Ready?" Seth asked.

"As I'll ever be," Serrin said.

"Let's go then."

Serrin focused on his destination, blinked out of existence, and reappeared on the fields before Findoor Castle. Seth appeared before him seconds later. It was earlier in the day there by a few hours, but where they would have heard the sounds of people from Findoor city, birds, insects and maybe even other animals, there was silence. The field was clear, though it was obvious that a battle had been waged there. The stone wall that had been raised in front of the castle was gone, with little more than a trace to show for it, but the most disturbing sight they saw was the banner being flown from the highest spire of the castle.

"Gladius's banner," Serrin said, pointing to the black flag with a silver lily and a snake wrapped around its stem.

"Let's go," Seth said. "Malia, Cedric and the others must be in some kind of trouble."

Seth led the way toward the front gate of the castle. The giant wood doors were open as they would normally be midday, but no traffic flowed in or out of the castle the way it used to. Still, there were people inside, all of who appeared to be working. "Be careful," Serrin said. "Something isn't right here."

They continued walking through the gates unquestioned. The people they passed ignored them, going about their work in a quiet, determined rush. Very few would even lift their gaze to meet Serrin's, and those who did shifted it back to their work just as fast. The Silver Steed, the old tavern that was always the center of citizen activity, was empty and quiet. No music or laughing patrons, no jovial talk or stories being told or hunters boasting about their most recent kill. "It's like a ghost town," Seth said to Serrin. "Except all the ghosts are here, still working."

The only sounds they heard were from work, and a few hushed voices of those who had no choice but to talk to their fellow citizens. "They're scared of something," Serrin said. "Findoor has never been a kingdom ruled by fear. Something is terribly wrong here."

When the pair reached the castle, Seth stopped in his tracks and gasped. Standing to either side of the main door heading into the castle proper were soldiers who looked like corpses. Their gray flesh appeared dried and pulled back from their teeth., and their empty eye sockets stared out at nothing. Expressionless corpses who forgot to fall over when their time was up. Serrin urged him forward. "Don't stop, and don't look at them. Speak no ill of the dead or defiled."

They passed through the doors unquestioned once again and walked straight to the stairs that would lead them to the throne room. As they walked through the castle they saw more of the gray-skinned wretches lurching about. Most of them were guards, but some looked like former runners, and others were dressed like councilors of the King's Court.

Seth stopped outside of the throne room and Serrin turned to face him. "When I left, the King had committed suicide, and Malia was to take the King's Trials to become the new Queen at Merek's suggestion," Seth said. "I don't know who we might find in there, as I thought the war was won."

"Whoever is in there, they wield dark magic. Very dark. We must use caution in dealing with them."

"Agreed," Seth said, and turned toward the door.

He led the way with Serrin following close behind him, and pushed the doors of the throne room open. It was almost identical to the last time Serrin had seen it, with banners and tapestries, and a lush red carpet leading to the throne set up on a platform. The only difference was a large silver circle traced into the floor. It was about fifty paces in diameter and centered on the throne where there was a figure cloaked in black with a deep hood pulled over his head. To either side of him were more of the gray-skinned corpses that populated the castle. Two more stood to either side of the doors, and closed them once Seth and Serrin were inside. The rest of the occupants of the room were very much alive. It appeared as though whoever sat on the throne had kept most of the King's council intact. Serrin looked at their faces, but they kept their eyes down and remained silent.

Seth approached the throne and spoke up in a clear, loud voice. "Who are you, and what are you doing on the Findoor throne?"

The dark figure lifted his head and laughed. Serrin didn't recognize the man, and guessed that Seth didn't either, as a look of confusion washed over his face. The man on the throne had short black hair and was clean-shaven. Serrin thought he looked a little like Garick Trill from his time.

"How long I have waited for this. How many times I tried to capture you, and here you come, walking right into my clutches," the man said. "The last Time Weaver, here in the King's Court once more. Come now, everyone. Let us give him the warm welcome he deserves."

The court erupted in cheers and applause from all the councilors in the room. Even the corpses moaned in approval until the man on the throne raised his hand. Then the room fell silent once more and everyone went back to staring at the floor.

Serrin was at a loss for words, but neither he nor Seth got a chance to speak before the man started speaking again. "Pardon my manners. We've not formally met," the man said, standing up from the throne and taking a step down off the platform. He was tall, had a moderate build, and carried himself well. "My name is Grian Trill, but you can both refer to me as 'Your Highness'."

"You bastard," Seth said, approaching Grian. "What have you done with Malia?"

Serrin tried to hold Seth back, but wasn't fast enough. He watched as Seth stepped inside the silver circle on the floor.

"The little blonde soldier you mean?" Grian said with a sneer. "If she's not dead, then she's rotting in a dungeon in Caldoor somewhere. You, on the other hand, are about to meet your goddess." A black flame erupted from Grian's hand as he spoke magical words of power. "Vimvitas Mortai."

He moved faster than Serrin expected him to, closing the gap between himself and Seth in the blink of an eye. Serrin summoned the power of fire to him in a focused blast and unleashed it at Grian, but watched in shock as the flames struck an invisible barrier created by the silver circle and dissipated around it.

Grian's hand plunged into Seth's chest without causing a wound, and Serrin thought for sure he was done for, but Grian screamed with pain and rage and ripped his hand from Seth's chest as fast as he plunged it in. Seth stood silent for a second, but didn't fall.

"You can't have that," Seth said. "You can't take it from me, it must be willingly given. Now it's my turn."

Seth held up his hands and blasted Grian with a power Serrin had never seen before. A column of flames combined with lightning and white holy light. The blast struck Grian and burnt away his robes to reveal full body armor beneath. The armor was black, with tiny filaments of every color worked through it. Serrin couldn't tell what the armor was made from, but it wasn't steel, or anything he'd ever seen. The closest thing he could come up with was plastic from Earth. The armor protected him from Seth's magic, even with his robes gone. When Seth ended his spell, Grian stood firm and smiled back at him.

"It would seem we are at an impasse," he said, "but never fear, you've only seen the edge of the tide. I will make you burn for what you've cost me. I'll make you beg for death, and you will give up what you have to me. If not for yourself, then for your little princess and her jester, for I will make them pay as well. I'll peel their flesh from their bones, bit by bit, and make you watch, and when I'm done, I'll put them back together and enslave them. They'll be my personal servants for all eternity."

Serrin tried to call Seth back, to warn him not to continue the confrontation, but he was too late. Seth cried out and unleashed another powerful magical assault on Grian which was deflected by his armor, and then Grian launched one of his own. A black mass flew from his hands and struck Seth in the chest. It came alive and wrapped around him, searing his flesh and reaching for the ground to bind him there. "Get away, Seth. Teleport," Serrin shouted, getting ready to do the same himself.

"I can't," Seth said through cries of pain. Serrin could see the strain on his face. He was using all his power to heal the wounds the black ooze was causing and couldn't free himself.

Serrin stepped forward into the circle and fired two blasts. One fire toward the mass wrapped around Seth, and the other that created a dome of solid ice around Grian. The dome froze and held Grian in place while Serrin focused on freeing Seth. By the time the ooze was gone, Grian was already breaking through the ice. "We have to go, he's far too powerful, even for us," Serrin said.

He focused on teleporting away, but something blocked him. The look on Seth's face told him he was having the same problem. "The circle," Seth said. "Get outside the circle!"

Both men ran toward the edge when something grabbed them from behind. Grian was still busy with the prison of ice, but the two wights that had stood to either side of Grian now seized them from behind. Their grip was like ice on Serrin's flesh, drawing all warmth from it and turning it gray like theirs. He launched flames at the one holding Seth and freed him. "Go, Seth. Go and get help from the council."

Seth landed on the floor in a heap outside the circle as the wights dragged Serrin back toward Grian. The remaining wights in the room came to life and approached Seth. Serrin could see that he didn't want to leave him behind, but shouted anyway. "Go!"

Just as three wights were about to grab hold of him, Seth disappeared, leaving an empty space for the surrounding air to fill.

# Chapter 4 - A New Council

Undead hordes chased Gladius and Tyriel all the way to the eastern border of Findoor. Once the pair crossed the border, the army retreated back into the kingdom. Tyriel watched and caught his breath. "What an odd behavior for an army," he said, wiping sweat from his forehead.

"I don't find it odd at all," Gladius said. "Whoever is controlling that army is trying to keep up the appearance of a functioning kingdom. They don't want to reveal to the outside world what is really going on. I don't know who's on the throne in Findoor right now, but whoever it is, they are either extremely powerful, or have extremely powerful friends."

"We may find some answers at Ducain's then. Let's make haste; Serrin and Seth are likely waiting for us already."

The two men set out on the road to Ducain's and found it to be easy travel so long as they stayed on the roads. The stretch that went from the Findoor border to the first fork was quiet. Once they passed the first southern fork, they passed the occasional caravan, but when questioned, they found none heading toward Findoor.

"If it were safe to use rifts, we could be there in minutes," Gladius said early one morning as they packed up their camp. They had stopped in a small town and traded services for supplies to keep them going until they reached Ducain's Keep. After performing several hours of healing services, they had more than enough gold to get them there.

"I suspect it will never be safe to use rift travel again," Tyriel said. "Seth and Serrin have repaired the damage, but the barrier that holds this universe together is like a blanket of scraps sewn together with a single thread. Break that thread, and the whole thing could come apart."

Gladius was about to say something in response but stopped, stared into the distance, and said, "Something is coming, should we take cover?"

Tyriel followed his gaze and spotted a golden figure gliding through the air. It was moving at a tremendous pace, but he recognized it right away. "It's a golden dragon. Could it be Morganath?"

The dragon moved with such speed that by the time Tyriel finished his question, it was directly above them and passing by. "I don't think there are any other gold dragons left," Gladius said. "A hundred years ago, dragons were sparse, and it was thought that Morganath was the last then."

"Can you fly up and get his attention?" Tyriel asked.

"Sadly, no," Gladius said. "Krycin robbed me of all but my first and true element when he defeated me."

"Seth. His name is Seth. Nobody in this time can know who you or Seth truly are. In fact, you should decide on a false name. If the wizards of Ducain's Keep discover your true identity, you will be put to death without a trial."

Gladius looked down and said, "You're right."

Both men watched the gold dragon fly off into the distance, toward Findoor. Once it was out of sight, Gladius looked at Tyriel and said, "Andran Riverson. That's what I shall be called."

"Very well, Andran. Let us go and be quick about it."

They finished packing up their things and set out on the road again toward Ducain's Keep. Their pace increased once Gladius agreed to use his magic to enhance their endurance and speed. They covered the distance to Ducain's Keep in half the time it would normally take. Looking down from the top of the mountains into the valley, they could see the Keep was in disarray. Several large groups of wizards had formed and were keeping their distance from each other. One of the corner towers had been knocked down in what looked like some kind of explosion, and the front gates of the keep were unguarded.

"What's going on here," Gladius asked. "It's like the council has been dissolved. They would never stand for this kind of segregation."

Tyriel started walking down toward the keep. "Let's go find out, shall we?"

The path leading down from the mountains was well-traveled and easy to navigate. Steep spots had stairs carved into the stone, and sometimes a chain that could be used to steady themselves. In most places it was just a smooth dusty path. They arrived at the gates in minutes and walked in, heading straight for the front doors of the keep. There were other wizards around, but Gladius and Tyriel looked like any other black and blue robed wizard, and so they passed through the grounds without question. Inside the keep was no less chaotic, with various arguments going on, most about who was going to lead who.

Gladius spoke as loud as he dared as they walked toward the council chamber. "Something has happened to the council. That's all I can make out."

"They've been slain. There is no head to this beast right now. I can hear some who are talking about possible leadership, but nothing is solidified. The last time this happened, my brother was the only one left. It appears that the destruction of the council was much more thorough this time."

Gladius came to a stop before the door to the council chamber. "What can we do? How can we help? Have Serrin and Seth not made it here?"

"If they had, they would have met us at the front gates I suspect," Tyriel said. "We're on our own, and I'm not much help as my skills with magic are limited."

"Shall we see what they've come up with?" Gladius asked, but didn't wait for an answer before he knocked.

They waited a few minutes in silence, but no answer came and no sound could be heard inside the chamber. "Is it empty?" Tyriel asked.

"Nay, the chamber is designed to keep their discussions silent from prying ears. The enchantments on this room date back to the construction of the keep, and are considered to be some of the most complex magic ever worked. Wizards have tried to break through them. Some have perished as a result. Others have gone mad. Only an official council member can open these doors from the outside." Gladius knocked again and waited.

After a few more minutes, the door opened and a slim young woman with long brown hair stepped out. Tyriel could hear arguments going on inside the room but there was so much chaos, he couldn't make out what they were arguing about.

The woman was shorter than both men by at least a hand and was slight, but her features were attractive, with almond shaped eyes and dark tanned skin. Tyriel noted that her features meant she was likely from Astara to the south. She wore green robes, marking her as a disciple of Torenna, but kept her hood down like Gladius and Tyriel. "Is there a reason you insist on interrupting this very important meeting of the Wizard High Council?" she asked.

Her accent confirmed her Astaran heritage. Gladius spoke up first and captured her attention. "My apologies for the disturbance. We come with very important news and are seeking information ourselves." Tyriel could almost feel the charisma in Gladius's voice as he spoke. "We were hoping we could offer the council a trade."

"I've not seen you two around here before. I know, because I would remember your face," she said, referring to Gladius's scarred face. "Identify yourself."

"My name is Andran Riverson," Gladius said, "and this is my good friend Tyriel. We've traveled from Findoor seeking aid."

The girl's eyes grew wide at the mention of Findoor. "You came out alive? We've not heard from Findoor in weeks. Not since the Dark Lord marched on Findoor. Do you bring news from the west?"

"There's the thing, really. We're trying to figure out what's happened to Findoor ourselves," Gladius said. "I didn't catch your name."

"Nadya Hamal, green council wizard. Perhaps we can help each other understand what has happened," she said.

"We have little to offer," Tyriel said, finally speaking up, "but we shall tell you what we know."

"Very well," Nadya said. "We will see you."

They all entered the council chamber together. Nadya took her seat in the green chair, and Tyriel and Gladius stepped into the circle in the center of the room.

"What is the meaning of this?" the black robed wizard said, standing up and glaring at Nadya.

"Sit down, Trysk," Nadya said. "Andran and Tyriel have come from Findoor. They have news they would share."

Trysk turned a suspicious gaze from Nadya, to Gladius, and then sat down.

Tyriel turned in a circle and measured up each member of the council. "I apologize for the intrusion. We have traveled long and hard from Findoor to seek information and help in understanding what has happened."

"As of now, we don't fully understand what is happening in Findoor," Nadya said. "The dead walk, that much we know. Months ago, the Wizard High Council approached a rogue wizard, Grian, who had amassed an army of Narshuks in the Badlands. This wizard singlehandedly defeated the entire council, and then led his army to conquer Findoor. At the same time, a Lyecian was discovered by the Findoor Arch-Magus and was pursued by both Merek and Grian. Once the Narshuk army reached the Losteron Plains, everything got hazy. Reports stopped flowing. We received information that the King had taken his own life, and vague reports that the Dark Lord himself had returned. It was said that the Lyecian, Seth Alkirk, challenged the Dark Lord, defeated him, and then disappeared. After that, we know nothing."

Tyriel listened close to all she had to say. When she finished, he spoke up. "We have been to Findoor Castle, though not inside. A great spell has been unleashed on Findoor, waking the dead and turning them against any and all intruders into the land. For the moment, they are staying within the borders of Findoor. For how long, I don't know."

"We are supposed to meet some friends here," Gladius said. "The Lyecian, Seth, and another. We expected that they would be here by now, but obviously they haven't made it yet. On our way here, we saw a gold dragon leaving for the west. Was that Morganath?"

"It was," Nadya said. "His rider was also looking for Seth, though he wouldn't give us information beyond that."

The room fell silent for a moment as each wizard, along with Tyriel, gave the situation some thought. The white wizard, Attowen, looked like he was about to speak when a rush of air burst from the center of the room between Tyriel and Gladius. A figure appeared there. A man wearing plain pants, a white tunic and simple leather boots appeared and collapsed to the ground. Tyriel leaped back and swung his scythe out from behind his back, ready to strike in the blink of an eye. When he focused on who was on the platform with him, he breathed a sigh of relief. "Seth, you're alive. Where is Serrin?"

Seth rested on the platform and caught his breath. When he could speak, he looked around at the council with a confused look on his face. Tyriel could see that Seth was trying to make sense of the situation. He put his scythe away, knelt down next to Seth and placed a hand on his back. "Easy, my friend. There is a new council. Tell us what you've seen."

"Grian," Seth said. "Grian has taken Findoor. Findoor is lost." His eyes were wild and lit up with something Tyriel had never seen there before. "He has Serrin. He has my father."

## Chapter 5 - Run and Hide

Sophie placed her hand on the knob of her apartment door and was about to leave when she heard a sound on the balcony. It sounded like somebody dropped a large sack of potatoes on the small concrete platform outside her sliding door. She turned around, but sheer white curtains covering the glass doors stopped her from seeing any kind of details. What she did see was a dark heap on the floor outside that made her heart jump into her throat. A shiver ran through her as the heap sat up. It had a head that it turned back and forth looking around, getting its bearings. She froze, unable to turn the door knob that would get her away from this potential intruder.

The figure outside went from sitting to standing, but wavered a bit, like it was having trouble keeping its balance, then it turned and knocked on the door.

The sharp sound of the figure's knuckles on the glass cut through the room and made Sophie hold her breath. She looked toward the kitchen to see if there was anything she could use as a weapon.

A second knock came, this one more urgent than the first. The figure outside the door wavered and listed to the left like it was going to fall over, but caught itself. She watched as she crept toward the kitchen to get her large chef's knife from the knife block.

There was a muffled voice coming from outside that sounded familiar to her. She listened and as it called again, she heard it yell. "Sophie."

Her heart leapt a second time and pounded in her ears, making it hard to hear. She forgot about the knife she was going for and walked to the kitchen door to listen. The voice called a second time as the figure pounded the glass, "Sophie!"

*Dave?* She thought. After Seth disappeared, Dave had spent a lot of time with her and they became good friends, but she hadn't seen or heard from him in weeks. Every effort she made to contact him had gone unanswered, so she had assumed he didn't want anything to do with her anymore, though she couldn't figure out what she did to deserve that kind of treatment. Now he was on her balcony, though he looked like he was in rough shape. *How did he get on my balcony?*

She took a step toward the door and watched as he fell to his knees. "Help me, please," he cried in a weak voice and put a hand on her window to keep himself from falling over.

*I must be dreaming or something,* she thought as she took another step forward. She placed her hands on the railing that separated her dining room from her living room. There was a step down and the balcony was on the other side. When she was sure it was actually Dave outside her door, she walked over to the opening in the railing, stepped down into her living room and crossed the room. Dave was still wavering outside her door when she unlocked it and slid it open.

"Oh my god, Dave. What's happened to you?"

His hair was scruffy and long and his face unshaven. He had dark circles under his eyes and his former, muscular build was depleted to almost dangerous levels. She reached down and offered him a hand and said, "Where have you been? And how did you get on my..."

Her question was cut off by the sight of blood on the side of his head and on her balcony. Dave tried to say something, but she stopped him. "Oh goodness, you're hurt. Come in here, can you walk?" She helped him up the best she could and got him into the apartment. He was out of breath, looked like he hadn't slept in days, and was bleeding from his foot. The wound on his head looked like it had clotted. She got him to her couch and lowered him into a reclined position. "Sit there and rest. I'll be right back with the first aid kit."

Sophie closed and locked her balcony door, ran to the kitchen and filled a large bowl with some warm water, and grabbed a clean cloth and her first aid kit from her bathroom. When she got back to Dave, he looked like he had passed out, but when she approached him, he lifted his head and opened his eyes. He tried to say something, but Sophie hushed him again. "Don't speak. We'll talk in a bit. Let me clean you up first."

She wet the cloth and wiped the dried blood from his head first. The cut was on his ear and wasn't deep, but it had bled a lot. Once that was cleaned up, she looked down at his foot, which had almost stopped bleeding. She cleaned blood from it the best she could and apologized each time Dave winced from the pain. There was a perfect dime-sized hole going from the top of his foot through to the bottom. "This looks like a bullet wound, Dave. We need to get you to a hospital."

Dave's eyes lit up in panic and he shook his head. "No, no hospitals. Just patch me up the best you can."

"I'll try, but this kit isn't really equipped to handle a wound like this." She took the water into the kitchen, dumped it out and ran fresh water, then returned to Dave. After another round of cleaning she opened the first aid kit and took out a small white bottle. "I need to disinfect it, Dave. This is gonna hurt, a lot."

He nodded and leaned his head back on her couch, bracing for the inevitable pain. She opened the bottle of alcohol and placed a towel under his foot to catch the run-off, and then poured the alcohol over his wound. He held still, but grunted and clutched the pillows on her couch to control himself. At one point she thought he might cry out, but he managed to stifle it. When she finished and the last of the alcohol ran off, Dave breathed a sigh of relief. She took out several clean gauze pads and a bandage she could wrap his foot in. When she finished wrapping the foot the best she could, it looked like nothing more than a sports injury, though the bleeding had started again a little bit.

There was a long moment of silence as she looked him over and he watched her, and then she got up, cleaned up the mess and came back to sit beside him on the couch.

"So let's start at the beginning. Where the hell have you been? Everyone has been worried sick about you, including me. I thought I'd done something wrong. You haven't been answering your phone or your door. You stopped going to work. What's up with that?" She wasn't angry. Her tone was concerned and she could tell he understood that.

"I'm sorry, Sophie. I've been researching something big and kind of got caught up in it."

"Research? That's it? You've been missing for weeks, and now you come to me looking like you've been a prisoner in a war camp, and all you can say is you're researching something? Give me some credit, Dave. Stop fucking around and tell me what's going on."

His demeanor changed with that, from too exhausted to even lift his head, to wide-eyed and alert. He sat up and looked her in the eye, and it almost scared her how he changed so suddenly. "Do you remember when Seth disappeared?"

"Of course I do. We were supposed to go out dancing that night. That was a long time ago. I remember it was the same day as that publicity stunt was going on. What does this have to do with Seth?"

Dave scoffed, which turned into a fit of coughing. When he recovered, he looked up at her with a darkness in his eyes. "Everything," he said. "This has everything to do with Seth. He had a book, something his father left him. The day he disappeared, he brought it to me. Said it was the first time he had ever been able to get it open. It had some kind of lock on it. The pages were covered with these weird glyphs, and I figured it was just some ancient language that I could get one of my buddies online to figure out for me. I scanned some pages and posted them online. But here's where things get really weird."

Dave paused while Sophie shifted so she could face Dave head on. When she was comfortable again, she said, "Go on."

"Nobody, not even the top cryptographers and linguists in the world had ever seen anything like it before. So I started working on it, along with a bunch of other people. We tried to decipher the code, and I succeeded, at least partially."

"Good for you," Sophie said. "But that doesn't explain what happened to you. How did you get shot? And how the hell did you get on my balcony?"

"Well, that's the really interesting part of this story. Turns out the language on those pages is not a single cipher, but many, all in some strange multi-dimensional symbolic script. The first layer was just a bunch of kid's stories, and I think that was there to keep people from discovering the truth. The layers after that, at first looked like gibberish. But the more I studied them, the more they made sense. It's magic, Sophie. Real magic." She could see Dave was getting excited at the prospect, but she still wanted to know the rest, so she raised her eyebrows and motioned with her hand for him to keep talking. "Right. I found two powers in that book that I could understand. One lets me move things without touching them. I found that one first, and have learned how to control it fairly well. The second is newer to me, and harder to control. It creates balls of fire that explode, and is very destructive. I hadn't had time to learn how to better control that one when the police came to my door. They were looking for me based on a missing persons report, and I guess I look pretty crappy, because they thought I was a user. They thought I was running a meth lab in my house. Things got hairy, I got upset, and next thing I know, there's fire shooting from my hands and the cop in front of me is vaporized. I ran, and flew, and landed here on your balcony because you were the first person I thought of that I could trust."

Dave was shaking now, so Sophie put her hand on his and spoke in a soothing tone. "I don't know what's going on with you, but this stuff sounds crazy. I'm sure you didn't vaporize a cop. Let's have some dinner, get a good night's sleep, and figure out what to do in the morning. Hopefully that foot of yours doesn't get infected or you could be in trouble."

"Maybe you're right. Maybe I've just been cooped up in my house for too long," Dave said with a smile.

"Right. Let me finish cleaning you up and then I'll make you something good and healthy. You look like you could use some good home cooking, and I've got just the thing." She smiled at him as she got up. "Wait there, and I'll be right back for you."

She got up without waiting for a response and walked into the dining room, took a chair and placed it in the bathroom in front of the sink. When she returned to the living room, Dave was struggling to his feet. "You did a good job on my foot. Still hurts a lot, but I think I might be able to walk on it." He put some weight on it and grimaced, then shifted back to his good foot. "Maybe not," he said and smiled.

"Hang on, I'll help you," Sophie said, crossing the room to meet him. She put his arm over her shoulders and supported him as he hobbled to the bathroom. When they got there, Dave eased himself down onto the chair. "Now, I'm no hairdresser, but this mop needs to go." She used a sheet to cover him up to his neck and retrieved a set of cordless clippers from under the sink. When Dave gave her a puzzled look, she said, "A little something one of my exes left behind."

The clippers came to life with a loud buzzing sound and before Dave could object, she was running it through his hair, shaving off large clumps of it. She used the shortest guard so that Dave would still have some hair left, but ran them over his whole head and shaved off as much as she could. When she was done, she leaned his head back and repeated the process on his face with the guard off, shaving his unkempt facial hair as close as she dared.

Twenty minutes later, she walked around to the front of him, brushed off any bits of hair from his head and face, pulled the sheet away from his neck, and looked at him. "You look almost respectable again."

Dave laughed. "Yeah, okay, you got me. I'm a mess."

"Let's get these clothes off you and get you bathed. You're not sitting at my table until you at least smell like a man and not a toxic waste heap."

"Ouch," Dave said. "What, you're gonna bathe me?"

"Well you're not about to do it yourself. You can barely stand. Besides, you wouldn't be the first guy I've seen naked. Don't be so modest."

Dave shrugged and relented to her. She started a bath filling and went back to him, stripping his dirty clothes off. Between the sweat, dirt and dried blood, she could tell they were ruined, so she bagged them up and left them by her door to take to the garbage chute. When she got back to Dave, she turned the water off. It was a bit of a struggle to get him into the tub while keeping his foot out of the water, but once he was settled, she started to wash him. She used the least smelly soap she had, knowing he would appreciate it, and when they were done, she helped him out of the tub and into her bedroom. She grabbed towels on the way to her bed and helped him dry off, then said, "I don't have any men's clothes, but I can go out and grab some for you a bit later. My robe will have to do for now."

She grabbed a white robe off the back of her door and handed it to him, which he wrapped around himself the best he could. It was a little small on him and tight around the shoulders. "Lie down, rest, and I'll make us something to eat, okay?"

"Yes, mom," Dave said with his usual sense of humor. She scowled at him and he laughed. "Thanks, Sophie. I mean it."

He laid down, and she was sure he was snoring before she left the room.

# Chapter 6 - Caldoor Hospitality

While the Caldoor soldiers rode horses and slept under warm blankets, Malia walked behind them, bound and chained. They stripped her of weapons and armor and left her to sleep on the ground with nothing but a tunic and pants in the cool autumn air. Traveling in a straight line toward Caldoor Castle, they walked through fields and forests, and over rocky hilltops. Reds, oranges and yellows streaked the leaves all around them as the days grew shorter.

They were halfway there when Malia was woken one night by the feeling of cold steel against her throat. Her instinct was to scream, but she stifled it when she heard a gruff soldier's voice. "If you make a sound, I'll be forced to silence you."

He turned her onto her belly and rested his weight on her legs to pin her down. With her hands bound in front of her, there was little she could do to fight him. "It been a long time since I had a woman like you," he whispered in her ear, leaning over her back and pressing into her so she could feel his erection. The smell of his breath carried alcohol with it, and the heat of it on her neck repulsed her.

With the tip of his blade stuck into the ground next to her neck, he rested the blade against her skin. "Now don't you move, or you'll get hurt," he said, lifting his weight. He used his free hand to pull her pants down around her thighs. "You are a beautiful piece of meat, yes you are."

His weight rested back down against her legs, and he shoved his hand down between her legs, letting his fingers grope inside of her. The violation made her shudder, and her heart raced as he probed deeper inside of her. "Lovely and warm. You're going to be a sweet treat."

He removed his hand and lifted it up to her face, holding his fingers under her nose. "You resist, but your sex smells so sweet, I think you want it."

She could smell herself on his fingers as he rubbed against her, arousing himself even more. He smeared his fingers against her lips, and she saw her chance. She opened her mouth, letting his fingers in. His middle finger slid between her lips, and she bit down as hard as she could. Her teeth pierced his flesh, cutting through callouses, muscle, and finally hitting the bone. He screamed and went to move the blade, but she bucked and flung her feet backward, hammering them into his back, and sending him flying forward. The sword fell from his grip, and he landed full-force onto her head, but she didn't let his finger go. Instead, she bit harder, feeling the bone crack under the pressure of her jaw.

The sound of boots hitting the ground was never sweeter to Malia as the soldier wrestled to free his hand from her mouth. She took one of his knees to her upper back, but she continued to bite and severed the finger just below the middle knuckle. He tumbled forward as his hand came free, and Malia rolled onto her back and sat up.

Three other soldiers surrounded her now, all with their swords drawn. The soldier who had tried to rape her was nursing his hand, and spewing a line of curses at her, some of which she'd never heard before. She ignored him, and spit the end of his finger onto the ground in front of her.

"What is the meaning of this?" the commander of the Caldoor troops asked as he broke through the lines of soldiers now surrounding her.

Malia used her shoulder to wipe the blood from her face, and tried the best she could to pull her pants up to cover herself. After spitting once, she looked up at the commander and said, "Tell your men that if they ever try anything like that again, they'll lose more than a finger next time."

"That little harlot were askin' for it, an' when I did her bidding, she went an' bit off my finger," the soldier said as he struggled to take his feet. He cradled his injured hand with his other and walked up behind Malia. One of his boots connected with her lower back, sending a wave of pain through her, but she felt satisfied that she took a piece of him in the exchange. "Filthy wench."

"Belfa, go to the other side of the camp, and remain there. You will put as much distance between yourself and General Corsair as possible for the remainder of our journey," the commander said. He turned away from Belfa and back to Malia without giving him a chance to say another word. "Get the general some new clothes, and a blanket. I want her delivered to our King intact, and unspoiled. I will personally remove the manhood of any soldier who tries to touch General Corsair again. Am I clear?"

"Yes, sir," a chorus of voices shouted. They sprang into action as their commander leaned down and removed the ropes that tied Malia's hands.

"My apologies, General. I won't make excuses for Belfa's behavior."

Malia straightened out her clothes and stood up. She glared at the commander, but said nothing.

The commander took the hint and had a tent set up for her, and fresh clothes and blankets delivered. Belfa was left to sleep without a tent or blankets for the remainder of their journey.

After that incident, the commander picked up the pace. The rest of the soldiers grew restless with a mission that they grumbled about under their breath, and Malia felt if they took much longer, that her life might be in danger. Only the commander kept the soldiers at bay. They reached the castle a week later, with no further incidents.

Caldoor Castle stood at the top of a large hill with the city below it at the base. It was a contrast to Findoor, where the city and castle rested behind the same walls. Here, the castle looked down on the city, like a parent looks down on a child, and the only inhabitants of the castle were royalty, staff, and servants.

Malia examined the castle as she walked through the city square. With her head held high, she endured the cries and jeers of the townsfolk. The soldiers leading her egged on the crowd and laughed when the rotten vegetables started to fly. Malia didn't flinch once.

At the side of the road, a pair of performers caught her attention. It was a man and a woman who were spinning blades, clashing them together and tossing them around. It was a display of extraordinary skill and it fascinated her, as she had never seen anyone juggle that well with normal objects, let alone full size swords.

The two stared into each other's eyes with such intensity that Malia's heart fluttered with the feeling of love between them. The swords flew back and forth, each one timed so that the hilt would face the other to catch it, and despite how dangerous the display was, Malia knew their skill meant they were in no real danger from each other.

She forgot where she was and slowed as she grew more engrossed by the display. The pair took turns performing stunts, each more amazing than the last. The man, who wore his long dirty blond hair tied back out of his face, would toss a blade twenty feet in the air, perform acrobatics in place and catch the descending blade, all while keeping the steady stream of swords flying back and forth to the woman.

The woman turned around so that her back faced him and continued to catch the swords being thrown at her back. As she caught them, she would flip them and toss them back to him over her shoulder. Malia lost herself in the show. The flying blades, the man and the woman who caught and threw them, and the love they shared when they looked in each other's eyes were all that mattered to her.

Her concentration was broken by the commander's voice. "They're beautiful, aren't they."

His comment caught her off-guard. "I have not seen such skill with a blade in all my life," she said, without taking her eyes off them.

"Blade slingers. A lost art, except for these two. They're out here every day, sometimes for hours. Nobody knows where they learned it, but they have two children they've been teaching."

Malia watched them for a few minutes more, but the initial captivation was lost. Her heart ached, knowing that she couldn't stand and watch them forever. She longed for Seth to be by her side so he could see them too. She was about to continue down the road when she noticed the rest of the soldiers were as mesmerized with the show as she was. A broad circle of soldiers had closed around the two slingers and some were making quiet exclamations of surprise each time they did something daring.

As the pair put on a show for the soldiers, Malia noticed a child playing with a dog at the other end of the circle. It looked innocent enough, but when the child threw a ball for the dog and it bounced into the performance area, an alarm went off in Malia's mind. The dog gave chase, bounding after it with a stupid dog grin on its face and ran between the two performers. One of the flying blades clipped the dog's ear and made it yelp and turn to run. The man caught his blades and dropped them to the ground with lightning speed, marking the end of his part of the show. At the same time, the woman on the other side struggled to catch the blades flying at her. One by one, with extraordinary accuracy she plucked the blades out of the air and let them drop to either side of her. The last blade, the one that clipped the dog's ear, flew past her, leaving her scrambling to catch it. Her hand closed on the hilt with the blade inches from the neck of one of the soldiers in the circle behind her.

She dropped the blade to the ground and lowered to her knees in apology. "Many pardons," she said to the soldier, despite the fact that he was uninjured.

The damage was done though. It was the same soldier who had lost most of a finger during the trip, and he looked as though he was ready to cut her down where she knelt. He drew his sword and leveled it at her neck, using the tip of it to raise her chin up. "You nearly killed me," he said, his tone snide and condescending. "Like to play with knives, do you? Perhaps we should take you in as well. We'll teach you a lesson in how to treat soldiers."

The woman's partner approached the soldiers with empty hands. "My apologies, good knight," he said. "We meant no harm and no harm has befallen anyone. The only blood drawn today is a few drops from a dog who has learned a lesson he won't soon forget. Let us go now, and this shall not happen again." He lowered his head in apology as well and awaited a response.

"Let you go? So as you can fling one of your blades into my back? I think not." The tip of his sword was still at the woman's chin and Malia could see the strain on her face to keep control and the fear in her eyes. "Looks like you both need a lesson in manners."

The commander approached them now. "Belfa, stand down. None were harmed, and they have apologized. You need not act like a brute in the company of such esteemed citizens."

Belfa looked up at his commander, anger twisting his face. "Stand down? You let a prisoner bite off my finger and go unpunished, and now you'll let these charlatans go as well. You've gone soft. Is this the kind of lawless country you want?"

The gap closed between the two men as the commander continued his careful approach. "Nay, Belfa. There are laws aplenty," he said. "You were unharmed in this incident, and it was clearly not her fault. Now stand down. That's an order."

"I'm tired of your orders," Belfa said, and spat in the woman's face. Malia's heart twisted in her chest as she watched him thrust his sword forward, plunging it into the woman's neck. "That is what happens when you break the law."

He withdrew the sword and blood poured from the wound. Her partner gaped for a moment, and then screamed, "No! Not my love." He collapsed to the ground next to her and caught her as she fell. Blood spread down the front of her in a wave and pooled on the ground. Malia wanted to rush to their aid. She wanted to cast every healing spell she could, but it would make no difference. All she could do was watch with a breaking heart as the woman's life flowed out the wound. "My darling Mara, my love," the man said as tears flowed down his face and he held her close.

The commander was about to take action when the man let Mara rest on the ground and laid each hand on a blade. "You'll pay," he said as he stood up. "You'll pay with your life."

The flash of steel was so fast Malia wasn't sure he'd even moved. The blades spun in the air, each one connecting with Belfa in what looked like an insignificant way. Cuts opened up on the shocked soldier's face, but the man didn't stop there. The blades flew in his hands, moving like they were part of him. Pieces of Belfa's armor fell to the ground, and then clothes until his chest was exposed. He stood there, facing the swordsman, dumbfounded.

"An eye for an eye," the man said, and thrust both swords into Belfa's chest. "A heart for a heart."

The commander drew his sword now, trying to take charge of the situation. "Stand down now, you've had your revenge."

The man turned toward the commander, his face twisted with rage. "Stand down? Like your soldier did? I have nothing now."

There was a quick motion from him and the swords were freed from Belfa's chest, letting the soldier fall to the ground. He spun the blades around and cut the commander's throat, felling him as well.

All the surrounding soldiers drew their swords and readied for battle, but he was too fast for them. Four more soldiers were slain before Malia could even tell what was going on. *He's so fast,* she thought, watching in wonder as he parried the swords of other soldiers who thrust them his way. Two more soldiers fell to his blades before they backed off and decided to take a different approach. He was far more skilled with a blade than any of them, and much faster. They circled him, trying to cut off his escape, and closed in around him, keeping their shields in front of them and forming a wall of steel.

It took seconds for him to find a weakness in this strategy and he used that weakness well. One soldier lowered his shield for a split second to check his position and took a blade to the eye. He fell screaming and left a hole in their circle. The man darted for the hole, spinning his blades to either side of him and cutting down the soldiers to either side of the hole. The circle was broken and he was free and running straight for Malia.

He was standing before her with his blades poised to attack when a strong, clear voice spoke. "Restringuntas."

A black bolt of energy struck the blade slinger from behind and sent him sprawling to the ground. His movement stopped and the swords clattered away from him. A black-robed figure stood at the far end of the clearing from them, staring at Malia and assessing the situation. She hadn't seen this man before, but had heard of him, and recognized him by the scar above his left eye. "Darian, the Black," Malia said under her breath. The Arch-Magus of Caldoor who was known to be heartless but fair.

A number of soldiers approached the blade slinger who was now motionless on the ground and readied their blades. Darian raised a hand and spoke in a deep commanding voice. "Lower your weapons. He will stand trial for his crimes. Belfa would have as well, had he not gotten himself killed." The black wizard walked in slow measured steps toward Malia, who remained still and silent. She kept her gaze fixed on him as he approached. His manner was confident, almost fearless, and he wore a smirk on his face as he measured her up. "What do we have here?" There was an air of power about him that Malia could feel as he approached. Merek had once spoken of him when he was offered the black seat on the Wizard High Council. Darian had refused, claiming he enjoyed his position as Arch-Magus far too much to give it up. "General Corsair, I presume," he said with a nod of respect.

"Darian," Malia said, remaining still.

"Guilty as charged. You have my most sincere apologies for your treatment." He touched a finger to the chains around her wrists and caused them to release and drop to the ground. "Our soldiers are not normally so incompetent. Please, follow me to the castle. My King anxiously awaits your visit."

Malia rubbed her bruised wrists and nodded. "As do I."

Darian turned and led the way to the castle without looking back. Malia could have run at that moment, but she knew if she did, she wouldn't get fifty paces before Darian struck her down. She walked after him, leaving the soldiers behind her to deal with the paralyzed blade slinger. "What will happen to him?" Malia asked as she caught up to Darian.

"He will be tried for his crimes. If he is found guilty, he will be executed. An attack on the King's soldiers, for any reason, is considered an attack on the King himself."

"Surely exceptions can be made. The poor man did nothing but defend his partner, whom he obviously loved a great deal. That lout of a soldier deserved what he got."

Darian stopped and turned to face Malia with a smile, though she suspected it was about as genuine as her apparent freedom. "And what of the ten other men who fell to his blades? They have wives and families, children who will have to grow up without their father. What shall we tell them when they come calling for his head? That we made an exception? That he was defending his wife? Had Jax only taken Belfa's life, I would have excused it outright. Maybe even commended him for putting the idiotic fool out of his misery. But eleven lives paid for one? No exceptions shall be made for that massacre."

"His name was Jax, then," Malia said. "I shall pray that Ignith lights Mara's way to her next life."

Darian was about to continue to the castle, but stopped when he heard the name of the god of fire. "You are a follower of Ignith?" he asked.

"Yes. He has been most generous with his gifts."

"Interesting," Darian said, reaching up to Malia's neck and taking hold of the gold pendent resting there. "Carrying such a beautiful charm, I would have thought you were a follower of Lyecha."

"It was a gift," Malia said.

"An interesting gift," Darian said, and led her the rest of the way to the castle.

The walk was lonely and cold up the path. Darian remained ahead of her, his robes fluttering in the cool autumn breeze. Her own clothes were dirty and ragged and did little to keep her warm. She did her best to ignore the temperature as he led her to the castle. The sky was overcast, allowing little sunlight through, and her boots were almost worn through, making each step more difficult than the last. The great doors of the castle were open before they reached them and Darian led her inside. He motioned to several servants and said, "Take General Corsair to her chamber and draw her a bath. Ensure that all of her requests are fulfilled and she is made comfortable. Until she is found guilty of any crime, she is to be treated as a guest of honor. I'll have the head of any who mistreat her while she is in our company."

Those who answered his summons scattered to do as they were told. One servant remained to show Malia to her quarters. Malia turned to Darian, and despite knowing she was still a prisoner of Caldoor, gave him a polite salute. "I thank you, Arch-Magus. Your kindness is well received."

Darian nodded and walked away, leaving her in the care of the servants.

The young fellow who remained led her to a room in the northern wing of the castle. It was a large room with luxurious furnishings and a private bath that was being filled by servants. Clean clothes were laid out on the bed, including a blue gown that Malia wrinkled her nose at. The servant must have seen her expression because he said, "Something the matter, milady?"

"No," Malia said. "Not really. I would prefer some more practical clothes to the gown though. It is beautiful, but I do not care for it."

"Very well," the servant said, and motioned to several others to take the gown away. "Traveling clothes then?"

"That will be fine, thank you." She walked over to the bath that was almost filled and removed her clothes heedless of the servants milling around her. They didn't appear to take notice and continued about their work as Malia climbed into the large basin and relaxed. It took little time for her to wash the grime of the road from her skin. All the while, servants around her worked, preparing her bed, bringing plates of food, and doing their utmost to make her comfortable.

As she relaxed in the bath, her thoughts strayed to the blade slinger and the tragic loss of his wife. He would be in the dungeons sitting on the hard stone floor, or maybe in a patch of straw. The only food he would get would be water and stale bread, just enough to keep him alive while he awaited trial. She looked over at the plates of fresh fruits, vegetables, and steaming hot meats. It made her sick to her stomach. *How can I dine like a king while he sits in the dungeons?* she thought.

She stood up and got out of the bath, accepting a towel from a servant. Clean, fluffy and warm; everything designed to make her comfortable while Jax sat in misery. "Pardon me," she said to the head servant who had led her into the room.

He came right away and presented himself to her. "Yes, milady."

"There was a prisoner brought in shortly after me, he would be in the dungeons now. I'd like him brought to me, I shall take full responsibility for him."

The servant looked shocked that she would even suggest such a thing and said, "I'm sorry milady. I can't do that."

"Then fetch me Arch-Magus Darian and I shall make the arrangements myself."

He hurried off to do her bidding while she dressed herself in the traveling clothes that were left on her bed in the gown's place. They were comfortable and of much higher quality than what she had worn under her armor. By the time she was done and resting on the edge of her bed, Darian entered the room.

"There was something you wanted to discuss?" he asked, getting straight to the point.

Malia stood up and approached him. "Yes. Jax, the blade slinger. Is he being held in the dungeons?"

"Indeed, he is," Darian said with a note of triumph in his voice.

"I want him moved up here. I shall share my room with him if I have to. I won't be treated differently than another prisoner."

"General Corsair, you are no prisoner here. Besides, his trial is finished. He now awaits his execution. Justice is swift in the land of Caldoor. Come with me. The King will see you now." Darian presented her with a pleasant smile.

"This is not justice," Malia said, standing a few paces from Darian. She looked into his eyes, but Darian revealed nothing about his emotions.

"My dear Malia, justice will be served in whatever way is our custom. Your words will not change that. Follow me, and speak with our King." He left the room without looking back. With no other option other than staying in the room as a prisoner, Malia followed him.

The audience chamber was much smaller than Findoor's, with fewer benches and a more intimate feel to it. Where the Findoor throne room had stone floors and walls, and few embellishments, this chamber was adorned with a softwood veneer and tapestries depicting great heroes of Galadir. King Farric Tendstone sat in an oak throne and spoke in hushed tones with a man who looked familiar to Malia. Farric was a young man about the same age as Malia, with dark hair and eyes and an air of strength that he projected to all those around him. It was said that he was inexperienced, and sometimes overly careful, but Darian was a close adviser and held a strong influence over him. When she approached and bowed down before the King, he waved the man away and smiled down at her. "Malia Corsair, daughter of Jaren Corsair, granddaughter of Jhet

Corsair, former general of the Findoor militia. Your grandfather was a celebrated hero of the Lyecian war, was he not?"

Malia lifted her head to look at Farric. "Yes, Your Highness. I can only hope to rise to his level of greatness some day. You say 'former general' but that is not the case. The men I command are the last of the Findoor militia, and I remain their general."

"So you admit it them?" Farric said, raising his eyebrows.

"We have come seeking help. A dangerous wizard has usurped the Findoor throne. Even as we speak, he grows in power and defiles the dead, raising an army to rival any ever seen on Galadir. If you do not act with haste, he will overrun your kingdom as swiftly as he took Findoor."

She watched his face as she spoke, but he revealed nothing. His face was blank but steady, and the only emotion portrayed was in his eyes. There was fear there.

"Lies," a man shouted from the benches to Malia's right. Both Malia and Farric turned to see who spoke. It was the man who had been waved away when Malia was first presented. "Lies from a murderer and a thief. I expect nothing more." The man stood up and walked toward the throne once more.

"Kern, sit down," Farric said in a stern and powerful voice, stopping the middle-aged man in his tracks. "Speak out of turn again, and I shall have you escorted from my court."

Kern hesitated, looking from Farric to the other side of the room. Malia followed his gaze to Darian, who returned a cold, blank stare back to Kern. After a second more, Kern slunk back to his seat, stared at the floor and said nothing more.

"As our most honored guest, Kern, has pointed out, Findoor's version of your story is much different. We have received a petition from the new King of Findoor," Farric said, holding up a parchment scroll. "It's signed and sealed by every Findoor councilor, and accuses you of the murder of King Verand, an attempt at usurping the throne yourself, and of leading an attack on Caldoor in the effort to start a war between us and Findoor."

"Outrageous," Malia said. A growing sense of dread gnawed away at her resolve. "Most of the men I led across your border were tired and hungry. We are in no position to start a war between anyone." She looked around at the entire court and saw faces filled with unspoken accusations. The weight of their stares was almost more than she could take. "Listen to reason. There is an army at your doorstep, one that I prevented from entering your kingdom by destroying the bridge. But they will not stop there. This army is living death. They do not eat or sleep. They do not rest. When they kill, the dead rise up and join them."

Farric looked alarmed at this revelation, but said nothing for a long moment. "If this is the case, why did our soldiers not see this army?"

"They retreated. I know not why."

"How convenient," Farric said, clearing the emotion from his face. There was a chuckle from the rest of the court. "So, an army of the dead chased you here, and then retreated at the last moment, just in time for our soldiers to miss them?"

Malia lowered her gaze in defeat. "Yes, Your Highness."

"What of the stolen sword? The relic that you carried when our soldiers forced your surrender?"

"Arch-Magus Merek gave it to me, as a gift."

Malia spotted Darian as he raised an eyebrow. He didn't look convinced, but curious about the sword.

Farric continued his interrogation, "Arch-Magus Merek is not known for giving away magical relics lightly. Darian brings me to understand that this sword was used by the Dark Lord himself during the Lyecian war. The new King of Findoor claims that you stole the sword, used it to slay Merek, and then Verand. In fact, it was this sword that helped you destroy the bridge into Caldoor as well, was it not?"

"Yes. The sword helped. I could not have achieved that level of power on my own. But I did not kill Merek or King Verand. Merek gave me the sword to help me with a task he assigned to me. I was to retrieve a Time Weaver from another world and bring him back to help us battle the wizard who now sits on the Findoor throne."

Farric laughed this time, a deep hearty laugh. "Please, Malia, I can take no more of your stories. A Time Weaver now? There hasn't been a Time Weaver on Galadir since the end of the Lyecian war. You know this as well as any in this room." Malia opened her mouth to say something, but Farric raised his hand to hush her. "I want to believe your story, but you are not making it easy. What I can tell you is this: I do not believe for a second that you killed Verand or Merek. Darian tells me that Verand took his own life, as reported to him by Merek. He also told me that even with the black steel sword, you would not have had the skill or the power to slay Merek. In that regard, there are inconsistencies in Findoor's account of this story. But one thing I do know is you admit to destroying the bridge, something that will cost Caldoor years in trade and tens of thousands of gold pieces to replace. It is considered an act of war, and as such, you will be treated as a war criminal. You will be taken to the dungeons, and if no further evidence arrives within three days to clear your name, you will be hanged for your crimes."

Malia's heart sank when she heard this. The strength threatened to leave her legs and she struggled to stay upright. Her eyes shifted to the Findoor councilor who sat at the side with a smug expression on his face. A fiery rage built up inside her that tempted her to bolt for her sword that she knew was only paces away, but she resisted, no matter how much the sword called to her.

## Chapter 7 – Evidence

While Malia was being arrested, Cedric bolted for Morganath and climbed onto the dragon's back. They launched into the air, leaving the Caldoor soldiers on the ground with no idea how to stop them. Morganath flew toward the North, but Cedric leaned into his neck so he would not be misheard.

"We're going to have to do something exceptionally dangerous," Cedric said, patting the dragon's neck.

"What are you planning, Bard?"

"Nothing we can't handle, but we're going to have to fly over Findoor again. We need to take a number of the defiled to Caldoor Castle, but I have to make a stop first. Remember that town we stopped in on our way to Findoor with Seth?"

"I remember the children there made me itchy from all their playing at my feet."

"We need to stop there again. I remember them having a falconer," Cedric said. He adjusted his cloak and mask that had gotten jostled during their hasty retreat. "I need to send a message to Ducain's Keep."

"As you wish, but know this, Bard. I grow impatient with being used as your personal courier. I continue only because Malia requests it, not you."

"I understand, and I don't blame you. A few more stops and I shall be out of your scales for good."

"Nothing would please me more," Morganath said, and sped up his flight toward the little town of Sampson. There were several days of uneventful travel before they reached the town, and when Morganath descended, Cedric noted that it was much the same scene, except the fields were harvested now, and the weather was cooler. Children ran out to meet them, and several adults, including the same burly man as before, Erith.

When Morganath landed, Cedric slid off his back with ease and approached Erith, standing tall. The look on Erith's face told him his welcome would not be so warm this time. "You've got a lot of nerve showing up here again," Erith said, clenching his hands into fists. "Didn't you and your lot cause enough trouble last time?"

Cedric let out a weak chuckle and bowed to Erith. "Please, pardon our intrusion once more. There shall be no trouble this time, I simply need to send a message from your falconer to Ducain's Keep, and I'll be on my way."

"How 'bout you skip the message and be on your way now," Erith said, scowling at Cedric and coming to a rest before him. Erith stood quite a bit taller than Cedric and was at least twice as strong by his estimates, if not more.

"Come now, my friend. Be reasonable. We could scarcely be held responsible for what happened last time. I certainly had no idea that we were being followed, let alone by somebody as hostile as Mr. Cy Cooper. Not only that, but Cy is dead now. Perished at the hands of our mutual friend Seth, so there won't be any trouble from him."

Erith opened his mouth to say something when a woman walked up behind him. "Erith, don't be rude to our guest. Let him do his business and be gone."

The big man turned to face the woman Cedric guessed was his wife. "Marta, we must be careful of outsiders. These times are troubled."

"Let him do his business, and be gone," Marta said in a much more stern tone this time. She was smaller than him, but he didn't further question her judgment.

"Very well," Erith said. He looked back toward Cedric and said, "Go on, send your message and be gone with you."

"I thank you kind sir and lady," Cedric said with another bow and flourish.

He hustled off toward the falconer and let himself in. A young man stood at a counter that was covered with parchment and ink and quills. When runners were too slow to send a message, and no wizard was nearby who could send a message using magic, falconers were the next choice. This one garnered much of the eastern Caldoor business, being the only falconer within a week's travel. Cedric approached the desk and gave a polite nod to the young man. "Good afternoon, I need to send a message to Ducain's Keep, and it must be sent with all haste."

"Ducain's huh?" the young man said. "Write your message, I'll look up how much it will cost while you do so, but I warn you, it won't be cheap. We've lost a few falcons over Findoor recently."

"Charge what you must, it is critical that this message arrive intact."

Cedric scrawled out a note on a bit of parchment, folded it, and pressed sealing wax onto it with his personal seal. By the time he finished, the young man had returned. "To get it to Ducain's will be twenty-four gold pieces."

"That much?" Cedric asked, gaping. "When you said it would be expensive, I didn't think you'd be robbing me blind. Very well, here." He removed a pouch from his pocket and emptied it onto the counter. "You're leaving me copperless, I hope you're happy." Cedric flashed the young man a knowing smile which he returned as a smirk.

"Have a safe journey," the young man said. "I'll take care of your message." He took the sealed message and walked to a back room, leaving Cedric in silence.

With that done, Cedric left the falconer's shop and walked back to Morganath, who seemed to be getting agitated with the children playing around his feet. As he made his approach, he called out to the kids. "Come now, children, let's leave the lovely dragon in peace. We must be off now."

The children responded with a groan, but did as they were told and ran back to their parents who were waiting a fair distance back. Cedric walked up beside Morganath and climbed up onto his neck again, giving him a pat. "You're a good sport, my friend. To Findoor now, for the less pleasant part of our trip."

"Indeed," Morganath said, grumbling to himself. "How do you propose to capture any of the defiled without us getting killed in the process? I'd rather burn them."

"You know as well as I do that Grian's army is much too big for us to take on alone. He will know about you by now, and that will make this extra tricky. But I have my magic, and a few other tricks up my sleeves. Leave it to me."

The two turned their attention to the east, heading toward the crevasse that separates Findoor and Caldoor. Several days later, Morganath signaled to Cedric that they were about to pass over the

Algorn Canyon. "Pick up the pace," Cedric said. "We don't want to dawdle in Findoor."

They flew over the hill that ran along the Findoor side of the canyon and Cedric caught his breath at the sight. Just over the hill, beyond the sight of Caldoor border guards, a massive army waited, all standing motionless. At the back of the army, there was a great beast preparing to launch itself into the air. With black horns and spines, red flesh, and black feathered wings, it appeared to be the Tordrake Gladius's simulacrum had summoned. "This can't be," Morganath bellowed as he made a dizzying approach.

"What's the problem? What is it?" Cedric asked.

"The Tordrake. Grian has animated it. This is going to be more difficult than I thought."

At that moment, the hideous, half-rotted creature launched itself into the air. On its back was a dark rider wearing a long, flowing cloak. Cedric couldn't make out who the rider was at first, but when they got closer, he gave an involuntary shudder. "It's Gladius, or rather, what's left of Gladius's body. Blast it, Morganath, this is dark magic unlike anything Galadir has ever seen."

Morganath pumped his wings faster to gain speed as the distance between the two flying beasts closed. Cedric felt Morganath's chest expand underneath him as the gold dragon drew in a great breath. When the animated Tordrake with its dark rider were within range, Morganath let out a great roar, belching what appeared to be liquid fire at the foul creature. At the same time, the Tordrake released its own breath weapon; a purple cloud of noxious gas that Cedric could smell even from a distance. It smelled of rotting and death, and embodied the entire army in one puff of smoke. The fire and gas struck between them, dissipating into nothing. The two creatures were on a collision course when Cedric struck Morganath's neck to get his attention. "Roll," Cedric shouted.

"I'll send you to the ground," Morganath said.

"Roll, do it now. I'll be fine."

As Morganath tucked his wings back to roll himself underneath the Tordrake, Cedric leapt into the air, propelling himself above the foul creature to land on its head. He ran down its neck to confront the shade, drawing his short sword as he went.

"Disciple of Grishtor, leave now and all shall be forgiven," the Gladius shade said in a hollow, mocking tone. Cedric got a chill up his spine when he heard it, but didn't stop his advance.

The power of death came to him with ease as he ran and he focused it into his sword. A black flame erupted around the blade as he spoke. "Impuleras," he said, using a spell that would dispel the dark energy, and drove the sword forward into the shade's face under its hood. There was an ear-piercing shriek, and the shade lashed out at Cedric as he tried to push past it. Dark energy flooded down the length of the blade and struck Cedric's hand, sending pain through every nerve, like the life had been drawn out of it all it once. He didn't break his stride though, and managed to break loose from a grapple and run down the back of the Tordrake. Morganath had emerged on the other side and was just flying away when Cedric made a second leap in an effort to land on the dragon's back.

For an instant Cedric hung in the air, soaring with Morganath beneath him. One beat of Morganath's wings propelled the dragon forward enough to leave nothing but open air and an ocean of living dead beneath Cedric.

"Blast it all," Cedric said as he fell from the sky. Morganath shrank in the sky above him, and with little left to do but fall, Cedric tried to gather his thoughts. The sound of the wind past his ears was numbed by the silence of the army below him. They didn't move or speak, shuffle or fidget. There was no coughing or sneezing or throat clearing. Not even a whisper. Cedric fell toward a blanket of silence. Thousands of defiled bodies, standing and waiting to kill at Grian's command. He was seconds from hitting the ground when Morganath swept by below him in a flash of gold. Cedric reached out and grasped the dragon's tail as he flew by. The sudden change in direction wrenched his arm, but he held tight and grabbed Morganath's tail with his other hand to reinforce his grip.

The wind swept past him, threatening to blow him away, but Morganath leveled out his flight and gave his tail a flick, sending Cedric flying up into the air and forward. He landed on Morganath's back and nearly fell before he crouched down and got a grip. He scrambled to Morganath's neck, sat down, and shouted, "Good timing."

"I have no interest in being responsible for your death, bard."

"Let's get what we came for. I have just the spell, but you'll need to snatch them up fast once I cast it."

"Just say the word," Morganath said, his voice booming below Cedric.

They came about once again and Cedric took a measure of where everything was. The Tordrake was nowhere to be seen since its rider was dispatched. The army below them didn't move, and so they made easy targets. Off to his right was a small group separated from the rest by a few paces. Cedric called on the power of death once more and said to Morganath, "Those few down there. Once I cast, snatch them up. You'll have only seconds to do it."

"Understood," Morganath said and turned in the air to swoop down on the group.

Cedric raised a hand and pointed it at the group, calling out the words to his spell. "Restringuntas cadavrai."

A ball of black energy flew from his palm and struck one of the foul creatures that wore Findoor armor. Black tendrils erupted from the ball of energy and wrapped around it and several others nearby. Once the spell wrapped the defiled, it squeezed them together and paralyzed them. Morganath swooped down and grabbed several of the closest ones and bolted straight up into the air to avoid attacks by several others who awoke at the first sign of an attack on them. His powerful wings took them high into the air, and his front claws wrapped around the paralyzed defiled bodies to hold them tight.

"Fly now, Morganath, to Caldoor Castle. As fast as the wind will take us."

"As you wish," Morganath said, pumping his wings as fast as he could toward the southwest.

5

Gladius and Nadya waited outside the guest room where Seth slept. He had gotten hysterical after he appeared in the council chamber, and so Trysk put him to sleep. They were assigned to stand watch over his room until he awoke. Gladius looked to Nadya as they got comfortable and said, "There are still three seats on the council unfilled."

Nadya smiled at him and nodded. "Yes. There is a struggle for both the red and blue seat. Tell me – you wear blue robes, and yet I see your face is scarred. How did that come about?"

Gladius shifted in his seat, feeling uncomfortable about the true story of the scars. He looked up into Nadya's expectant eyes and gave a nervous laugh. "An accident. That is all. An idiot played with fire once, and I got burned. The scars cover most of my body."

Her eyes lost their curious gleam and took on a look of pity as she thought about his answer. "They must have been terrible wounds to have left such scars. The good lady Philana heals most injuries leaving only the smallest of scars."

"My goddess has been generous with her gifts," Gladius said, "but I believe she intended for me to learn a lesson, and a hard lesson it has been. I care not to discuss it further."

"Fair enough," Nadya said. "The council intends to offer the gold chair to Seth."

"Good," Gladius said. "There isn't a person on Galadir or beyond more deserving of such an honor. He is not only a powerful Lyecian, but also a good man."

"Have you traveled with him long?" Nadya again took on a curious gleam in her eyes that Gladius couldn't help but be attracted to.

"Not really, and yet we go way back. He saved my life once, and he didn't have to. I certainly didn't deserve to be saved." There was regret in his voice, and Gladius knew it, so he changed his tone. "Besides, he has thrice saved Galadir from disaster, and still he continues. He could have returned to his own world when he learned to control his powers, and yet, he remains."

Before Nadya could speak another word, a sound inside the room startled them. Gladius was on his feet in an instant and through the door to find Seth on his feet and dressed. "You're awake. Are you well?"

Seth nodded and walked toward them. "Yeah, I feel much better. Sorry 'bout that."

Nadya smiled and welcomed him out of the room. "Don't mention it. We know what kind of stress you've been under, and the shock of your loss would be terrible. The council is already discussing what to do about Findoor and Grian. We've all been very worried about you. I have to say, it is a real pleasure to finally meet you. Word of your existence spread fast through the wizarding world."

"I'd love to exchange pleasantries, but Malia is in danger, and we must rescue Serrin," Seth said. "I can't lose my father again."

"We will, my friend," Gladius said. "But we must be careful. Grian wields a dangerous army and must have considerable power to have amassed so many defiled so quickly. There are few Lyecians who could wield that kind of power, let alone a normal human. With careful planning, we'll free Serrin, and with any luck, destroy Grian in the process."

"I'm confused," Nadya said, looking back and forth between the two men. "You keep referring to your father as Serrin, but I thought your father was Krycin? You look just like him, I didn't think there was any doubt."

"Krycin was a hero from long ago. He doesn't exist anymore," Seth said with some hesitation. "My true father always was Serrin. The confusion came from my resemblance to Krycin, and the fact that up until recently, I didn't know who my father really was."

"Interesting. We had our scholars research the name Serrin," Nadya said. Her voice indicated some suspicion, and her eyes matched it. "We can find no reference in history to his name. Not only that, but we can find no reference to any of your names. The only name we were able to find was Tyriel's, and it was a single, obscure reference from the Lyecian war. I must apologize, but after what happened with Grian, the council is extra careful about who they conduct business with. Trysk is worried, and there will be more questions. Our records are considered to be some of the best in Galadir, and we collect copies of the records from all magic academies as well. It's difficult to believe that none of you, save one, have ever appeared in anyone's records."

Gladius cracked a reassuring smile at her. "There's only two possible explanations for this. Either we aren't who we say we are, or we aren't from Galadir."

Nadya shook her head and smiled. "You don't have to convince me. I'm easily one of the most reasonable wizards on the council. It's Trysk you have to convince, and I'm afraid that isn't going to be easy. I simply want you to be prepared when you step before the council."

"Thank you," Seth said, and hesitated. "Sorry, I didn't catch your name."

"My apologies. I am Nadya Hamal, green council wizard. Our introduction in the council chamber was cut short, and since then I have discussed you with your friend Andran here."

"It's good to meet you. Let's go to the council and get the formalities over with so we can start taking action. I need help. I don't think I can defeat Grian alone."

Both Nadya and Gladius nodded and the three of them headed to the council chamber to meet the rest of the Wizard High Council.

# Chapter 8 - The Lab

It was early morning, but the lab buried deep under the military compound in Denton, Iowa was anything but quiet. Mathers stood on an observation deck as he watched dozens of scientists mill around a platform that had been built in the middle of the room. Control panels surrounded the platform housing screens that lit up with numbers and stats. Mathers could never make sense of the details, so all he wanted was the bottom line from these scientists.

At the far end of the platform were two small tubes filled with red liquid – synthesized blood from Seth's DNA samples. Mathers' lead scientist had explained the process to him, but he seldom understood scientific descriptions. He just remembered the scientist saying it would work.

He hailed one of the lead scientists over to him and called down, "Get me MacPherson, would ya?"

The scientist nodded. "Right away, sir."

Mathers waited for several minutes before John MacPherson arrived. He looked nervous and under-slept, but that was nothing unusual about him. MacPherson was always nervous about something. Mathers didn't let it bother him because the man was brilliant.

"Are you sure this thing is gonna work?" Mathers asked.

"Why, yes, yes, of course sir. When we were trying to create a portal, we would have had to breach and hold open the wormhole to the other world. But this time, we're not holding it open, we're just pulling something through."

"And how can you be sure you're going to get Alkirk? I don't need another monster running around here destroying the place."

"Well, sir," MacPherson said, motioning to the platform. "Alkirk is special. His body has a unique energy signature that sets him apart from others. The girl's DNA has magic potential, but nothing like Alkirk's. I suspect that most people in the other world have some kind of magic potential, but Alkirk radiates energy, all the time. It's some kind of self-regenerative cycle that his DNA has. If we had no records of when Alkirk was born, there would be no way to detect how old he truly is. We use this energy signature to target the wormhole, and then draw him back using his own power."

Mathers clapped him hard on the shoulder and smiled. "I knew you could pull it off. Now, how do we stop him from flying away like he did last time? We need him."

"That was actually easier than the portal itself. Once we have Alkirk on the platform, we have a pair of bracers that we will clamp onto him. They'll disrupt his ability to produce another wormhole and keep him from running. Of course, there's no way to stop him from using his magic. I'm afraid to say that, based on our tests, his abilities are quite substantial." MacPherson avoided eye contact while saying that. Mathers guessed it was because he thought he was going to catch hell.

"When can we get started?" Mathers asked.

"We have several more hours of warm-up cycles to do, and I want to run some more tests on the power grid to make sure it's going to stand up to our demand during the operation. If we lose power partway through this, we could kill him."

"Take all the time you need, but have it ready to perform by tomorrow morning."

"Yes, sir," MacPherson said. "That should be more than enough time."

"Very good, you're dismissed," Mathers said, going back to watching the team below him run more tests on the machine.

Reports continued to flow in about people doing strange things. Some able to fly, some lighting fires without knowing it. Mathers didn't know how to handle it other than by pulling somebody in who had dealt with this stuff before. Had he not seen the portal himself, had he not seen Alkirk regenerate before his eyes from a blast that would have vaporized a normal man, had he not seen Alkirk stand up and fly back into the portal to close it, he would never have believed these things were possible. He had seen it, and it haunted his nightmares every night since. It changed everything.

5

Sophie decided to sleep on the couch and let Dave sleep as long as he needed to. He woke up around dinner time the next day and stumbled out of her room limping, but under his own power. She gave him a bright, warm smile when she saw that his eyes looked better. The red had left them and the dark circles underneath were gone. He looked more like himself, even if he was much thinner. "Good morning, or should I say evening," she said.

"Hey," was all Dave managed as he limped into the bathroom and closed the door.

He emerged a few minutes later and made his way to the dining room table where Sophie sat with her laptop open. "Hungry at all?" she asked as he sat down.

"Oh my god, starving. I could eat a horse."

"Good, because I have something special cooking, just for you," Sophie said and got up. She walked into the kitchen, pulled the lid off the pot on the stove and served up some steaming hot chili into a large bowl for him. She delivered it to him along with some toast.

Dave inhaled the steam coming from his bowl and smiled. "That smells amazing, what do you put in it to make it smell so good?"

"Never mind that," Sophie said, placing the toast on the table next to his bowl. "Eat up. You need it. Vegetables, carbs, lots of protein, everything your body is starved for right now."

"Thanks, I appreciate this."

"Don't mention it. I was looking for an excuse to make it anyway." She sat down at the table, pulled herself in, and resumed her work on her laptop.

After a few minutes of silent eating and the occasional grunt of approval, Dave looked up from his meal. "You didn't take a day off on my account, did you?"

"I called in and told them I'd work from home," she said, motioning to the laptop. "I wanted to be here when you woke up. I have to admit, last night you sounded pretty crazy. I chalked it up to delirium or something. I've tried to figure out an explanation, but everything I come up with doesn't explain how you got on my balcony yesterday. You didn't climb all the way up here with that foot did you? Though it would certainly explain the delirium."

Dave shook his head. "No, I told you the truth last night. I wasn't delirious, I was just tired and panicked. I have a clear head now, thanks to you."

"So you expect me to believe that you flew onto my balcony?"

"I can show you if you like," Dave said.

"Give it your best shot, just don't jump off the balcony. I didn't fix you up last night just to have to peel you up off the parking lot today."

Dave pointed at a salt shaker across the table and said, "Watch."

His face changed from relaxed, to intense concentration, and then he spoke a single word. "Incitatas."

The salt shaker flew from one end of the table to the other and into his hand.

"Holy shit," Sophie said, leaping up from the table and sending her chair into the wall.

Dave laughed and stood up as well. "I know, I felt the same way the first time it happened. I don't know what it is, or how to explain it, but I can create fire in the same way. I just don't have the same kind of control over it."

Sophie took a step to bring her to the edge of the table and examined the salt shaker, picking it up and turning it in her hands. "So you really did it then, what you said last night?"

There was a moment of silence before Dave said, "Yeah." He shifted his gaze around the room, trying to avoid her eyes, but she placed a hand on his chin and directed him to look at her.

"It's not your fault, understand?"

"But it is," Dave said. "If I hadn't been obsessing over those stupid pages. If I had paid more attention to the world around me, or taken a shower, or showed my face in the last..." He stopped and thought for a second, "...I don't know how long, it wouldn't have happened."

"Jesus, Dave. You need to turn yourself in."

"And what? Tell them I didn't mean to vaporize a police officer? It was an accident? I'll be questioned for ten years on what I used to do it, and then spend the rest of my life in a prison, or worse, in a lab with them sticking me with needles and running tests. No thank you. Not interested. What's Plan B?"

Sophie moved her hand from Dave's chin to his cheek and stared into his eyes. There was something there she'd never seen before. Genuine worry. Dave was never worried about anything that she knew of. "We'll figure it out. Do you know anyone who might be able to help?"

He looked thoughtful for a second, then let out a big sigh. "If Seth were here, he'd know what to do."

Hearing Seth's name made her heart sink. She'd almost put him out of her head, but now his memory came back full force. "I miss him too," she said. "I wish the police would do more, but they say he contacted them shortly after he disappeared and told them he'd moved away with his mother."

"Yeah. I don't really know who else to turn to. That's why I came to you."

Sophie thought of something and got a smile on her face. "What about the guys at the club? You always used to go on about how they were your 'boys' and they 'got your back'."

Dave's eyes lit up at the mention of the club. "You are a genius." He put one hand on each side of her head and kissed her forehead. "If there's anyone who knows how to make somebody disappear, it's those guys."

"Okay, should we go now?" Sophie asked, looking to her balcony and seeing the dying sunlight.

"No, we'll have to wait till dark. The club won't even open till nine, and, well, what day is it?" Dave got a sheepish look on his face as he asked.

"Friday. I was planning to go out tonight anyway. I was gonna go out last night, but I called my girls and canceled. Should I give them a call?"

"Yeah, that sounds good. We'll go in as a group, it'll be less conspicuous that way. In the meantime," Dave said, tracing a finger down her neck and sending a shiver up her spine. "I'm going to sit down and eat about three bowls of this wonderful chili of yours. Man, am I starving." He laughed and broke away from her and sat back down at the table.

"You jerk," Sophie said, and laughed as well. "All right, eat as much as you want. You need it."

Despite his joking, he dug into the bowl.

## Chapter 9 – A Message Delivered

The rest of the Wizard High Council were discussing the remaining two seats when Seth, Gladius, Tyriel and Nadya entered. Nadya took her seat in the green chair and the rest of them took a place in the center of the room.

Trysk spoke up with a strong, clear voice. "Seth Alkirk, your identity is already confirmed by our good friend, the Arch-Magus of Findoor, Merek. Though we have not heard from him in weeks, it does not change who you are. As the only confirmed living Lyecian, we offer you the gold chair on the council. The position is yours by a unanimous vote."

Seth looked around the room. Everyone looked to him with expectant faces, and he knew if he refused the position, it would cause more problems. "I accept," he said. "On the condition that Serrin will take my place once we free him."

"I cannot promise that, but you are free to resign the position at any time. Until then, we will look to you as our leader, as the council has always done."

Seth took his place on the gold chair and now faced Gladius and Tyriel.

"Our second order of business, is the identity of these two," Trysk said. "Andran, there are no records of your training at any academy under the council's control. I find this hard to believe, as the Wizard High Council collects records from almost every academy on Galadir."

Gladius opened his mouth to say something, but Seth cut him off with a raised hand. "Andran is a good friend of mine, and comes from another world. There will be no records of him. But I assure the council, there is no more powerful blue wizard on Galadir. If it is

67

within my power, I would appoint him to the blue seat on the council, as his knowledge and power would be a great asset to all wizards."

Trysk's expression turned from suspicion to anger at this, but Nadya was the first to speak, raising her hand at Trysk. "It is within your power, but use caution. An appointment without a vote is quite unusual. Normally, we would vote on all new members."

"I understand," Seth said, looking around at all the council members. "But these are unusual circumstances."

Gladius raised his hand at that moment and interjected. "Let it be known that if there are any who challenge this appointment, I am happy to follow standard procedures for challenges. I do not wish to divide our ranks over leadership concerns. I am honored that Seth thinks so highly of my abilities, and am happy to accept this role."

There was a scoff from the gray wizard, and Trysk stood up. "Of course he won't refuse. What right-minded wizard would?"

"Merek did," Attowen, the white wizard, said. "Nobody can say that Merek was out of his mind. In fact, in my life, a number of wizards have refused a spot on the council. Sit down, Trysk. If Seth wishes to appoint Andran to the Wizard High Council, we must support him."

"I agree," Nadya said.

"As do I," the yellow wizard, Merisill said, speaking for the first time since Seth entered the room. She was taller than Nadya and had strong facial features and cheek bones. Her light brown hair was short and hung loose about her face.

"Well," Trysk said. "It would appear there is more faith in you than I originally thought. Know this: I shall be keeping a close eye on Andran in any way I can. Your identity may not be in question, but I personally find Andran's story a little too far-fetched."

"Far-fetched?" Seth said with a laugh. "Before I knew of Galadir, I lived on another world where there is no magic, no dragons, and no beasts that want to rip us to shreds. People live mundane lives, and I spent my days sitting in a quiet office writing code, and I was happy. Try being taken from your home, and forced into a world you didn't know existed. Try being told that everything you thought about your life, everything you *knew* was true about your life was actually a lie. I could barely hail a cab before I came here, now I can stop time. People where I come from dream about having powers like this. They make up stories and movies, and play games where they can pretend to have powers like this, but nobody does. And you sit there in your black robes, and tell me that this..." Seth motioned to the room in general and all those present. "...is too far-fetched?"

Trysk said nothing. He sat and stared back at Seth, his knuckles white from gripping the arms of the chair. Nadya smiled and motioned for Gladius to take his seat. "If we're done with that business, perhaps we should move on to the more pressing issues," she said, motioning for Seth to take the lead.

"Right. Findoor is under the control of a wizard named Grian. He hunted me, and is part of the reason I'm here today. He now has a hostage and a way to neutralize my abilities."

A gasp ran through the room from all except Gladius, who gave Seth a curious look. "How?"

"I'm not sure how he did it, but it had something to do with a silver circle on the floor of Findoor's throne room."

"A reality anchor," Gladius said. "If Grian can cast a reality anchor, it means he has gained the use of seven of the eight elements. There is a way to break a reality anchor, but you would need the Lyecian tome in order to do it."

"Oh my god, the book," Seth said, his heart surging with panic. "I forgot all about the book in all the commotion."

"What book do you speak of?" Trysk asked, scowling at the pair.

"A Lyecian book of magic," Seth said. "It was left to me by my father, and can only be opened by a Lyecian. It contains some of the most powerful spells Galadir has ever known. Merek told me it was written by Lyecians long ago, and up until the Lyecian war, was held by the Wizard High Council for safe keeping."

Nadya perked up and smiled. "I remember this. History has it that Gladius stole the book from the forbidden zone, and it was later recovered by Cy Cooper, who then delivered it to Krycin. Nobody knew what happened to it after that, as Krycin was the last known keeper of the book, and he disappeared."

Seth nodded. "Yes, and Krycin gave it to my father, who gave it to me. I'm not sure where it is now, or who has it. It was left on the battlefield after I defeated Gladius in Findoor. I forgot about it in all the commotion."

"That was weeks ago," Trysk said. "Where have you been since then anyway?"

"That's not important. Right now, we need somebody to find the book. Andran, perhaps you can take on that task. You know the book."

"I'll go with you," Tyriel said, speaking for the first time since their meeting began. "I'm not much of a wizard, but I know the book you speak of as well, and I am good with a blade."

"I, as well," Nadya said. "If you are from another world, as you say, then having somebody from this world will serve you well."

Seth looked at the three. "That sounds reasonable. Trysk, can you and Attowen look into ways to defend against the coming undead army?"

Trysk looked from Seth to Attowen and nodded. "As you wish. I'm certain there are spells in the forbidden zone that can help us."

"Okay, good," Seth said. "The rest of us will..."

His last thought was interrupted by a frantic banging on the door. Seth paused a second, having lost his train of thought and heard the banging again. The rest of the group looked at him and so he stood up, walked to the door and opened it. Outside was a runner with a falcon on his arm.

"Pardon my intrusion," the runner said. He was trying to catch his breath as he spoke but Seth could still understand him. "A message for Seth Alkirk. I was told he would be up here."

"That's me," Seth said, a little confused.

The runner removed a small piece of parchment from a tube attached to the bird's leg and handed it to Seth. "Here you are. I believe the message is quite urgent, as it came on one of the fastest falcons I know from Caldoor."

"Thanks," Seth said, accepting the parchment. He closed the council chamber door and turned around. "Who else knows I'm here?" Seth asked.

"Just whoever you've told, and a few selected wizards around here," Trysk said.

"Then how could somebody from Caldoor know I'm here?"

Everybody in the room looked around at each other with confused looks on their faces. While they did, Seth opened the piece of parchment and read it. When he was done, he looked up at them.

"Everyone who is not working on something else should figure out what to do about Findoor," Seth said. "I'll join you as soon as I can, there's somewhere I have to be."

Without waiting for a response from them, he concentrated for a moment, and disappeared.

# Chapter 10 – Entrapment

Tension ran high in the lab buried deep below the military base in Denton. Mathers watched as men and women in white coats scrambled everywhere doing final checks before they activated the machine. John MacPherson approached Mathers and said, "Are you sure you want to be here for this? If something goes wrong, this could get extremely dangerous."

Mathers scoffed. "Son, I've seen some of the worst places on earth. This should be a walk in the park. Besides, I thought you said this would be stable?"

"Yes, sir. Stable for sure. But we have no idea how Mr. Alkirk is going to react to being pulled here."

"Don't worry about that," Mathers said. "I have insurance." He patted the holster on his hip that held his military-issued sidearm.

"If you say so, sir. I think we're just about ready." John turned and signaled to somebody at the main control panel and got a thumbs-up back. He left Mathers to watch from the balcony that overlooked the platform and went down to check the screen they used for targeting.

Mathers had requested a large screen be installed on the observation deck so that he could see what they were doing, and now watched as the wormhole generator closed in on Seth's energy signature.

"Charge up the phase generator," John called from the main control panel. Another scientist typed a command into a computer and the lights around the main platform came to life. A hum came from it that filled the room. Mathers had felt that hum once before, when the man in black had opened the portal. It made him uncomfortable, like the very essence of his body was being shaken at a molecular level, but he was confident his team had everything under control.

Every eye in the room was either on a screen watching numbers and stats, or watching the platform. The screen before Mathers showed him a bright spot that represented Seth's signature, and a wire frame tube that was the wormhole they would create to pull him back.

"Adjusting predictive analysis to compensate for movement," John shouted. Mathers saw the light on the screen was indeed moving, but only a little. "Power up the quantum entangler."

Another scientist below typed a command into a computer and more lights turned on around the platform. There were four spires that had been added around the platform that would create the beginning of the wormhole. The other end would be controlled by the targeting system.

"Stand by with the anchoring bracers," John said.

Mathers had authorized a number of soldiers to be here as well, who now stood by with the bracers that would keep Seth from escaping once he was there. They stood close by the platform to rush in once they saw Seth appear.

"Charge up the pulse generator. Targeting system locked in."

Everyone in the room hushed now in anticipation of John's next order. Mathers watched as the end of the wormhole on his screen was directed around Seth's energy signature. There was a sound in the room that overwhelmed the humming. It was a high pitched whine that grew in intensity as they waited. The more intense the whine got, the brighter the wormhole on the screen became.

"Ready," John said, with his hand over a green button. Two other scientists on the floor around the platform also had their hands over green buttons. "On my mark. Three... Two... One..."

Mathers looked on in anticipation, expecting John to call "mark" and the whole thing to be over with, but he hesitated. When he looked down at the screen, he realized why. The light that represented Seth was no longer there.

"Shit," John said. "He's moved. He just jumped. Recalibrating."

His actions were frantic on the keyboard, trying to adjust for the change in position. The screen showed the end of the wormhole moving to find the signature again. A small point of light appeared on the screen and grew.

"I've got him. Locking him in," John said. The image on the screen reflected it, and then the bright light disappeared again, only to reappear dimmer elsewhere on the screen. "God damn it. He's jumped again. Compensating."

The targeting system found Seth again and locked on. The whine in the room combined with the steady hum that shook Mathers to the bone was almost unbearable. He shook his head, but couldn't focus on the screen anymore, so he looked down at the platform. A bright light appeared in the center of the platform and grew in intensity.

"Mark," John shouted, and hammered the green button. The other two did the same and the machine came to life.

The light in the center of the platform grew brighter and more intense, leaving spots on Mathers' vision, but he couldn't turn away from it. The screaming whine went away as the power cells discharged. Everything appeared to be going as planned until an alarm went off on one of the screens on the floor. A big red "danger" band was flashing on the screen.

"Damn it to hell," John said, but didn't take his eyes off the screen in front of him. "More power. We need more power. There's almost twice as much mass as we anticipated."

White coats ran in every direction, working to compensate. Cables were hooked up, switches thrown, and the light in the center of the platform seemed as bright as the sun. The lights in the lab dimmed as the machine drew power from the main grid. Sparks flew off several control panels and the shouts of the lab workers all blended together in a mad panic to make the machine work.

The screen in front of Mathers shut down, along with several banks of lights. More sparks flew from the machine, and the light faltered. There was a scream at one point, but Mathers couldn't tell where it had come from. Another cable was attached to the machine and the light grew again.

There was an explosion, and a pulse emitted from the platform. Every electronic device in the room burst into a shower of sparks, and the power failed. All the lights went out, shrouding the entire lab in darkness. Mathers thought about the emergency lighting, but that didn't come on either. There was a struggle on the platform, and some shouting that Mathers couldn't make out.

When the room went quiet, he heard a soldier's voice. "Two people came through. There's two of them."

5

Morganath flew like the wind to the southwest toward Caldoor. Cedric could see the city laid out at the base of the hill when Morganath slowed. "Set down outside of the city," Cedric said. "I don't want to raise any alarms."

"As you wish," Morganath said, his voice rumbling through his body.

He dropped from the sky at a steady pace, aiming for a field a fair distance outside of the city. Ten feet from the ground he back-winged and slowed his descent. The wind almost ripped Cedric from the dragon's neck, but he managed to hold on. Morganath released the paralyzed bodies and let them fall to the ground and landed about twenty paces away from them. Cedric slid from Morganath's neck, checked his bow and quiver, and then turned to face the massive gold dragon. "Wait here, but do not endanger yourself. Flee if you must. I'll bring the officials this way with Malia once I've rescued her."

"I'm in no danger here. I shall wait."

Cedric turned and began the long trek through the field to the city. Unlike Findoor, Caldoor city had no walls around the outer reaches of the city. The residents would enter the walled inner portion of the city each day to work, and return home each night. Many who lived there thought this set up was bad for their protection, but the King had denied all requests to extend the walls beyond the current boundaries, claiming the cost would be too great to bear in a time of peace.

The city was quieter than Cedric thought it would be. It took him far less time to reach the castle side than it should have on a normal busy day, but understood why when he arrived. A large crowd had gathered around the gallows, which stood on the edge of the city just off the path that led to the castle. Three ropes were suspended from the main support, one for each person that would be hanged that day. There was no platform and no stairs. The prisoners would be hoisted up onto horses, fitted with the rope, and then the horse pulled out from under them. If their neck didn't break the moment they fell, they would hang until they either suffocated, or in more extreme cases, until they died of thirst. Cedric knew well enough that their necks seldom broke, and whether they suffocated or not would depend on how tight the rope was fitted.

A contingency of soldiers emerged from the castle, escorting three prisoners to the gallows. One was a man with dark hair, one was a man with light hair, and Cedric knew the third without thinking. Her wild blonde hair blew in the breeze, and she walked tall with her head held high. She was dressed in typical gray prison clothes like the other two, but looked stronger than them. More defiant. "Malia," he said under his breath.

He watched the proceedings from a distance and waited. Three horses were brought out from the stables and led to the gallows where they awaited their doomed prisoners. The man with the dark hair reached the gallows first and lost control. His screams and pleads for mercy echoed off the most distant buildings and seemed to surround Cedric as he waited. The man claimed innocence and begged for his life, but was given no respite by the soldiers who led him.

The lighter haired man arrived at the gallows next. His steps were forced, but not by the soldiers around him. Cedric could tell he was forcing himself to walk. He stared at nothing and didn't appear to notice what was going on around him. His expression was blank, even as he was hoisted up onto the horse's back and fitted with the rope. *This is a man who's lost everything,* Cedric thought. He felt pity for the man, but couldn't explain why. There was no sadness or anger in the man's face. No remorse. There was nothing. Just an emotionless shell. The soldier who fitted his rope pulled it tight around his neck, enough to press into the skin.

Malia arrived last. She maintained her defiance all the way to the gallows, and though she looked worried as well, she didn't give them the satisfaction of losing control. The first man with the dark hair was still shouting and begging for his life as Malia was helped up onto the back of the horse. "Good girl," Cedric said in a whisper.

A black-robed man, who had followed the soldiers and prisoners down the path, came to a stop. He cleared his voice and called for quiet which hushed the crowd in an instant, except for the dark-haired man. A soldier next to him used the hilt of his sword to smack the man in the head and knocked him out, which left the whole congregation in silence. "There you are Darian," Cedric said.

"You have each been found guilty of crimes against our fair Kingdom, and for that, you shall be hanged until you are dead," Darian said to the prisoners. "If you have anything to say for yourself, speak now."

There was silence from the remaining two conscious prisoners. At that moment, Cedric broke into a run toward the horses and shouted, "Stop! For the sake of justice, stop what you are doing."

He ran up to the gallows and approached Darian and the other soldiers, who had drawn their swords and prepared for an attack as he ran. Cedric raised his hands to show that he had no intention of attacking. "Come now, Darian," Cedric said. "You can't honestly believe that General Corsair is guilty of any crime."

"You've got a lot of nerve showing your face around here, bard," Darian said. "All for a convicted criminal who led an invasion force into Caldoor?"

Cedric smiled and tapped his mask. "As a technicality, I'm not showing my face. But listen to reason. General Corsair has done nothing wrong. Quite the contrary, actually. Her little display at the bridge was an effort to protect the Kingdom of Caldoor, not invade it."

Darian raised an eyebrow and lifted a hand to stop the advancing soldiers. Cedric stood his ground and flashed a smile up at Malia who was watching him in silence. "I hope you've brought proof of this claim," Darian said, walking with slow, deliberate steps toward Cedric. "Otherwise, you'll be joining them on the gallows. There's always room for one more rope, especially for a loopy thief who masquerades as a bard."

"Of course. I wouldn't think of coming here without the required proof. Outside of town there are several of the foul creatures Grian has animated. Over the border to the north, there are thousands of the things. Now I'll let you guess why Grian would amass such an army. It's either the biggest and worst party in history, or an invasion force waiting to cross the canyon and add Caldoor's people to its ranks."

Darian looked from Cedric to Malia and then motioned for several of his soldiers to follow him. "Show me," he said and approached the masked bard.

Cedric led Darian and the soldiers to where Morganath waited. By the time they reached the defiled bodies, Cedric's spell was wearing off and they were beginning to move again. The rotting corpses shifted and squirmed, trying to get to their feet again. The soldiers who accompanied Darian all ran forward, surrounded the small group of creatures and readied their attacks. Darian held up a hand and said, "Save your strength."

"As you can see, the reports of the dead walking are not so exaggerated," Cedric said.

"This is the work of pure evil. You say these are from Findoor?"

"Do you think I dressed them up in that armor all by myself?" Cedric asked with a smirk.

One of the creatures that rose to its feet wore a breast plate with a crown and sword on it, marking it as a soldier of Findoor. Darian made a sound of disgust, pointed at the creature, and said, "Impuleras." A black ball of energy flew from his hand and struck the creature in the chest, sending it flying to the ground. There was no further movement from the creature, that was now nothing more than a corpse. Darian repeated the process with the remaining bodies. "Show these bodies the proper respect they deserve," he said to his soldiers. "Burn them."

Cedric motioned for Morganath to take care of it and the dragon grumbled. "Gladly."

All the men moved out of the way as Morganath let out a stream of fire that engulfed the bodies and reduced them to ash.

"It would appear both I and my King have been duped by Grian," Darian said. "Malia shall be freed. My business with you shall wait for another day."

He turned away from Cedric and motioned for his soldiers to follow him. As they walked away, Cedric heard a roar from the crowd at the north end of the city and fear rushed through his heart. Without waiting for Darian, he bolted into a sprint toward the city. "The prisoners," he shouted back at Darian. "They've begun the executions."

By the time Cedric got to the gallows, the dark-haired man was already dead. It appeared as though his neck had snapped the moment he fell. The lighter-haired man was dangling from his rope, struggling against it, very much alive. The crowd was going wild watching him struggle and cheering on the soldier behind Malia's horse. He raised his hand and egged on the crowd as he prepared to strike the horse to make it move.

Cedric pulled his bow from his shoulder and nocked an arrow as quickly as he could, taking aim at the rope above Malia's head. With a deep breath, he steadied his aim and whispered a prayer to Hadra. The soldier slapped the horse, and he loosed his arrow.

5

Relief filled Malia's heart as she listened to Cedric convince Darian to hear him out. She watched with anticipation as Cedric, Darian and several soldiers walked away. The wait on the horse was excruciating as the entire population of the city stood in silence and watched her. After a long wait, some of the people started to get restless. There were shouts in the crowd from a few hotheads who were out for blood. The fear of her impending execution took over once more when one of the younger soldiers slapped the horse beneath the dark-haired man. She turned away, unable to watch as his limp body fell and his neck snapped with a sickening crack.

The crowd went wild over this and the young soldier reveled in his newfound fame. He slapped the second horse, and Jax fell. His neck didn't break and he hung there by the rope gasping for breath.

People cheered and yelled, calling for the soldier to continue. There was no reasoning with them and nothing she could do with her hands tied and a rope around her neck. If Cedric and Darian didn't return soon, there would be no prisoners left to save.

The soldier approached her horse and gave it a smack. She felt its back slide against her inner thighs and then open air. She closed her eyes and expected a sudden stop, pain, or something, but all she felt was a bit of a tug from the rope and she continued to fall. Soldiers reacted fast as she fell toward the ground. Her rope had snapped, but before she reached the ground, she felt arms around her, catching her. A strong, familiar embrace wrapped around her. She opened her eyes and caught a glimpse of Seth just before everything went dark.

Her entire body exploded with pain, like her universe was being ripped away around her. She saw a blue light, and then nothing.

$$\mathfrak{H}$$

When Seth opened the piece of parchment handed to him by the runner in the council chamber, the last thing he expected was this:

> Seth,
> A city at the base of a hill. A castle on top, surrounded by fields of green and gold. West, near where we met, awaits your love.
> Cedric

When he finished reading, he handed out a directive to the council, and focused on the place Cedric had described. Curiosity welled up inside of him, bringing with it questions. *How does Cedric know I'm here? And how does he know I can teleport, or what I need to teleport?*

The questions would have to wait until he could talk to the strange masked bard, but the memory of the conversation he had at the entrance to Morganath's lair came back to him. It would be one hundred years ago now. *Does Cedric remember that, and if so, does he know who I really am?*

He drew the power of time and space to him and disappeared from the council chamber just as he felt a tingling sensation all over his body. Bright afternoon light took him off his guard as he forgot about the time difference between the two locations. When his eyes adjusted, he saw the city and castle before him. A crowd had gathered on the edge of the city on the castle side. The gallows stood there with two people already hanged and a third about to be. The blonde hair was unmistakable. "Malia," Seth said, and focused on her position just as the soldier struck the horse beneath her. Again he felt the tingling sensation over his entire body, but had little time to worry about it. His intention was to appear below her, grab her legs as she fell, and teleport away.

When he appeared below her, she fell right into his arms. The rope had snapped, though Seth didn't have time to contemplate why. He focused on teleporting away with her, but before he could use the power, the tingling sensation exploded into searing pain as every nerve lit up. He felt his body being pulled by some unseen force and almost lost his grip on Malia. Using the power of life, he created a barrier around the two of them so that whatever was pulling him would pull both of them.

The pain eased as soon as the shell was up and the world fell away around them, melting into the blue aether that existed between worlds. He held tight to Malia who was now looking up at his face with a smile on her lips. For a short time the two of them floated through the aether, pulled by a strange force toward another universe. The force faltered, and Seth tried to free them from its grip, calling on the power of time and space to push them back to Galadir. A struggle began between him and the force that pulled them. He almost broke free, but a surge finished the job and pulled them through the barrier of another universe.

Everything went dark around him, but he could feel Malia in his arms and the floor under his feet. Silence surrounded him for a split second as he dropped his barrier. He went to say something to Malia when hands closed around his left arm and began to pull.

"Shit," Seth said as he lost his grip on Malia. He knew she fell, but didn't hear her hit the floor.

Another pair of hands grabbed his right arm and he began to struggle against the grip. *Two people, maybe three,* Seth thought as he fought against them.

"I've got him," one of his assailants said, trying to hold his arm steady.

"Unhand me, you brute," he heard Malia say. There was an impact, the sound of a fist hitting flesh, and then a loud grunt from a male voice.

Seth thought better of trying to out-muscle the people who held him. Instead, he focused on moving himself out of their reach and tried to teleport. Before he could, somebody clamped something cold and hard onto his arm. When his ability activated nothing happened. He remained frozen in the grip of two men.

He could hear the struggle Malia was giving them. There was another impact, and another grunt from a male voice. Seconds later, the struggle was over. Seth relaxed and stopped fighting, knowing both he and Malia were beat.

A voice called out in the darkness. "Two people came through. There's two of them."

Seth didn't recognize the voice, but his main concern was Malia. "Are you okay, Malia?"

There was a pause that sent a chill through him, but relief came he heard her voice. "Yes. I am fine, though restrained."

"I missed you," Seth said, not really knowing what else to say.

"I missed you as well. I was not sure I would see you again."

"How touching," a voice said above them. This voice was familiar, though Seth had only heard it once, and it seemed a very long time ago. "Somebody get me a god damned flashlight or lantern or something."

After a short pause, dim light flooded from a battery-powered lantern on a balcony above where they stood. Seth saw the platform beneath him and computers and equipment all around him. Two soldiers held him by the arms, and another two held Malia across from him. The noose hung limp around her neck with the end of the rope frayed where it had snapped. He tried to make out who was above him holding the lantern, but could only see a silhouette. It was a man, that much he could make out from the broad shoulders and heavy build.

"Welcome back, Seth," the man said as he walked over to a flight of stairs and descended. All around the room, men and women in white coats began cleaning up the mess. The soldiers in the room, dressed in green combat uniforms, remained still with assault rifles pointed at Seth and Malia.

"Earth," Seth said in a very matter-of-fact voice. "I'm on Earth. How did you get me here?"

"You two caused quite the stir the last time you were here. Cost us millions to cover up. Had I been able to, I would have arrested you on the spot." The man approached Seth on the platform now, and he could finally make out who it was.

The memories flooded back to him, as clear as day.

> "Boy, you're lucky you're not dead," the military man said. He offered Seth a hand. "Can you stand?"
>
> "I think so, yeah."
>
> Seth took the man's hand and hauled himself up off the ground. Now facing him, Seth saw his name tag which read "Mathers". He turned and looked around at the rest of the soldiers standing around him. Mathers offered him a hand and said, "General Neil Mathers, US Army. And you must be Seth Alkirk."
>
> "Yeah, good to meet you," Seth said, shaking his hand.
>
> "You really aren't human, are you?" Mathers asked, doing away with tact and pleasantries. "I mean, I didn't believe it at first, but now that I've seen for myself, I really can't deny it. What exactly were you trying to do up there, before you nearly got yourself killed?"
>
> Sparing a glance toward the rift, Seth looked back at the General and said, "Trying to close it. Trying to save the world."
>
> "Is there anything we can do?"
>
> Seth flashed him a grin. "Yeah. Stand back, and try not to die."

"Mathers. General Neil Mathers," Seth said. "It's been a long time."

Mathers gave him a funny look. "It hasn't been that long. A few months maybe. But you look a lot older. Who might this lovely young woman be? I recognize her from the video footage."

"This is General Malia Corsair of the Findoor Militia. Cut the crap, Mathers. Why are we here?"

"Well, *she* isn't supposed to be here," Mathers said. "We were trying to get you. Apparently, she came along for the ride."

"I brought her," Seth said. He turned to face Malia. "I couldn't lose you again."

She had been scowling with a look of anger in her eyes up until that point, but now the anger melted away and she smiled. "Thank you," she said to Seth, then turned to face Mathers. "It is good to meet you, General."

Seth shrugged away from the two soldiers holding him. "Get off me, I'm not going to hurt anyone." He looked at the soldiers holding Malia and said, "Let her go too. Put the guns away, I don't want to fight you. It wouldn't be a fair fight."

Mathers motioned for them to do as he said and they let Malia go. "I suppose with twelve fully armed soldiers in the room, you're right."

"Yep," Seth said with a grin. "You'd need way more soldiers than that."

# Chapter 11 - Torture

Serrin stood in a prison of pure energy that had been created by Grian in the center of the circle in the throne room. It was ancient Lyecian magic that Grian had summoned, designed to sap away the occupant's own power in order to fuel the cage. Any time Serrin tried to summon magical energy, it was drained away and only made the cage more powerful. The circle kept him from teleporting, and so he stood, silent and stationary.

"Who are you?" Grian asked, but Serrin refused to answer. When Grian grew tired of waiting for an answer, he said, "I know you're a Lyecian, because I saw you appear out in the field. Your valiant sacrifice to let Seth go means you must be related somehow. Are you Krycin? You look nothing like the pictures and paintings."

He remained silent and stared at Grian, wishing him dead with each passing second.

"Answer me," Grian screamed with such rage that Serrin jumped. Grian wore a twisted expression of hate. "Answer me, or I'll peel the flesh from your bones, bit by bit and feed it to my pets. I'll make you suffer a fate far worse than death, because when I'm done, I'll force your animated corpse to do my bidding for all eternity. One way or the other, you will serve me."

It took a moment of thought, but Serrin decided he would be more useful to Seth alive than dead, or worse. "My name is Serrin, and yes, I'm Lyecian."

"Good. Now we're getting somewhere. Where did you come from? Merek and I searched for years and never once found another Lyecian until Seth appeared on the dead world. Where were you hiding, and how many more of you are there?" Grian's voice was powerful, confident, but Serrin heard something more. Fear. There was an edge of fear to his voice.

"I haven't been hiding," Serrin said with a hint of derision to his voice. "I was brought forward, by Krycin."

Grian smiled. "So there *are* more, and Merek was right. Krycin could travel through time. Where is he now? And what is your relation to Seth?"

"I don't know where Krycin is now. He brought me here, and then disappeared. There is no relationship between us." Serrin hoped Grian would buy the lies.

"Ha, we'll see about that. Seth is no ordinary Lyecian. He's something more. I should have been able to take his powers. I should have been able to take his soul, but I couldn't. What's inside him? What is Seth?"

The tension had now left Grian's voice, and the fear. Serrin took it as a sign that he was buying the lies, at least in part. "I don't know. I thought Seth was just another Lyecian. If there's something more to him, you'll have to ask him yourself."

"Oh, don't worry. I will. Once I capture him, I'll figure out a way to extract that beautiful shard from him, and then I'll have the ultimate power, and nobody will ever stand in my way."

Curiosity crept into Serrin's mind along with the fear. *I knew Seth was special, but what is this shard he speaks of? Perhaps that's why Seth can move through time,* Serrin thought.

"Join me," Grian said, interrupting Serrin's thoughts. "You seem like an intelligent man. Join me, and we can rule together. With your Lyecian powers, even Seth wouldn't be able to defeat us. All the wizards in all the worlds wouldn't be able to defeat us together."

Grian looked into Serrin's eyes with a hopeful expression. Serrin didn't need to think about a response. "You defile the dead, usurp the Findoor throne, attack and imprison me, and then ask for my allegiance? Are you mad?"

"Mad? My soldiers do not need to eat or sleep. They don't get tired or complain. If you cut off an arm or a hand, they continue to fight. If you cut them in half, they continue to fight. Compared to traditional soldiers, they are superior in almost every way. So who is mad? It took me hours to assemble my army, it would have taken another ruler weeks or even months to assemble an army of the same size, and the resources required to sustain the army would be unattainable. What you call mad, I call efficient."

"I call it an abomination," Serrin said. "No wizard has ever raised such an army before."

"No wizard has ever been as powerful as I am now," Grian said. "Even the Dark Lord Gladius was not able to take Findoor, and he had two chances."

"That's not going to matter if there's nothing and nobody left to rule. Lord Gladius knew this, which is why he ruled a living army. You've lost touch with reality. You think you can have a world with an undead army, but you can't. Everything will die, and there will be nobody left to call you King. You'll be the most powerful wizard on Galadir, because you'll be the *only* wizard on Galadir."

Grian laughed and turned away from Serrin. He looked out at the court, which was still assembled in the throne room. "Tell me, is there one here who does not call me King?"

The room went silent, with all eyes on Grian.

He turned back to Serrin and smiled. "You see? They are loyal."

"Do not mistake fear for loyalty," Serrin said. "They fear what you would do to them should they defy you, and rightly so. I fear you as well. Not because of your power, but because of your insanity. You are deluded. Drunk with power. I can only hope that the power consumes you."

Serrin watched the smile on Grian's face turn to anger. "Adigas poenai," he shouted, pointing a finger at Serrin. Raw, unhindered pain seared through every nerve in Serrin's body. He screamed and fell to the floor of the cage, convulsing as every muscle reacted to the torturing magic. Had he been able to speak, he would have begged Grian to stop. He would have done anything to make the pain stop. His eyes burned, and his throat grew dry from screaming. His skin felt like it was on fire, but there was none. Just magical energy surging through him until consciousness left him.

# Chapter 12 - Revelations

Cedric let out an excited shout when his arrow struck true. Malia fell free of the gallows into the arms of Seth, who had appeared there rather suddenly. His excitement was cut short when both of them were consumed by a strange blue light. A bubble formed around them, and they disappeared, like they were being pulled out of the universe. "Well that wasn't supposed to happen," Cedric said. The light-haired man continued to fight for breath as he hung from the gallows next to where Malia had been. Cedric cleared his head and nocked a second arrow, taking aim at the rope above him. While all the soldiers and people of the city reeled at the disappearance of one prisoner, Cedric calmed his nerves and let his second shot fly.

The arrow severed the rope, sending the man to the ground. He collapsed in a fit of coughs and fought at the rope around his neck. Most of the soldiers around him were still stunned by the disappearance of Malia, but some were catching on. Before they could take action though, Darian walked by Cedric and approached the gallows. His hands were outstretched to either side of him as he appeared to be gathering energy, and then he raised them in a clap and spoke the word, "Tonitras."

When Darian's hands struck together, there was a burst of light and a clap of thunder so loud it made Cedric's ears ring. It also stunned the soldiers and the audience. He didn't wait for a reaction, but instead shouted with an amplified voice, "Go home, everyone. This show is over. General Malia Corsair and her army are exonerated of all wrongdoing."

There was a collective groan from the audience, but not a single person hesitated, except for a little girl who ran to the light haired man who was still lifting himself off the ground. Cedric watched as the girl, who was no more than eight or nine years old, helped the man off the ground, and then wrapped her arms around him and squeezed him tight.

Cedric approached the scene with Darian as the soldier who was responsible for the premature hangings tried to get away. Darian stepped toward the younger soldier who tripped over his own feet, sprawling onto the ground. He rolled over to face Darian, who said, "I suppose you think you're funny, treating prisoners with such disrespect?"

"N-no, sir, Arch-Magus," the young man said.

"You could have killed an innocent person today. Thankfully, there were no doubts about his guilt," Darian said, motioning to the man still hanging from the gallows. "But General Corsair's innocence was certainly in question, and you ignored that in favor of a few seconds of fame. For that, I have no qualms with trading one life for another. In the coming months, Jax Fellstar shall be far more valuable to Caldoor than a runt like you."

"Please," the young man begged.

Darian ignored him, pointed a finger at him as he tried to scramble away, and said, "Obitas nexasa mortai."

A black bolt of energy flew from his fingers into the young soldier's chest and snuffed out his life. Darian turned back to the other soldiers with an unapologetic look on his face. "Clean this refuse up, and get the word out to the border where General Corsair's army is being held. They are free to go, but are invited to Caldoor city and shall be welcomed as heroes."

"Yes, Arch-Magus," the senior soldier said, and barked orders at his men to get the mess cleaned up as quickly as possible.

Cedric approached Jax with a smile. "Luck is with you today," he said. "A strong breeze on my arrow, and your life would have been forfeit."

"I thank you," Jax said, his voice still rough. A red bruise had formed around his neck where the rope had squeezed and his eyes were shot with blood, but he was otherwise okay.

Darian approached the pair and said, "Come. You both dine with the King tonight."

Jax looked at him as if he were insulted. "Dine with the King? You think that will bring her back?"

"Not at all," Darian said, his voice changing. Where he usually spoke with a hard elegance, now his voice filled with compassion. Cedric admired the wizard's control. "Nothing can ever bring your wife back. You have my most sincere apologies for all your suffering. Nevertheless, your debt is paid, one life for another. You are free to go."

There was little hesitation in Jax's actions. He turned and urged the young girl to go home and followed after her.

"Please," Darian said, "hear me out."

Jax paused, but didn't turn around.

"There is an army poised to invade Caldoor, or so the bard and General Corsair say. I have been presented with sufficient evidence to believe them. I am willing to give you a command position. Your skills with a blade are unmatched. Won't you please stay, at least for dinner, and talk about it?"

Cedric watched Jax contemplate the offer. When he walked away without a word, Cedric raised a hand to Darian and followed, catching up. "Come now," Cedric said. "I know not your story, but when you are spared a hanging in favor of a command position, one does not toss that aside lightly. Not even myself, and I take very little seriously."

"I care not for his offer," Jax said. "I just want to go back to my children and try to pick up the pieces of my life."

"Okay," Cedric said, still walking next to him. "Have it your way."

He walked next to Jax for some time as they passed through the city to the far side. When the silence was too much, Cedric broke it and said, "Have you lived here long?"

"Only since I completed my training. What does it matter to you?"

"Oh, it doesn't," Cedric said. "But I figured if we're walking together, we might as well talk about something. What did you train for?"

"I'm a blade slinger," Jax said, increasing his pace down the flagstone road.

"A blade slinger? I thought the art was lost. You're very young to be a master."

"I'm not a master. I was an apprentice, but my master died, and I have found no other to take his place. I will train my children as I have been trained, but the art is dying."

"I thought it lost already," Cedric said. His legs burned with the effort of keeping up with Jax, but he dared not give up yet. "It will be lost, though."

"Not so long as I live," Jax said, slowing his pace. Cedric guessed that Jax's legs were as tired as his own.

"Of that, you are right. But that won't be long now, so there's nothing to worry about. Go home, and spend your last days with your children. Grian will rule all this land soon enough."

Jax stopped in his tracks and turned to face Cedric. "Is it true? Is there really an army of the dead waiting to invade Caldoor?"

"I've seen it with my own eyes," Cedric said, taking on a serious tone, one that he reserved for only the most serious of situations.

"How many?"

"Beyond my ability to count. Thousands. Malia came here to not only warn Caldoor, but to request their aid. From what I've seen, even the strong Caldoor military might not be enough." Cedric backed up a step, adjusted his mask, and smoothed out his cloak. "We need every soldier we can get, and we need them to be trained and ready for what they are about to face. Otherwise, we stand little chance of resisting the invasion."

"All right," Jax said, looking at the ground.

"All right?"

"I shall join you, and lend my swords. But not for Darian, and not for Caldoor. I shall fight for Findoor and General Corsair." He lifted his head up and met Cedric's gaze. "And my children."

Cedric smiled and clapped him on the shoulder. "We are glad to have you. Come. Let us get a decent meal out of this kingdom, and I shall break the news to Darian. Malia's army will be coming here. It isn't much, but it's all we have. No more than five hundred men and women, most of whom have had little to eat or drink since we left Findoor Castle."

"I shall join you at the castle," Jax said. "I must tend to my children and ensure they are cared for while I am away."

"Very well," Cedric said. He walked away with a smile on his face as he made his way back to Caldoor Castle.

5

Darian the Black re-entered Caldoor Castle after Cedric walked away. His lab rested deep beneath Caldoor Castle and it took him some time to navigate the twisting and turning hallways and stairs to get there. Once he arrived, he was almost guaranteed none would disturb him. Even runners disliked coming to the musty old subterranean wing that Darian called home.

The lab spanned a large area under the castle and had been created by Darian when he first accepted the position of Arch-Magus. Tables made from Ardan trees lined the walls, as magic always functioned better in the presence of Ardan wood. There were shelves filled with books and tools, and containers of all shapes and sizes with all manner of items in them.

The black steel sword that had been confiscated from Malia waited for him on one of the tables. He'd heard of the sword, discovered by Merek long before the Lyecian war, stolen by Gladius and wielded by him when he faced Krycin, and eventually forgotten about until now. Items with magical properties were hard to find and very few held any kind of good in them. He was curious how such an artifact would find its way into Malia's possession.

"Show me your secrets," Darian said to the sword. "What power do you hold?"

With some trepidation, he moved his hand over the sword without touching it. There was a warmth radiating from it, but no hostility. It felt as though the sword was beckoning him to take hold of it. To wrap his fingers around its hilt and lift it over his head. It wanted to be wielded in combat, it wanted glory and triumph. "A heart of fire," Darian said. He resisted the urge to pick up or even touch the sword. "You'll see only death in me. They don't call me Darian the Black for nothing."

The sword went cold. Dormant. The desire Darian had felt in the sword faded like a dream when one first wakes. He tried to think of how it felt, but couldn't even imagine it. He doubted himself, thinking he was mistaken, perhaps.

"You are a tricky one. I can see why Merek kept you hidden all these years. With the right master, you would be a brilliant sight to behold."

He went to pull his hand away from the sword and felt all the warmth drain from it at once. Pain shot through his hand and up his arm, causing him to snatch it back away from the sword and jump back several steps. The sword flared to life, turning bright red and throwing off vast quantities of heat. Flames burst from the sword, and the table beneath it began to smolder. Darian stared in disbelief as the table was consumed in seconds, leaving the sword to clatter to the floor. It was white-hot now, throwing off waves of heat and forcing Darian to step back several more steps.

"Grishtor curse you," he said, watching the stone floor begin to melt around the sword. "The right master, indeed. Malia was your master, wasn't she?"

The heat began to fade, and the sword returned to its original black color. It rested in a shallow crater created when the stone melted.

"I dare not attempt to wield you. We would not get along, and I'm no good with a sword. But you and Malia, I admire your work on the bridge. Such power could not be achieved by her alone."

There was a knock at his lab door that broke his focus on the sword. There was some hesitation in the knock and it was light-handed. A runner, he suspected. Darian looked around the room and saw the cloud of smoke that had gathered near the ceiling. With a shrug, he walked to the door to answer it.

Waiting in the musty hallway was a young female runner who looked far more nervous than she should have been. Darian expected people to be a little uneasy near his lab, but she was shifting from foot to foot and looking around everywhere but at his door. Her gaze was on the hallway leading away from the lab, and her mind was so distracted that she didn't notice his door open until he cleared his throat.

"You have a message?" Darian asked.

She started and snapped her head in his direction, her eyes wide with fear. "Yes, Arch-Magus."

"Well, what is it? I don't have all day."

"Dinner is served. His Highness requests your presence," she said. She looked at him only as long as she had to, then turned her head toward the floor.

Darian let out a great sigh. "Very well. I'll be there in a moment."

He closed the door without hearing another word from her and walked back to where the sword rested on the floor. With a pair of heavy leather gloves, he picked up the black steel sword. Despite the floor being quite hot still, the sword had cooled and could be handled. He dared not touch it with his bare skin though. "Your power would be quite intoxicating, wouldn't it?" He asked, carrying the sword to another table. "Your master is still alive, though I know not where the Lyecian has taken her."

With the sword resting on the table, he placed the gloves back on the shelf. "You are bound to fire. There must be more, then."

He placed his hand over the sword and felt its familiar warmth. Taking that as an affirmative, he continued his questions. "One for each element?"

The warmth continued, though more subtle this time.

"An element is missing from your ranks? Which is it?"

He thought for a long moment, going over each element and their strengths. "Time. Of course, what would a Time Weaver need of a powerful sword like you. So seven brothers. Seven swords. I wonder if Merek knew this as well."

The possibilities ran through his head. A sword of death with power like this would make him one of the greatest wizards on Galadir. He smiled to himself at the thought of it. "Seems it's time to make a trip to Ducain's Keep after all," he said, and walked toward the door.

## Chapter 13 – Cleaning Up

Soldiers surrounded Seth and Malia as they stood on the platform, but when Mathers walked away to take care of the power situation and get a status report from the scientists, nothing else mattered but each other. Seth walked over to Malia and wrapped his arms around her, pulling her into a warm embrace. "I thought I was gonna lose you," Seth said as he stared into her gray eyes.

"I thought I had lost you. Where have you been?"

"Long story. Not one I care to recite in present company." He looked down at the gold pendant around her neck and smiled. "I see you got my message."

"I found it after you disappeared to close the rift. I have worn it ever since, with hope that I could return it to you." She reached up to unclasp it and take it off, but Seth stopped her.

"You keep it," he said. "Consider it a promise. No matter what happens, I'll always be here for you. I'll always come back for you."

The smile that lit up her face warmed his heart. He leaned in to kiss her, but stopped when he heard Mathers clear his throat behind him.

"The power won't be on for a while yet," Mathers said. "Follow me. We'll walk."

§

Twelve floors, two flights of stairs each. Twenty-four flights of stairs, fifteen steps per flight. That meant three-hundred-sixty steps to the surface of the military compound. By the time Seth, Malia, Mathers and the rest of the soldiers made it to the top, they were all exhausted except for Malia. Seth admired her strength as she climbed the stairs without complaint while many of the other soldiers lamented the loss of power, and thus the loss of the elevator. Smiling to himself, Seth wondered if she even knew what an elevator was.

When they reached the top and had all caught their breath, Seth looked around at what appeared to be an ordinary office building. It might have passed for his old office at Griffin had it not been for all the people in army fatigues.

"So are we prisoners?" Seth asked as Mathers led them down a hallway.

"Not in the normal sense of the word. You will be allowed to go free, so long as you do what we ask of you. If you don't, well, let's just say things will get unpleasant." Mathers looked down at the bracer on Seth's arm as he spoke, then back in front of him so he could keep track of where he was leading them.

They walked through some twists and turns and made it to an office at the end of a long hallway. Each person they passed watched them with amused interest. Malia still wore the prison outfit, which looked like something a homeless person might wear on the streets. Seth wore a simple white tunic and black trousers, along with leather boots. They stood out amongst all the army personnel who were in clean and pressed army uniforms.

Mathers opened the door and led them into an office. Two soldiers came in with them and closed the door behind them. Mathers crossed the room and rounded his desk to sit in the chair behind it. "Have a seat," he said, motioning to several chairs resting in front of his desk.

Seth raised an eyebrow at him and looked at the two soldiers standing inside the office door. One was on each side of the door, and both were equipped with assault rifles. "Are they really necessary?" he asked, turning back to Mathers.

"Insurance. In case you're not inclined to cooperate."

"Sad excuse for insurance," Seth said. "You have no idea who you're dealing with."

"These are some of the most highly trained marines in the United States, son. They're here because I know exactly who I'm dealing with."

Seth focused his mind and willed time to stop. When he was sure nothing would move, he walked over to the two soldiers and took the assault rifles from their hands. He placed them on Mathers' desk and went back for their sidearms and any other weapons they carried.

When they were laid out in front of Mathers, he returned to his original position and willed time to start again.

The startled reaction from the soldiers behind him brought a smirk to his face, but Mathers made him laugh. "Good god, how'd you do that?" he said, jumping back from his desk and leaping to his feet.

"Look," Seth said, taking a step toward the desk. All the humor left his face, and his voice took on a serious tone. "I don't know who you think you are, but I suggest you stop fucking around and get to the point."

Mathers took one more look at the weapons and said to the soldiers at the door, "You're dismissed."

They left the room without saying a word.

"Okay, Alkirk. Have it your way."

Both Seth and Malia sat down in chairs in front of his desk and listened.

"Several weeks ago, we started receiving reports of people who could do strange things. Fires starting without fuel or spark, lightning fired from fingertips, whole people frozen solid. Each of these incidents have a common key. They all encountered a certain set of images that were posted on the Internet."

Malia spared a sideways glance at Seth, who caught it out of the corner of his eye. "You're talking about magic," Seth said. "Humans, performing magic?"

"If you want to call it that, yes. The images in question are right here." Mathers passed some pictures to Seth that made him gasp.

"Oh no," he said, flipping through the five printed images. "No, this isn't good."

"That is High Lyecian," Malia said. "Where did those come from?"

"I forgot about these," Seth said, looking them over one more time. "They're scans of the Lyecian book." A blank expression washed over his face as another realization came to him. His heart filled with hope. "The book. Malia, do you know where it is?"

Malia looked pensive for a moment. "I do not know. You were the last to use it. It must have been forgotten in all the excitement."

Mathers spoke up and interrupted them. "What book? And why isn't this good?"

"This isn't good," Seth said, turning back to face the general, "because the book in question is basically a manual on how to summon and control magic, along with some of the most powerful spells ever discovered on Galadir. If somebody were to discover how to open it, and translate it, that person could destroy worlds. They could be the ruler of a universe. The pages you have here, they are basic spells, along with one on how to awaken suppressed talent."

"Hang on," Mathers said. "You mean, if somebody were to read these pages, they could discover how to use magic?"

"Yeah, that looks like the case. The fact that you are seeing this happen confirms it. We need to get these images off the Internet. If the wrong person figures this out, or the wrong group, Earth will be in serious danger."

"That's what I need you for. The two of you handled that beast that came through before."

"The Narshuk," Malia said.

"If that's what you call it, yes," Mathers said. "I need the two of you to round up these people." He laid a small stack of papers down in front of them, each with a person's picture, name, and a bunch of other information on how to find the person. "They are the ones who have discovered the secrets of the pages. I've stacked them in order of their potential for danger, with the one on top being the most important."

Seth gaped at the first photo, his jaw hanging open in surprise. "Dave."

"Yes, we believe he's the source of the photos. He also vaporized a police officer, and has since disappeared."

"I think I know where he is," Seth said. "We're going to need new clothes. We won't exactly fit in. Got any cash?"

Mathers smiled and nodded. "Of course." He pulled a small briefcase out of a drawer in his desk and set it on top of all the papers. In one smooth motion, he popped the locks, opened the case, and turned it around to show them. "Prepaid cell phone, I have the number so I can contact you. Prepaid credit card with more than enough money to do you. ID cards that will convince anyone who asks, and this." He lifted a small revolver out of a pocket in the case and showed Seth. "Just in case."

Seth scoffed at the revolver. "We won't be needing that."

"Regardless, I'd like you to take it along," Mathers said.

Seth took the gun from Mathers and inspected it. "I wouldn't even know how to fire it. Trust me, it won't be necessary."

"You seem very confident in your abilities."

"Let's be clear, General Neil Mathers," Seth said with a snide tone. "I've taken on some of the most powerful wizards on Galadir and lived to tell the tale. I can slow and stop time, and teleport instantly from one place to another. I'm the only Lyecian ever to be able to wield all eight elements. That pea shooter of yours is useless in my hands. Besides, where I'm going, carrying a gun is a no-no."

Mathers let out a sigh. "Okay, have it your way." He put the revolver back on his desk and closed the case. "My people are currently making the same case for you," he said to Malia. "We hadn't anticipated having two people to prepare for."

Seth cleared his head and took a deep breath. "I have one more request."

"What's that?" Mathers asked.

"Remove the leash," Seth said, holding up the bracer. "From both of us."

"I don't think I can do that. What would stop you from bolting the second I took them off?"

"Trust. If we're going to work together, we have to trust each other. But you must understand, I have obligations elsewhere as well. My father is being held captive, Malia's kingdom has been usurped, and somehow I have to help set things right. I need to be able to come and go at my leisure, but I assure you, from one man to another, that I will help you fix this. It was my fault it happened and I wouldn't be able to live with myself if this caused a war or worse on Earth."

When Seth mentioned his father, Malia snapped her gaze to him and eyed him with a curious expression. Seth placed a hand on hers to reassure her that he would explain later.

Mathers appeared to consider the request, and then nodded. "Okay. You saved us once by closing the portal. I'll trust you. But if you betray that trust, I promise you, I'll never stop hunting you, and next time, I won't let you go." He pulled a key chain from his pocket and sifted through the many keys until he found one that looked like it would fit in the lock on the bracer. Once the bracer was removed, Seth felt like a weight was lifted off his shoulders. Mathers removed the bracer from Malia's arm as well.

Seth looked at Malia and smiled. "Let's go shopping."

§

Seth, Malia, and Private Dana Jackson left the military compound once Malia's case was ready. Dana drove them into town so they could find some clothes that would help them blend in better.

Downtown Denton was a small but bustling place. Stores lined the streets, and people milled along the sidewalks, moving from place to place. Many buildings had other businesses in the upper floors as well. A shopper could find just about anything if they took the time to look. Clothing was among the most popular stores and Dana led them to a place where Malia could find something young and modern that would compliment her features. Seth waited in a chair outside the fitting rooms while the two women worked out an outfit.

She finished their trip in a designer pair of blue jeans that looked like they were made for her, and a fit black t-shirt with a plaid button-up shirt over top. Dana took her old clothes and stuffed them into the bag and handed it to the cashier. "Just trash these. She won't need them anymore."

They left the store and walked down the street toward the mall at the end. "I'll pick up some clothes in there," Seth said to them.

"That's fine, you know your way around, right?" Dana asked.

"Yeah, if you ladies have somewhere to be."

"I'm going to take her to have something done with her hair."

Malia looked at her confused. "What is wrong with my hair?"

Seth laughed and looked at her long, wild blonde hair that flowed down her back. "Nothing, Malia. But it would be better if it were styled to fit in a little better. Besides, we're going to be dancing later, so you should probably get it put up in some way."

Dana smiled at her and took her hand. "Don't worry, we won't cut it, if that's what you're worried about. We're just going to make it a little more manageable."

"Very well. How long shall it take? And where shall we meet up?" Malia asked, looking at Seth.

"I'll meet you here. In an hour?"

"That should be enough time. If we're not here, just wait longer. She has a lot of hair."

Seth parted from them and walked to the big mall at the end of the street. There was a department store inside where he could find clothes and anything else he needed. He looked down at his wrist and realized he had no way to tell when an hour had passed. *First stop, Jewelery,* he thought to himself. Some things were moved since he had last been there and it took him a few minutes of walking around before he found what he was looking for. A jewelery counter sat at the very center of the store with racks of wristwatches on display. He went over and browsed the watches for a few minutes before he found one that suited him. A steel watch band, multiple time zones, and both analog and digital time displays.

100

The case that held it was locked and no associate was in sight. He looked around a bit before he spotted a woman outside the counter talking to another customer. When she finished with that person, he approached her. "Excuse me," he said, with a smile.

The woman turned around, looked at him and wrinkled her nose, then scoffed and walked away back behind the counter.

Her reaction caught Seth off guard and it took a minute for him to recover. By the time he worked himself up to approach her again, she was dealing with another customer, a well-dressed man who was looking at diamonds. She was sweet to him, smiling and willing to show him anything he wanted to see. Again, Seth waited until she was done before approaching.

"Excuse me, I need some help," he said.

She looked at him once more and wrinkled her nose again. "You sure do," she said. Her voice had a bit of southern to it, but it had mixed with a midwest accent which Seth guessed was the result of living in the south when she was young. "I'm sorry sir, you'll have to go to the mission across the road if you're looking for handouts."

"I'm not looking for handouts," Seth said, raising his voice. "I'm looking to buy a watch, are you going to help me or not?"

"Oh," she said. A flush appeared on her cheeks and she turned her eyes away from him. "I'm so sorry. I thought you were a homeless person. We get them in here sometimes. It's the reason we've had to lock everything up. Give me one moment and I'll get you what you need."

She walked over to the cash register, out of earshot of Seth, and picked up the phone. Despite being a fair distance from him, she put a hand up over her mouth when she talked and made no secret of what she was doing. *She's calling security. Fantastic,* Seth thought.

When she returned, she wore a fake smile and said, "Now, how can I help you?"

Seth walked over to the case that held the watch he wanted and pointed it out. "I want this one, here."

"An excellent choice." There was a jingle as she fumbled with keys and then dropped them. Seth suspected she was stalling, but took a deep breath to keep his cool.

When she finally got the keys straight, found the right one, and was opening the case, Seth heard a deep male voice behind him. "Excuse me, sir? I'm going to have to ask you to leave."

Seth turned around to face the man and was surprised to see a very large, very tall security guard standing before him. "Perhaps the associate here misunderstood me," Seth said. "I'm here to buy a watch and some clothes. I don't want any trouble."

"If you don't want any trouble, then you'll leave quietly. This is a place of business, we don't need your kind causing trouble and stealing things. The exit is that way," he said. "Go now, and we'll be discreet about this."

"I'm not going anywhere until I've gotten what I came for," Seth said. He could feel anger welling up inside him, and he regretted separating from Dana and Malia. "Escort me if you like, I'll pay for everything, but I have no intention of leaving empty-handed."

The guard nodded to the girl behind the counter and she proceeded to take the watch out of the case for Seth. He turned back to her as she reached down to get a box for him.

"Oh, that won't be necessary. I'll just wear it out. Here," Seth said, handing her the card Mathers had given him. "That should cover it."

She scurried away, watch and card in hand to ring it in, and Seth turned back to the guard. He took a deep breath and said, "Are the homeless in this city really that big of a problem?"

"Sure are," the big man said. "Ever since they started expanding that base just out of town. Been buying up land, putting farmers out of business cuz crops won't grow around the base, and nothing new will move into town. People are afraid, and the homeless population has been growing."

"Ahh," Seth said. He understood why they acted the way they did. He looked down at his own clothes and realized that he did look very much like a homeless man in his dirty tunic and trousers. He looked back up at the guard and said, "I'm not homeless. I've been to hell and back, but I'm far from homeless."

"Sorry bout this," he said. "We got rules we gotta follow now. Corporate was tired of losing merchandise. No hard feelings, right?"

"No worries," Seth said.

The girl returned and handed Seth the watch and his card back. "So sorry for the confusion, Mr. Alkirk," she said. "I hope you'll shop here again."

Seth smiled and nodded at her, put the watch on his wrist and kept the receipts. He turned back to the guard and said, "Think you could escort me around the store until I can get some proper clothes? I'm not interested in any more trouble."

"Sure thing, Mr. Alkirk."

"Call me Seth."

The guard smiled at him, a big toothy smile that showed a mouth full of missing teeth except for the very front ones. He looked like he'd been working a long shift because he had a good five-o-clock shadow going on, and a face pocked with scars from years of shaving with dull razors. Seth guessed that his job barely paid the bills. "You can call me Rudy," the guard said.

"Okay, Rudy. Where is menswear?"

"Follow me," he said, and took off faster than Seth expected him to go.

He followed Rudy through the store to the far corner where there were racks of men's clothing on display and fitting rooms in the corner. Seth looked through the pants and picked out a pair of black cargos, then found some t-shirts that would fit him. He took the lot to the change room and got dressed, pulling the tags off and keeping them so the cashier could ring him through. When he emerged from the dressing room, Rudy flashed him a smile. "Looking much better, Seth."

"Thanks. Where can I find a coat? It's getting cold out this time of year, isn't it?"

"Sure is. Gets right chilly at night. Come with me, I know where you can find a good one."

Again, Seth followed him through the store to a display of thin but warm jackets that were touted as the latest technology in outerwear. "These look awesome," Seth said, picking a black one off the shelf.

He tried it on, right there in the aisle over top of his clothes. It fit well, and felt warm enough for the temperature outside. "Okay, this should do. Where do I pay for this stuff?"

"Right at the front of the store. I'll keep you company, since you're wearing your purchases. Strictly speaking, I'm not allowed to let you do that, but I'll make an exception." He gave Seth another of his less-than-toothy smiles and led him to the cashiers at the front of the store.

"Thanks, Rudy. You've been a big help," Seth said.

"No problem. Take care."

Once Seth got through the cashier, with Rudy reassuring the cashier that everything was in order, he left the mall and went back to the meeting place. Dana and Malia were nowhere in sight, so Seth crossed the street to a coffee shop, sat down at a table where he could see outside, and ordered an extra large.

His coffee arrived moments later in a white paper cup, with a plastic lid. He marveled at the convenience of it, as it was something he hadn't had in months. He took a sip of the beverage and savored the taste of the bitter drink. He never realized how much he took coffee for granted.

Twenty minutes later, Dana and Malia arrived at the rendezvous point. It took Seth a moment to realize it was Malia because she looked so different. The sides of her hair were french braided to the back of her head. The rest of her hair was tied back with the two braids and left to hang down the middle of her back. She had makeup done as well, but it was modest, and highlighted her features.

Seth grabbed two more coffees and went out to meet them. Malia smiled as he approached. "You look quite handsome," she said.

He laughed and felt his cheeks burn. "You took my breath away," he said. "Here, try this." He took one of the cups from the tray and handed it to her, then gave the other to Dana.

Malia looked at the cup with curiosity. "How do I try it?" She asked, fiddling with the lid.

"Oh, sorry," Seth said. He'd forgotten that she'd never seen a take-out cup before. "Watch." He reached over and pulled the tab on the lid, lifted it up, and folded it back to latch it to the lid.

"How clever," Malia said with a smile. She lifted the cup to her lips and took a sip. The expression on her face was hard to read, but Seth thought she looked nostalgic. "It tastes similar to the tar-leaf tea that comes from southern Astara. But it is very expensive, and is consumed only on special occasions."

"We call it coffee, and it's very common here. It's been months since I've had any," Seth said.

Dana raised her cup to the two of them. "To coffee, and tar-leaf tea."

"Indeed," Malia said, and raised her cup as well.

Seth raised his cup and nodded. "So now what? I think we could all use a shower or something. At least, I could. Running water is something of a luxury in Galadir as well. In fact, I can't remember seeing it anywhere but Alkirk Manor."

"We can go back to the base, but that's a long drive."

"Why don't we go back to my house?" Seth asked. "I assume it's still my house?"

Dana nodded. "When you disappeared, General Mathers had the house appropriated. I don't think anyone has been there since the original investigation though."

"Let's go then," Seth said, leading the way back to Dana's car.

# Chapter 14 – A Miscalculation

Cedric and Jax sat side by side at the head table in the main banquet hall of Caldoor Castle. King Farric and Darian sat at the center of the table facing out toward a large gathering of citizens. Rows of tables furnished the room and the aroma of fresh baked bread and spit-fired meat filled the air. Residents occupied every seat in a hall that, on any other night, would be empty other than the King and a few close advisors. The constant drone of people talking made it nearly impossible for Cedric to listen to his hosts who were trying to say something to him.

"Cedric, our honored guest," Darian said. "Won't you please remove your mask and cloak and make yourself comfortable?"

"I'm forbidden to do so, as you well know," Cedric said. "But rest assured, I am comfortable. How are the Findoor troops? Have they begun their journey here yet?"

"Letters to that effect have been deployed by falcon to the former site of the bridge. They will be on their way here by morning. I assume that with General Malia missing, her first commander, Ceridan, will be taking charge of her troops?"

"Yes, Commander Ceridan is more than capable of managing her troops. How do you plan to defend against the coming army? How many wizards have you assembled? How many troops?" Cedric asked. His first concern was making sure there would be adequate time to prepare for the coming attack. "Do you have any plans to go after Grian himself?"

"Come now, Cedric," Farric said through a mouthful of food. He swallowed and continued. "War plans can wait. Orders will be deployed first thing in the morning. I'm certain our well-trained army can handle what's coming."

"Tomorrow?" Cedric asked, raising his voice. "You plan on waiting until tomorrow? Perhaps you don't fully understand what you are up against. The army that is marching on Caldoor doesn't eat. It doesn't sleep. There are no politics, no ranks, no emotions. It was created by magic, is driven by magic, and will not stop to wait for you to be ready. If you do nothing now, it will sweep across your land as it did in Findoor and leave nothing in its wake. Verand was a fool who allowed his court to decide when to deploy troops against the better judgment of his advisors. Findoor paid the price for that foolishness. This army is at your doorstep now. Don't wait until it's too late."

During his speech, the entire room fell silent and every person in the room now looked at Cedric, who realized he was standing and berating their King. The young King also appeared to notice, as he cleared his throat to respond. "Very well. I shall send word tonight. Every able-bodied person will be required to do their duty for their kingdom. Darian, do what you can to assemble any wizards who are capable of fighting such an army."

"As you wish, Your Highness," Darian said. His tone was flat and his face unamused, but Cedric had never known Darian to refuse an order from his King.

"Will that appease you, bard?" King Farric asked.

"Yes, thank you. I wish only to help, as I have always done." He flashed Darian a sly smile, who returned a cool glare. "One last thing, Your Highness."

"What is it?"

"We must find Seth Alkirk and Malia. The Time Weaver may be our only real hope of stopping Grian, and as of earlier today, he disappeared with Malia. I know not where he might have taken her, but with Darian's help, perhaps we can find a clue."

"I am more than happy to help him," Darian said. "I'm interested in meeting this Time Weaver myself."

"There you go," Farric said, and looked out to all the people gathered before him. "Enough of this, though. Let us celebrate our Findoor friends tonight, for opening our eyes before it was too late."

A rowdy cheer came up from the crowd and everybody dug into their meals. All except Cedric and Jax, who picked away at the food in front of them. Cedric leaned toward Jax and said, "Not hungry either?"

"Nay," Jax said. "I fear the danger is being misunderstood." He lowered his voice so that Cedric could barely hear it. "The Caldoor army is not as heavily armed or well trained as Farric is led to believe. They will make a valiant effort, but if this enemy you speak of is as powerful as you say, Caldoor might already be lost."

"Indeed," Cedric said in the same hushed voice. "We must find Seth and Malia."

They finished their dinner in silence, picking away at their meat and vegetables. The bread was the highlight of the meal. It was fresh baked that day and made from Caldoor grains which were the kingdom's chief export. When the hall had cleared of most citizens, Darian invited both Cedric and Jax down to his lab to discuss Malia and Seth.

Cedric looked around at the dark corridor leading to the lab and noted the musty smell and undecorated walls. "Not much for pleasantries down here, are you Darian?" he asked with a smirk.

"Pleasantries are for kings and princes. I conduct business down here, most of which the average person has no place knowing anything about." Darian opened the lab door with the wave of his hand and motioned for Cedric and Jax to enter.

Once the three of them were inside, Darian said, "Where did Seth come from?"

"His parents are from Galadir, though his exact lineage I'm uncertain of. I know he carries the Alkirk name. Seth himself grew up on the dead world."

"He might have taken Malia there. Was there anything unusual about his disappearance at the Gallows besides the obvious?" Darian asked.

Jax spoke at that moment, startling the other two men out of their discussion. "I don't think he went willingly."

"What would give you that impression?" Darian asked.

"When Seth appeared, there was nothing. He simply appeared below her. But when they disappeared, there was a blue flash of light, and a wave of energy."

"Curious," Cedric said.

"Curious indeed," Darian said. "If that's true, then you are correct. He was summoned, and Malia was caught in it by accident. Their lives may be in danger."

"Send us there," Cedric said. It came out without him thinking and he almost regretted saying it once it was out.

"Send you there? To the dead world?" Darian asked. "I'm unsure whether this is courage or stupidity, but we know so little about the dead world or who lives there. Can you be certain you can find them?"

Cedric shrugged. "Little is certain these days, but we must try. If Jax and I work together, we stand a good chance. If we do nothing, I am certain they won't be found."

"Are you in agreement, Jax? Do not make this decision lightly, for you may not return." Darian asked.

"Yes. I would be honored to work alongside Cedric."

"Go then, prepare yourselves, and meet back here in an hour. I shall make preparations to open a rift. Once you get there, your only hope of returning here is with the Time Weaver. Find Seth, and he can bring you home."

"Understood," Cedric said. "Come, Jax. Let's get you some weapons."

# Chapter 15 - The Lyric

Dave and Sophie left her apartment with a bunch of her friends and took one of their cars. Sophie introduced him as her boyfriend, which made him smile. She took extra care to make herself up before they left and Dave thought she looked more beautiful than ever. Her hair was tied back for a night of dancing and she wore eyeliner and mascara that made her blue eyes stand out. Red lipstick and a little bit of blush, combined with an outfit that showed her pale white flesh in all the right places and Dave wished he could tell her friends to go away and just have her to himself for the night.

He caught his breath and said, "When we get to the club, I gotta go talk to my boys upstairs. You ladies go ahead and order some drinks and have fun. I'll get them to put it all on a tab in my name. Tonight is on me."

They all went down to the parking lot and got in the car. Dave took the middle position in the back seat so that he wouldn't be spotted on the way. By now, he and Sophie had seen reports with his picture on the news. The police were looking for him and claimed he was wanted for murder.

The drive there was uneventful. They parked as close to the club as they could, but it was a busy night and the streets in the downtown area were already filled with cars. The four girls got out first, with Sophie looking in at him. "Coming?"

"Yeah," Dave said. "Just a little nervous. If somebody sees me and recognizes me, we're done."

"Don't worry. Everyone in the club will be so drunk, or worse, that they'll barely know their own name. You think they'll remember some random news report they saw earlier today?"

"True enough," Dave said. "Okay, let's do this."

He got out of the car and hobbled the best he could with an injured foot. Walking in the middle of the four girls, they made casual conversation so as not to attract attention and arrived at the entrance to the club. There was a lineup out the door at the club already with a large bouncer at the front. Some people got in and some were turned away. Dave turned to Sophie and said, "Let me take care of this. We'll be dancing in no time."

He led the way, limping past the line of people waiting and straight to the bouncer at the door. "Louie, my man," Dave said with a smile. His heart was pounding while he said it, but he did his best not to show it. "Spare some love for me and my crew? I gotta talk to the big man."

Louie looked down at Dave and scoffed. "Big man ain't seein' no one tonight."

"Come on, man. You guys are my boys, and I'm in a jam, deep. Help a brother out?"

"Heard about your jam. Big man don't want no part of it. Back of the line," Louie said, taking a step forward. He was a much bigger man than Dave and had been known to throw guys bigger than Dave around like rag dolls when they got unruly.

Sophie pushed past Dave and stood facing Louie, looking up into his eyes. "I don't know who you think you are, but you tell the 'Big Man' that if he doesn't see Dave right now, we're gonna have a very serious problem. If you know the 'jam' that Dave is in, you know we can make this a real big mess in a real big hurry."

Dave saw the fear in Louie's eyes. He mumbled something into a microphone clipped to his collar, waited a second, and then looked down at Dave and Sophie. "Go ahead. All of you. Big man will see you, Dave, and only you."

Dave put on a smile for the bouncer. "Cool, man. Cool. I owe you."

"No, you owe her," Louie said, pointing at Sophie. "Your lady there got spunk. Go on, before the Big Man changes his mind."

The group walked past him and entered the club, much to the chagrin of the many people waiting in line. Inside the club the music pounded. An electronic house-style music with a strong bass line that kept the patrons of the club moving all night. The dance floor was out of sight from the entrance, but the music was clear no matter what corner of the club you were in. Dave looked at Sophie and smiled. "Take your girls and go have fun. I shouldn't be long."

Sophie nodded. "Be careful. These guys aren't your typical gangsters."

"Don't worry 'bout me. I got it covered," Dave said with a smile.

"Yeah, sure you do. Like you had Louie covered too, right?" She flashed him a grin and walked away.

Dave went to the left where the stairs to the second floor were. There was no door, and no guard at the bottom of the stairs, but he knew his every move was being monitored. He climbed the stairs one at a time, favoring his good foot, and went through the door at the top. It opened into a long hallway with doors on either side. At the end of the hall was a door marked with a big gold star. *Great,* he thought. He limped his way down the hall and tried to ignore sounds of torture and sex behind each door. Some of the club's VIPs had fantasies and fetishes that Dave found weird, and often disturbing. The owners of the club did it all under the table, and because they dealt with some of the most powerful people in the city and surrounding cities, nobody touched them.

When he reached the end of the hall, the door with the star opened without him needing to knock. Inside was a room that looked like any other office. There were filing cabinets, a large wood desk, a blank whiteboard, and several well-dressed men sitting in chairs around the room. Dave also noticed guns. Lots of guns.

Every person in the room had at least one gun. Some of them two or three. The desk was also covered with guns and there were some hanging on the walls. There were also what Dave guessed might be explosives on top of one filing cabinet.

Hanging from the ceiling were several exotic plants that looked very out of place.

The man behind the desk, a white guy with black hair and a thin mustache cleared his throat. "How's it going, Dave?"

"I'll be honest with you, Ricky. I've been better. Think you can set my girls up with a tab? I'm good for it."

"Already done. You better be good for it. You know it ain't a good idea to owe me money."

"No problem," Dave said, waving a hand at him. "I need to lay low for a while. Disappear, ya know? It may require some travel, under the radar. Think you can hook me up?"

"That depends." Ricky stood up from his chair and walked around his desk. "What are you running from?"

"You know what," Dave said. He tried to hold Ricky's gaze, but couldn't. He looked down at the floor as Ricky approached.

"Word on the street is, you're wanted for icing a cop. That true? I didn't believe it myself. I mean, I know you, man. I know what you're capable of. We're practically brothers. Murder ain't your style."

"It was an accident," Dave said, lifting his head so he could look Ricky in the eyes again.

Ricky burst out laughing along with the other three guys in the room. It was so sudden that it startled Dave and made him jump, which sent pain through his foot. "An accident, huh?"

"That's my story, and I'm stickin' to it."

"My guy on the inside says you vaporized one of 'em. Nothing left but his shoes and sidearm. That's some accident. They say you were cookin' up some meth. That true?"

Dave took a deep breath and closed his eyes. "No, no meth."

Ricky chuckled and hit Dave's shoulder with his fist which hurt more than he would have expected. "Relax, man. I knew you weren't creepin' on my turf. So, weapons then. Something that can vaporize a human, no trace, in a single hit. Some kind of designer explosive?"

"No," Dave said. The first pangs of regret had started to creep into his mind. These guys wouldn't stop until he told them what they wanted to hear. "No, nothing like that." He thought for a second, and an idea came to him. "Look, I need a place to hang out, and you want what I got. It can be used as a weapon, but it's not a weapon really. I think that's a pretty decent bargain? You harbor a fugitive for a bit, and in return, you get yourself a new toy to play with."

"Alright, alright, I see how it is. You drive a hard bargain, but I'm sure an arrangement can be made. There's some rooms in the basement where you can crash for a bit. I'll get you what you need to make me a weapon that can make some bad people go 'poof', and everyone will be happy. I'm only doin' this cuz we go back a long way, my man. Don't make me regret it."

Dave smiled and took a deep breath. He realized he'd been holding his breath but he had what he needed now, even if he had to teach some of Ricky's goons the same trick. "You won't regret it. I can't thank you enough. I'm gonna need my computer stuff from my house. All my hard drives. That's where my research is. I won't be able to do anything without it."

"Leave it to me," Ricky said. He motioned for one of the guys in the office to approach. "Nelson, get this man what he's asked for. All of his equipment from his house, and anything seized by the cops." He motioned for another to approach. "Go downstairs and make sure the guest suite is clean, and I mean really clean. Treat this man like family. Treat him better than family. He's a close personal friend of mine, so if you offend him, you'll be offending me. Got it?"

The man nodded and left the room in a hurry.

Ricky turned to face the third man. "Take Dave here downstairs, reunite him with his lady friends, and make sure he has a good time. If he's stayin' here, he and all his guests are eatin' and drinkin' on my dime. Go on, man, have a good time. We'll have everything here by morning."

Dave opened his mouth to say something when he heard a commotion outside the office. There were shouts and gun shots fired. One bullet came through the office door, whizzed past Dave's ear, and came to a stop in the far wall. He felt the wind of the bullet as it went by and dropped himself to the floor. Ricky pulled two hand guns from holsters and aimed them at the door. "Stay down, man. This is gonna get ugly."

He jumped back and slid across the surface of his desk to get behind it, knocking various weapons onto the floor in the process. Dave had already made it half way around the desk when more bullets were fired through the door. Ricky waited with his guns ready and aimed at the door.

5

Seth's house was almost exactly as he had left it. The lawn was a little overgrown and nobody had been by to pick up the newspapers, which left a small pile of them on his front step. What gardens were there had long since died off, and hedges and shrubs around his yard were overgrown.

"Would it have killed them to send somebody out to tend to my yard?" Seth asked with a smile.

"Before you get out," Dana said, looking serious. "The story of your disappearance is that you and your mother have gone on an extended vacation overseas together. That's what's been told to everyone who's filed a missing persons report. If you get questioned by a neighbor, go with that. If they want details, make up something believable and write it down."

"Good to know," Seth said. "Why with my mother?"

"Because she hasn't been seen since the day you disappeared."

"Oh." Concern crept into Seth's heart when he heard that, but he also knew he had little time to dwell on it. "All right. Come on in, Malia. I'll show you around."

They all got out of the car and walked to the front door. Seth reached into the garden beside the door and picked up a rock, turned it over, and opened a compartment in the bottom. He pulled a key from it and used it to open the door. Seth led the way inside and flipped the entryway lights on as the sun was just starting its final descent on the horizon.

The inside of the house wasn't in too bad of a shape other than a bit of dust on everything. Malia looked up in wonder at the light on the ceiling. "I thought this world had no magic?"

Seth laughed and said, "That's not magic. It's just a light. Electricity."

She walked in and removed her shoes and jacket and made room for Dana to do the same. Seth led the way into the house. "You'll have to pardon the dust, I haven't been here in a while."

He flipped lights on as he went and showed Malia around – kitchen, living room, hallway, bedrooms, and finally the bathroom. She looked around in awe as he showed her his home. "You are so rich compared to the people of Galadir. Lights such as these are powered by permanent magic and are reserved for nobles and those who can afford them."

She looked around the bathroom, at the bathtub and shower, the toilet, the sink. Seth walked over to the sink and turned a faucet to let the water flow. A steady stream ran from the spout and into the sink, only to flow down the drain. Malia gasped in surprise. "Where does the water come from? Where does it go?"

Seth laughed again. "All these things we take for granted. Every house has electricity, water and sewage. There's gas as well, for heating the house when it's cold out." He pointed to the vent where the warm air would blow from. "Speaking of which, I should turn the heat on. It's a little cold in here, and it's going to get colder."

"To be able to just turn the heat on when it is cold. That would be a wonder in most homes. I would very much love to stay here longer. Not many people on Galadir get to experience this level of luxury." She walked over to the toilet and pointed to it. "What is this for?"

"Oh," Seth said, snickering. "That's a toilet. If you need to, uhm, pee. That's where you do it. When you're done, just push this lever..." Seth reached down and pushed the flush lever. The water came to life in the bowl, swirling and flowing down the drain. Malia jumped again and smiled at it. "... and it all goes away."

"Your tradesmen have thought of everything," Malia said, still smiling. She motioned to the bathtub and said, "This must be your wash basin."

"We call it a bathtub, and that's a shower," Seth said pointing at the shower head. "Once you get the water temperature where you want it, pull that button up, and it will turn on and rain water down on you so you can wash up."

She felt the plastic shower curtain, looked around, and ran a hand over the laminated counter, then touched the light switch cover plate. "What is this? I see it everywhere in here, but I've never seen a material like it before. The cup that held my drink earlier, the lid was made of it as well. Galadir has nothing like it."

"Plastic. We make a lot of things out of it. It's cheap, easy to work with, and can be made into almost any shape."

Seth motioned for her to follow and led her into his bedroom. Dana was in the living room and it sounded like she was watching TV. His bedroom was in the same condition he had left it so long ago when he first opened the Lyecian book. He walked in and sat down on his bed and patted the mattress beside him. "Come in, sit down. We have some time now, and I have some things to talk to you about."

Malia took a seat beside him on the bed. Bounced once to test it, and then turned and smiled at him. "It seems everything in your house is luxurious."

"In reality, I'm just middle class," Seth said. "Lower middle class really. Before I met you, I was working as a software developer, and just starting to work my way up in the company. I didn't make a lot of money, and everything I did make went into savings or into my house. The morning my powers emerged from suppression, my whole life changed, and I realize now that I can't go back to this."

"I am sorry your life has changed so much in so little time," she said, looking back at him and meeting his gaze.

Their eyes locked on each other and for a moment, Seth felt his stomach rise into his throat. What he had to say could change everything between them, but he had to be honest. "Don't be sorry. I'm not. I did it to myself."

Her face turned curious. "To yourself? How could you have done all this to yourself?"

"This is what I have to tell you. I hope you understand, that no matter what I say now, my feelings for you haven't changed. Throughout my ordeal, my only thoughts were getting back to you."

"Tell me, Seth. What is it that bothers you so?" Her face was now a mix of curiosity and concern. Her gray eyes pleaded with him to get on with it, but he was having a hard time figuring out what to say.

"Okay, it's a bit confusing, so I'll start at what I perceive as the beginning. My father didn't leave me. I took him away. It was the only way to save Galadir. I grew up on Earth, but Galadir is where I was born, and where my heart rests now."

"I do not understand, how could you have taken Krycin away? You were five years old, were you not?"

"Yes, and no. Everybody thought Krycin was my father because I looked so much like him. The truth is, I am Krycin. My father's name is Serrin, and you'll find no records of his existence because I made sure there were none." He rubbed at his wrist where the mark of Hadra still remained, a symbol of a price he had yet to pay for what she had done for him. "I couldn't afford to leave any trace of where I had taken my family. The day I took Serrin away, I suppressed the powers of a much younger me so that Cy wouldn't find him, or rather, me. Serrin came forward with me, to the present, and helped me repair the last of the damage that Gladius's simulacrum caused."

Malia let go of his hands and backed away from him. "What you are telling me is not possible. You would have to travel through time, and no wizard or Lyecian can do that, no matter how powerful they grow."

"I can, and I have. I won't do it again. When I did it this time, I caused a war that wiped out almost every Lyecian on Galadir. Please understand, I'm not just a Lyecian. There's something more in me, and there are more out there like me."

"How," she said, with a note of anger. "How can this be? The Lyecian war was one hundred years ago. Please, Seth, help me understand, because I do not."

Seth recounted the events of his adventure since he closed the rift created by Cy. Waking up on the beach with no memories, befriending the blue wizard Gladius, being chased by the fates, and the eventual fall out with Gladius and the final battle. He was nearing the end of his story when he got to the part where he returned to the present. "I didn't return alone. I brought two others with me. Tyriel Ceorn, the reaper who chased me at first. He gave up his powers so that I could repair the damage that I'd done to the time line. The other was Gladius himself."

Malia gasped and jumped to her feet. "No. No, we killed him. Krycin killed him. He is dead, and gone, and we will never have to

worry about his evil again. Please say this is so, and that you jest."
She backed up a step, her face filled with fear.

"No. No joking. Your history doesn't say that Krycin killed
Gladius. It says that Krycin *defeated* Gladius. And I did. I nearly killed
him, but I couldn't bring myself to do it. There was another presence,
something darker, that was controlling him. When I defeated him, I
broke that bond. The man I brought forward is nothing but a young
man who is much wiser for his mistakes. Everyone deserves a chance
at redemption."

Uncertainty clouded her face. Seth saw the conflict on her face. "I
admire your strength," she said after a long pause. "I would not have
been able to find it in myself to forgive him." She stepped forward
again and reached down to him. Seth took her hands and stood up,
face-to-face with her.

"So now... now we have two messes to clean up," Seth said. "We
have a mess here, with humans learning to use magic, and we have
Grian in charge of Findoor, leading an army of undead."

"We cannot be everywhere, but I know that Cedric and Ceridan
will do what they can to continue the fight for Findoor, even in my
absence."

"There is also the new Wizard High Council, who is searching for
a way to undo what Grian has done."

Malia smiled at this. "Then Findoor is in good hands."

"Grian has my father as well."

"Bait on a hook," Malia said. "He will not kill him. He will use him
to lure you in. If he knows who and what you are, he will stop at
nothing to capture you and acquire what power you have."

"So for now, we take care of Earth. We stick to the plan. Which
means, I need a shower and a shave." He flashed Malia a smile, and
she grabbed him and pressed her lips against his.

It took Seth by surprise and was a far more intense kiss than any
before it. When they parted, Seth was speechless. Malia laughed and
said, "That is for being honest with me. I can tell it took great
strength to recount, and I want you to understand that I do not
blame you for the Lyecian war. Gladius made his choices, regardless
of his motivation. With or without your presence, he would have
chosen the same; he would simply have found the motivation in
something else."

"Thanks. That actually makes me feel better," Seth said. He
gathered up his things and went to the bathroom for a shower. When

he was done, he walked back to his room wrapped in a towel to get dressed and found Malia flipping through some of his books.

"I know, it doesn't make for very interesting reading," Seth said of the software engineering textbook she was looking at. "But it's what I was good at."

She looked up from the book at Seth and said, "That much I do understand. Many have asked me why I continue on my path in the military rather than starting a family like most women my age. It is what I am good at."

"I don't know why, but a sword in your hand has never looked unnatural."

Malia stood up and returned the book to the shelf. "Where can I find the towels, and I shall get washed up as well."

"The closet in the hallway. Third shelf," Seth said. "I'll be here, getting dressed."

When both of them were ready, they walked back into the living room hand in hand and approached the couch where Dana was watching sitcoms. She turned to face them and clapped. "You two look fantastic!"

"Thanks, Dana," Seth said and walked to the couch to sit down.

Malia stared at the television, a look of fascination on her face. "I had no idea you had scrying pools in your world," she said. "How do you keep the water from flowing out?" She walked over and touched the LCD screen and jumped back in surprise when multi-colored ripples moved over its surface.

"Easy," Seth said. "It's not a scrying pool. We call it a television. You're watching a recording, not a live performance. It's for entertainment."

She backed up a step and watched the characters on the screen for a few minutes, looking quite amazed. "This is remarkable, though I would prefer a play, or concert. There is nothing like really being there."

"What else do you do for entertainment in your world?" Dana asked.

"Well, we have contests of skill, jousting, swordplay. Those who can afford them read books, but they are a luxury. Children have games they play, but most adults are too busy working to indulge in entertainment. Of course, there is dancing, a few times a year."

"Your world fascinates me, Malia. Someday, I would love to visit. Maybe when you two are done here?"

Seth smiled at the prospect, but shook his head. "You wouldn't like it. It took me a long time to get used to, but I had no choice. I also had a lot of help, and a lot of magic. I couldn't imagine how somebody from Earth would cope." He looked at his watch to check the time. "It's getting late, we should get going to the club. If Dave is anywhere, that's where he'll be. He has connections up there. Some guy he used to go to school with."

"Okay, The two of you go in and get Dave," Dana said. "I'll wait in the parking lot."

There was a moment of silence as Seth considered this, then he shook his head. "No. Go back to the base. We'll meet you there."

"You know I can't do that," Dana said. "I'm supposed to be escorting you everywhere."

"Yeah, yeah, making sure we get the job done. I'm telling you, the job will get done faster if you drop us off and go back to the base. I gave Mathers my word that I would do this, and I will. Not just for him, but for everyone on this planet. Magic is not a force to be played with. It's not a toy. I've seen magic kill thousands. In the wrong hands on Earth, it could kill millions. So we do this my way, and it will get done. Understand?"

Dana backed down, looking somewhat sheepish. "Okay, you're the boss. How do you plan on getting back to the base then?"

"Don't worry about us. I'll make sure we get back," Seth said.

With that, the three of them left the house. Seth turned off all the lights and locked the door behind him. As he walked to the car, one of his neighbors pulled into his driveway. He got out of his car and looked over the roof at Seth with a surprised expression on his face.

"Seth! How was the vacation?" he asked.

"Phil! Hey, it was good," Seth said. "Can't talk now though. We're going out to the club. We'll catch up later, okay?"

"No problem," Phil said. "Don't want to keep the ladies waiting." He flashed Seth a wink and a smile and went into his house.

Seth got in the car and they left his house behind. He looked back at it once, wondering how long it would be this time before he got back to it again.

S

Just after nine, Seth and Malia arrived at the club. Dana dropped them off around the corner and Seth led as they walked the rest of the way to the end of the line. Music boomed out the front doors and they could see a large bouncer controlling the crowd. The line moved fast, but mostly because the bouncer was being picky about who he let in. Anyone who was underdressed or who looked or smelled like they'd already been drinking was turned away. Seth knew from experience that some nights this meant turning away nine out of every ten people who approached the bouncer. *Louie is his name,* he thought as he neared the front of the line with Malia next to him.

When it was their turn, Seth put on a big smile and grasped Malia's hand. "Just here for a good time," he said to the bouncer.

Louie looked him up and down, and then checked out Malia. A slow whistle left his lips as his eyes went from Malia's face to her chest, down to her hips and finally her legs. "I don't know where you picked her up, but you better hold on to her tight," he said in his deep voice.

Seth laughed and wrapped his arm around Malia's waist, pulling her close. "I have no intention of letting her go."

He shot a glance at Malia's face and saw that she was smiling and nodding. Playing along, despite the fact that their conversation was a bit degrading. She was moving her body to the beat already, and she looked at Louie and said, "I just want to dance."

Seth was surprised that she could play along so well, but kept his eyes on Louie. He hesitated for a moment. It looked like he was thinking about something. *Just let us in,* Seth thought.

"Your accent," Louie said. "Where you from?"

He addressed Malia directly, and Seth's heart jumped into his throat. He'd gotten so used to hearing her accent that he didn't notice it anymore. It never occurred to him to come up with a cover story for her.

"New Jersey," She said, surprising Seth.

"Don't sound like no Jersey accent to me, but whatever. Go on in, lovebirds."

They wasted no time leaving him behind. Once they were in the doors and on their way to the main club, Seth looked at her and said, "New Jersey?"

"Yes," Malia said. "I saw it on the back of one of your books."

He breathed a sigh of relief. "I'm glad you have good observation skills, because I totally blew that for us."

She laughed and kept walking through the doors to the bar and dance floor. Seth watched her as she walked several steps ahead of him, her body moving to the rhythm of the music. With her hair back in braids, he could see her long neck and high cheek bones. She looked exotic compared to most women in the club, which was something Seth found very attractive. He followed along behind, but wasn't into the electronic music as much as she was.

The pounding bass line always disoriented him and if he spent too long in the club it would make him sick to his stomach. It didn't appear to be bothering Malia at all. She paused and took Seth's hand. "Come, Seth," she said with a big smile on her face. "This music, it is wonderful. I have not heard anything like it before. Let us dance, we have time."

Before he could object, she pulled him out onto the dance floor and was checking out the moves of some of the other women, learning from them. She was very good at picking up the local dances, and several times got very close to Seth, pressing her body against his. He did his best to match her skill, but was never a very good dancer. Just the same, many people backed away to give them room. Malia laughed and kept it up, adding her own flares to the dancing and enjoying the attention they were getting. Seth took her hand and spun her in place, then pulled her into a tight embrace and swayed to the music with her body against his.

"You're good at this," he said in her ear.

"When you have little for entertainment, dancing becomes much more important to you," she said back to him.

With his head next to hers, Seth was able to see past her. In the crowd behind her, he saw a familiar face that stopped him in his tracks. Dirty blonde hair and blue eyes stared back at him, but she didn't look happy to see him this time.

"Excuse me for a minute," Seth said to Malia. "Enjoy yourself."

He let go of her and walked to where he'd seen Sophie's face, but she was already gone. He looked around and saw her back as she fled into the hallways where the bathrooms were. As quickly as he could, he pursued her, weaving through the crowd and trying not to step on anyone's toes. When he reached the back hallway, Sophie was standing about six feet in with her back against the wall. Her eyes were closed, and he could tell she was trying to hold back tears.

"Sophie," he said.

She looked at him with an icy glare. "You're back."

"Not for long. Hey, I know I stood you up, and I'm sorry."

"Sorry? You're sorry? I thought we were good. I thought you had a great time on your birthday, and I was so excited to see you. We were good together, Seth, and we would have been great together again. Then you disappear. Not a word, not a call. No 'hi', 'bye' or 'go fuck yourself'. You just left, without a trace. What part of that am I supposed to be okay with? And where the hell have you been for three months?"

Seth took a step back. It hadn't occurred to him how his disappearance would affect other people in his life. Now that he thought about it, his sudden reappearance would come as a shock to most. "I didn't have a choice. If I told you the truth, you wouldn't believe me, so I'll tell you what I've been told to tell everyone. I was on an extended vacation."

She scoffed. "Extended vacation, my ass. Who the hell does that? Who leaves their home, their job, their entire life behind, and goes on vacation without a word to anyone? Dave and I have been worried sick about you. But you know what the worst part is? You didn't even call when you were back in town. You just show up here with some slut on your arm, and act like this should all be okay. It's not okay, Seth. Dave's gonna be pissed at you."

Her words cut like knives through his heart, but he bit his tongue and took a deep breath to calm his anger. "Okay, you win. I'm a jerk. You're absolutely right. Where is Dave, and I'll go talk to him now."

Sophie appeared to calm herself a bit when he said that and pulled herself away from the wall. "He's upstairs, with his 'boys'. Some kind of business he had to attend to. I'm sure he'll be down at some point." She took another deep breath and wiped away the tears that were running down her cheeks now. "Come here. I'm sorry I freaked out on you, and I'm sorry I called your friend a slut. That was out of line."

Seth walked over to her and gave her a hug. "To be honest, it's good to see a friendly face, relatively speaking." He took a step back from her and bumped into somebody behind him. When he turned around, he saw Malia, and smiled. "Hey, you never know who you might bump into in one of these clubs. Malia, this is Sophie, a good friend of mine. Sophie, this is my girlfriend, Malia."

"It is a pleasure to meet you," Malia said. "Have you and Seth been friends long?"

Sophie smiled at her, though Seth suspected it was fake. "We used to date, actually. A long time ago. It's good to see you Seth, you look good. It was a pleasure meeting you as well, Malia."

She walked by them, but Seth turned and called out as she walked away, "Maybe you can show Malia around while I go find Dave. She's not from around here."

"Yeah, sure," Sophie said, and motioned for Malia to follow her.

"Are you certain this will be okay?" Malia asked.

Seth leaned into Malia and whispered in her ear. "Things may get crazy in here once I grab Dave. Take care of Sophie and get her out of here if things go wrong." Malia nodded, but said nothing, prompting Seth to speak up so Sophie could hear. "Okay, I'll see you in a bit then. Have fun."

He walked away, moving through the crowd and leaving Malia with Sophie. When he got to the front doors, he walked out into the entryway and turned toward the stairs that were off to the side.

The moment Seth reached the top of the stairs, he knew there would be trouble. The nearest two doors opened right away and two thugs stepped out. "No guests on the top floor," one said, and moved to block Seth's path. His face was marred by a scar on his cheek. The other thug, a much larger brute, took up the rest of the hallway and ensured he couldn't pass.

"Hey guys, I'm just looking for a buddy of mine," Seth said. He was trying to sound calm and cool, but he thought he sounded more like a nervous wreck. Despite all he'd been through, guns still scared him, and these two thugs were armed and dangerous.

"Look for him somewhere else," Scar said.

Seth continued to approach them, trying to keep his cool. "His name is Dave, have you seen him?"

Scar drew a semi-automatic pistol and pointed it at Seth. "I said scram. Don't make me get ugly with you."

At the end of the hall, two men emerged from a room and closed the door behind them. When they turned back, they stared at the scene before them, stunned. "What the hell is going on out here?" The bigger one asked.

There was a moment of silence as Seth stopped and drew the power of life to him. He looked from Scar to Brute and let the corner of his mouth turn up in a slight smile. "You have no idea how ugly this is going to get."

He focused the magic, creating a shield of glimmering white energy in front of him. Scar pulled the trigger, but the bullet ricocheted off the shield and hit Brute in the upper arm. He let out a shout and fell to his knees holding his arm. The two men at the far end of the hall ducked to either side and scrambled to get their guns out. Scar pulled the trigger several more times, each time sending a bullet flying back in his direction.

Seth called on the power of fire and held his hand out in front of him. A flaming ball shot forward and hit Scar in the chest, sending him to the floor screaming and rolling to put out the flames that consumed his shirt. Both Scar and Brute scrambled to get away from Seth as he advanced toward the end of the hall. The other two men had their guns out and started to fire, sending bullets in every direction as they reflected off the shield. One bullet struck the man on the left in the head, splattering blood on the wall behind him. He slumped to the floor, but the other continued to fire.

A second ricochet struck the other man in the chest, killing him and ending the gunfight.

"Tell me where he is, and nobody else will get hurt," Seth said to Scar.

"What the hell are you?" Scar yelled as he got to his feet.

Seth continued walking toward them, the energy shield moving with him. "I asked you a question. Where is Dave? I don't want to hurt anyone else, but we're not leaving without him."

Scar looked worried. Brute was still cradling his arm and shaking his head. "Okay," Scar said. "Okay. A guy came in not long ago, went in the big guy's office. Right through this door." He motioned to the door behind him that was now riddled with bullet holes.

"Thanks," Seth said, calling on the power of death. "Now, sleep." He thrust his hand forward and sent two bolts of black energy at the men. They struck true, and both fell to the floor unconscious.

He tried the door and found it locked. It took him a moment to draw the power he needed, and then focused on the hardware on the door. It turned red hot and melted, running down the front and back of the door leaving a scorched trail behind it. With a push, the door swung open. He heard the pops of the guns being fired before his instincts kicked in and slowed time. The bullets flew through the air in slow motion, allowing Seth to dodge and weave around them. He entered the room with time slowed and willed it to stop. The whole scene froze, with one man behind a large wood desk holding a sub-machine gun, and another off to Seth's right with a hand gun. Dave was on the floor and it looked like he was trying to get behind the desk.

Seth walked around the desk to the guy with the bigger gun and removed it from his hands. He put it under the desk where it wouldn't hurt anyone when he started time again. The other guy would be firing at a wall, so he left him and worried about Dave. He leaned down and laid a hand on Dave's shoulder, willing time to start for him only.

There was a moment of confusion as Dave tried to scramble behind the desk, and then he stopped. Seth stood over him, smiling.

Dave looked up and met Seth's eyes, then jumped back, startled. "Jesus Christ," he said with a wild look in his eyes. "Seth, what the fuck?"

"Hi, Dave," Seth said. "You need to come with me. I'll explain everything later."

"The hell I do. What the fuck is going on here?" He looked around at the frozen room, the bullets hanging in the air, and the two men frozen like statues. "What? How? Are you doing this?" He looked back at Seth, who grinned down at him and offered him a hand.

"Yes, I'm doing this, and yes, you do need to come with me. Whether you want to or not."

"Jesus man. All right," Dave said, looking worried. "What about Sophie?"

"I'll come back for her. She'll be okay, I've got a friend taking care of her," Seth said. He concentrated on the parking lot of the base and they ceased to exist on the second floor of the club. They appeared just outside the main building of the military base, where Dave doubled over and vomited on the ground.

# Chapter 16 - Strangers in a Strange Land

The rift Darian opened was only large enough for one to pass through at a time. Jax volunteered to go first, as he was the superior swordsman and could handle anything on the other end while Cedric caught up. When Cedric emerged at the other end, Jax was standing on a stone walkway next to a small canal that was several paces wide. He took note of his surroundings before the light from the rift was gone: stone walls, floor and ceiling, with steel pipes and cables running down the walls, extending away from them in either direction. The rift closed and left them in darkness with a dampness in the air and an unpleasant smell surrounding them.

"With no magic, the people of this world must be primitive," said Jax, who was also assessing his surroundings.

"Don't be so sure of that. I've heard Seth describe his world, and though they do not have magic, they do have a great many other wondrous things. I would very much like to spend some time here, learning what I can, but alas, there is a kingdom to save. Perhaps someday." Cedric looked up and down the tunnel searching for a clue as to what direction to go when he spotted a small beam of light coming from a hole in the ceiling about a hundred paces down. "This way. There's a light over there."

Cedric led the way this time, stepping with care on the narrow walkway. When he arrived at the light, he looked up to see a round steel plate with two holes in it where the light flooded down.

"Sewers," Cedric said. "Of all the places Darian could have dropped us, he would drop us in some kind of sewer system."

"But what's up there?"

The light flickered and they heard a rhythmic double thump from above them.

"I'm unsure, but we can't stay down here," Cedric said. He looked at the wall and saw rungs that he could use as a ladder. Without another word, he began to climb. When he reached the top, he pushed on the plate. It took almost all of his strength to lift it out of its place and slide it to one side. Sunlight flooded down into the tunnel below him and fresh air rushed in. He went to peek his head up to look around when he heard a loud screeching sound and a shadow passed over the opening.

"Jesus, are you trying to get yourself killed?" He heard a young woman say.

Another step up brought him above ground where he could see who the voice belonged to. "My apologies," Cedric said. "If I had my choice, I wouldn't have chosen this as a starting point."

The girl was standing outside of a large horseless carriage of some kind and was dressed in shorts and a small top that showed off her midriff. The temperature above ground was just warm enough to justify her attire, though Cedric had never seen a woman dress like that before. Her hair was short and dark brown, and she had blue eyes. Her build was average, but lean. Cedric could tell she was fit, probably from running as she had well-muscled legs.

"What are you doing down there, anyway? Do you work for the city? I just about took your head off."

"Tis a long story," Cedric said, lifting himself up one more step. The girl walked over to him and offered him a hand, which he took and climbed the rest of the way out.

"You're not some kind of terrorist, are you?" Cedric watched her eyes as she looked him up and down. "Or are you trick-or-treating?"

"I don't understand what you mean," Cedric said. He glanced behind him as Jax climbed out of the hole. "Perhaps you can be of help to us. We're looking for somebody by the name of Seth Alkirk. Do you know him or where we might find information on him?"

"Oh," she said, surprised. "There's more of you. How many are there? I think I should call the cops." She backed up several steps with fear in her eyes, looking down at something behind Cedric.

He turned and saw the swords hung from Jax's belt. When he turned back, she had opened the door to her carriage and was getting ready to get in. "Please, milady. Do not be alarmed. We have no intentions of harming you or anyone else."

She paused and looked back at Cedric's masked face. "Okay, if you say so," she said, looking as though she wanted to leave.

Cedric bowed low and said, "My name is Cedric, and my associate here is Jax. We are mere travelers and would not dream of bringing harm to a fair maiden such as yourself."

"Sure. Cedric and Jax. Got it," she said, and relaxed slightly. "But don't call me 'milady'. My name is Alexis. My friends call me Alex. Who did you say you were looking for again?"

"Seth Alkirk. He's very important," Cedric said. "It is a pleasure to meet you, Alexis."

"Gimme a sec and I'll Google your friend," she said as she took a small black box out of her pocket. She ran her finger over the surface of the box and tapped it a number of times. Just when curiosity was getting the better of Cedric, she lifted her head with a smile. "There's one here on Facebook. Says he lives in Denton, Iowa."

Cedric approached her and looked at the little black box in her hand. On it was an image of Seth and some information about him. "What is this? It's too small to be a scrying pool, yet you have an image of Seth on it. That is, indeed, the man we are looking for. How do we find him? Can you show me what he's doing now?"

"Whoa, slow down. I've only ever heard of scrying in D&D. Don't you guys know what a cell phone is?"

Cedric shook his head, as did Jax. Both men looked at it in wonder, and Jax finally spoke. "You were right. They aren't primitive at all, just different. Even more wondrous than I expected."

"You guys are weird," she said and looked around.

Cedric followed her gaze and saw several more horseless carriages coming.

"Hey, we should get off the road. Put the manhole cover back and let's do this on the sidewalk, okay?" Alex said, beating Cedric to the thought.

"You are right. I shall put the cover back. Jax, go with Alex and I'll follow momentarily."

She pointed to a paved strip off to the side of the road and Jax walked to it while Alex moved her carriage. Cedric got the cover back on the sewer and walked off the road just as the next carriage went by. As he approached the two waiting on the paved walkway, he said, "You didn't answer my other question. Can you show me what Seth is doing now, and precisely where he is?"

There was a pause between them as Alex gave him another funny look with a lifted eyebrow. "No, I can't do that. All I can show you is what he's posted on the Internet."

"What a shame. Can you tell us how to get to the Kingdom of Iowa then? What direction should we walk?" Cedric asked.

"Kingdom? You guys seriously sound like you're playing D&D," Alex said, laughing. "Iowa is hardly a kingdom. It's a state. If you walk, it'll take you forever. Here, I'll look up some directions for you." She tapped a few more times on her cell phone and brought up a map. Cedric watched her as she controlled her cell phone as easily as he could play his lute. "You guys really aren't from around here, are you?"

"Nay," Cedric said. "We're from a world called Galadir. Seth is as well, though he was raised here. An evil wizard has taken over our kingdom, and Seth is the only person who can help us defeat this wizard and reclaim what is ours."

Alex stopped and looked up at him, her face full of doubt. As she stared into Cedric's eyes the doubt faded. "Why do I get the impression that you're telling the truth?"

"I have no reason to lie to you," Cedric said. "Our world is in peril, this is no time for jokes or make believe."

"You need a better story. I don't know if you really are who you say you are, but somebody even a little more skeptical than me would have walked away from you by now. Can you guys do anything? Dance? Sing?"

"Yes, of course. I am a bard by trade, I live to perform, both song and story. Jax here is an artist with blades."

Alex continued working on her cell phone to bring up the directions they required, and said, "So you're buskers then. Traveling street performers. If anyone else asks you, tell them that."

"That is a splendid idea," Cedric said. "You are wise beyond your years."

"Okay, here we go," Alex said, showing Cedric the little screen. "I-15 will take you all the way from here to Iowa. Once you get there, just ask somebody for directions to Denton and I'm sure they can help you out."

"Oh," Cedric said, his tone disappointed. "I thought you could take us. I can pay you, and you look like you're just bursting for an adventure."

She laughed and shook her head. "Oh no. I couldn't. What would I tell my boss? I can't just go off on some road trip. But if you have money, you can always get a bus or something. I'd be happy to take you to the bus station."

Cedric thought for a moment and turned on the charm. "Come now, Alex. You would leave the two of us, foreigners in a strange land, without a guide, without direction, to fend for ourselves? How about this," he said, reaching into a pouch in his belt. He drew his hand out and opened it before her. In the palm of his hand were five gold coins. "I'll give you five gold now, and five when we get there? It's more than generous. An escort in my world would cost a tenth of that."

Alex's eyes grew wide when she saw the gold. It was stamped with the symbol of a crown with a sword through it on one side and a man's face on the other. "Is this real gold?" she asked.

"But of course it is. What else would I give you?" Cedric asked in return.

"I don't think I've ever seen this much gold in one place, other than a jewelery store. This must be worth like, two thousand bucks."

"I'm unsure what livestock has to do with it, but it is certainly nothing to scoff at, and that's only half of what I'll pay you. I trust that will more than adequately cover your time and lost work? It's dreadfully important that we get to Seth with as little fuss as possible."

"Okay, okay, I'll take you. Both of you. Stow your things in my trunk and hop in." She pressed a button on a small black box hanging from her key chain and a hatch opened in the back of her carriage. Both Jax and Cedric removed their weapons and gear and placed them in the trunk. Alex closed the lid and said, "I'm only doing this because you guys really do look stuck. Just don't make me regret it."

"We shan't milady," Cedric said with a smile. "I suspect it will be the adventure of a lifetime."

"That's what I'm afraid of," Alex said, returning his smile. "I have to make a stop at home first, and make a couple phone calls before we can head out."

"Very well. We'll wait in your carriage while you run your errands."

"Carriage? My car you mean. If you're going to try to fit in, you'll need to learn the vocabulary. Don't you have cars on Galadir?" Her tone was teasing as she got back in the car.

Cedric and Jax walked to the other side and they got in, with Cedric taking the front seat. "Nay, we do not have such wonders. But we have others. That box that you keep referring to, what is that? I should dearly love to have one when I go back to Galadir. It seems to know everything. You called it a cell phone?"

"Oh, yes, my phone. I practically live on my phone. It's used for communication, and entertainment. I can take pictures with it, and video, and I can get on the Internet with it, which is what I've been doing for you."

"Internet?" he asked.

"Yeah. It's a global computer network. You can find practically anything on the Internet," Alex said as she started her car and began to drive it.

"Truly astounding. I remember Seth once saying that he was a computer programmer. Does that mean he is an architect of the Internet?"

"Oh, I don't know. There are lots of different types of programmers. So what's so special about this Seth guy? When I read his Facebook profile, he seemed pretty normal to me."

"Seth is a very special person. Far from normal, though I'm uncertain if your world is ready to know who and what he really is."

Alex asked no further questions of Seth after that, but Cedric thought she looked like she was in deep thought for the rest of their drive. They pulled into a small paved area in front of a house and she looked over at Cedric. "I have to go and make some phone calls, and change, and pack up some stuff. Can you wait here?"

"Certainly, milady," Cedric said.

She got out of the car and went in the house, leaving Cedric and Jax to wait in the car. Cedric shifted so that he could see Jax. "So? What do you think?"

"I think we don't fit in, but she will be a great benefit to us," Jax said. "Provided this is where Seth has gone. If not, then we have made a grave mistake even coming here."

"What's life without a little risk?" Cedric asked with a broad smile. "Besides, it's a little late to be having doubts now. Let's focus on the task at hand."

"You're right. We're here now. At least this world doesn't seem particularly hostile."

Alex emerged from her house at that moment and closed the door behind her. She had changed clothes into something a little less revealing and carried a backpack on one shoulder. The trunk lid popped open by itself startling Cedric and she tossed her backpack in with their belongings, then got back in the car. "Hey, we have to stop to buy gas before we head out. Do you guys want to grab a bite to eat too? It's a long drive. We'll have to stop to rest at some point, unless you guys know how to drive."

Cedric shook his head. "Nay. I can ride horse and dragon with the best of them, but not a horseless carriage."

Alex giggled and shook her head. "Dragons now? Next you're going to tell me that magic and wizards are real. I'm starting to feel like Harry Potter." Cedric opened his mouth to say something, but Alex put a finger over his lips. "Don't say it. If you say it, I'll kick you out of the car right now. I already feel crazy just for entertaining this. I mean, two strange men come out of the sewer and need a ride to Iowa? That's weird enough. But you, with your 'nay's and 'shall's and funny clothes and swords and bows; there's only so much weird a girl can take."

"Very well," Cedric said, removing her finger from his lips. Her hand was soft and delicate, like the hand of a noble woman. "I give you my word, no harm will befall you. Jax and I will do our utmost to protect you."

"Thanks," She said. "But really, what danger is there in Iowa?"

"None, I hope," Cedric said.

Alex started the car, they backed out of the drive, and set off down the street. A few minutes later, Alex pulled into a place where other people had carriages hooked up to big metal boxes with hoses. "Wait here, I'll just be a minute."

She got out and hooked up one of the hoses to her car. Cedric watched the numbers on the metal box count up and finally stop. Alex hung up the end of the hose and walked into the building nearby. In a carriage in front of them, two little girls were peering out the back window at Cedric, staring. He watched them for a moment, looking into their eyes, and then opened his door.

"Where are you going?" Jax asked.

"I shall be but a moment," Cedric said with a sly smile.

He got out and walked toward the car with the children in it. They watched him the whole time as he approached their door. When he arrived, he held out his hand before the window. In his palm rested a small black seed. The seed shifted and shook, and a small root and leaf sprouted out of it. The root worked its way into Cedric's hand, and the leaf grew straight up on a small stem. The whole thing was pure black, and the children were delighted. As the plant grew, more roots plunged into Cedric's hand, and the stem grew longer, sprouting more black leaves. A moment later, a bud appeared.

The children in the car were fascinated and couldn't take their eyes off the plant that was growing from Cedric's hand. The bud swelled and the plant grew taller. When the bud was so large that the stem could barely hold it up anymore, it opened, blooming into a great feathery rainbow flower. The children squealed with delight at the rainbow colors and cheered for more. Cedric was about to show them another trick when there was a shout from the building where Alex went.

"Hey," a big man said. "Get the hell away from my car."

The flower, stem and roots withered away and dissolved into dust as Cedric lowered his hand and looked toward the man. "My apologies, I simply wished to entertain."

The big man approached Cedric fast and said, "Yeah, well entertain somewhere else, you masked freak. What is this, Halloween already?"

Cedric backed up a step, unsure of how to proceed. "Come now, there's no need for name calling. No harm has been done. Again, I apologize if I was out of line."

More people were taking note of the exchange now. The big man reached out and grabbed the front of Cedric's tunic and gave him a shake. "No harm yet, but what were you trying to do? Lure my kids out of my car? Do you think I'm an idiot? I see the news. Predators like you have no place in our society."

He shoved Cedric and sent him sprawling to the ground. Alex came running out of the building at that moment and put herself between the big man and Cedric. "Leave him alone," she said. "Get in your car and piss off, before I call the cops."

The big man hesitated and looked around. Cedric noticed that other people were watching now, some of them shaking their heads. The man's shoulders slumped and he backed down. Cedric got up off the ground and brushed himself off as the man walked around his car, got in and drove away. Alex turned to him and said, "I thought I told you to stay in the car?"

"On the contrary," Cedric said. "You simply said 'wait here', and here I waited. But I simply can't resist bringing a smile to a child's face."

"Next time, wait in the car. You can't do stuff like that here. People get scary about their kids."

"Indeed. Lesson learned. I shan't do that again," Cedric said, and got back in the car.

Alex got in the driver's seat and started the car. "Here we go," she said, giving Cedric a sideways smile. "Off to Iowa."

## Chapter 17 - The Quickrot Plague

Gladius walked ahead of Tyriel and Nadya through the halls of Ducain's Keep, leading them to the forbidden library in the basement. "I know there is a map down there that can help us," he said, excited to be able to enter the area without fear of retribution.

"How do you know what's in there?" Nadya asked, trying to keep up.

"I just know. You speak the name of the object or person you want to find, and it will show you where it is. It's a very dangerous artifact in the wrong hands." Gladius rushed down a set of stairs leaving his companions behind him. When he reached the bottom he turned down a dark corridor that led to the ancient library. His mind wandered through memories of the last time he was there, when he'd had his first confrontation with Lebriel, and when his own father had banished him to the Eastern Badlands. Bitterness crept into his mind, but he pushed it back as best he could as he approached the library door.

It was just as he remembered it: a heavy oak door with silver runes traced up one side and down the other. *The council must have replaced it after I destroyed it all those years ago*, he thought. With one finger, he traced the runes one at a time, reciting the names of the runes as he went. When he completed the task, the door swung open on its own. He was about to enter when Nadya and Tyriel caught up.

"Goodness, Andran," Nadya said. "What has you so excited?"

He almost told her the true reason, that it was his thirst for the power he once had that drove him. But he caught himself, and said, "I am eager to help my friend, that is all."

"Slow down," she said with a smile. "The books aren't going anywhere."

"I know that. But time is of the essence."

"Andran is right, we should make haste," Tyriel said. "Though use caution when using any artifacts in this room. Many of them come with a high cost."

"You two know an awful lot about the forbidden zone, for never having been in it," Nadya said, pushing past them and entering the library. Gladius followed her and took a deep breath of the musty stale air. While she went about looking through the shelves, Gladius went straight for the scroll rack and sifted through them until he found the one he was looking for.

He pulled a black scroll case from the rack and took it over to an ancient wood table. The case opened without trouble and revealed a scroll inside made of old yellowed parchment. Using care not to damage it, Gladius unrolled it onto the table and used weights to hold down the corners. On one end of the scroll there was a small metal barb with the words THE COUNCIL'S BLOOD SHALL POINT THE WAY TO YOUR HEART'S DESIRE written around it. The rest of the scroll was blank. Gladius took his finger and placed it on the barb, pressing down so that it pierced his flesh. "Show me the Lyecian book," Gladius said.

The barb bit deeper into his flesh sending pain through his finger and up his hand. He could feel the blood being drawn from the wound. As the blood flowed over the barb, it spread out on the scroll and formed into lines and pictures. A map became clear after a few moments showing Findoor, Caldoor and the Badlands. The barb sank deeper still into Gladius's finger, pulling more blood into the scroll. A line ran from where Ducain's Keep would be, down through Findoor and into the Eastern Badlands, where it formed a tiny picture of a book.

Gladius gasped and pulled his finger from the scroll. When he did, the image on the scroll disappeared, leaving the parchment blank once again. He looked up to realize that both Tyriel and Nadya were watching him.

"To the Badlands, then," Nadya said.

"I cannot go there," Gladius said. "Anywhere but there."

"What's the matter, Andran," Nadya said in a teasing tone. "Afraid of a few Narshuks? With the way Seth talked about you, I would have thought you could handle it."

"Oh, I can. I'm not afraid of the Narshuks," Gladius said. "I'm only afraid of one, assuming he is still alive."

"The book was probably picked up by one of those animals during their retreat from Findoor and they're using it as bedding now," Nadya said.

Anger swelled inside Gladius, driven by a compassion he had for the Narshuk people. "Do not speak of them as such," he snapped at her. "They are not animals. It is the Wizard High Council that keeps them the way they are, and it is something I will be working to change at my first opportunity. They have power. More than you could ever imagine. If their shamans have this book now, and they have it open, they will be quite dangerous."

"How could they have it open?" Tyriel asked. "Doesn't it require a Lyecian to open it?"

"Yes, that's what Seth said. But he also said he was using it at the end of the battle for Findoor. If it was left open on the field and forgotten, one of them could have picked it up." Gladius wrapped a handkerchief around his finger and pressed it tight to stop the bleeding from the cut the scroll gave him. "If the Narshuks attacked Findoor, then they were united, and if they were united, there's only one Narshuk who could have done it."

"I don't normally think of them as individuals," Nadya said. "They have always been animals to me, something to be kept penned up and controlled."

"That's what the old council would have taught you," Gladius said, his voice still marked with anger. "I've lived with them, fought with them, and seen what they can do and what compassion they can have. Yes, they fight amongst themselves and sometimes kill each other, but that's their way. They value strength above all else, and those who show weakness in their ranks deserve to die. But they are not animals, and will *not* be treated as such."

Nadya took a step back, her face showing her surprise at the sudden outburst. "As you wish," she said. "If they have the book, won't they still have to translate it?"

Gladius took a deep breath and centered himself. "Yes, and that is no easy task. The book is written in High Lyecian, which is a complex language. But do not underestimate them. If my old friend is still alive, he would have the intelligence to do it. It is only a matter of time."

Tyriel stood up tall and placed the scroll back in its case, then deposited it back on the rack. "We should leave immediately," he said, turning back to Gladius. "We have little time to spare. Grian grows more powerful with every moment. I'm unsure where Seth has gone, but we can leave a message for him to join us when he returns."

"Agreed," Nadya said. "I shall inform the rest of the council that we shall leave for the Eastern Badlands immediately. Gather provisions and meet me at the front gates."

"Thank you, Nadya," Gladius said. "Bring a black cloak with a deep hood. If the Narshuks discover we are council wizards, we are as good as dead."

Gladius and Tyriel left the library to gather provisions for their journey into the Badlands. When Nadya was out of earshot, Gladius looked to Tyriel and said, "Do you think Scrag is still alive after all these years?"

"It's possible, though he must be ancient and crippled by now. Seventy or eighty years is old for a Narshuk. It's extremely rare that they live to see a hundred years or more."

"Supposing he's still alive, what do I do if he recognizes me?"

Tyriel stopped in his tracks and appeared to be thinking. When he looked back up at Gladius, his face was serious. "Run."

"Comforting," Gladius said, and carried on down the hallway. The pair gathered three packs with provisions to last them several days' travel, and several empty water skins. Gladius also took a longsword from the armories. When they were ready, Nadya was already at the front gates waiting.

"There you are," Nadya said. "I'm going to transport us to the Eastern Badlands, somewhere close to the point that was marked on the map. Do you have a plan for how we'll find the book once we're there?"

"Yes," Gladius said. "I know the Badlands. I know where they will have taken it if they have it."

Nadya narrowed her eyes at Gladius. "How do you know so much about the Badlands and the Narshuks?"

"I've spent some time there," Gladius said. "That's all you need to know."

"Very well," she said, and began to chant. She weaved her transport spell that burst above the three companions and descended around them like a dome. The curtain of energy wavered for a moment making the outside unrecognizable, and then lifted, leaving them on an outcropping of rock.

All around them was the desolate landscape of the Badlands. A blanket of dark gray cloud hung overhead, but it was obvious from the dried plants that struggled for life that it seldom rained. Gladius took a deep breath of the dry air and exhaled slowly. "It's been a long time since I've been here. Call it what you will, but this place almost feels like home to me."

Nadya gave him a funny look and shook her head. "Not for a million gold would I live here."

"We must go before we are discovered by wandering Narshuks, or worse," Tyriel said. "Andran, you said you knew where they would take the book if they had it. Can you get your bearings enough to figure out what direction to go?"

Gladius looked around, measuring up landmarks, and spotted a cave not far away. "Down here," Gladius said, and began winding his way down off the plateau to the rocky cave below. He remembered the scene as if it were yesterday. The inside of the cave, and sleeping on the hard stone. Waking up to hear the Narshuks arguing outside the cave, and one who fell to another's challenge. The small Narshuk whose fur was streaked with gray. *Pledge me your life and soul in service to me alone, and I shall mend the wounds you are dying from. Anything less than that, and I shall walk away and let you die. Do we have an accord?*

Nadya's voice pulled him out of the memory. "Do you know this place?"

Gladius was startled by how little the area had changed over a hundred years. "Yes. We have two days' travel to the village. Follow me, quickly and quietly. Narshuks have keen hearing and can smell blood and sweat from miles away. Their hunting packs are known to travel far and wide in search of food. If we are confronted, let me handle it. I know how to talk to them."

The three companions set out from the cave, heading south. As they walked, Nadya asked questions of Gladius while Tyriel followed behind. Gladius noted that she was interested in learning more about Narshuk culture, and he was happy to share. The three companions kept their hoods pulled over their heads to hide their identity, but Gladius knew that their size alone would give them away as human if they encountered any Narshuks. The nights were long, dark and cold, and the steady wind that swept over the Badlands chilled the three companions to the bone. They avoided lighting fires though, for fear that they would give themselves away before they made it to their destination.

By the middle of the second day, Gladius spotted the little plot of huts that was built around a small, natural spring. Water was scarce in the Badlands, and when the companions had run out, Gladius used his magic to produce more. But the Narshuks had no such magic, and

Gladius knew it. "This is it," Gladius said, raising his hand to tell his companions to stop.

Nadya took a place on one side of Gladius while Tyriel stood on his other side. "If they are on alert," Tyriel said, "won't they already knew we're approaching?"

"Yes," Gladius said. "It's been too quiet. Look down at the village. There's no activity. No smoke from fires, no Narshuks moving from place to place. It looks deserted, and yet there are furs hung to dry, and the huts are intact."

"Could they be hiding?" Nadya asked.

Gladius jerked his gaze toward her with a glare that would have withered the heart of the most seasoned soldier. "Narshuk's don't hide," he snapped. "Not even when injured."

"Then where are they?" Nadya asked.

There was a long moment of silence between them while Gladius looked into her almond-shaped eyes and searched for an answer. "I don't know, but we won't find out by standing around here."

Gladius led the way down to the village. It was also much the same as Gladius remembered it. Many of the huts had either been moved or rebuilt over time, but they were all the same style, and the circle where the Narshuks held their rituals was still in the same place. It appeared in good repair, but the only sound they heard was their own footsteps against the stone. Even the wind stopped, leaving them in eerie silence as they looked for some sign of life. A slight smell of death hung in the air, but nothing moved.

"Where are they?" Nadya asked, looking around.

Gladius approached the nearest hut and pushed aside the grass that acted as a door covering. The putrid stench he was met with almost made him vomit. He coughed and drew his cloak up over his mouth and nose, and despite his watering eyes, he stepped into the hut. There was a heap at the far end of the hut where a Narshuk would have slept. The sound of buzzing insects could be heard clearly from the doorway, but Gladius needed confirmation. When he pulled aside the furs that covered the heap, there was a half-rotted corpse of a Narshuk. Its eyes were empty and its body bloated as it decomposed under the fur. The smell of death overwhelmed Gladius and he turned and ran from the hut. When he emerged into the open air, he collapsed to the ground, dropped the cloak from his face and was unable to stop his body from emptying his stomach onto the ground.

"Torenna help you," Nadya said, running to his aid. "What happened here, Andran?"

"They're dead," Gladius said through a fit of coughs. "They're all dead. Quickrot, or something like it." When he managed to compose himself, he looked up to see both Tyriel and Nadya standing over him. Tyriel was holding a hand down to him, which he took and used Tyriel's help to get to his feet. "I think the whole village is plagued with it. But I don't understand, Narshuks are supposed to be immune to quickrot. Something is wrong here."

Gladius rinsed his mouth out with fresh water and took a drink before deciding to proceed with a search of the entire village. "Come with me," he said. "If there is anyone alive, it will be in the shamans' huts."

He walked through the village and noticed a few other Narshuks lying on the ground rotting. The smell of death became much more prominent as he drew closer to the shamans' huts where they would normally have kept their sick or dying. Gladius approached the door of the first hut and heard movement inside. The rough growls and grumblings of Narshuks, and shuffling, as though whoever was moving could not take proper steps. Gladius drew aside the grass curtain and stepped inside. Before him were three Narshuks. Two looked like typical shamans, and the third he barely recognized. It had mostly gray fur that was matted and scruffy. One eye was completely clouded over and the other had the beginnings of it. He was shorter and smaller than the other two, but they listened to him and followed his orders when he spoke. *Scrag,* Gladius thought as his heart jumped up into his throat.

All three Narshuks had seen Gladius, but none reacted. Instead, they carried on with their work. Gladius took a step forward and saw a great many stone bowls and wood tools covered with black sludge that the Narshuks were working with. "You're looking for a cure," Gladius said in the Narshuk tongue.

"If I could see better, I could do more," Scrag said without looking up. He was holding down a small rodent and force-feeding it some of the black sludge. The rodent's squeals of terror and eventual strangled cries told Gladius that whatever Scrag was trying to accomplish had been unsuccessful. He finally looked up from his work with a rather curious look on his face. "I've seen you die twice, and yet you stand before me once more. Do my eyes and ears deceive me?"

"No, Scrag. It's me. You've grown old."

"Yet you remain young," Scrag said, and broke into a fit of coughs. "Stop insulting me and tell me what you want."

"I need the Lyecian book," Gladius said.

"I need a Lyecian. Can you grant that?" Scrag asked, lifting his head and glaring at Gladius.

There was a long moment of silence while Gladius and Scrag stared at each other. The rest of the Narshuks stopped moving and turned to see what was going on, and Nadya stood behind Gladius, waiting with held breath. It was like there was a thread between Gladius and Scrag being pulled so tight it was ready to snap.

"You can't have it," Scrag said, breaking the silence. He turned back to his work and swept the now dead rodent off the table. He turned to one of the other Narshuks in the room and said, "Catch me another."

The other Narshuk stomped out the back door of the hut leaving only one other Narshuk and Scrag.

"If I give you the book, my people will die," Scrag said as he pulled another bowl near to him and started work on another variant of his 'cure'.

"What happened here?" Gladius asked.

"That wretch, Grian. That's what happened. He defiles the dead, and spreads disease. When I figure out the cure, I'm going to walk into Findoor and carve the flesh from his bones, bit by bit."

"Then we have a common enemy. The Lyecian has returned and is leading the new council. There is a second one being held at Findoor Castle by Grian. Without the book, we have no hope of defeating Grian. Fight with me, like you once did."

Scrag paused in his work and turned his head slowly toward Gladius. "You mean for you?"

"No," Gladius said. "You once swore an oath to serve me. A lifetime for a life."

Gladius paused as Scrag stood up to his full height. Despite being smaller than most Narshuks, Scrag was still half a man taller than Gladius, and dwarfed him. Scrag approached Gladius with his fist clenched, but Gladius raised his hand. "I release you from your oath. Fight *with* me, and free your people. No obligations, no strings attached."

"What happened to you?" Scrag asked. "You were once a warrior."

"I grew up," Gladius said. He felt a hand on his shoulder and turned to see Nadya behind him.

"Everything all right?" she asked.

"Yes, fine. Though I'm not sure we're going to get much help here. We'll just have to send Seth here to get the book." He hoped Nadya would pick up on his bluff.

There was a moment of hesitation, and then Nadya said, "Very well. Let's just hope there's some Narshuks left by the time we come back with him."

Gladius led the way out of the hut with Nadya in tow. Tyriel waited outside and approached the two as they emerged. "Do they have the book?" he asked.

"They do," Gladius said.

"What is their price?" Tyriel asked.

Gladius raised a hand to silence him and waited a moment. After some silence, Scrag emerged from the hut carrying the Lyecian book. "My price is this," Scrag said in the common tongue, though he stumbled over the words. "Help me find a cure for this plague, and I will fight by your side. With you, not for you."

"Agreed," Gladius said.

He approached Scrag with his arm extended to shake hands on the deal when a commotion came from the edge of the village. There was a rumbling sound, and barks and howls that grew louder by the second. Scrag looked around with a panicked expression on his face. "The others. Take the book and get out while you can."

Scrag tossed the book at Gladius and walked back into the hut. Gladius looked around at Nadya and Tyriel. "Take the book and get out of the village. I'll buy you some time. Seth can use the book to break the reality anchor around Grian."

"Andran, you'll be killed," Nadya said, her face filled with concern.

"I can take care of myself," Gladius said. "Go. You don't have much time."

Nadya took the book from Gladius and left with Tyriel, heading away from the approaching Narshuks. Gladius walked toward them, intending to meet them at the ritual circle. When he arrived there, Narshuks were already gathering around the circle. The largest of them walked to the center of the circle and looked around at the others who were still filing in. His eyes met Gladius's and a sneer appeared on his face as he let out a long, slow growl. "What is this?" he shouted in Narshuk.

Gladius stood tall and entered the circle. "What is your purpose here? This village is doomed."

"I don't answer to you, runt," the big Narshuk said. Gladius looked up at the beast who was at least twice as tall as himself and wore leather straps adorned with bones of all kinds. Some Narshuk, and some human.

"But you do answer to the elder of the village, and I speak on his behalf."

"Nobody speaks for elder Scrag," the big Narshuk said.

There was a commotion at the edge of the circle to Gladius's left, and then Scrag emerged from the crowd and stepped into the circle. "He speaks the truth, Kroog," Scrag said.

Kroog stooped down so that his claws were almost on the ground and narrowed his eyes at Scrag. "Then you have truly gone mad, allowing a runt of a human to speak for you."

"The Narshuks were once a proud and noble race, who had respect for their elders and valued strength above words," Gladius said. "Show me that strength, for I challenge you." He took hold of the edge of his black cloak and pulled it from his shoulders, revealing his scarred appearance and his blue robes beneath.

Silence fell over the crowd of Narshuks as Kroog turned to face Gladius once more. The beast's face twisted into a distorted smile and he let out a strangled sound that might have been a laugh. Without warning, Kroog launched himself at Gladius with his claws and teeth bared. Gladius had time enough to duck and roll, but didn't avoid the attack altogether. He felt claws rake across his back, slicing through flesh and muscle. His robes were wet with blood before his got to his feet again.

"Restitas," Gladius said, drawing the power of water to him and focusing it into the wounds. They sealed up, and the pain disappeared before it became a distraction. He looked up in time to see Kroog preparing to make another run at him. Gladius drew more power to him and whispered the words, "Gelumas armaturai."

Blue light flooded from his hands and spread out over his body, encasing him in a suit of armor made of ice. He wrapped his hand around the hilt of his longsword and longed for the warm feeling the black steel sword used to bring him. It took him off guard because it was the first time he'd thought about it since Seth had defeated him. The distraction was enough to let Kroog take a good swipe at him. Claws struck his chest plate and sent Gladius flying back into the Narshuks behind him. His chest plate was cracked in three places, but Gladius had no time to recast his spell. Instead, he focused on an attack of his own.

He struggled to his feet again as Kroog approached and formed another spell in his mind. Kroog was three steps from him when he spoke the word. "Exsiccatas."

A blue light flashed from his hand and struck Kroog. The light surrounded the beast and brought him to his knees, causing him to let out a great roar that shook Gladius to the bone. It didn't break the spell though, and despite Kroog's repeated attempts to get to his feet again, he couldn't, as all the moisture was drained from his body.

Gladius approached him this time and watched as Kroog fell to the ground. "You are defeated," Gladius said.

Kroog shook his head in defiance, though his eyes were sunken in and his exposed flesh was now tight and cracking. The blood that flowed from the splits was thick and viscous and a dark crimson color.

"Kroog, you are defeated," Gladius repeated, using a more firm tone this time.

There was silence in the circle other than Kroog's labored breaths. He coughed once as he tried to say something, and then raised his hand in defeat with his last ounce of strength.

Gladius ended his spell and knelt down next to Kroog who was just clinging to life.

"I do not wish to have another death on my conscience, there are far too many already," he said to Kroog who stared back at him. Gladius could see the beast pleading for his life with his eyes, though he couldn't speak.

It took a moment for Gladius to gather the strength, but when he did, he spoke a healing word and channeled the power of water into Kroog to heal him. His wounds closed, leaving a network of thin scars over his body where his flesh had split, and he was able to lift himself up from the ground.

There was a tense moment as Kroog stared back into Gladius's eyes, and then he stood up and walked to the edge of the circle. "Stop," Gladius said.

Kroog paused, but didn't turn around.

"I concede my challenge to you," Gladius said. "I have no interest in ruling you or your people."

A grumble flowed through the surrounding Narshuks as Gladius invoked the little-used Narshuk custom that allowed him to win a challenge without taking control. Kroog stood up tall and returned to the center of the circle with Gladius, facing him this time. "You honor me," Kroog said, descending to one knee before Gladius. Even lowered as such, he was taller than Gladius.

"A long time ago, I made a mistake, but a good friend of mine taught me a lesson in humility, and compassion," Gladius said. He looked around at all the Narshuks, and continued. "To the north, in Findoor, the black wizard Grian has amassed an army of the dead that he will use to wipe out all of Galadir. If we are to defeat his army, we must stand together, united. Not just the Narshuk tribes, but all of us. Even as we speak, the new Wizard High Council is preparing to take action from the east, and soldiers from Findoor have traveled west into Caldoor to get help there. We can lead the charge from the south, fighting together."

Scrag entered the circle, hobbling, but standing as tall as he could. "Bring us the Lyecian. Get him to help us cure the plague, and we will fight."

Kroog gave a nod to Scrag in agreement.

"It shall be done," Gladius said, and walked toward the edge of the circle.

Before he could leave, he heard Kroog's voice behind him. "Wizard, what do we call you?"

Gladius turned around and said, "Andran. My name is Andran Riverson."

# Chapter 18 - Exit Strategy

The music pounded in Malia's ears, making it hard for her to hear the introductions to Sophie's friends. One of them handed her a drink that she called a Mo-hee-toe, which Malia accepted and took a few sips of. The flavor was unfamiliar to her, but she could tell there was alcohol in it. A quick glance around the room told her that many of the people in the club were either drunk or well on their way to being drunk. She stayed close to Sophie and moved to the music, losing track of time, until a commotion at the back of the room caught her attention.

She stood on her tip toes to look over the crowd and see what was going on. There were screams, and the crowd started to move toward the main entrance. Malia spotted two large men at the far end of the room, each holding a metal object that struck up a memory. When she pulled Seth through the rift the first time, she had been hit with a projectile weapon that went through her armor and shattered her knee. The men were holding similar weapons, and one of them was coming their way.

Malia tapped Sophie on the shoulder and said, "It is time to go."

"What do you mean," Sophie said. "We've barely gotten started."

"If we do not leave now, we may not be able to," Malia said, and motioned her to follow.

There was already a steady stream of people heading toward the exit. When Sophie saw what was going on, she charged ahead of Malia trying to get to the door as well. Malia put a hand on her shoulder and said, "Do not rush. Seth must have found Dave. They will be looking for us. Stay by my side and I will keep you safe."

Sophie paused and Malia could see a mixture of fear and confusion in her eyes. "Why do they want us?"

"Because we came in with Seth and Dave. Stay by my side," Malia said, and continued making her way toward the door at a steady rate. Ahead of her, the clamor for the exit was turning into a brawl, which Malia had anticipated. More and more people in the club were running now, and people were screaming.

Malia looked back and saw several more men enter through the back, each holding a projectile weapon. Her heart began to race as panic crept in like smoke under a door, clouding her judgment. She hesitated and reached for a sword hilt that wasn't there. The panic inside her surged as her hand found nothing. Sophie was beside her, saying something to her, but she couldn't hear it over the sound of her heartbeat. "The door. Move steady toward the door," Malia said, and urged Sophie on. They were twenty paces from the door now, and almost clear of the dance floor. The music had stopped and most of the flashing lights were turned off in favor of normal white lights. It became easier to see where she was going and what she was doing, but that didn't help when more men appeared at the door, halting the crowd.

"Shit," Sophie said, coming to a dead stop.

"Is there any other way out?" Malia asked her.

"There has to be," Sophie said. "Fire escapes. There must be fire exits around here somewhere."

The crowd around them was moving in every direction as people panicked. Malia looked around and spotted several doors with signs over them. With the nearest one in her sights, she motioned for Sophie to follow her. There was only thirty paces between her and the door, but even that much proved to be a challenge. People bumped into them and refused to move. Panic surrounded them as men with weapons closed in. The crowd began to thin when the men started letting people out after being inspected.

Malia glanced around her to take her bearings and note where the men were, and saw that one of them was positioning himself between them and the fire exit. He held his weapon at the ready, but Malia wasn't about to give up. She called on the power of fire and focused it into the palm of her hand. "Fumabuntas," she said, and manifested several small objects that began to smoke the moment they appeared. She tossed them in varying directions and the smoke billowed out from them, filling the air and making it hard to see. She seized Sophie's arm and charged forward through the haze.

There were screams and shouts all around her. Some were from frightened people who just wanted to get away, and others were from the men who were hunting for them. The smoke made it almost impossible to see anything beyond a few paces in front of them and grew thicker by the second.

When they were near the fire exit, Malia heard the man stationed there say, "There you are, pretty girl. That's far enough."

He held the weapon pointed at Malia's chest. She didn't stop her advance though. Instead, she drew in more energy, focused it on the weapon he held, and said, "Crucintas."

The handle of the weapon blazed with heat and light, searing the man's hand and causing him to toss the weapon aside and yell, "Son of a bitch." It skittered across the floor and let out a number of pops before the glowing faded. Malia reached the man while he was still nursing his burnt hand and swung a tight fist at his face. The impact let out a loud smacking sound as it took him off guard and sent him flying against the wall to the left of the door. Malia watched as the back of his head hit a large metal cylinder and he fell to the ground, unconscious.

There was a voice behind her, saying something with a frantic tone, but Malia couldn't make it out before a large fist struck her in the side, sending pain through her ribs and knocking her back. Another powerful pair of hands caught her and grabbed hold of her arms from behind. She had time to see the dark skin of the hands holding her before a fist connected with her stomach. The air escaped her lungs and refused to enter again. She caught a glimpse of a large, dark-haired man in front of her before the man holding her wrestled her back. "Don't struggle now, you're only making it harder on yourself."

Sophie was nearby, but out of view. Malia could hear her sobbing and pleading for her life. Several more men gathered around, and the man holding her spoke up once more. "This one's got spirit, boys."

Using the man's tight grip as an anchor, Malia lifted her legs off the ground, putting all her weight on his arms, and drove both of her feet backward, kicking with all her might. Her right foot struck true, and his weight, combined with her own weight and momentum caused his right knee to snap the wrong way. Both Malia and the man collapsed, though she was able to break free of his grip as his attention turned to his injured leg. She rolled forward and brought herself to her feet again, trying to ignore the pain in her abdomen while she drew more power to her. Three men surrounded her now, and were closing in as Malia struggled to make her magic work.

The dark-haired man spoke again. "Damn, she's got more than spirit. She just busted Louie's leg."

"I'm gonna bust her up for that," another man said. He had lighter hair, and a much heavier build than the dark haired man. Malia was used to fighting other men, but these thugs were much heavier built than anyone in Findoor.

She longed to have her sword in her hand as the power of fire grew inside her. The more it built, the easier the power flowed. The light-haired man took a swing at Malia, and she ducked below it, trying not to lose focus on the energy flowing into her. The third man laughed and said, "She's quick, Greg. Don't let her get away." His tone was mocking, but it told her that despite her performance so far, they still underestimated her.

Both the dark-haired man and Greg approached her at the same time, and Malia backed up toward the third man behind her, letting them close in. They were all chuckling when her spell came to fruition and she shouted, "Incendras."

As the magical energy released from her body, Malia focused it into a wave of fire that spread out in a small but intense circle around her. All three men were caught in the blast that left a scorched circle on the tiled floor. Their clothes vaporized and their hair and flesh caught fire. Skin blistered and burnt, and the three of them collapsed to the floor letting out piercing shrieks that echoed throughout the club. Malia scanned the area and watched as the smoke from her previous spell cleared. At the far end of the room stood a man with black hair and a thin mustache. He had one hand on Sophie's hair, holding her on her knees. His other hand held a weapon that he was pointing at her head. "That's quite enough," he said. His voice was calm, though his eyes held an anger and intensity that robbed her of her confidence.

"Let her go," Malia said, taking a step forward.

"Oh no," the man said. He yanked on Sophie's hair to emphasize his next words. "I think I'll keep her right where she is. That was a neat trick you did there. Allow me to introduce myself. My name is Ricky, and I own this here establishment. Your boyfriend caused me some trouble and lost me three of my boys. Now you come here and cost me three more, and Louie is gonna need some serious work before he can walk again. You tell me how I should feel about that."

Malia looked from Ricky to Sophie and watched the tears roll down Sophie's cheeks. Had she not been silenced by Ricky pulling on her hair, she would be in hysterics, but Malia could see the pain and pleading in her eyes. "What do you want from me?" Malia asked.

"Simple, really. Teach me that trick of yours. What is it, a close range incendiary device? Some kind of explosive? What is your secret?"

"I can no sooner teach you to do that than I could sprout wings and fly with the Fioraden," Malia said. "It has taken me a lifetime of training to learn what I know."

More men arrived as the two talked and Malia knew that if she didn't offer him something in return, that neither she, nor Sophie would make it out alive. "You better start talkin' sweetheart," Ricky said, "or I'm gonna splatter your friend's brains all over the floor over here."

"You do not understand," Malia said. "It is not something one can learn without first being born with some potential."

"Then how did Dave do it?" Ricky screamed. He took a step toward Malia without letting go of Sophie's hair. "Doesn't it seem funny to you, that somebody I've known my whole life, somebody who has never shown this kind of... talent before, can now vaporize a cop with a single word?"

"Dave's abilities are unnatural," Malia said. "He could just as easily vaporize himself without the proper training."

"Natural. Unnatural. I don't care if you gotta strap me down and inject me with drugs. I want to do what you and Dave did, and I always get what I want."

Malia tried to think of ways to stall or disarm him without hurting Sophie in the process. She focused her mind on calling forth another spell, one that could potentially disarm Ricky, and struggled to draw sufficient energy to cast it. Her hand again went for the spot where her sword would normally sit, but found nothing. Her heart sank as the magical energy trickled away, her body too fatigued to gather it.

Her shoulders slumped in defeat as several of Ricky's goons surrounded her, and she refused to fight, lest she further endanger Sophie.

"It's amazing what happens when I have the right leverage," Ricky said with a smirk on his face. "Show this little mouse what happens to people who cross Ricky Tate."

Malia was prepared for the first fist that pounded into her abdomen. She doubled over, gasping for air, but didn't cry out. Fists struck her several more times before she collapsed to the floor. She could hear Sophie pleading with Ricky to make them stop, but her vision blurred as tears filled her eyes. Darkness was taking her when she heard a blast from behind her and the ground shook.

5

Seth looked around the parking lot of the military compound and saw nobody else around. "Wait here and don't move," Seth said to Dave. "I'm going back for the girls."

"Oh no," Dave said. "No you don't. I don't know how you got here, or what you're doing, but you owe me an explanation. I haven't seen you for months, and then you whisk in all fire and light, and do something with time, and then zip us away? What the hell is going on, man?"

"I..." Seth said, and thought about what he could say. "Look, I know I've been gone for a while, but I promise, it wasn't by choice. I don't have time to explain right now, because it's a very long story, but it's a story I need to tell you, because you're now part of it, and it's my fault."

Dave closed his eyes and shook his head. "I'm so confused, dude."

"I know," Seth said. "It gets easier to accept, but I really need to go. The girls may be in trouble. You know how those guys are."

"Oh geez, yeah, I know how they are."

"What were you doing there, anyway? Those guys are nothing but trouble. I don't even like going to the club, let alone talking to them upstairs."

"Aw man, Seth. I'm in trouble," Dave said. "Deep trouble."

There was a moment of silence between them as Dave tried to find the right words. Seth thought he looked like he wanted to walk around, but there was something wrong with his foot.

"I vaporized a cop, Seth," Dave said. "One second he was there, the next he was gone. Poof, just like that."

Seth had never seen Dave so upset before. Their friendship had spanned a long number of years, and Dave had always been the strong one, the confident one, always the guy getting them into, and out of, trouble. Seth felt like he was always along for the ride, but now he was driving, and he wasn't sure what to do. "I'm sorry, man. We'll catch up once I get the girls, okay? We'll get this all worked out."

"Okay, okay, I got it. Go get the ladies, I'll wait here," Dave said. He had a smile on his face, but Seth could tell it was forced.

"I'll be right back," Seth said, and focused on the entryway to the club.

When he appeared, there was a scene of panic around him. People stampeded out of the club screaming about men with guns. He tried to work his way through the crowd, but there were too many people going the wrong direction. "Sophie, Malia," he shouted, but there was no response. People were pressing in from all sides trying to escape the building. He made it to the front door, but couldn't go any further, and couldn't see over the people rushing out. "Damn it," he said, and closed his eyes to focus himself. He tried to will time to stop, but the rush of people around him and bumping into him kept him from clearing his mind. Frustration took over, and he called on the power of air, focusing it into a blast that blew people out of the way and cleared the front door.

With a clear path, Seth advanced into the club and was met with more people who were all rushing toward the door. Several thugs were braced in the inner doorway, blocking the way into the dance floor and bar, and Seth could see smoke circling the ceiling, but no fire. "Malia," he said, and his heart jumped into his throat.

The power of fire came to him with little effort, and he focused it into a small ball that he threw at the thugs. When it struck one of them, it exploded, and sent both of them flying in opposite directions.

Seth advanced on the door and heard a crack as he walked through it. His instincts took over and time slowed down, revealing a bullet flying toward his face. He shifted to the right and let the bullet fly past him.

"Oh, that was even cooler than what she did," a familiar voice said from across the room. "Let's see that again."

There was another crack, and time slowed again. Seth moved to the left to avoid the second bullet flying toward him, and continued his advance. Ahead of him, Ricky held Sophie by the hair and had a gun pointed at Seth. Malia was on the floor, motionless other than the rise and fall of her breathing, with three men standing over her.

"Let her go, Ricky," Seth said.

"Or what, you'll dodge some more bullets? Set some more fires? Come on, show me what you can do. It's a great big old super hero party down here at The Lyric tonight." Ricky wore a smile and trained the gun on Seth again.

He paused his advance on Ricky and cleared his mind, willing time to stop. It obeyed this time, and everyone in the room stood like statues. It was all Seth could do to keep from wiping the smirk off Ricky's face with a ball of fire, but he stopped himself, and walked over to Malia instead.

He shoved the three men around her, tipping them so that they would fall when time resumed, and leaned down. With one hand on her shoulder, he resumed time for her only, and called on the power of water to cast healing energy into her. Malia's gray eyes opened with fear in them, but that melted away the moment she saw Seth's face.

"You have returned," She said. "I was beginning to think you had forgotten us."

"Sorry, Dave talks too much. Let's get Sophie and get out of here."

Seth helped her to her feet, and they both approached the front of the room where Sophie was being held. There were tears frozen on Sophie's face, and Seth could see the terror in her eyes.

It took little effort to manipulate Ricky's hand so he could free her hair, and then Seth rested a hand on her shoulder and started time for her as well. She gasped and screamed as time resumed, and Seth guessed she was surprised at his sudden appearance in front of her. He knelt down before her, looked into her eyes and said, "It's okay, Sophie. Everything's gonna be okay. We have to go now. It's going to be a little disorienting, but we'll be safe when it's all over, okay?"

She almost broke into hysterics, but somehow, Seth's gaze and the sound of his voice calmed her. She sniffed once, and her voice hitched as she tried to speak. "Okay," was all she could manage before her tears started again. Malia joined the pair and Seth took her hand. With his other hand still on Sophie's shoulder, he focused again on the parking lot of the military base and the three of them ceased to exist in the club.

Sophie cried out something that Seth couldn't understand, and then slumped to the ground in a fit of sobs. Malia looked like she was struggling to orient herself and keep her stomach from emptying itself all over the asphalt. Seth got up and looked around for Dave, who was standing not far from him, leaning against a car.

"Dude, you gotta show me how to do that," Dave said with a grin.

"You can't do what I do," Seth said. "Any magic you can use was awakened by a spell you deciphered in the pages you scanned from my book. We need to see the General, and then Malia and I have to go back. There are other people who need our help."

"Whoa, hold on there, buddy. You've been gone a long time. We've been best buds forever, and you didn't even tell me where or when you were leaving. What's going on?"

"I found my father," Seth said, looking into Dave's eyes.

There was a moment of silence as Seth watched Dave's face. "Wait, like, your real dad? Like, missing for twenty-five years dad?"

"Yeah. My real dad. Turns out, he was twenty-five years ago, waiting for me the whole time. Now he's in trouble, and we need to get back so we can help him and Malia's kingdom."

"Dude, you're not making any sense."

"I told you, it's a long story," Seth said.

He looked back down at Sophie who was beginning to get herself under control. She looked up at Seth through red, tear-filled eyes. "Seth, how did we get here?"

Seth spoke in a soft, reassuring voice. "I brought us here. You're safe now. Dave's here too."

She looked around and up at Dave who reached down with one hand and took hers. "Right here, babe. Still in one piece, thanks to Seth." Dave went to pull Sophie up off the ground, but flinched as he put weight on his foot. "Damn it," he said as he almost lost his grip on Sophie.

Seth steadied the two of them and looked at Dave's foot. "Are you hurt?"

"I had a bit of an accident a couple nights ago. I'll live," Dave said with a smile.

"Here," Seth said, laying a hand on Dave's shoulder. He focused on the power of water and channeled the blue energy into Dave's body.

"Jesus," Dave said as he jumped back with a start that made them all flinch.

Seth smiled at him and pointed at his foot. Dave looked down and stomped twice with the foot he had previously avoided putting weight on. "Okay, no jokes," Dave said. "How'd you do that? I mean, one second I'm in a club filled with flying bullets, then next I'm in a parking lot on a military compound that none of us are supposed to be on. One second I have a bullet hole in my foot, and the next I don't. I've never been more confused in my life, but whatever super-powers we seem to have, Seth, you've obviously got the better half."

"Come on," Seth said, motioning for the group to follow him. "Let's go meet the general, and then I can explain everything."

Seth led the way into the main office building. The guard at the front door gave Seth and Malia a nod and waved them through. Seth vouched for Dave and Sophie, and the four proceeded to Mathers' office. His door was open, and he was sitting at his desk reading reports. When the four of them walked in, Mathers looked up and smiled. It was an unnatural look for him, as Seth had never seen him do anything but scowl.

"I see you found our man," Mathers said.

"Yeah, piece of cake," Seth said. "Though there may be a bit of a mess to clean up at The Lyric. Lots of people saw us use magic, and Ricky..."

He was having trouble finding the words when Dave cut him off. "Ricky wants what we have. He's going to have his guys go after my computer that was seized by the local cops when they raided my house. If he gets it, can he do what I did?"

Mathers looked at Seth for an answer. "Well? What are we dealing with here, Alkirk?"

"The images are already on the web. I don't see how you can contain it, but Ricky is definitely not a guy you want using powers like that."

Seth caught a glimpse of Sophie as she backed away from the group and sat down in a chair at the edge of the room. Malia went with her and tried to comfort her. Dave on the other hand was so excited, he was jumping out of his skin. "Come on, Seth, you said you would explain everything. This is the General, I assume?" He turned to face Mathers and offered his hand. "Hi, I'm Dave. Good to meet you. Now tell me what the fuck is going on here."

"Easy, Dave," Seth said. "I'll start at the beginning, I think, for everyone's benefit, because some of this, even the General hasn't heard yet." Everyone in the room looked at Seth and awaited his story, and so he began. "I'm not human, and I'm not from Earth. My family is from an alternate world in a parallel dimension to ours. A planet called Galadir, in a solar system that, as far as I can tell, is much like our own. Their history and culture however are much different than ours. I'm a Lyecian, a race that can manipulate and control time and space, though with the exception of my father, I may be the only one left.

"The people of Galadir have all grown and evolved with the ability to use Magic. They're still human, but there's something different about them. People of earth may have at one time been like them, but at some point in history, all the magic was either vacated or suppressed in our world. Galadir is very much different. In some ways, they are less refined than us. Their technology sits around medieval times for us. But in others, they are far more advanced. They have a council of wizards who govern, control, and teach the use of magic."

Dave interjected at this point and said, "So how did you come to live here then? If your folks were from this other world, and you were some kind of super-powered wizard, why didn't they keep you there?"

"It was too dangerous," Seth said. "I was the last of the Lyecians, after a war nearly wiped us out. They brought me here to keep me safe, and give me a better life." He paused for a moment to let everyone digest that for a moment, then continued. "I know it sounds crazy, but consider what you've already seen me do, and that's just a small portion of my powers. Here's the problem now: Pandora's Box is open. Magic exists, and because of my ignorance, and Dave's curiosity and intelligence, the whole world is going to figure it out eventually. Malia and I will stay long enough to teach Dave how to properly harness and use the power. After that, you're on your own. If it's on the Internet now, there's no stopping it."

"You're right," Mathers said. "Despite our best efforts, we can't purge those images from the Internet. They are propagating faster than our experts can delete them, and the conspiracy theorists are all over it, pointing fingers at the government and stirring up mud about it. Trying to get rid of the images is drawing more attention to them."

"The best thing you can do now," Seth said, "is be prepared. People with magic are going to start appearing everywhere. So why not start training your soldiers to deal with it now? Once we train Dave, he can take over and train others on how to use it."

"What about me?" Sophie said from the back of the room, near the door. "I never asked to be part of this. Dave pulled me in. I don't have *powers* and I don't want them. I just want to go home."

Seth watched Mathers' face as it went from its usual stern all-business look to a more softened, tender appearance. "I'm very sorry you've been dragged into this, ma'am. We'll have one of our doctors look you over, and then you're free to go."

"I can't help but notice that nobody has actually *asked* me what I want," Dave said. "But hey, it's just my life. Go on and plan it however you want. I'll just play along."

Everyone in the room fell silent after hearing this. Seth looked at Dave and saw the pain in his eyes, even though he put on a tough guy shell. He walked over to Dave and led him aside. "Hey, I know how you feel, man. I grew up thinking I was human. Lived my whole life, and then everything changed on me. You used to go on and on about how if you had super powers like the comic book heroes we used to read about, that you would change the world. Here's your chance. I know it's scary as hell, but you have friends who are going to help you, and the U.S. military to back you up. I can't think of anyone else I would want heading up this project. Let's do this, Dave. Let's change the world."

Dave looked like he was thinking long and hard about the prospect. After a while, he looked up at Seth and said, "That does sound pretty cool, huh?"

"Once you get used to the idea," Seth said, "it's the most amazing thing in the world."

"Alright. I'll do it. When do we start?"

"Right now," Seth said with a smile.

## Chapter 19 – Slipping Away

Serrin sat on the floor of the Findoor throne room in the center of the force cage. The bars hummed with an almost living power and any time he so much as thought about using magic, he could feel the cage sap his strength away. He ignored everything outside of the cage, including any further questioning from Grian, who seldom left the throne room. The only thing he watched with any interest were the undead things that Grian had created. They stood by his side, day and night. They took no food, drank no water, and didn't even breathe. There was an occasional gasp or moan from them, but otherwise they showed little interest in anything going on around them. They caught Serrin's interest because of the occasional glance they spared toward him.

There was no instruction from Grian to watch Serrin, and Serrin moved very little from his cross-legged position in the center of the cage, but something in their black, empty eye sockets told him that he needed to watch them. Their touch was deadly to any living thing and even Lyecians were affected by it, though it took longer to drain the life away from a Lyecian. Serrin had watched several humans as they were hugged by these creatures – an embrace of death that stole their life force and turned them into another of the foul creatures.

Serrin didn't fear them. Had he been able to use magic, he could easily vaporize them. His interest was due to pity. They were once living men and women, and were now forced to continue their existence in an eternal unlife.

He was watching these creatures when something Grian said caught his attention.

"What do you mean 'She still lives'?" Grian shouted at his court.

"Your Highness, the bard and the dragon brought evidence at the last moment that subverted our letter. He also destroyed the Dark Lord in a raid on our border. Caldoor is mobilizing their troops for defense, and the element of surprise is lost."

Grian took a deep breath, like he was trying to calm himself after receiving the bad news. There was an eerie silence in the room, and then Grian shouted, "Obitas nexasa mortai."

A ball of black fire erupted from his hand and struck the councilor in the chest, snuffing out his life and causing him to fall to the floor in a loose heap. There was a grumble in the room that went silent the moment Grian looked up at them. "Send word to the nobles: there is an opening on the King's Court."

The rest of the court laughed at this, but a runner was dispatched to do just that. Grian paced at the front of the room and for the first time since Serrin had arrived in the castle, Grian looked as though he was losing control. Serrin watched with interest over the next few minutes as Grian walked back and forth in front of the throne. The dark wizard's pace increased as he did so and Serrin could see the anger welling up inside of him. It took him and the entire court by surprise when he stopped.

"Prepare my mount. I'll be leading the invasion across the Algorn Canyon," Grian said to the court. He stormed out of the room and the court filed out behind him, leaving only the defiled creatures standing in silence several paces away from the force cage.

For the first time since he had been captured, Serrin realized he was left without a living guard. *Good*, he thought. *With Grian distracted, I can find a way out of this place.*

He thought long and hard about the mechanics of the force cage and how it worked, and tested the bars of energy once. The moment his skin touched them, the bar flared to life and seared into his flesh, leaving a deep burn on the finger he had touched it with. He tore a strip of fabric from his tunic to bind the wound and then a thought occurred to him. His gaze shifted up to the defiled creatures who were standing a short distance away, and he removed his entire shirt, wrapping it around his hand and arm so that no flesh was exposed.

"Hey," he said through the bars of the cage. There was no response from the creatures, but Serrin knew they could hear him. "Hey, you two. Come here." One of the creatures turned to face Serrin, its empty eyes burning into Serrin's soul. "I'm going to try to escape, and you're going to help me," Serrin said, and extended his covered hand and arm between the bars toward the creatures.

The one facing him took a step forward and reached out with its hand, gasping as it did so.

"That's right, come and feed. It's the living energy you thirst for, isn't it?"

It continued its approach as the second of them turned to see what was going on. Serrin reached out as far as he could between the bars without hurting himself, leaving inches between him and the creature. It lurched forward and wrapped its fingers around Serrin's covered hand. Its grip was like a vice, and sent pain coursing through Serrin's arm. Even through the cloth covering, Serrin could feel his life energy being drained by the creature. With the creature's grip on his arm, he pulled back as hard as he could, using his body weight to carry the creature into the bars of the force cage. The creature struck the cage, and the bars lit up with power, searing through what remained of the creature's body and carving it into pieces as Serrin pulled it through. Black sludge oozed from its wounds as pieces of it fell to the ground. Smoke rose from the last of its body as it collapsed in a heap of gore. Serrin shook the creature's hand off of his arm and rubbed the sore spot that remained.

"That takes care of one of you," Serrin said, looking at the other one that was now turned and looking straight at him. A shudder ran through his spine as he felt the hate radiating from the creature. It wasn't a directed hate of what he had done to its cohort, but more a hate of the life force inside of him. The creature was bound to servitude and denied its release from life. It should have died when Grian attacked it, but instead, Grian perpetuated its life as an abomination. The vile creature could do nothing but what it was ordered to. "You want release. Come, join your friend. I'll help you."

A gasp came from the creature, and the empty sockets that were its eye changed somehow. There was a pleading sense to it that Serrin could feel. It hated its own existence, and could do nothing about it. It stood its ground, unable to follow the order of anyone but Grian.

"Very well. We'll do this the old fashioned way." He looked at the bars once more, and tried to summon the power of water, only to have it drained away from him. The bars flared up, consuming the energy faster than Serrin could summon it. "It thrives on magic. Perhaps I'll take a page from my son's book of tricks."

He sat down and closed his eyes, focusing his mind on suppressing his powers. When Seth had suppressed his own powers, he had done it one element at a time. Serrin now focused on the element of water, pushing the power away from himself. It drained away, leaving an emptiness inside of him. Next, he pushed away the element of air, and expanded the void inside of him. *How did Seth live like this for so long,* he thought as he continued the process and suppressed the element of life.

Each time he suppressed an element, the cage bars would dim and grow weaker. He watched the creature, still standing several paces away, and was comforted by the fact that it didn't move. Fire was the next to go, and once it was suppressed, the bars of the force cage were little more than dim strands of energy that acted as a net, keeping him contained. At last, Serrin pushed the element of time away, suppressing the last of his magic.

The bars of the force cage faltered and failed, leaving Serrin sitting on the floor in the center of the silver circle. The creature took a step forward, but appeared to be resisting whatever magic Grian had cast on it. Its orders were to guard Serrin, but the scrap of living soul that remained in the creature fought that, and it was winning. Serrin got up as fast as he could and ran out of the silver circle. The creature lurched one step at a time, trying to follow him.

"Thank you," Serrin said. "I'll come back for you."

He turned toward the door of the throne room and ran without looking back. A moan escaped the room as Serrin walked through the corridor in search of a room where he could find some clothes. His instinct told him to teleport out, but when he tried to call on the power, nothing came. He found a small room used by runners who were staying overnight at the castle and searched for clothes that would fit. There was a runner's uniform that was a little too big, but would work to get him out of the castle. He shed his clothes and put on the uniform, then took a good look at the arm the creature had grabbed. There was a blackened hand print where it had held his arm, and the flesh was starting to fester. It was raw and painful, but a quick cloth wrapping and a pair of gloves hid the wound. He found a knife that he slid into his belt, and put on a pair of boots that were a little too tight. Once he was ready, he left the room, walking fast but not frantic through the castle, making his way toward the front gates.

He was about to exit the front doors into the main courtyard when he spotted several horses outside, and Grian in his full armor preparing to mount. It was all he could do to stop himself from launching into the yard and firing everything he had at the wizard, but even at the thought of casting a spell, he remembered the emptiness inside of him. His powers wouldn't work. After some thought, Serrin backed away from the door and walked down the corridor to where runners would normally get their assignments.

A lanky young man sat at a table with papers spread out before him. He looked no more than twenty, and was busy organizing runs that would be sent out that evening. Serrin approached the table and said, "Do you happen to have anything going out just now?"

The young man looked up at Serrin and narrowed his eyes. "I haven't seen you around before, but you're too old to be new. Where are you from?"

Serrin thought for a moment and said, "The eastern reaches of Tandoor. If possible, I'd like to head back that way."

"Right," the young man said, and lifted a brow. He looked over the assignments before him, shuffled a few around, and then picked up three and handed them to Serrin. "These are all going your way."

"Thank you," Serrin said, accepting the papers. One of the stops was Ducain's Keep, which would take him right where he wanted to go. He left the room and followed several other runners to a back exit that led down to the stables. Runners were used to moving quickly and running at top speed for extended periods of time. The ones Serrin followed were no exception and it was all he could do to keep up with them.

When he arrived in the stables, there were several horses in full riding gear waiting already. Serrin surged forward and took the one in front without waiting for approval and leaped onto its back, urging it up to a full gallop before he had cleared the stable doors. He burst out into the midday sun and kicked the side of the horse to keep it moving at top speed through the city and out the front gates. When he was out in the fields in front of Findoor Castle, he realized that he hadn't been breathing and gasped as he took in the fresh afternoon air. With autumn setting in, it was cool on his skin, but he had never felt so alive.

After a quick review of the sun, he pointed the horse off toward the east and began his long journey toward Ducain's Keep.

᷍

Grian shouted orders at the young squires around him, getting ready to leave when a runner approached him bearing a scroll from the councilors. He accepted the scroll and sent the runner and the squires away before opening it. There was only one reason that the councilors would send him news by runner rather than in person, and it wasn't because it was good news. When he was alone in the main courtyard of the castle, he opened the scroll and read it. His demeanor changed from calm and collected, to panicked as he jumped from the back of the warhorse he was on and approached the front gates of the castle.

The parchment scroll landed on the ground in a crumpled ball as Grian cast the required spells to open a rift. Lightning arced from its edges onto the ground around it, and Grian stepped in, allowing it to close behind him.

# Chapter 20 – The Battle of Algorn Canyon

Ceridan and his soldiers led the way to the northeast border of Caldoor. Each morning and night they took some time to train Caldoor soldiers on how to battle the undead army that awaited them. At the crest of the last hill before the Algorn Canyon, Ceridan stood with Darian the Black and surveyed the battlefield, which lay between them and the canyon. Their plan was to keep the undead creatures from crossing into Caldoor land, and if they did, push them into the canyon. For now, there was no movement on the far side of the canyon, and some of the Caldoor troops behind Ceridan were questioning whether there was an army there at all.

"It's there, I promise you," Ceridan said. "Grian is a coward; he hides in Findoor Castle and directs them from afar. He will hold back until he is sure of his success."

"Sounds like a brilliant strategist, to me," Darian said, with a half smile.

"Grian is a vile snake. A poser and defiler. He scarcely deserves a name for what he's done. My kingdom is in ruins because of him, and I will not rest until I've run my sword through his chest."

"Very well," Darian said, but his voice held no apology for his words.

Ceridan was about to order a fallback when a blue light appeared on the other side of the canyon. Lightning arced out from the light and burned up the grass on the ground as a tear spread open and the blue aether between worlds could be seen. Seconds later, a figure clad in black armor stepped out of the rift, and it closed behind him.

"Is that Grian?" Ceridan asked, watching as the dark figure walked toward the edge of the canyon.

"Brilliant," Darian said, and walked away toward the wizards at the back of the army.

"Ready," Ceridan shouted, and motioned to the flag bearers to come forward. Several soldiers came to him, and he said, "I need you to spread out, and if one of you falls, the others must cover the gaps. Communication will be key in this battle."

The soldiers acknowledged his orders and walked away to spread out across the front lines. Ceridan drew his sword and raised it into the air. Across the canyon, the dark figure raised his hands at the same time. The ground began to shake and shudder as the green energy of earth flowed from his hands and into the ground beneath him. Large columns of stone, like massive teeth, grew from the edge of the canyon on his side and extended toward the Caldoor side. From Ceridan's position, it looked like the canyon was a massive mouth with jagged teeth biting at the sky.

The first of the columns struck the canyon wall on the Caldoor side and sent a shudder through the earth that made Ceridan and everyone around him steady themselves. A land bridge was formed over the canyon where no crossing was possible before. More of the columns struck, each time creating a deafening boom that echoed for miles. The columns grew together and created a solid bridge that was double the width of Caldoor Castle and stronger than anything their wizards would be able to destroy before half of Grian's army flowed over it.

Murmurs ran through the gathering of troops on the Caldoor side, some coming from the remaining Findoor troops, but more coming from the Caldoor soldiers who had never seen such a display of magic before.

"Hold your ground," Ceridan shouted, hoisting his sword higher into the air. "Grian is all about show. If we break rank now, we are already defeated. You're going to see some things that no man should ever see. Grian's army may appear man or Narshuk, but do not be fooled. They are magical automations, nothing more."

The troops behind Ceridan fell silent and formed into ranks. The initial shock of what Grian had done had worn off, and Ceridan's words brought them back from the brink of panic. He watched Grian for some time without saying a word, until Grian walked back to the top of the hill on the Findoor side and made a strange motion with his hands, as if he were waving the soil itself to march forward. There was a rumbling sound that came from his direction again, this time softer, and more rhythmic. Ceridan was beginning to think

Grian was calling forth an army of rats when a tide of undead spilled over the hill top toward the stone bridge.

It was silent except for the marching feet and scuffling of arms against their sides. The rumbling grew louder as more came. Thousands of the defiled creatures approached the assembled Caldoor and Findoor armies.

"Archers, ready," Ceridan shouted and watched as his flagmen raised their banners. Lines of archers took to the front lines and nocked arrows that had heads packed with tinder. A wizard stood at the end of the line and fired several sparks which went down the line, igniting the tinder and setting the arrows ablaze. "Fire at will," Ceridan cried, and the banners were dropped.

Arrows flew into the air leaving black streamers of smoke behind them. They descended on the first wave of undead, lighting many on fire, but the creatures were unmoved by the puncture wounds. The fires spread and several hundred were consumed by flames before they went out, stomped out by their comrades who continued to walk forward despite their fallen allies.

"It's not enough," Ceridan said. He looked around for Darian, but couldn't find him among the soldiers. While he searched, archers loosed another volley of flaming arrows that set more fires among the undead army. "Hold steady," Ceridan said. "We must hold this ground, or Caldoor will be lost. Fight with everything you have."

The black army of the dead continued its approach, slow but steady. Had Ceridan not fought them once already, he would have been more flustered by an army that exhibited no emotional reaction to their attacks. There were no screams of dying soldiers, nor flailing that could spread the fire to others. They simply fell and burned to ash, with others taking their place in the lines. Grian stood atop the hill watching the display, and though Ceridan couldn't see his face, he knew the Defiler was smiling back at him.

"Smile at this, you bastard," Ceridan said under his breath and removed a small tube from his pocket that Darian had given him. It was a device Darian said he could use to signal Morganath to attack, and so he pointed it into the air and pulled the twine that hung from the bottom of it.

A burst of light like a small fireball erupted from the end of the tube and flew up into the air. When it reached several hundred feet, it exploded in a burst that could be seen from miles. Moments later, a golden form erupted from a nearby stand of trees and let out a great roar that shook the ground. The Caldoor army let out a cheer as

Morganath flew into the air toward the oncoming army, making a pass at the front lines of it. When he reached the first of the walking dead, he exhaled a stream of liquid fire that covered hundreds of the creatures and reduced them to ash in seconds.

*The bodies must be drying out,* thought Ceridan as he watched Morganath make a second pass and destroy several hundred more of them. The fires spread now as the animated corpses piled up into giant flaming pyres. Still, the creatures continued to walk, many right into the fires to meet their doom. Yet, more approached the front lines of Ceridan's troops. Archers were now firing flaming arrows point blank into the creatures.

Ceridan drew his sword and raised it into the air. Flagmen followed suit, raising the infantry banners. All across the lines, swords were drawn, and the army engaged the walking dead. Ceridan charged into them, waving his sword with wild strikes and taking the heads off of creatures with every swing. The creatures didn't flinch or fall back, but kept coming despite his ferocious attacks. One clawed at his arm and he flung his sword on a back swing, shattering its skull. Another reached for his throat, only to have its arm removed. With a second hit, Ceridan cleaved the creature in two and moved on.

The picture was similar all around him, though there were occasional screams as one of their own fell to the creatures.

Black smoke hung in the air from the burning corpses and brought tears to Ceridan's eyes, but he dared not blink, for death was all around him. The smell of the burning bodies was almost unbearable, and Morganath continued his passes to thin the undead army even as they engaged it hand-to-hand. There was no time left to see what Grian was doing. All Ceridan could do was keep swinging his sword, and pray that it would end.

§

Grian kept watch over the attack until the smoke grew too thick for him to see. Though the dragon had taken out a chunk of the initial advance, Grian looked behind him and saw thousands more waiting for their turn to cross. With his invasion well in hand, he began to draw the magical energy required to get him back to Findoor Castle. He was about to begin casting, when a bolt of black fire flew at him, striking him in the chest and disrupting his focus.

The built up energy inside of him burned in his flesh and muscles, bringing him to his knees. There was nowhere for the energy to go as it released all at once and he could feel his body heat up from the inside out. Blisters formed on his skin under his armor, and he screamed with pain and rage.

"You are powerful, I'll give you that," said a familiar voice, though it was a voice he hadn't heard in a long time. "But you are undisciplined. Perhaps you should have remained Merek's pupil just a little longer, and you would have known what to do with that energy. Instead, you get to cook inside your armor."

"Darian," Grian said, pushing himself back up to his feet. "Enjoy it. You won't catch me off guard a second time."

"Oh, I know. I won't need to. You've already done half my job for me," Darian said. Grian watched as Darian approached him with slow, deliberate steps. "Had you just remained quiet and stayed on your own side of the border, I wouldn't have to do this. We're both disciples of Grishtor. We're fighting for the same cause, and you know it."

"I don't fight for him anymore," Grian said. "I don't fight for any god. That's your singular miscalculation, Darian. You fail to see the bigger picture." He drew in the power of life, and focused it into a single blast, which he unleashed toward Darian all at once. "Sanctatas."

The light struck Darian in the chest and sent him flying back into a crowd of undead. They ignored him and continued their walk toward Caldoor. Grian dusted himself off and said, "You should have brought friends."

There was a moment of silence while Grian organized his thoughts, and then something struck him from behind. Before he could turn around to see what it was, another struck him in the chest. It was a ball of black energy focused on him, and not far away was a black-robed wizard, drawing energy in for another attack. A third hit him from the right and make him stagger.

"I did bring friends," Darian said, as he emerged from the stream of undead. He fired a fourth energy ball, which hit Grian in the chest. Two more struck him before he could focus on Darian and form a coherent thought.

When Grian looked around, there were at least seven wizards all around him and the attacks were coming in at a steady pace from every direction. He couldn't clear his mind long enough to cast a spell and each hit was draining a little more of his life away.

There was a ring on his index finger; something he had been saving for his next encounter with Seth, but if he didn't do something soon, he would be finished. He clenched his fist and focused on the ring to activate it. The world around him swam for a moment and then a white shell of energy formed around him. When the shell dissolved, he stood before Findoor Castle with nobody else around him. He walked back to the castle, and back to the lab deep below it where his research would continue.

5

Darian smirked as the sphere appeared and then dissolved, leaving empty space in its place. His plan had worked perfectly, though they still had Grian's army to deal with. He looked out over the battlefield and watched as thousands of the dead creatures continued to flow into Caldoor. His army was doing their best to hold it off, but Morganath had exhausted his breath, and the men were getting tired as more and more of the creatures crossed the stone bridge.

"We need a green wizard," Darian said. His small band of wizards all looked at each other and then back to him, but none said a word. "Yes, I know. We'll have to make due. Summon up everything you can and focus it on a single point. If we can't take the whole bridge down, we may be able to at least slow them down."

He pointed at one part of the bridge that looked particularly rocky. "There. Focus your fire there. Draw everything you can and focus it into a single explosive blast. Ready?"

The others nodded and lowered their heads in concentration. Darian did the same, calling on the power of death for a single explosive burst of power. When he had everything he could draw, the others were ready. Darian raised his hand and a black ball of crackling energy appeared in his hand. "Impuleras," he said, and launched the ball out toward the bridge. The others did the same, sending eight energy balls to strike one part of the bridge. All but one hit its mark and sent a rumble through the ground as the rocky bridge gave out under the assault. Half of the stone bridge shattered and fell into the canyon, leaving a much smaller path for Grian's army to cross.

He looked out over the field once more, trying to find Ceridan, but couldn't. The battle had descended into chaos, and he had nearly exhausted himself. "We're going to need a miracle," Darian said, trying to catch his breath.

# Chapter 21 – Finding an Old Friend

The sudden quiet woke Cedric from an uncomfortable sleep. It took him a moment to get his bearings. He sat up in a confined space with windows all around him. Alex was next to him, but it was dark out now, and the only light came from a small spot on the ceiling of the car. There was a pain in his neck from sleeping with his head to the side.

"Wakey, wakey," Alex said, prodding his shoulder. A flash of light from her phone brought him back to reality. "I'm cooked. It's like, almost midnight and I need some sleep. I'm not used to driving this far in a day."

"Where are we?" Cedric asked, looking around.

"Holiday Inn, near Richfield, Utah. We're about a third of the way there. With a good night's sleep, we should make it to Denton by tomorrow night. Come on, wake up sleeping beauty back there and let's get a room for the night."

Cedric glanced at the back seat and saw Jax slumped over, sound asleep. He got out of the car, opened the back door and leaned over to shake Jax awake, but the moment he laid a hand on Jax's shoulder, the young man's eyes snapped open and he screamed, "No, not my Mara."

There was a struggle as Jax fought against Cedric's grip, and then he stopped and calmed himself. "You are having nightmares," Cedric said.

"Is it any wonder?" Jax asked. "It's the first time I've slept since they killed her, and though I took my vengeance out on him, I don't feel at peace with it."

Cedric stood up and looked around, but couldn't see Alex anywhere. "Your secret is safe with me, my friend."

"I don't care," Jax said, with a flat tone. "You weren't there. You didn't see the injustice of it all. It wasn't even her fault, it was that mangy mutt that ran in on our show. The soldier wasn't even hurt by it, yet I had to stand by and watch him cut her throat. They all stood by and did nothing while he killed my Mara."

Tears formed in Jax's eyes, and Cedric realized that these must be his first tears since it happened. "Is that why you were up for execution?"

"Yes. I killed nine of them in total. It should have been many more."

"It wouldn't bring her back. Take it from a disciple of Grishtor, no amount of death will create life anew. But you can help save lives. Many of them."

Cedric heard somebody walk up behind him and assumed it was Alex based on the light steps. It took him by surprise when a man's voice said, "Alright, love birds. Stand up, get out of the car, and give me all your money."

"You have got to be kidding me," Cedric said as he stood up and faced the owner of the voice. The man he faced was bigger than himself, heavily muscled, and holding a large knife.

"I never kid. What is this, Halloween? Take that mask off, and give me every penny."

Cedric took his money pouch from his belt and handed it to the man, then stepped aside so that Jax could get out of the car. With a quick shuffle, Jax was out and standing before the man, looking at the knife with a smirk.

"What's so funny, freak?" The man said, thrusting the knife toward Jax. Had Cedric not been watching, he would never believe it happened. Jax kicked his leg up and struck the handle of the knife, sending it flying into the air. The man had enough time to form an expression of shock before Jax snatched the knife out of the air and slammed it blade down into the man's outstretched hand. Cedric's money bag fell to the ground as the man stepped back, an expression of shock on his face as he looked at his hand, now impaled with the knife. Blood droplets were already falling from the tip of the knife.

"Restringuntas," Cedric said, and fired a bolt of black energy at the man. It struck him in the chest and wrapped around him, paralyzing his entire body. His inability to move threw him off balance and he fell to the side. The only sound he made was a muffled thump as his body hit the pavement.

"Oh-em-gee... Did you just kill that guy?" Alex said from the other side of the car.

Cedric shot a half smile her way and said, "Fear not, he is simply paralyzed. A few minutes and he'll be just fine. Until then, he can lie there and think about his actions." He walked over and knelt down beside the paralyzed man and whispered to him, "While I've been known, on occasion, to take an item or two that doesn't belong to me, one must be certain that one is not getting himself in over his head."

Though the man couldn't move, Cedric could see the terror in his eyes, and knew he would be a changed man. He grabbed his money bag and returned it to his belt, then walked around the car to join Alex, grinning the whole time.

"Oh no," she said. "You're not getting off that easy. How did you do that? I mean, you don't just paralyze somebody like that. Nobody does that."

"If I tell you, do you promise not to kick me out of the car?" Cedric asked.

Alex breathed a big sigh and said, "Forget it. Forget I asked. I don't want to know. Let's just go get some rest. We still have a long drive ahead of us tomorrow."

A loud groan from the other side of the car told Cedric that his would-be mugger was now free to move. He walked back around and saw the man curled up on the ground cradling his injured hand. "You'll want to get that looked at by a healer. Perhaps next time, you'll put more thought into your actions."

Cedric offered the man a hand to help him up, but he batted it away and scrambled across the pavement to get away. When he did manage to get to his feet, he stumbled once, ran, fell, picked himself up again, and disappeared into the night with the knife still lodged in his hand. Alex removed a backpack from her trunk and allowed Jax and Cedric to grab their gear, then locked the car and led them to two doors.

"You guys will have to share a room, okay?"

"Of course," Cedric said. "Sleep well, milady."

Alex gave him a key, and then went into her own room and closed the door. Cedric opened their room and looked around. He couldn't make out much detail in the dim light, but could see a bed large enough for him and Jax, and some other furnishings to make people feel at home. It wasn't much different than rooms at inns in Findoor or Caldoor, with the exception that he couldn't see a lantern anywhere. A quick glance over at Alex's window showed a light on in her room, so Cedric walked over to her door and knocked. The door opened right away, revealing Alex's surprised face. "What's the matter? Everything okay?"

Cedric spotted several lights on in her room, but they didn't look like any lantern he'd ever seen before. Instead, they looked more like the permanent magical lights used in some castles. "Begging your pardon, milady. Could you show me how to ignite the lanterns in my room?"

Her face grew momentarily confused, but then a smile spread across her face. "Oh, you mean the lights? You seriously don't know how to turn on the lights?" She giggled at this, and Cedric felt his face burn with embarrassment. "Sorry," Alex said, clearing the smile from her face. "Here..." She reached over to a switch on the wall and flipped it down and back up. The lights turned off and back on again.

Cedric let out a gasp of surprise and clapped his hands together. "Remarkable. Truly remarkable. Certainly better than burning my fingers trying to light a lamp. I thank you." He bent over into a little bow and backed away a step. "Good night to you, milady."

Alex rolled her eyes and said, "Good night, Cedric."

Her door closed, and Cedric returned to his room, flipping the lights on and startling Jax. "Truly amazing, this world," Cedric said with a smile. "Now we can eat."

The pair had a small meal of trail rations from their packs, and then went to sleep in the bed that was far more comfortable than anything Cedric had ever slept on.

5

Cedric awoke to a knock at the door. Sunlight flooded in through the window. He got out of bed and saw that Jax was already up and sitting in a chair, looking out the window at the parking lot. Cedric opened the door to find Alex outside. "Time to go, boys," she said. She held her phone up and it made a strange sound, similar to what she had done the night before when he first woke up. "We're already later in the day than I wanted to be."

"Indeed," Cedric said. "What exactly are you doing with that?"

She grinned at him and turned the phone around so he could see the screen. On it was a picture of himself. "I'm taking pictures of you guys and our trip. I take pictures of everything, but this is the most interesting thing to happen to me in a long time."

"I see," Cedric said with a nod. "Give us a moment. We will meet you at your car."

"Did you sleep in that mask?" Alex asked, giving Cedric a funny look.

"Yes," Cedric said, with a dry, flat tone.

Alex leaned forward and tried to look under the edge of the mask. "Do you ever take it off? Are you like, all gross and stuff underneath?"

"Nay. It is part of my order. I swore an oath when I joined, and gave up who I was to become who I am. If I remove the mask, I break that oath." The line of questioning was familiar to Cedric, but always made him uncomfortable. Alex must have sensed this, because she backed up a step and flashed him a smile.

"All right," she said. "Hurry up. We still need to grab something to eat."

She walked away and Cedric looked toward Jax. "Did you sleep at all?"

"No," Jax said. "I tried, but I had already slept in the car and I don't think I can face those dreams again."

"Give it time, my friend. In time the pain will ease."

Jax stood up and approached Cedric. "I think that's what I'm afraid of."

Both men collected their things and left the room. A few moments later, Alex was driving them to get some food. They stopped at what Cedric assumed was a small tavern or something, though he couldn't tell if they served ale or not. The three of them walked in and sat down at a table, and a young waitress walked up. "What'll it be?" She asked.

Alex took a quick look over the menu and said, "Three country breakfasts, and make em all over-easy."

"No problem," the waitress said, but her tone was dry and bored. She walked away and shouted something into the kitchen that was both loud and unintelligible, and then returned to her position behind the counter.

"Once we get to Denton, how do we find Seth?" Cedric asked. "We're not even sure he's there, but it is our best guess."

"Well," Alex said, taking out her phone. "We can always look up his name in the phone book. What's his last name again?"

"Alkirk."

"Right," she said, and tapped on her phone screen a few times. "Okay, so there's no S. Alkirk in the phone book, but there's a J. & M. Alkirk in the same city. They may be related."

"Perhaps," Cedric said. "It's worth a shot."

"Then that settles it," Alex said. "We'll go there first when we get to Denton, and figure out the rest as we go, right?"

"That's my kind of plan," Cedric said, with a smile.

Jax appeared to listen to their conversation, but remained quiet. Even when their food came, he ate in silence while Cedric raved about the meal. When they were done, they paid and left the diner, ignoring all the people who stared at Cedric and his mask. The remainder of the journey was uneventful, as Cedric opted to stay in the car other than for meals, and they drove almost non-stop until they reached Denton. The sun had set by the time they got there, and Alex complained that her legs were getting tired from driving. She pulled to the side of the road once to check directions on her phone, and said, "I sent Seth a message on Facebook this morning, but he hasn't responded. At least if he does check his messages, he'll know you're looking for him."

"A good idea. Thank you, Alex," Cedric said. "Let's get to that house and see if they know anything about Seth."

Fifteen minutes later they pulled up in front of a small house. Cedric got out first and walked toward the front door. The grass in front of the house was long and poorly maintained compared the rest of the houses in the neighborhood, and the gardens to either side of the path that led to the front door were overgrown with what Cedric assumed were weeds. The inside of the house was dark, and the night air was cooler than Cedric was used to. As he approached the front door, he thought he glimpsed a slight movement in one of the windows, but shrugged it off and knocked on the door. Jax and Alex walked up behind him while he waited for an answer.

After a few minutes, Alex said, "I don't think anyone's home."

"There's somebody here," Cedric said. "You just can't see them." He backed away from the door and called on the power of fire, focusing it into his hand. "Incendras," he said, and fired a small ball of fire at the door, which blasted a hole in it.

Alex jumped back, and said, "Jesus. What the hell was that?"

Cedric stepped forward and reached through the hole to unlock the door, then pushed the door open. "Just my way of saying 'hello'," Cedric said with a grin. "Wait here, I'll only be a minute."

He entered the dark house and saw a shadow move down a hallway at the far end of the room. With his bow at the ready and an arrow nocked, he followed the shadowy form down the hall to the room at the end. When he entered the doorway, he could see the shadow inside the room.

"I know you're there. Show yourself," he said, watching the shadow form for signs of movement.

"Incendras."

He heard the word before the ball of fire struck his chest. Next thing he knew, his back hit the wall behind him and there was an intense burning pain in his chest.

The shadowy form ran past him before he could get up, but Cedric thought fast and focused the power of death into a bolt. "Restringuntas."

The energy struck the shadow, knocking it to the floor. Cedric struggled to his feet through the pain of the burns on his chest and walked over to the shadow form. It was a slight figure, smaller than an average man. *A woman*, Cedric thought. He gathered the power of death to him, willing it to strip away her enchantments that hid her from view, and said, "Depellendas."

A blue light erupted from her and the shadow melted away, revealing a middle-aged woman. Jax entered the house with his swords at the ready, but Cedric held up his hand. "That won't be necessary," he said, and approached the woman on the floor. Gray hair surrounded a face that Cedric recognized from long ago. Time had taken its toll on her body, but he would know her green eyes anywhere. "Catrina."

"It's been thirty years since anyone has used that name," she said, her voice trembling.

He offered her a hand which she accepted and he pulled her up off the floor, though it hurt him to do so. The burns on his chest had grown quite painful. "It's been over a hundred since I've seen you, but only several months since I've looked into your eyes."

Catrina looked confused as she responded. "Over a hundred? How can that be? Serrin consulted with you when he worked on his summoning research, and that was before the Lyecian war, thirty years ago."

"My dear, the Lyecian war was over a hundred years ago."

She stepped back, a shocked expression on her face. "That can't be. Krycin brought us here thirty years ago, to get away from all the war and politics. To raise our son in peace. I still curse his name when I think about it."

Cedric approached her with outstretched hands and took hers in his. "Time does not flow true for you then. Why are you hiding? You have no need to hide in this world."

"I thought you were him. I thought you were Cy."

"Then you have nothing to fear. Cy is dead, destroyed by your own son," Cedric said. He remembered the night of the ball, when Cy had attacked Findoor Castle. It was the first time he truly believed that Seth could be a hero.

"Seth?" Catrina asked. "Where is he? Is he okay? When did he encounter Cy?"

"Easy, now. We have much to discuss. We are looking for Seth ourselves, and now I am in need of a healer," he said, looking down at his chest.

Alex poked her head in the door at that moment and gasped. "Oh my god, what happened to you," she said, rushing to Cedric and ignoring Catrina. "You've been burnt, and it looks bad. We need to get you to a doctor."

"I can bind the wound for you," Catrina said. "But I cannot heal it."

Cedric looked from one woman to the other and smiled. "Don't worry about my wounds. It is far more important that we find Seth. We have reason to believe that he has come to this world, and we are in dire need of him on Galadir."

"So it is true, then?" Catrina asked, taking a step back. "Somebody did come for him?"

"Indeed," Cedric said. "Fortunately for him, the right people returned with him. Had Grian gotten him before his powers had fully matured, our conversation would be very different right now, if it would have ever happened at all."

"When I saw the Narshuk on the news, I didn't think it possible. I went into hiding, and prayed to Lyecha that she would protect him. Then tonight, there was the disturbance downtown. I thought Cy had returned." Tears rolled down her cheeks and she swayed back and forth like she might fall. Alex moved to steady her and Jax took up a position on her other side. They walked her to a couch and sat her down.

"Do you have a first aid kit?" Alex asked her.

"Yes, in the hall closet," Catrina said. Alex walked away and Cedric sat down near her.

"Disturbance? What sort of disturbance?"

"A club downtown. People were describing events that sounded like more magic. We've been hiding from Cy ever since we came to Earth. That's why Serrin left twenty-five years ago."

Alex returned carrying a small white box with a red cross on the front of it. She placed it on a nearby table and looked at Cedric. "Lie down. I can at least cover this so it doesn't get infected." She eased Cedric down onto the couch and lifted what was left of his shirt. Taking great care, she applied bandages to the burns the best she could. While she did this, Cedric continued to talk.

"Serrin? Is that his name. My mind keeps wanting to think his name was Krycin, but I knew that wasn't right. I knew there was another name. Krycin was the hero of the war, but there was no way that Seth was Krycin's son."

Catrina laughed when he said that. "No, of course not. What fool believes that?"

"All of Galadir," Cedric said, without a hint of humor in his voice.

"The very idea that I would lay with that vile maggot. The only reason I allowed him to bring us to Earth was because Serrin trusted him."

"You cannot believe that of Krycin," Cedric said, trying to look up at her. When he did, Alex pushed him back down and he resigned himself to her care. "Krycin is well respected on Galadir. He was a hero and saved many lives."

"He was a snake, and a fool," Catrina said. "He should have left me dead."

Cedric let out a great sigh. "I'd heard stories about the miracles Krycin had performed. How he raised the dead, and healed the sick. I didn't believe them. Thought them exaggerations of his deeds."

"He did many things, and he failed many times. But let's discuss other, more important matters. You say Seth has returned?"

"We think so. Jax and I were sent here to find him," Cedric said. He looked over at Jax and tried to get up, but was again pushed down by Alex.

"Stop moving or you're going to make this worse," Alex said in a stern tone.

"Forgive my manners," Cedric said. "Catrina, this is Jax, my companion and one of the last remaining blade slingers of Galadir."

Catrina bowed her head to Jax. "It is a pleasure to meet you."

"The pleasure is mine," Jax said.

"After the Narshuk attack, things changed in this city. The military moved in, and there have been frequent patrols. We were told a cover story for what happened, but nobody really believes it." Catrina looked down at the smooth hardwood floors. "If he came back, the military will probably be the first to know. They've been experimenting with things they don't understand, and I fear they might do real damage."

"Well then, that sounds like a good place to start," Cedric said.

Alex placed one last bandage on Cedric's chest and said, "There. That's the best you'll get without going to a hospital. There was a base just outside of town that we passed on our way here. Is that where they've been experimenting?"

"Yes," Catrina said as Cedric sat up.

"My goodness, my manners have failed me again," Cedric said with a grin. "Alex, this is an old friend of mine, Catrina Alkirk. Catrina, this is Alex, our escort. Now, if we leave right away, how long will it take us to get to the base?"

"A half hour maybe," Alex said. She took out her phone and tapped a few times, then looked back up. "Thirty-five minutes according to this. But you can't just walk onto a military compound."

"Then let's go. If there's a chance they know where Seth is, or how to find him, that's where we need to be," Cedric said, getting to his feet. "We can worry about how to get in when we get there."

"Can I come with you?" Catrina asked. "I haven't seen Seth in months, and I've been so worried about him."

"But of course," Cedric said. "So long as Alex is all right with it. It is, after all, her car."

"Yes, please," Alex said. "There's plenty of room in the back seat."

"Off to the compound, then," Cedric said, leading the way out of Catrina's house.

# Chapter 22 – Going Home

"It's no use, I just can't control it," Dave said, after incinerating a third mannequin. "You both make it look so easy."

"I assure you, my abilities are the product of years of study," Malia said. "You are trying to master this in one night, and that is not possible."

"Then how come Seth is so good at it? I know he hasn't spent his life studying magic, and he knocks the socks off of both of us."

"You can't measure your abilities in comparison to mine," Seth said. "I'm not human. The limits that define your abilities don't exist for me. But you are lucky. You can use two elements, which is uncommon on Galadir. Most normal people can only use one." Seth watched as Dave breathed a sigh and closed his eyes. It was a fast meditation technique that Malia had taught him in order to help him clear his mind. He raised his hands toward the fourth mannequin and took a single, deliberate breath. "Now, slowly, concentrate on what you want to accomplish. Visualize it in your mind. The energy of fire is red, so see the energy in your mind as a red flow that travels to you and focuses in your hand."

A glow appeared around Dave's hand, red and fiery. Seth could see the strain on his face as he fought to control the energy and form it into a small ball of fire. His task was to disarm the mannequin, which was holding a fake pistol aimed at him.

With a quiet, calm voice, Seth said, "Now let it go, all at once, focused into a tight beam."

The fire in Dave's hand erupted toward the mannequin in a straight line and struck the gun. The flames continued up its arm and consumed it up to the shoulder, leaving nothing but dust drifting to the ground.

Seth watched Dave open his eyes in the silent room to see the results of his spell. He wasn't ready for the exuberant cheer that Dave let out. "Yeah, man," Dave hollered. "That's what I'm talkin' about."

"It is a start," Malia said, with a smile.

Seth was about to say something when General Mathers walked in with a concerned look on his face. He didn't wait to be addressed, but walked straight up to Seth and said, "Alkirk, we need you up top. There's some crackpot asking for you by name. Night guards said they didn't see a soul pass through the gates, and we've got nothing on surveillance. We would have arrested him on the spot, but he knocked out four guards in under thirty seconds and insisted on speaking with you."

"Okay, I'm coming," Seth said. He went to follow Mathers out, but stopped when he saw Malia was about to come with him. "I'd prefer it if you stayed here," he said to her.

"And I would prefer to come with you," Malia said.

"It could be dangerous, we have no idea who is up there, and besides, Dave still needs some instruction."

"Oh, no, I'll be fine, Seth," Dave said, waving them both off. "I'm going to practice a while longer."

Malia scowled at Seth and said, "It is not for you to say whether I can put myself in danger or not. I'm a grown woman, and the general of an army. I am capable of making my own decisions."

Before Seth could say another word, Malia had already left the room and was heading toward the elevator. Seth went to follow her, but Mathers put his arm out to stop him. "Let me give you some advice, son. Don't ever try to make up a woman's mind for her, especially a woman like her. You'll only push her away."

"Thanks," Seth said. "I'll keep that in mind."

"Just trying to help you out," Mathers said, with a sly smile. "She's a fine young woman. Treat her right." He lowered his arm and let Seth pass, following close behind. They could hear small explosions coming from the training room right up until the elevator doors closed. Malia gave Seth a cool stare, but said nothing, which left them all in awkward silence.

They reached the ground floor moments later and left the elevator, making their way to the front entrance of the building. Seth led now and was curious about who could be there, and how they knew his name. His questions were answered when he approached the lobby and saw the tall, thin figure standing there in all black, with a mask over his face.

"Cedric," Seth said with a smile, and sped up.

Malia ran past him and flung her arms around the bard, who seemed off guard at the sudden emotional state of the two. When Malia released him from her embrace, he backed up a step, looked at Seth and said, "Indeed. But use caution, as you might wear out my name, and it's such a bother to find a new one."

"That joke is so old it's wearing out," Seth said with a smile.

"I trust you have a better idea of who you are now?" Cedric asked. The corner of his mouth was turned up in a half smile, but there was a look in his eyes that told Seth his appearance there was not a social visit.

"I do," Seth said. "What are you doing here? How did you get here from Galadir?"

"That was my thought as well," Malia said. "How is it that you came here?"

"How I got here is a long story for another day. Let me simply state that it has been quite an adventure. Your world is very strange and wondrous," Cedric said. "Darian sent me here to find the two of you. Grian is set to invade Caldoor with his army and may have begun already. We need you, Seth, to battle the vile wizard, and Malia to lead her army. There is little time to waste."

Seth turned to Mathers and shrugged. "This is it," Seth said with an apologetic smile. "We have to go. Do you think you have enough help now with Dave in hand?"

"I think we'll manage. We can always recruit more," Mathers said. "How do I contact you if we need you again?"

"You don't," Seth said. "There's no easy way to communicate across worlds. But rest assured, I'll be back to check on things someday. Right now, there's another world that needs us."

"Go on, then. Don't be a stranger," Mathers said, and waved them off. "Get on with it, I'm not one for long goodbyes."

Seth turned back to Cedric and said, "Ready? We can be there in seconds."

Cedric raised his hand to stop Seth. "Nay, not yet. There are a number of others outside who are waiting to meet you."

He turned around and walked out through the front door. Seth and Malia followed close behind and were surprised to see a small car parked in the parking lot with three other people around it. The first, Seth recognized as the man who was at the gallows with Malia when he rescued her. The second was a young woman he had never seen before, and the third he would know anywhere. "Mom!"

His mother looked at him, her face confused. She looked as though she was battling some kind of internal conflict. "Krycin," she said, in a whisper. "No, you're not my son. You're that bastard, Krycin." She moved back a step, her eyes full of anger and fear. A tear rolled down her cheek as she appeared to be summoning magical power. She raised a hand and said, "Incendras."

Seth raised a shield before him just in time to block a ball of fire that she sent at him. "Mom, it's me. It's Seth," he said, but she wasn't listening anymore.

He walked toward her, stepping to the side to keep other people out of her blast radius. She spoke again, and said, "Tremefascas." The ground shuddered and the paved surface of the parking lot split open, breaking the asphalt into large chunks. Several of these chunks launched at Seth, and his instincts kicked in, slowing time around him. He ducked his head under one, and side-stepped another, but the third clipped his forehead and left a large gash.

"Please, Mom," Seth said. "Listen. I know I look different, and I sound different, but this is who I've become."

Blood dripped from his forehead into his eyes, and he focused on the power of water to heal the wound. It closed up, leaving a tiny mark where the rock had first hit. He stepped toward her, but she spoke again. "Indespectas."

She disappeared, becoming invisible before Seth could get any closer to her. He closed his eyes and called on the power of shadow to reveal her location, but he was too late. She was standing before him, mere inches away, and before he had the chance to react, she spoke again. "Obitas nexasa mortai."

The words echoed in Seth's ears as her hand touched his arm and he felt the cold embrace of death seize his soul. Darkness flooded in around him as he struggled to cling to life. There were shouts all around him, but he couldn't make out what they were saying. A single word cut through the darkness and brought him back. "Restringuntas."

There was a blast before him, and his mother's body flew back and landed on the ground, paralyzed. Seth shook his head and looked around at all the people around him. Cedric was standing beside him with a concerned look on his face. "We almost lost you there. Are you well?"

"Yes, I'm fine now," Seth said. "Thanks."

"It's like she was under some kind of spell," Cedric said.

"There's only one person who's ever had that kind of hate toward me," Seth said. He approached Catrina and knelt down beside her. When he looked into her eyes, it startled him. All he could see was darkness and hate. "I'm going to find out what's wrong with you, Mom. I'm going to fix things."

The power of life came easy to him now and he willed the white magic into her body to show him what was wrong. Inside her head he saw a black thread, like a snake, working its way through her brain. It constricted around her mind and controlled her actions under specific circumstances. Seth focused his white magic on this thread and neutralized it, little by little, until there was nothing left.

"You're going to be okay, Mom," he said as the paralysis began to fade.

She blinked and looked like she was confused. "Krycin," she said, but thought for a moment. "No... Seth. You look so much older."

"I know. It's time to go home now."

"Home? I just came from home," she said, sitting up.

"No, not your house. Home. Galadir."

Her eyes lit up, the green in them brightening, and she smiled. "It's been so long since I've been home, and you've grown so much."

Seth helped her up off the ground and turned to face the others. As he did, the young woman he didn't recognize spoke up. "Okay, I'm not even going to pretend to know what's going on here." She looked from Seth to Malia and then back to Seth. "You must be Seth," she said as she walked toward him.

"I am," Seth said, shaking her hand. "You are?"

Cedric approached and cut in before she could say anything. As he did he bumped into Seth and flinched. "Seth, this is Alexis, though she prefers Alex. She helped us find you, and brought us here."

"It's good to meet you, Alex," Seth said, releasing her hand. He looked toward Cedric and scowled at the bard who was obviously trying to cover something up. "Are you wounded?"

"'Tis nothing," Cedric said. "I don't like to complain."

"Let's see it," Seth said.

"I'm not sure that's a good idea," Alex said. "It's a pretty bad burn, and could get infected."

"I know what I'm doing," Seth said. "Come on, Cedric. Let's see it."

With a sigh, Cedric lifted the front of the spare shirt he had put on. The bandages covering his wounds were soaked through as the wounds wept, and Seth could tell this was more serious than Cedric had let on. He removed the bandages with care and shook his head when he saw the severity of the burns.

"Hold still," Seth said. Calling on the power of water, Seth poured the energy into Cedric's chest. A blue glow flowed from Seth's hands and surrounded the wounds. The redness faded and new skin formed. When there was nothing left but some pale scars, Seth stopped and looked up. "Good as new."

"Jesus," Alex said, rushing forward. She ran a finger over Cedric's chest where the wounds had been, looked up at Seth and said, "How?"

"I would explain it," Cedric said, "but you keep telling me not to."

"Let me handle this," Seth said to Cedric. "Before I had a chance to talk to General Mathers in there, I didn't understand it myself. We call it magic, but it's not, really. All around us, and everywhere in the universe, there's microwave radiation that is residual from when the universe was created. People from Galadir have a genetic anomaly that allows them to harness that energy, store it, and release it in various ways. They call it spell casting, and it can do all sorts of things, from creating fire, to healing wounds, to destroying entire worlds."

"So, it's magic, but not magic," Alex said with a smile. "I was never very good at science."

"You're taking it better than I did," Seth said. He looked around at everyone else and said, "So we have myself, Cedric, Malia, and of course my mom. Who is this?" He gestured to Jax who had been watching the whole scene quietly. "I recognize you from when I caught Malia. From that castle."

"My name is Jax Fellstar, and I am at your service. I have pledged my service to the remaining soldiers of Findoor, which means Malia is my general." He gave a deep bow toward Malia, and then stood back up.

"It's good to meet you. So you'll be coming back with us. What about you, Alex? You up for an even bigger adventure?"

She let out a weak laugh and shook her head. "Not a chance. But hey, if you're ever in L.A., drop me a line and we'll hang out. Any of you. It's been a slice, peeps. But I've got a life to get back to."

"Your loss," Seth said, and shrugged. "Do you need a quick ride back home? L.A. is a long way from here."

"I've got my car, it'll take me about two days to get back if I take my time."

"I could get you there tonight," Seth said.

Alex looked toward Cedric and said, "Can he do that? Just, like, zip me away back home?"

"If he says he can, I would trust him," Cedric said with a nod. "I've never known Seth to overstate his abilities. Before you go, I must make good on my promise." He reached into his money bag, drew out a handful of coins, and took Alex's hand. "Take this, with my most sincere gratitude. You've earned every copper of it."

She looked down at the handful of coins with wide eyes. "Oh, Cedric. This is too much. Our agreement was for five, and I would have been fine without that."

"Speak no more," Cedric said. "I won't take it back, so you're stuck with it now." He gave her a wink through his mask and backed up a step. "May Grishtor ever treat you well."

Alex ran forward and threw her arms around Cedric in a big hug that looked like it took him off guard. After a moment, Cedric returned the embrace. Seth was amused by how good they looked together as a couple.

When she released him, Seth approached Alex and said, "How strong is your stomach?"

Alex's face washed over with confusion at the unusual question. "Uhm... strong?"

"Good," Seth said, and placed a hand on her shoulder as well as her car. He closed his eyes and focused on the city on the southwest coast, with the Hollywood sign on the hill. They ceased to exist in the parking lot of the military compound and appeared in a parking lot on Hollywood Boulevard. Alex stumbled back a step and looked around. Her face held a look of revulsion, like she was trying not to throw up. After a moment, she composed herself and looked at Seth.

"What the hell was that?"

"Teleportation. Instant point-to-point travel. It comes in handy if I know where I'm going. Takes some getting used to, though."

"I'll say; I just about lost my dinner."

"So listen," Seth said. "We're all going back to Galadir, but this isn't the last you're going to hear about magic. It's very real, and very dangerous, and in the wrong hands, it could be devastating to this world. If you know what's good for you, you'll steer clear of it. Understand?"

"Yeah, I get it. It's weird, but I get it," Alex said. She backed up a step to go to her car, but Seth thought she looked like she had something more to say.

"Come on, out with it," Seth said with a smile.

"Well, Cedric told me that you grew up on Earth, but you have all these crazy powers. How did you hide them?"

"For most of my life, I was human, just like you. My powers were suppressed for a long time. Longer than they should have been."

"Wow. How do you cope with learning all this? I'm having trouble believing it, and I'm on the outside. I couldn't imagine being in the middle of it all like you are."

"To be honest, I'm still figuring that out," Seth said. He smiled at her and shrugged. "Maybe someday I'll get a handle on it. Take care, okay?"

"Yeah, sure. You too," Alex said, and looked like she was still thinking about something. "If you guys ever get back here, look me up. I mean it." She took out a scrap of paper and a pen from her purse, wrote something down, and handed the paper to Seth.

"We will," Seth said, and tucked the paper in his pocket.

Seth watched Alex get in her car, and once she had it started, focused on the parking lot at the military base and teleported back. When he appeared, he looked around at the rest of his companions and said, "So, back to Galadir then. Where am I taking us?"

"I need my armor and sword before I can enter battle," Malia said. "If I am right, Darian still has it at Caldoor Castle."

"I will accompany you to the front lines of the battle when we go," Jax said. "If Grian's army is as dangerous as Cedric says it is, you will need every warrior you can get."

"Splendid," Cedric said. "I shall stay with Catrina at Caldoor Castle, as I don't believe I shall be much use in this battle. Ceridan had planned to bring Morganath into the battle as well. Take us to Caldoor Castle, and then you, Malia and Jax go and join Ceridan at the front lines."

Seth nodded in agreement. "You okay with that, Mom?"

"Yes, Cedric and I have some catching up to do."

"Everyone hold hands," Seth said. Once they were all linked together, Seth concentrated on the castle he had seen when he rescued Malia, and they all disappeared.

# Chapter 23 - Wraiths and Wizards

A white dome of energy lifted from around Gladius, Tyriel and Nadya, revealing the outer grounds of Ducain's Keep. The area was quiet and still in the afternoon air, and not a soul could be seen outside. There was little sunlight, as the clouds above were blocking it, threatening rain. Gladius took in a deep breath and exhaled slowly, enjoying the crisp feel of the autumn air in his lungs.

"It's too quiet," Nadya said, looking around.

Gladius looked around and shrugged. "It's late afternoon. Besides, they're probably afraid to get rained on."

He listened for a moment, but heard nothing. No birds, no people. The cool breeze made the only sound, and his realization of the eerie silence made the air feel colder still. He shivered as it worked its way through his robes.

"No," Tyriel said. "This is different." His hand had found the handle of his scythe, and he removed it from its place on his back.

Gladius scanned the area and took a few steps toward the keep. "I see nothing unusual, other than a lack of wizards."

"It's never this quiet at the keep," Nadya said, following Gladius. "Even on the most terrible days, there is at least a candle lit in a window somewhere with a wizard studying."

When Gladius looked over the keep once more, he saw there was indeed not a single window lit. The entire keep was dark and quiet and still. He continued to lead the way toward the front gates, keeping a spell ready in his head just in case. Tyriel stayed close, but Nadya lagged behind. Gladius entered the gates first and saw something that disturbed him. Scattered around the courtyard were robes of all colors, settled on the ground like the owners had vanished and left them to fall. The air grew colder still as they approached the keep and Gladius could see his breath now before him.

"What is this?" Gladius asked, watching the clouds of moisture escape his lips.

Tyriel looked as though he would answer when an ear-piercing shriek came from behind them. Gladius turned in time to see Nadya taken from behind by a dark form. Its body looked much like Tyriel, with flowing, incorporeal features, but the hands that grasped Nadya were bone-white with sharp claws in the ends that dug into her flesh. Tyriel was faster than Gladius and moved like the wind to help her. He swung his scythe at the creature that clung to her and buried the blade in its head. It dissolved into black mist and dissipated around her, leaving her to collapse.

Gladius ran to her side, but wasn't able to help her before three more of the creatures lifted out of the ground around them. Tyriel took another swing and dispersed a second one, then backed up a step to put some distance between himself and Gladius.

There was a moment of silence as the remaining two creatures made their approach, but Gladius had no intention of waiting for an attack. He drew the power of water to him and said, "Congelascas." Several balls of blue energy fired at the nearest creature and exploded in spheres of frost on contact. The spell would normally have been devastating to a living creature, but the black form didn't appear to notice the impact of the spell. Tyriel spun and sunk his Scythe into a third one as Gladius gathered his thoughts.

"We need to move," he said to Tyriel. Nadya lay on the ground at his feet, her skin as pale as the creature who touched her. She took shallow, quick breaths, and Gladius could tell she was in a state of shock.

"Go," Tyriel shouted as several more of the creatures appeared. "Get Nadya to safety. I'll hold them off."

There was a flash of a blade and the nearest creature to Gladius dispersed into the air. He reached down and lifted Nadya into his arms and began the long trek toward the front doors of the keep. He could hear Tyriel behind him grunting and swinging his scythe to destroy the creatures. The doors were still twenty paces away when one of the creatures lifted up out of the ground before him. It moved with the same slow, steady patience as the rest of them. Its silent motion overwhelmed Gladius far faster than he expected, and though Nadya wasn't heavy, her weight still hindered his movements. He took a step back away from the creature and tried to draw the energy to cast a spell, but before he could, a blast of white light struck the creature and it exploded into a shower of sparks around Gladius.

"Philana save me," Gladius said as he stumbled back a step, surprised. He turned to see where the blast came from and spotted a figure at the top of the mountain pass that led down to the keep from Findoor. When he looked around, it surprised him to see at least two dozen of the black forms drifting toward him and Tyriel, threatening to overwhelm them. The figure in the distance raised its hands and sent a shower of white lights into the air. They rained down on the creatures, spreading out to cover the whole area. Each time a light touched one of the black forms, it exploded and sent more of the white lights in every direction around it. Seconds later, the courtyard was free of them, and the figure was coming down the hill toward them.

"Who is it?" Tyriel asked. His breathing was fast from his exertion, and Gladius could tell they lived now by a stroke of luck.

"I'm not sure, but I think we're about to find out."

The person came into better view, revealing a runner's uniform with the hood pulled over his head. He rode a horse that bore the Findoor crest, but he was not an undead creature like they had fought in Findoor before. He sat tall on the horse, and demonstrated control over the element of life. "Count your blessings that I made it here when I did," the runner said. His voice was familiar, but it had been a while since Gladius had heard it.

"To whom do we owe our lives?" Gladius asked. He adjusted Nadya in his arms, who was still clinging to life, but was fading.

The runner pulled his hood back revealing red-brown hair streaked with gray, and a strong, yet familiar jaw line. "You owe me nothing," he said as he came to a halt and dismounted the horse.

"Serrin," Gladius said. "The gods favor us. Can you help her?"

Serrin approached and knelt down before them. He looked over Nadya and saw her white skin. Her body was beginning to shake as the heat left her. "Her life force has been partially drained. I'm not certain she can be helped now, but let's get her into the keep before more wraiths get here."

"Agreed," Gladius said. He stood up with Nadya in his arms and approached the front door of the keep. Tyriel was already there, pounding on the door. After a few moments, the door opened a crack and a white robed wizard peered out. "Hurry up and open the door, you imbecile. We're under attack."

The door swung open, and Gladius saw Trysk inside. He was out of breath and looked as though he had run all the way from the council chamber to the front entrance. "Andran, has she been touched by one of them?"

"Yes. She's badly wounded and needs help." Gladius went to carry her in, but Trysk blocked his path.

"No," he said. "She must remain outside."

"What are you talking about? She needs our help. If we don't act fast, she'll die." Gladius tried to work his way around Trysk, but the black-robed wizard continued to block his way in.

"I can't let you bring her in here. We've already lost a great many good wizards to the wraiths today. She *will* turn, and she *will* attack, and we will all die if we let her in. Council wizard or no, she must remain outside the keep."

"You're a heartless bastard, Trysk." Gladius backed up a step so that he could take Nadya outside.

"I'm a smart bastard, and you know it." He turned to the white-robed wizard next to him and said, "Go and get Attowen. He will be able to help."

Gladius left the entrance to the keep without another word and carried Nadya over to where Tyriel stood. "We can't lie her on the ground. The wraiths can travel under it. Can you take her while Serrin and I set up wards to protect against them?"

"Gladly," Tyriel said, holding out his arms. He lifted her unconscious form away from Gladius and moved away toward the keep.

With his arms now free, Gladius approached Serrin who was already casting defensive spells to keep the remaining wraiths at bay. "How did you escape, anyway? Seth told me there was a reality anchor around you."

"Yes," Serrin said, "and a force cage. But Grian is not as smart as he seems. He didn't realize that a force cage will not contain a non-magic user."

"You suppressed your powers?" Gladius asked.

"Indeed. They have not fully returned yet, but I have limited use of them again. Do you know where Seth is now? We need to let him know that I'm okay."

"I'm not sure. He received a message during the last council meeting and said there was somewhere he had to be. That was before we went to the Badlands." Gladius thought for a moment about where he might be. "I'm going to talk to Trysk. There's something I need Seth to do as well."

He walked back toward the keep and gave Attowen a nod as they crossed paths. The white wizard's face was lined with concern over one of his comrades, but gave him a friendly smile anyway. Gladius entered the keep and marched all the way to the council chamber. Inside, Trysk, Merisill and the gray wizard Kenda were discussing something in hushed voices. When Gladius entered the chamber, they all went silent and sat at attention.

"Oh come now," Gladius said. "Don't stop on my account."

Trysk stood up and approached Gladius. "Fine. I'll continue. You're hiding something, Andran. I know you are. When I figure it out, I will expose you to the council and have you expelled. You may have befriended the Lyecian, but you haven't got all of us fooled with your stories."

"Just like a black wizard, full of suspicion. How do we know it was Grian who sent the wraiths. Perhaps it was you, or one of your students. Anything to gain a little power, right?" Gladius stepped toe to toe with Trysk and looked him in the eyes. "You don't scare me, black wizard. I've faced far more terrible foes and lived to tell the tale."

"Time will tell. What is your business here?"

"I came to see if there was any word from Seth. I've recovered the Lyecian tome, as I said I would."

Trysk backed up a step without breaking eye contact. "We've had no direct word from him, but Arch-Magus Darian in Caldoor informed us that he has sent two people to the dead world to find him. Grian is on the move, with his armies poised to invade Caldoor. They may be doing so right now. Darian believes that if they don't receive the help of the Lyecian, their kingdom will be overrun."

"So Grian is busy, even though he appears inactive," Gladius said. "The Eastern Badlands are facing an outbreak of quickrot that is killing Narshuks by the hundreds and spreading fast. That's where I found the book."

"Ha! I knew those animals would fall to their own filthy disease. Let them rot, we have no use for them."

"Grishtor take your tongue," Gladius said. As he did, he caught the surprised expressions of the other two wizards in the room as well. Their gazes were not fixed on him, but on Trysk. "You dare speak ill of your own god's creations? Or have you forgotten what color robe you wear?"

There was a moment of silence in the chamber. Gladius watched Trysk's eyes, which revealed a deep contemplation of what he had said. "What use are they?" Trysk asked.

"More than a narrow-minded snake such as yourself could ever know. When they gather, we tear them apart. When they try to assert their place in the world, we knock them back and confine them to that gods' forsaken land. They are strong, and wise, and could be a great and powerful nation if only we wizards would step out of the way and allow them." Gladius began pacing around the room as he spoke. The other three council wizards watched and listened as he did. "Instead, they live in squalor, fighting amongst themselves for the smallest scraps of food. They struggle to survive in the harshest environment on Galadir, and we sit in luxury here in Ducain's Keep. That's going to change, and it starts now. We will send what help we can to the Narshuks, and when I do see Seth, I will send him there as well. Once that plague is wiped out, the Narshuks will fight with us to wipe out Grian and his army."

A quiet filled the room as Gladius took a breath, and then there was a clapping sound. Two hands coming together in a slow, steady rhythm. Gladius spun to see where the sound was coming from, but had a good idea who it was already. Trysk stared back at him, clapping his hands, with a wide grin.

"Impassioned words. You put on a great performance, Andran." The smile left his face and he narrowed his eyes. "Isn't it funny how someone from another world knows so much about us and our practices?"

Gladius's heart jumped at this, though he did his best to hide his reaction from the rest of the wizards.

"How can a wizard, of whom we have no records, know so much about the Narshuks and be so attached to them?" Trysk asked the other two in the room. "You wanted proof that he is lying? He's just handed it to you. I've been communing with Grishtor, who told me exactly how to get the truth about you. Who are you, really?"

"It matters not," Gladius said. He swallowed once, but his throat was dry. "All that matters is that I'm here to help you. I've made mistakes, and made peace with who I was. That's not who I am now. The Narshuks are being wiped out, and if we don't help them, this disease could wipe us all out."

"Andran is right, Trysk," Merisill said. "It doesn't matter who he was. He is Andran now, and he has given us no reason to believe his intentions are anything but good. If Seth trusts him, then we should as well."

"Trust must be earned, not freely given," Trysk said. "I won't trust him based on recommendation alone."

"You're right," Gladius said. "Trust must be earned. So give me a chance to earn it. I have the Lyecian tome, just as we discussed. Now we must figure out what to do about Grian." He paused and thought for a moment, then said, "Oh, and the man outside who saved our hides from the wraiths? That's Serrin. That's Seth's father, who was captured by Grian."

Kenda stood up and approached Gladius with a confused expression. "How did he escape?"

"Serrin is not only a powerful Lyecian, he's also one of the most intelligent," Gladius said. "When Grian was busy with other business, he foiled Grian's protections by suppressing his powers. They have not fully returned yet, but he is a capable wizard."

"We must call a meeting of the council, then," Trysk said. "We must adjust our plans. Seth can't be in three places at once."

"Agreed," Merisill said. "Any action must be agreed upon by all present council members."

"I'll go get Attowen and check on Nadya," Gladius said. "Perhaps Serrin and Attowen together can come up with a way to cure her."

"We'll wait here," Trysk said.

Gladius left the room without another word and returned to the front entrance where Nadya was being treated. Serrin and Attowen were sitting next to a cot that had been set up. Nadya lay unconscious on the cot, but the color had somewhat returned to her skin. Both the wizards sitting next to her looked exhausted.

"How is she?" Gladius asked.

Serrin looked up at Gladius with an expression that did not bring hope to his heart. "She's stable, for now. I'm not sure how long it will last though. Both Attowen and I have done everything we can. I'm afraid the only person who can help her now is Seth."

"Thank you, both of you, for your efforts. The council must convene now to discuss the most recent developments in our situations. Serrin, I think it would be best if you joined us as well, as this involves you and your son."

"Very well," Serrin said, and stood up.

Gladius waited while Attowen discussed Nadya's condition with another white-robed wizard. "Send a runner if her condition changes in the slightest," the old wizard said to his much younger counterpart. "We must stay ahead of her injury, or she will be lost to us forever."

"Understood, Magus. I shall not leave her side," the younger wizard said.

The three men walked back up to the council chamber, ready to discuss the fate of Ducain's Keep and all the wizards inside. Gladius held the door for Serrin and Attowen, and followed them in, pulling the door closed behind him.

# Chapter 24 - Firestorm

Ceridan fought with every ounce of strength he had. Undead bodies had piled up all around him, some still twitching. Each swing of his sword brought down more, but the tide of creatures over the bridge seemed to have no end. His muscles ached with the effort as he tried to make some room between himself and the creatures so he could survey the situation. He wasn't sure if there were any of his soldiers left standing, or if there was even a reason to fight anymore.

He stepped backward to avoid the lashing claws of one of the creatures and tripped, his foot snagged on the body of another. Try as he might, it was too late to save his balance. He fell back, watching the world tip, and landed with a thud on his back that took his breath away. The undead soldiers descended on him without mercy, tearing at his armor and trying to disarm him so they could claim him into their ranks. Ceridan struggled with one who was trying to bite his face through his helmet. The thing's teeth were jagged and turning black with decay. He threw a punch, which was little more than a thrash of his arm and connected with its face. The skin of its cheek sloughed off exposing jawbone and molars, but it did little to dissuade the creature from attacking.

Part of his armor on his calf gave way and he felt the cool air flow over his skin as the steel plate was removed and leather was torn. Seconds later, there was searing pain through the muscle as teeth sank into it, trying to take as much as it could in one bite. A second creature swooped down on the exposed flesh in a frenzy. Ceridan grasped his sword as tight as he could and swung wild at the first of them. His aim was off, but the blade still hacked into its chest and forced it to let go of his leg. He swung a second time, moving the blade up and caught the second creature in the face, slicing through its jaw and up through its head. It fell back and joined the others that were littered around the area. He was about to brace himself to get up when he heard an unusual sound.

Behind him, and out of his field of vision there was a hissing, sucking sound, and he felt the air grow warm as it rushed past him. *Fire*, he thought, and rolled as hard as he could to protect his face and exposed leg. Just as he went face-down in a puddle of gore, he felt the firestorm flow over him. The back of his armor heated up and scorched the leather underneath the plates. A few spots charred the leather to the point that it burned his skin and left blisters, but when the flames dispersed, he lifted his head in a fit of coughs.

His sword was forgotten in favor of getting the gore-filled helmet off. Some of his hair had been charred by the heat, and he gagged several times before he was able to clear his eyes and mouth. When he was finally able to see, the area around him was clear of the undead and covered with ash. The battle wasn't done, but his immediate danger had passed and it gave him a chance to survey the area. Soldiers still fought around him, but the firestorm had cleared a path fifty paces wide and a hundred long of the creatures, destroying hundreds of them. Had it been dragon's breath, he knew he would be dead, so he looked around for the source of the spell.

Walking toward him was a familiar figure clad in full plate Findoor armor with a crown and sword emblem on the chest plate. The armor was crafted for a female warrior as she wore a chain skirt around her waist, and in her hand was the black steel sword.

"Malia," he shouted, and dropped to his knees. "Thank the gods."

"Ceridan?" she asked as she lifted the visor on her helmet. "You look like one of them. Are you well?"

He laughed. A deep hearty laugh that he had trouble controlling. Malia gave him a concerned look as she reached him and offered her hand. "Yes," he said. "Yes, I'm well. Nothing a good healer can't fix, though you nearly vaporized me."

"My apologies. I am still learning to control the power this sword has granted me. I had no idea there were still soldiers alive out here."

"Is it that bad?" Ceridan asked. A quick look around at the piles of ash being trampled by the approaching undead gave him his answer. "Never mind. What are your orders, General?"

"Regroup. Call a retreat. I have sent somebody into the masses to collect any soldiers still alive. Seth is going to cut off the flow of undead into Caldoor."

"Very well," Ceridan said and picked up his sword.

"What of your helm?" Malia asked, looking at it on the ground.

"It can stay there," he said, with a smile. Malia turned her attention to the coming undead while Ceridan shouted as loud as he could, "Soldiers, fall back and regroup!"

He and Malia worked their way through the horde to get ahead of them and give their soldiers a rallying point. Ceridan found one of their flags lying on the ground and hoisted it up into the air as he walked. When they came to a stop several hundred paced away from the advancing undead, Ceridan could see movement in the horde. One particular soldier led the charge wearing only leather armor. It would have bothered him, but the soldier fought with two swords that spun and cleaved through the undead like they were mere flies around him. The swords spun with such speed and accuracy that the soldier was hardly touched by the creatures around him. This allowed him to cut a swath through the horde and broke the line to allow the remaining Caldoor and Findoor soldiers to reach Malia and Ceridan.

"Where is Seth?" Ceridan asked. "I thought he was going to take care of the bridge?"

Malia lifted a hand and pointed to a tiny figure in the sky above the Algorn Canyon. He looked like he was trying to position himself above the bridge, but as Malia was about to say something, a great beast appeared out of nowhere. It was as if the beast, what used to be the Tordrake, had materialized out of nothing. Seth was already focused on a spell and had no time to react before the beast plowed into him.

"Seth," Malia shouted, but it was already too late.

⟆

Seth left Malia and Jax on the ground to rally their troops while he went to cut off their route across the canyon. He called on the power of air to lift him up into the sky and flew to the bridge to survey the stones jutting out the side of the canyon. When he had a good idea of what was required, he began calling on the earth element to gather the power required to destroy it. A sudden sharp pain in his back that carried through to his front disrupted the spell as the horn of something very large impaled him from back to front.

"Shit," Seth gasped as the energy coursed through his body and lit up every nerve. His body was being pushed through the sky now, by whatever had hit him. All he could see was the protruding cone from his abdomen that had impaled him. The pain was blinding and made it too hard to call on any of his powers.

There was smoke around him and he thought it might be Malia torching the undead until he realized it was coming from his own body. *Focus*, Seth thought, but it was easier to think than accomplish. He was being carried far away from the canyon, but he couldn't tell in what direction they were heading. *Clear your mind and focus.*

He closed his eyes and tried to block out the pain, to seize time and control it. Nothing happened at first, and caused panic to seize his already racing heart. Blood poured from his wound, and he wasn't sure he could feel his legs or feet. *Clear your mind and focus on what you want,* a voice said in his head. Krycin's voice.

He struggled with his mind, with racing thoughts of dying, and failing Galadir. Failing Malia. *I can't fail,* he thought, and pushed those thoughts aside. He centered his mind on one name, the name that had gotten him through the most difficult challenge of his life. *Krycin.*

The power flowed to him, though his vision was getting hazy and his head swam. Time slowed and then stopped, leaving him suspended in the air, impaled on the creature's horn. Energy infused his body, restoring his strength and lifting him away from the creature. The power of water flowed through him, mending his wounds. The power of life surrounded him, encasing him in his crystal armor, and when he held out his hand, the sword of light appeared.

He turned around to face the creature that had struck him and saw the Tordrake, or what was left of it. "God damn it," Seth said as he willed time to flow again.

The Tordrake had been moving at top speed when time had stopped. Now it rocketed toward Seth. He readied his sword and slammed it into the beast's head as it struck him. The impact exploded with light that penetrated the creature's skull and ran through its body. Seth held on to the sword and channeled more energy into it. Spears of light shot from the Tordrake as its body crumpled with the impact. It was all Seth could do to hold his position, but as the momentum faded, pieces of the creature fell away into the mountains below. When he was free of it, he focused his thoughts on the Algorn Canyon and the stone bridge that Grian's horde was crossing, and disappeared.

He reappeared above the bridge and saw what was left of the Findoor and Caldoor troops engaging the undead masses in one last attempt to hold the position. There weren't many of them, and their line was faltering. Seth let the sword of light fall and called on the power of earth, focusing it into his fist. He dropped from the sky headfirst, diving toward the stone bridge and as he struck it, he unleashed the power he had harnessed into a single concussive blast that shattered the bridge into nothing more than small pebbles, sending it raining into the canyon below. Hundreds of the undead creatures fell in after it.

Seth carried all the way through the bridge until he was underneath it, and then swung his way out of the canyon before the rock could fall on him. There were still masses of undead in Caldoor to deal with, and he intended on making it easier on the troops who were fighting for their lives. Malia was in there fighting alongside them now, leading them to what he hoped would be victory, but they were far outnumbered, even with the main army cut off.

There was little time to think about what he was doing. His powers were faltering from fatigue and he couldn't afford to make a precision attack. He found himself looking at the north edge of the undead army, and summoned all the power he could. With the element of fire fueling his spell, he unleashed a massive wave of fire that spread across the field before him. Undead were vaporized in its path, leaving behind a field of black soot and smoke. The wave rolled on with Seth pumping power into it despite the burning sensation in his head that told him he was overexerting himself. Something warm ran from his nose and dripped down the front of him, and still he continued fueling the spell as the wave consumed the undead.

When his strength gave out, the wave dissipated and left a few hundred of the wretches for the remaining soldiers to deal with. Seth dropped to his knees and put a hand to his nose to wipe away whatever was running from it. His hand came away covered in bright crimson blood that continued to pour from his face. He felt as thought he were crying, but knew it wasn't tears that flowed from his eyes. Blood dripped from his ears as well, but before he could summon any more power to heal himself, the world spun around him, sending him sprawling to the ground, and a curtain of black washed over him.

5

Malia thought for sure the Tordrake had killed Seth when the impact occurred. She could see him slump over when the creature's horn impaled his body and all the will to fight washed away from her. They had no backup plan. Seth was supposed to destroy the bridge, but now he was being carried away by something that was supposed to be dead.

Her thoughts got the better of her, and one of the undead creatures reached her, plowing into her body and knocking her back off her feet. Soldiers all around her descended on the creature, but it was Ceridan who struck the killing blow and took the thing's head off. Its body fell limp on top of Malia and was lifted off before she could begin to struggle.

"General, are you well?" Ceridan asked, offering her a hand.

She took it and allowed him to hoist her up off the ground. "Yes, though I am not sure Seth is. The Defiler has animated the Tordrake, of all the disgusting things. He was struck out of the sky and carried away. We will have to come up with another plan to hold the border."

"There aren't enough of us left," Ceridan said, his voice filled with worry. "We fight to the death, or we retreat."

Malia wrapped her fingers around the hilt of the black steel sword and felt the warmth in it. It beckoned her to fight on. To defeat the onslaught of undead creatures and claim her place in the halls of heroes alongside Seth and Krycin. She fought away the invading thoughts but they had already taken root. *What has he done to deserve to be there over you,* a voice said in her head. *What does he have to offer this world that you cannot give?*

"We fight on," Malia said. "Hold the line and fight on. If we die on the battlefield today, we die as heroes who staved off an invading force against incredible odds."

She drew her sword and dove into the action once more. The moment the sword was out it blazed to life with fire and heat radiating from the blade. She drew the power of fire and swung. There were no words in her mind, and no structure to the spell. It was raw power drawn through her and into the sword, which then erupted from the blade in a fan of fire that swept through dozens of the creatures, vaporizing them into black smoke. She was about to swing again when she saw a blinding light appear above the stone bridge. Seconds later, the light dropped into the bridge and sent a shock wave out that caused the ground to shake and forced her and all her soldiers to catch their balance.

The bridge was destroyed, and she knew who did it. She didn't need to see his face to know that Seth had returned. Her feelings were conflicted though, as she was happy he was alive, but upset that he could have cost them lives with a stunt like that. Just when her lines were getting back into the battle, she saw the flames rise up at the north end of the battlefield. It was a tidal wave of fire sweeping across the field vaporizing everything in its path, and some of her troops were in the way.

"Fall back," She called as loud as she could. The call was carried across the line before she had the chance to fall back herself. Others down the line had noticed the wave of fire coming toward them and were now running for their lives to get away from it. The undead were unchanged. They continued to plod along until the fire took them.

Most of her troops made it out of the fire's path, and it spread across the battlefield, destroying the creatures. Black smoke filled the air, and the smell of death drifted around them all. Very few undead remained now, and Malia put herself to work destroying them with short blasts of fire from her sword. The rest of her troops followed suit and wiped out what remained of the undead army in minutes.

Ceridan stood next to Malia as she surveyed the destruction. "Look for survivors. There may be some still out there." The field was a blackened, trampled mess, and the smoke was just starting to clear. "Not that Seth left much opportunity for that." She paused as she said that and shook her head. "Find Seth as well. I do not know what he was thinking unleashing a spell like that, but I would like to find out."

"Understood," Ceridan said with a nod. "Just, don't be too hard on him. He did save our lives."

"He could have just as easily killed us all," Malia said. The amount of anger in her voice surprised her, but she continued regardless. "Yes, he is powerful now, but that does not mean he should not consider other lives before he casts. There is more to war than casting the biggest spell."

She expected a response from Ceridan, but he said nothing. The look on his face was enough. After a brief moment of silent reflection, he walked away and joined the rest of the troops in looking for survivors. Malia remained where she was, looking out over the battlefield, and wondered what to do next.

## Chapter 25 – The Watcher at the Gates

Grian had no idea how long he had been in the lab underneath Findoor Castle. He stood in a familiar room with a pool in the center and a musty smell hanging in the air. His focus now was learning from his mistakes. Several miscalculations had cost him dearly and set his plans back, but he was nothing if not determined. Around the pool sat several figures who were at one time human. Their flesh had since turned black and dried to their bones, but they remained vigilant at the sides of the pool, awaiting Grian's instructions.

"Tell me," Grian said to the surface of the water, "how did the Lyecian escape? The force cage should have been impenetrable by any magical means."

*No magical means were used,* a chorus of voices responded to him in his head.

It would take a long time to get used to them invading his mind, and he wondered how Merek had done it without going insane. The cryptic answers they returned grated on his nerves. If it would do any good, he would have beaten each one of them for giving such obtuse answers to his questions, but it would be like beating a shield for failing to protect him.

"Then what means *did* he use?"

*Anti-magic.*

The word made no sense. Anger welled up inside Grian as he took another step toward the pool and drew in the gray magic of shadow. He held out his hand over the water and let the energy pour onto the surface while he chanted several incantations he had memorized while working with Merek. An image coalesced in the well showing the Lyecian and how he escaped, but Grian still couldn't figure out how he made the force cage disappear.

"I don't understand. The force cage is designed to hold any magical being. It should not have failed."

*Though a powerful magical being he was, he left a human.*

A light went off in Grian's head. "He suppressed his powers. I didn't think he would have it in him to do it. Which means he may not yet have them back." He backed away from the edge of the pool and let his spell dissipate. With slow, careful steps he walked around the room. He made no sound as he traversed the room and when he came to rest where he started, he said, "What is Seth?"

*The Traveler.*

"Yes, I know that. I figured that much out on my own. He's the one we've all been waiting for, ever since the prophecy was written. Has he been to the realm of the gods? Has he opened the way to the Crossroads?"

*Twice he has visited the Crossroads, though he has not opened the way.*

The answer again confused Grian. "How could he get there if he didn't open the way?"

*The way was opened for him.*

"What is the shard inside him?"

*A fatespark.* The voices grew quiet, like they were getting tired.

"One more question, and you can rest. How do I get this fatespark for myself?"

There was a hesitation from the Scryes, something Grian had never known to happen with Merek. He channeled more energy into the connection between them, hoping to get an answer from them. "Well? How?"

The Scryes' eyes lit up with magical energy and pulsed, but no answer came. Grian sensed fear in the room. Not of him, but of something else. He fought with them in his mind, strengthening the bond between them with more energy still. The one nearest to him opened its mouth and let out a shriek that filled the room and shook Grian to his core. He almost lost his focus on the magic he was channeling to them, but held on. He was prepared when the second started to shriek, and another. The sound reverberated off the walls and made the stone floor vibrate, yet Grian couldn't let it go now. There was something they knew, but refused to tell him out of fear, and he needed to know it. Deep inside him, he knew this would be the key. What would make all his plans come to fruition.

"Tell me," Grian shouted at them, and sent another surge of gray energy into them. Their eyes smoked and their skin cracked and split. Voices flooded Grian's mind as they tried to sever the connection, but it was all nonsense. They were actively fighting him now.

Grian got down on his knees at the edge of the pool and plunged his hands into the water, sending a surge of energy into the well that connected them all. One of the Scrye's head's exploded from the stress, leaving it to slump over. No magic would animate it again, but Grian paid no attention. He wanted his answer, and could feel it coming. The walls they tried to build between their minds were coming apart. A second head exploded and its body burst into flames from the magical stress.

The remaining Scryes gave in and let down their defenses, allowing the flood of magical energy to flow through them. A single word screamed in Grian's head before the remaining Scryes succumbed to the magic and burst into flames.

*Jarador.*

§

"This is highly irregular, Your Highness," one councilor said to Grian as he tried to keep up with the dark wizard.

"If I wanted your opinion, I would give it to you," Grian said. He continued down the hall toward the main entrance of the castle. "What I want is for you to carry out my orders, or I will find somebody else who will."

"The farmers of the land are already stretched to their limits. It's women and children tending to the land. The wars this kingdom has faced have robbed it of its laborers, and the farms normally tithe only thirty percent of their crop to Findoor Castle. Anything over fifty percent and you will have starving farmers, and you are asking them to give up over eighty percent of their crops?"

Grian stopped and turned to face the pudgy councilor who had to struggle to keep from knocking into the wizard. He recoiled from Grian and put a hand up over his face. "I'm not *asking* them to tithe eighty percent," Grian said. "I'm telling them that if they don't, there shall be dire consequences. It's going to be a long, hard winter here in Findoor Castle."

"Very well, Your Highness," the councilor said. There was a slight waver to his voice, and his eyes welled up with tears. It made Grian sick to look at him.

"Here is the list of items I need before I make my next move." He handed the councilor the list who took it with a shaky hand. "Get that stuff to me before nightfall, and there shall be a reward for you."

"You're very kind, Your Highness," the councilor said, and ran off with the list as fast as his short legs could carry him. He reminded Grian of the creatures the Narshuks sometimes hunted for food. They ran about on short legs and waddled through mud puddles and the dirtiest parts of the Badlands to find their own food, often running their long snouts through dust and mud to find the grubs they craved.

"Disgusting," Grian said, and shook his head. He carried on to his original destination, which was the front gates where a small army of skeletons waited for direction. As he approached the gates, he heard a sound from the shadows to the left where the guard station used to be. It might have been a word in some language, but it came out as a choke and he knew who it was.

He approached the old guard station without fear and peered into the darkness within. "What do you want, old man?"

The voice returned was weak and scratchy, like it came from a dry throat. "You know not the forces you are meddling with, Grian."

"And you would know?"

"I know enough not to tamper with things I don't understand." There was a cough from the darkness, and a retching sound.

"You've always doubted me," Grian said. "Even now, as I stand before you, the King of Findoor, and the most powerful wizard this world has ever known. Still you think I'm weak?"

"In your ignorance lies your undoing. You think you've already won, but you forget Krycin."

"Oh yes, the noble Krycin. He hasn't been seen in a hundred years. He's not coming back, which leaves whom to stand in my way?"

"Krycin's power was mighty, but restrained. I knew it even back then. His power is rivaled only by his son, Seth. Mark my words, Grian. You might control me, but you cannot control the traveler. He defeated the Dark Lord Gladius, he will defeat you as well."

"Still believing in old fairy tales, huh?" Grain asked with a smug grin. "The Scryes have spoken on that. The Traveler hasn't opened the way to the Crossroads. It was opened *for* him. The prophecy is a lie, and you know it."

"What has not come to pass does not prove or disprove the prophecy's validity." The voice in the darkness coughed again, and made a long, wheezy gasp. "It will occur. It's just a matter of time."

"Bah," Grian said, raising a hand in dismissal. "Wives' tales. Tell me, are you ready with the remaining troops?"

"What do you plan to do with them?"

"Ducain's. We are going to take Ducain's Keep. I have a name I need to look up."

There was a cackle in the darkness, followed by a strangled coughing fit, and then more cackling. The sound was almost inhuman, and it made the hairs stand up on the back of Grian's neck. "You *are* insane."

"Will they be ready or not?" Grian shouted at the murky blackness contained within the old guard house. His nerves were beginning to fray, and he knew it showed in his tone.

"Your anger is wasted on me. I do your bidding because I must. Yes, they will be ready, not that it will matter."

Grian was the one to laugh this time, though it wasn't as boisterous as his counterpart's laughter. "You have always been short-sighted. All I need them to do is lead the charge. Kill as many wizards as they can, and leave the rest to me."

"Now you would have me kill my own kind? Does your atrocity know no limits?" The voice in the darkness wheezed and sounded out of breath.

"My genius knows no bounds. As for you, I need you to guard the castle while I'm gone. Nobody gets in or out. Nobody passes these front gates. Do you understand?"

"I understand."

Grian smiled to himself and walked through the gates.

Standing in the grass was row upon row of skeletons. Most of which were blackened or dirty, some with rotted cloth over them, others with old rusted armor, weapons or shields. Without a word, Grian focused the dark energy that controlled them and directed them to the east. Toward Ducain's Keep.

# Chapter 26 - Shades and Indiscretions

An envelope of silence surrounded Seth and he wondered if the battle was done. Pain split through his head, but he didn't move. In a way, the silence comforted him and relieved the pressure he felt to make everything right. For a long time he lay with his eyes closed, shut against the world and all its troubles. The first sound he heard was an old scratchy voice as the owner cleared his throat. Somebody waited for him and he had little interest in who it was. Instead, he wished for the pain in his head to subside and enjoyed the darkness his closed eyes provided him.

"You can't stay like that forever," the voice said, breaking the silence once again. The voice sounded ancient and hoarse, but familiar.

Without opening his eyes, Seth said, "I'm tired."

"You're tired. That's all you have to say for yourself?"

"Yes."

"Get up, fatewalker."

Recognition surged through Seth's mind. That name. He'd been called fatewalker before, but couldn't place where or when. There were similar circumstances though. A battle that left him in darkness. He opened his eyes, expecting to see a battlefield before him. A room with a bed wouldn't have surprised him either. What he saw was more darkness, and an old man wearing a red robe covered with silver runes.

"Who are you?" Seth asked, blinking to clear the rest of his vision.

"You don't remember me? Has it been that long?" The old man's voice cracked which sent him into a fit of coughs, but Seth made no move to help him. Fear gripped his heart.

"I remember you, but that doesn't tell me who you are."

215

"Fair enough. Few know my true name, for I hid it away long ago. I'm sure if you asked your precious Lyecha, she would tell you. They all know and fear me." There was a sly smile on the old man's creased face. Every inch of his skin was covered with the deep folds of age. It was hard for Seth to tell what the man might have looked like when he was younger.

"Lyecha is afraid of nothing," Seth said. "She's a goddess, and more powerful than you and me combined."

"You assume too much, fatewalker," the old man said with a sneer. "Enough talk. It took me over a hundred years to break free of that pesky prison you trapped me in. Now I can finish what I started back then."

Seth wasn't expecting the sudden movements and only had time to raise his arms over his face when the old man plunged a hand covered with black fire into Seth's chest. An electric surge traveled through his body as every nerve lit up. He heard a scream and realized it was his own as the old man wrestled with something inside of him. It took only seconds, but it felt like an eternity before the old man let go and fell back, leaving Seth to lie on the ground in agony and out of breath.

"Well," the old man said. "It seems we've reached an impasse."

"You can't take that," Seth said once he caught his breath enough to speak. "Nobody can. It must be given freely."

"Then you are now in a very dangerous position, fatewalker." The old man got up and walked with shaky steps to stand over him. "You have something I want."

"You can't have it," Seth said. With renewed strength, Seth lunged toward the old man and pushed him away, causing him to fall backward and land in a heap of robes.

"This isn't over, fatewalker. You think you can push me around, but you're wrong. Mark my words, you'll give me that fatespark. Your friends will turn against you. The council will come after you, seeking the power that you have and they crave. Everything you've ever loved or held dear will be destroyed or corrupted. Even the *gods* as you call them will abandon you. When I'm done with you, you'll beg me to take the fatespark and wish you'd never been born."

Fear gripped Seth's heart and caused it to race. The icy grip of panic took hold and he looked around, only to find himself wrapped in darkness. He closed his eyes and felt his position change, though he hadn't moved. A cold sweat broke out all over his body and he struggled against the darkness, trying to find his way out. Images flashed through his mind: Malia and an unknown armored man holding each other, Grian holding Serrin by the throat and draining the life from him, wave upon wave of undead sweeping across the world, killing everything in their path. A light appeared before him and he willed himself toward it, trying to escape the dreams. Consciousness returned in a surge so sudden it caused a scream to escape his lungs.

$\zeta$

Malia sat by Seth's cot waiting for him to regain consciousness. The healers told her they had done all they could for him and that the unnatural sleep he was in was self-inflicted. A movement at the corner of her eye caught her attention, and she turned to see Ceridan entering the infirmary tent.

"Is there any change?" He asked, looking down at her with concern in his eyes.

"Nay. He has not moved in days, though the healers say he is physically fine."

"General, I insist that you come and get some proper rest. We can post a watch here that can inform us of any changes in his condition, but you are no good to Findoor or Seth if you have not slept or eaten a decent meal."

She stood up to face Ceridan and heaved a sigh. She hadn't realized how long it had been since she had slept, but he made a good point. When they found Seth, he had been near death with burns covering a large portion of his body. The healers stabilized his condition, and Seth's own regenerative abilities had healed the rest. She expected him to wake up as soon as his wounds were healed, but he hadn't.

"I do not want to leave him," she said, looking at Seth. "Perhaps you could bring me a meal?"

A finger touched her chin and guided her gaze back to Ceridan. His fingers lingered on her skin and he shook his head. "Come now. If his condition hasn't changed in these last three days, he shall be fine while you fetch some food and sleep."

There was a look in his eyes that went beyond concern for her health. It made her heart flutter for just an instant. Ceridan was an attractive man by anyone's standards, but she had never thought of him as anything but a comrade. Her heart belonged to Seth, or so she thought. As Ceridan took a step closer, a vague hint of doubt crept over her, wiggling its way in and squirming through everything she thought she knew. She felt Ceridan's breath on her cheek as he wrapped an arm around her waist. *He's just trying to get you to eat,* she thought, but his actions sent a tremor through her. "I... I cannot..." she said, trying to protest. She placed her hands on his chest plate to try and push him away, but she made little effort.

He wrapped his other arm around her and pulled her closer. "I can't let you starve yourself." His voice was a whisper now. She looked up into his eyes and saw a hunger that had never been there before. It both startled her and enticed her. After the battle they just fought, and the events of the last few months, it was nice to have a man want her. His lips were inches from hers, which made her heart beat faster. She moved her hands from his chest to his neck. The rest of the world, the war, all her troubles in the world faded away as Ceridan pulled her closer into his embrace.

The instant Seth sat bolt upright and screamed, it startled both her and Ceridan out of the moment. They jerked their heads toward Seth and saw him in bed, his skin beaded with sweat and a panicked look in his eyes. His breathing was fast, like he had just been running, though Malia knew he had barely moved up until that point. Their eyes met, and Seth's expression went from fear and panic, to pain as he realized what was before him.

Malia broke away from Ceridan, but she knew it was too late. She could almost hear Seth's heart break, and it brought tears to her eyes. She ran to the side of his bed and knelt down beside him. "You are awake," she said.

Seth's gaze moved from her to Ceridan and back again. Tears welled up in his eyes, and one rolled down his cheek. He looked like he was searching for something to say, but couldn't find the words.

"Please, Seth, say something," Malia said, placing one hand on his, trying to comfort him.

There was a sense of loss around them, like something had been taken from them that could never be regained. Seth opened his mouth and gasped for air. "How... How could you?"

Malia tried to make sense of the situation, but didn't have time to form a response. She felt the magical energy coalesce around them, and then Seth disappeared, leaving an empty space for the surrounding air to fill. The blanket that had covered him for three days collapsed onto the cot, and she laid her head down on it, breathing in his scent as it faded. She felt a hand on her shoulder, but made no move to escape the comforting touch. Instead, she wept as her heart tore in two.

5

Night had fallen on Alkirk Manor when Seth appeared on the roof. It was the one place he was sure he could be alone. The evening air was cool on his skin, but not cool enough to keep his emotions from overwhelming him. He sat at the edge of the roof, his eyes burning with tears, and tried to breathe and calm himself.

"That old man, he was there a hundred years ago," Seth said. "He was controlling Gladius. Now he's after my fatespark."

He inhaled deeply and let it out, watching as his breath formed a small cloud before his eyes. As it dissipated, he noticed the sky above the old lab was lit up with swirling colors. He watched it for a few minutes and thought it looked a bit like the northern lights on Earth, but the colors swirled rather than just dancing in waves.

"This must be what that old barkeep was talking about," Seth said, using his sleeve to dry his eyes. He watched it for a long time, sitting on the roof of his family's house, little puffs of cloud escaping as he breathed. The colors didn't change much as time went on. There was no specific pattern to it, and it didn't grow or shrink at all. More than anything, it gave Seth something to look at while he sorted out his thoughts.

"I need to figure out who that old man is," he said, suddenly realizing that he'd been talking to himself. "Cedric will know. He knows everything."

He focused his mind on the last place he saw Cedric, and disappeared from the rooftop, leaving the manor and the swirling colored lights in peace and silence.

Seth appeared in a chamber with stone walls and floor. Cedric sat at a small desk on one side, writing with a quill and parchment. There was some light from a window on one side, but it provided little help to Cedric's efforts, so he had an oil lantern burning on the hutch above where he worked. Seth's appearance in the room didn't move Cedric, though Seth was sure the sound of the rushing air would give him away. Tears were still present on his cheeks and his eyes were red. His strength had not fully returned yet, but he was able to hold himself up, though his legs were a little wobbly.

"It's about time you showed up," Cedric said, without lifting his head.

"What do you mean?" Seth asked and sniffed. He was still upset enough that his nose was trying to run.

Cedric turned around and flashed Seth a smile from underneath his mask. "Never you mind. Your presence is required at Ducain's

Keep. The Wizard High Council is convening, and they expect you to be there."

"Why do they need me?"

Seth remembered just after he spoke, but Cedric was a fast talker and beat him to the punch. "You *are* the current gold wizard on the council, are you not?"

"Yes. Sorry, I have a lot on my mind."

"This world needs you," Cedric said, getting up from his chair. "There's no time for personal comfort, no time to sit around and feel sorry for yourself. Keep fighting, keep moving, because if you don't, people will suffer and die."

Anger welled up inside Seth. First he catches Malia with another man, and now Cedric was berating him. He couldn't contain the torrent of emotions anymore. "No you listen to me. I've been running and fighting ever since my thirtieth birthday. I've been shot at, burned, teleported, slashed, stabbed and have regenerated from it all. I can't count the number of people I've saved already, and it was all because somebody *else* said I had to. I've been doing what everyone else expects of me for far too long. I'm tired. More tired than I've ever been. Hell, I'm not even sure who I am anymore. I came here because I thought you were my friend, because I needed somebody to talk to, but it turns out you're just as big an asshole as everyone else. Everyone keeps going on like I *have* to do what I've been doing, like I have no choice. The truth is, I *do* have a choice, and I'm choosing to stop, and rest."

He turned away from Cedric and stormed toward the door. When his hand grasped the handle of the door, he heard Cedric laughing and clapping behind him. He spun with such ferocity that even Cedric jumped. "What? What the hell is so god damned funny?"

"At last, you see the light. You always have had a choice. We all do." Cedric walked toward him, the smile still on his face. "What's important is what we do with the choices we have. And no, knowing the outcome doesn't make it easier. Quite the opposite, because it can give the illusion that you have no choice. But I'll tell you a secret, something that you will never hear from the Fates or any reaper or wizard on Galadir: Time is not a fixed sequence of events, but rather, a series of self-correcting cause and effect."

Confusion replaced anger as Seth tried to figure out what Cedric was saying. "So..."

"So make your choice, my friend," Cedric said. "There will always be somebody to fight the war."

Cedric approached Seth, slapped him on the shoulder and took the door from his hand. He pulled it open and motioned for Seth to leave.

"Wait," Seth said, looking from Cedric to the floor. "I need to talk to you. About Malia, and somebody else." The anger had made him forget about his heartbreak for the moment, but now it came flooding back.

"What about her? I heard you barely survived the last battle. That must have been hard on her."

"Yeah... I mean," Seth said, pausing to think about what Cedric had actually said. "I didn't think of it that way."

"We all make our choices, Seth. In most cases, things that seem like a good idea at the time, often aren't, though we may lack the wisdom to see that."

"Now you're starting to sound like Merek."

"I aim to please."

"Well, you've helped with one problem. Here's the other. Twice now I've been confronted by what appears to be an old man. Never out in the open, but at the peak of a battle, or while I'm unconscious, he's there."

Cedric looked curious, but there was something else in his eyes. A spark of recognition that Seth could see even behind the mask. "What color robes does he wear?"

"Red, with silver symbols embroidered into it," Seth said, approaching Cedric with hope in his heart that he would get an answer.

"My apologies, Seth. I know nothing of this man," Cedric said. His voice trembled as he spoke, and the confidence Seth was so used to hearing was gone.

"You're a terrible liar."

"There is nothing I can tell you about this man you speak of, and that is the truth. Forget him. Stay away from him. If you meet again, wake yourself up. Block him out of your head."

There was fear in Cedric's eyes. It was the first time Seth had ever seen the bard truly afraid of something. He had seen Seth through many of his first adventures, witnessed some of the most terrible battles, and always walked with confidence, but at the mention of this old man, he was afraid.

"It's not that simple. I feel pursued, like if I fall asleep, he's going to be there waiting for me. Every time I close my eyes, his face is there, mocking me. Whoever he is, he's after something, and he's not going to stop until he gets it. If you know who he is, tell me."

Cedric heaved a sigh, like he was trying to prepare himself for what he was about to say, and after pulling the door closed and looking around the room for something Seth couldn't see, he spoke. "If it's who I think it is, his name is Jarador, though I never thought him real. If he is real, stay away from him. That's all I can tell you. Now please, put it out of your head, and never mention it again."

"Okay, consider it done."

"Good then," Cedric said, switching back to his old self. "Now, there was the business of the council?"

"Yes, I'm going." Seth began to walk through the door, but stopped part way through. "Oh, and I've made my choice."

"Is that so?"

"I've decided," Seth said, with a bit of a smirk, "that this world needs to learn to fight its own battles, but there's no reason why I can't nudge them in the right direction."

"Spoken like a true hero."

Seth closed his eyes and focused, willing himself to teleport once more.

# Chapter 27 - Walking Away

Serrin sat on the gold chair in the council chamber and looked out at five other wizards. He was ready to call the meeting to order as the acting gold wizard. A touch of nostalgia hit him. It had been over five years since he had sat in that chair, though for the rest of Galadir, it had been over a hundred. Nobody knew who he was or where he came from, and now the only reason he was in the gold chair on the council was because there were no others to take his place.

He opened his mouth to say something, but didn't get a word out. At the center of the room, the air was displaced as Seth appeared with a loud popping sound. Exclamations of surprise came from all wizards in the room.

Seth looked around and stopped when his gaze met Serrin's. "Dad?" he asked, confused.

Serrin was speechless for the moment, and tried to come up with something to say. In the end, only a single word came out. "Son."

"I didn't think I'd ever see you again. How?"

"It's a long story that I can explain another time," Serrin said with a smile. "For now, it's good to see you."

Serrin watched as Trysk stood up and narrowed his eyes at Seth. "It's about time you joined us," the black wizard said. "I was beginning to think you had forgotten about your obligations."

Silence filled the room as Seth's gaze snapped toward Trysk. "Obligations? Oh no. I have no obligations to you, or anyone else on Galadir. In fact, I intend to eliminate the one last tie I have to anything here." He turned back to Serrin, who now wore a smile. "I'm not sure how you broke free from Grian, but this proves to me that the people of this world do not need me as much as they think they do. I'm glad you're okay. From this moment forward, I relinquish my chair on the Wizard High Council to Serrin Alkirk."

"This is an outrage," Trysk yelled, and took a step forward. "You can't just turn your back on your world. Grian commands an army the likes of which Galadir has never seen. How do we fight that?"

Serrin looked from Trysk to Seth to see his reaction, but was surprised when Gladius stood up and joined him. "Seth, we're in trouble. You gave us no word of where you were going, or when you'd be back. I made a commitment to the Narshuks that you would help them, and now one of our own has been critically wounded and may die if you don't help her." There was patience in Gladius's voice, but there was an edge to it as well. "Trysk is right, you have obligations to this council, even if you resign your position."

Seth looked from one man to the other. Serrin could feel a storm brewing in the room, and was trying to figure out a way to dampen it. His thoughts weren't fast enough though, and Seth exploded. "What the hell do I owe you? What did I ever do to put myself in the debt of anyone here? Or anyone on this world for that matter." His voice reached a volume that made Trysk and Gladius recoil from him. "I may have been born here on Galadir, but I lived most of my life on Earth. I'm a programmer, not a wizard."

"Seth, listen to reason," Gladius said, approaching him. He placed a hand on Seth's shoulder and squeezed. "At least help us with this last battle. Help us defeat Grian. You owe us that much."

Seth batted his hand away, and said, "Go to hell. I owe you nothing."

A moment of silence told Serrin that the final words had been said. He opened his mouth to say something, but Seth disappeared once more, leaving the council without his help. With a sigh, Serrin said, "I will speak with him. Something more is going on here. For now, Andran and Attowen should go and tend to Nadya. Do what you can for her. Trysk, take a partner and go to the Badlands. See what you can do about the Narshuks. If we are to battle Grian and his army, we will need every warrior we can find. The rest of you, take some wizards and scout the surrounding kingdoms. Request that they send reinforcements to the Findoor border, every man they can spare. I'll look for Seth and try to get him to see reason."

He didn't wait for acknowledgement before he focused on a place he thought Seth might be, and teleported away.

5

Seth sat back on the sloped edge of the shingled roof that protected Alkirk Manor. Two stories up gave him a great view of the caldera, and a cool breeze helped to settle his temper. The grass in the caldera was overgrown and threatened to swallow the ruins of the lab that had sat vacant for a hundred years. The lights over the lab were gone now, but the breeze created a whispering sound that was soothing to Seth. He closed his eyes and leaned back, taking deep breaths of the fresh air.

He wasn't sure how long he sat like that, listening to the whisper of the grass and the occasional chirp of a bird, but a sound below him of air being displaced told him he'd been followed.

"Seth?" he heard Serrin shout. Then silence. Seth guessed his father was waiting for him to respond so that he could talk him into changing his mind. He sat in silence. "Seth, I know you're here. Talk to me."

"What do you want?" Seth asked. Perhaps if he told his father what he wanted to hear he would go away.

"I know there's something else bothering you. Come down and talk about it."

Seth stood up at the edge of the roof and looked down at his father who was standing several paces from the front door. One step forward and he was in mid air, using the power of air to help him drift down without harm. "You know," Seth said, "six months ago I wouldn't have dreamed of climbing onto a second story roof, let alone jumping off of it."

"Galadir has a funny way of doing that to people. The luxuries of Earth tame the best of us. We tend to forget who we are or where we came from. It happened to me as well." Serrin approached Seth with slow, measured steps, trying to get as close as he could. Seth turned away from him before he could finish his approach. "When you came to get me, I had all but forgotten I could use magic at all."

"What does that have to do with anything?" Seth asked.

"The Wizard High Council is full of themselves. They always have been. Power hungry, ambitious, always struggling for superiority. You present to them a situation they've never had before: you're more powerful than any of them, and there's nothing they can do about it. It would be easy for you to go back to Earth and forget that all of this exists, but it won't change who you are."

"You don't know what it's like," Seth said, turning to face Serrin. "Everyone who knows who I am gets this look in their eyes like I have all the answers, I can make all their troubles go away, I'm the salvation of the fucking universe. But I can't be that person. Not anymore."

"You have to be," Serrin said. "If you don't play that part, nobody else can take your place."

"See? Even you're doing it. I'm not a hero. I never was. I was just in the right place at the right time. And the one time I tried to be a hero, do you know what happened? I nearly wiped out our entire race."

"Seth," Serrin took a step forward and caught Seth's gaze. There was a wisdom in Serrin's eyes that Seth didn't want to see. "You had no way of knowing what the consequences of your actions would be."

"I thought I knew what I was doing. I thought I could handle all of this, but I don't think I can. I'm not strong enough, not without her."

A look of understanding washed over Serrin's face. "Ah, so that's the problem. My son, women will be our rise and fall. Whatever happened between you and her, go, talk to her, and tell her how you feel. She will understand."

"I don't think she'll care. I knew I was never good enough for her," Seth said. Tears welled up in his eyes. He tried to fight them back, but the stinging was too much, and now they fell, rolling down his cheeks to escape onto the ground. "No. This world needs to learn to stand on its own. I'm not always going to be here when a wizard goes crazy and starts killing people. I can't live my life in fear that somebody is going to come after me."

Sadness filled Serrin's expression, but he didn't argue further. "Very well. We will launch the best defense we can, and hopefully that is enough. Take care of yourself, son."

Seth turned away from him, unable to stand to look at the pain in his eyes. "Winning a war isn't the responsibility of one person. It never should have been. It should never be again."

He heard a popping sound from behind him that told him his father was gone. A feeling of loneliness crept into Seth's heart that brought more tears. He looked up in the sky and saw unfamiliar stars. Night birds were fluttering about, catching insects in the air. Seth had never been one to watch nature, but he thought that now might be a good time to start. He focused his mind on a destination and teleported away from the Arvok Caldera.

5

Serrin reappeared in the council chamber. To his surprise, Trysk was still sitting in the black seat, looking pensive. The room was otherwise silent, and the doors were shut, unusual when there was no meeting going on. He looked at Trysk and said, "I thought I gave you orders?"

Trysk looked up with a glint in his eyes that Serrin didn't like. "I don't recognize your authority," the scheming black wizard said. "In fact, I don't trust you. How do we know you aren't working for Grian? How can we trust you, when the bastard might have set you free himself?"

"I've already gone over how I freed myself. There's nothing I can do if you don't believe me, but we do have laws and you are required to follow them the same as anyone else. Carry out my orders, or there will be consequences."

"Like what? You'll kill me? Wouldn't that be too convenient. Go on, then. Do it, because I have no intention of trying to speak with those filthy dogs down in the Badlands. Let them rot."

Serrin moved faster than he thought he could, approaching Trysk and grabbing him by the robes at his neck. He hauled the stunned wizard off his seat and dragged him to the door, slamming him against it. "You listen here, disciple of Grishtor. If you don't follow my orders, you'll get no punishment from me. But the rest of the council will be happy to have a piece of you, and when they're finished, I'll call down your god's wrath upon you. The disrespect you show for your god's people, for your peers, and for your craft will incur a retribution of such fury, that if you live through it, you'll wish you were dead. Am I clear?"

There was fear in Trysk's eyes. Real fear. Serrin wasn't sure which part scared him most, but he suspected it was the wrath of his own god. Grishtor could be tricky and particularly cruel when he wanted to be. "Perfectly," Trysk said in a shaky voice.

Serrin released his robes and said, "Then go do as you've been instructed."

Trysk scrambled with the door, struggling to get it open in his panicked state. When he managed it, he was met with Attowen and Gladius on the other side. They looked surprised to see him. Without waiting for words, Trysk pushed past them and hurried away from the council chamber. Attowen gave him a curious look, then turned back to Serrin. "Well," the old wizard said, "that would make two miracles today then."

"What do you mean?" Serrin asked.

"You managed to put the fear into that arrogant wretch, and somehow, Nadya is getting better."

"Getting better? You must be mistaken, there is no getting better from a wraith's touch," Serrin said. "Are you certain?"

Gladius approached him with a smile. "I saw it with my own eyes. I didn't believe it myself, but somehow, her condition is improving and the transformation is reversing. I think she should be better by tomorrow morning and possibly even ready to resume her duties."

"I'm relieved to hear that, but we must figure out what has cured her. This is significant."

Attowen approached Serrin with a sombre look on his face. "'Tis a gift from Anam."

"Perhaps," Serrin said. "Keep her under watch. If she is able to get up and resume her duties in the morning, we will accept Anam's gift and carry on with our plans."

"Praise the White King," Attowen said, using the more formal title for his god. He gave a little bow and drew a circle in the air with his finger, the best approximation for the symbol of Anam he could produce, and then left with Gladius to return to Nadya's side.

Serrin left the council chamber and decided to go for a walk to clear his head.

# Chapter 28 – A Night Around the Fire

"How could you?" Malia said to Ceridan, pushing him away. Her tears flowed without hindrance as she couldn't bear to hold it in anymore. "Had I known you were going to do that, I would have sent you away."

Ceridan flinched, as though her words physically hurt him. He said nothing, but stood his ground in the entryway of the tent.

"Get out," Malia said, though it came out more harsh than she meant it. It was her fault as well, and she knew it. Ceridan had done what any man would have done. She'd seen the way he looked at her, and had resisted his handsome features and strong physique all through their travels. But she was fragile, and with the uncertainty about Seth's condition, she didn't know what to do.

She looked up and saw Ceridan still standing in the entryway. "Leave me be," Malia snapped at him. "I wish to be alone."

Ceridan walked away and Malia had every intention of laying herself down on the cot and crying herself to sleep, when Darian's black-robed presence filled the entryway. "Milady," he said in his most formal tone. "A word?"

"What do you want, Darian?"

His face revealed nothing as he stepped into the tent and closed the flap. "Under normal circumstances, being on Caldoor land would subject you to Caldoor laws, and Caldoor rule. In this case, however, my wise King has granted you full leave to lead the charge against Grian with the support of every soldier we can muster."

"Your King is most gracious," Malia said, taking a handkerchief and blotting the tears from her cheeks. "Is that all?"

He took a step toward her and shook his head. "The Time Weaver, where is he?"

"I do not know," she said. "He disappeared shortly after he woke."

"Then, am I to assume he will not be helping us again?"

Malia felt another wave of tears coming, and swallowed hard to keep them from coming out. It felt like swallowing a stone, but she had to control herself. "I would not count on it."

"Very well. My scouts tell me that Grian is on the move toward Ducain's Keep. The defiled have left our borders and now gather to the east. It is such distance, that I doubt there will be much of a battle left by the time we get there, but," he emphasized the last word, narrowing his eyes. "A much more enticing target lies much closer than Ducain's."

She knew what he meant before he finished the sentence. "Findoor Castle. Has he truly left it unguarded?"

"According to my scouts, yes. Only a few wights remain, and they should be simple to defeat."

"There's more, though, isn't there?" There was always more with Darian. They didn't call him Darian the Black for nothing.

"A simple gesture of good faith, is all. My most intrepid King requests that in return for our soldiers and our wizards, you grant him payment of half the gold in the Findoor coffers."

The breath drained out of her as though she had been punched in the gut. He must have seen the shock on her face, because he walked up to her and offered her a hand to steady herself. She took it, and looked him in the eye.

"Of course," Darian said, "if you are unwilling to make that gesture, we will also accept payment in land, or..." He trailed off at the end, as though she wouldn't be interested in the third option.

"Or what? Thus far, your terms are preposterous." She composed herself and released Darian's arm, allowing him to back away a step.

"The Time Weaver."

"You would ask me to plunder my kingdom, or betray my love?"

"It seems to me that you already betrayed him. What would be the difference."

His words cut like a knife. She was in no position to discuss these terms, and yet she had the distinct impression that Darian would not leave without an answer. "You..." She was going to say something derogatory to him, but managed to stop herself. Instead, she said, "Your terms are unacceptable. I shall take my remaining soldiers and retake Findoor Castle by myself. I thank you, your King, and all the soldiers of your army for your offer, but I refuse to cripple my kingdom in order to save it."

There was a moment of silence between them. Malia watched Darian's face carefully, but he revealed little in his cold, stony gaze. "Merek told me you had integrity. Frankly, I didn't believe him when I saw your arms around Commander Ceridan, but I am proven wrong."

His words left her speechless. Anger welled up inside her, but she fought it back, thinking better of lashing out at the black wizard. "If that is all," Malia said, "I have work to do."

"That is all," Darian said with a pleasant smile. He left the tent, making sure that he closed the flap behind him. It gave Malia some privacy, and allowed her a chance to sit down and let her tears flow.

༄

When Malia woke up on the cot with a blanket tucked over her, she scowled and threw it off. It was dark, but beyond that, she couldn't tell how long she had slept. The tent had no lanterns lit, so she had to find her way to the entrance by feeling the walls. She stumbled once over the chair she had sat in next to the cot before making it to the opening with the canvas door.

The sounds outside told her there were still plenty of soldiers awake and making merry after their victory. Many had died in the battle, but many more still lived to fight another day, and that was worth celebrating. When she pulled back the door, she could see the entire camp lit by fires that were surrounded by soldiers. Many had casks of ale or wine that had been brought from Caldoor Castle, and several fires had animals roasting over them on spits. The smell of burning wood and roasting meat momentarily made her forget where she was as she remembered the last big feast she attended; the New Star Festival in Findoor. That brought back memories of Seth, and their dance together, and the wonderful night they had after Cy was destroyed. She hadn't worn a dress since, nor had she danced or laughed or sang. Her days were filled with running and fighting. Nights brought hiding, and sometimes more battles. Times had been tough, and now they would have to get ready to venture back into her now-hostile homeland. There was a stinging in her eyes as tears welled up once more.

"My darling daughter." Her father's voice carried over several men singing around a nearby fire. She could see him approach in her peripheral vision, but if she looked at him, she knew she would burst into tears.

"Father," she said, staring at nothing in particular.

"I thought you had retired for the night. You fought hard today."

"What are you doing here? You were supposed to stay back at Caldoor where it was safe."

"When you didn't return, they called for every able-bodied man to join the fight," he said, taking a place beside her and staring in the same direction as her. "I figured it was high time I earned my keep."

"You could have been killed."

"But I wasn't. I stayed back with the reserves. I hoped I would see you show up." There was a question in his voice and mannerism that she thought he was holding back. He kept shifting his eyes between her face and the stars that she was watching.

"Seth took me on quite an adventure."

"He seems like a good man. A powerful wizard, that's for sure."

Malia gave in and turned to face her father, choking back her tears so her men wouldn't see her cry. "Yes. Merek said he was possibly the most powerful to ever live. But he is careless."

"He loves you?"

"I..." she said, and paused. "He did. I cannot be certain now."

"If he really loves you, no matter what has happened, nothing will change."

She heard boisterous laughter coming from the direction of the fire. Ceridan was laughing with some of the other commanders, recounting old stories of tournaments and battles long ago fought and won, or lost. "You spoke to Ceridan."

"He spoke with me. Seemed concerned about something that happened between you and him. He was pretty shaken up over it."

"I don't think Seth is coming back." The sadness of that admission reopened the wound in her heart and threatened to overwhelm her again.

Her father took a step closer to her and raised his hand to her cheek. His skin was tough and leathery from years of farm work, but it offered a comfort that only a father could provide. "We all make mistakes. I can't count the number of times I've been angry with your mother, or your mother was angry with me. We still loved each other, no matter what. If Seth is half the man you've told me he is, he will be back."

Emotions overwhelmed her, and she threw herself into her father's arms, hugging him tight. "Thank you, father."

"There's no need to thank me," Jaren said. "Come, sit by the fire and have something to eat. I'm certain you can find something to smile about. Just being alive tonight is a gift from the Lady Torenna. We should all give thanks."

Malia released her father and followed him to the fire, sitting down across from Ceridan. He looked up at her with a cautious glance, but said nothing. One of the other men welcomed her to the fire. "General Corsair, I trust you rested well?"

"Yes, Barnaby, thank you."

"Ceridan there has been a real pleasure, dealing with all the official business so as to let you rest."

Malia turned her gaze to Ceridan and lifted one brow. Barnaby's tone told her he knew what had happened, which made her wonder who else might know. She felt her cheeks burn with embarrassment and hoped the yellow-red glow from the fire would hide it. "I appreciate you all letting me sleep, but Ceridan, you did not have to cover me up. I would have been plenty warm without the blankets."

Ceridan returned her gaze with a confused look. "I don't know what you mean, General. There were no blankets on you when I checked on you hours ago, and we have ensured that nobody has been in or out of the tent since then."

"Did you not place blankets over me while I slept? You must have."

"I swear to you, I didn't. After Darian left, all was quiet in the tent. I checked on you a short while after, and found you asleep, but I didn't enter. You needed the sleep, so I let you rest, and kept all others out of the tent while you did so."

Malia looked around at the others at the fire, and they all shrugged and nodded toward Ceridan to confirm what he said. "No matter, then," Malia said, and felt a grumble in her stomach. She couldn't remember the last time she had eaten a decent meal, and the smell of the meat roasting over the fires whet her appetite. "Where can I get some food, I am starved."

"Right this way, General," Barnaby said, getting up. He led Malia toward a much larger fire about fifty paces away. "They got a right feast going on over here, with the best roast buck you ever had."

She approached an area that had folding tables laid out and several men at them serving up plates of food. There were plenty of vegetables that had been roasted or boiled and mashed, and at the end of the table was a large side of meat from an animal that might have resembled a horse when it lived. When she approached, each person who noticed her gave her a salute and went about their business. Many of the Findoor men had not eaten a decent meal in days, so the feast was welcomed by all. "General Corsair," the head chef said with a broad smile across his face. He was a heavier-built man than most in the camp, but to say he was round would be a fallacy. He was as round as their meager provisions had allowed him to be during their escape from Findoor, and she suspected at the beginning he had been much more portly. "Please, come have a taste of this. I've saved the most tender portion of the buck just for you."

"Thank you, but," she started to say, but he was already carving several large slices from a piece of meat he had set aside to keep warm. He placed four thick slices on a plate and offered it to her. "I appreciate your effort, Sarron is it?" He nodded, and she continued before he could protest. "Please, take back half of what you have given me, and distribute the rest amongst the troops. I may be hungry, but I am afraid it will take some time before my appetite is ready for this much food. Allow the rest of the men the pleasure of your wonderful cooking."

"As you wish, General. You are truly kind." He flashed her a big toothy smile and hollered out to the rest of the camp to come and get it. Malia took her plate, now lighter by half, and added vegetables. Barnaby joined her in getting food and they both returned to the fire where her father and Ceridan sat laughing over a story one of the commanders was telling.

Malia sat and listened while she ate, but only finished a small portion of what was on her plate before the story ended and the company around the fire went quiet. She took the opportunity to speak to them. "Men, we may have won this battle, but we still have hard times ahead of us. The Time Weaver has left us once more, and may not return. Caldoor asks that we drain our kingdoms coffers by half in gold or in land in order to help us, an offer which I have politely declined. There are not many of us left, but there is good news.

"Darian the Black informed me that the Defiler is making a move on Ducain's Keep and has taken most of his army with him. I wish to return to Findoor Castle while it is left unguarded and retake what is rightfully ours. I will not force any man to make that trek again, especially since we can't be sure that all of the defiled have been destroyed or taken to the east, but I will appreciate any and all who come. I will also ask Morganath to accompany us. Where is Morganath, anyway?"

"I'm not sure. I haven't seen him since mid-battle. Do you know if there is anyone alive within the Findoor borders?" Ceridan asked.

"I do not," Malia said. "But earlier reports told us that the Defiler was trying to run the kingdom as though nothing was wrong. I can't see any reason why he would kill the citizens of Findoor."

"How many soldiers do we have left?"

"Perhaps five hundred, if that. It will be dangerous, but I think we can take the castle if it is under minimal guard. We must act smart and come up with a plan."

"General," Barnaby spoke up, to everyone's surprise. "Begging your pardon, but with not more than five hundred soldiers, if there is more than we expect, this might well be a disaster. How are we to know this ain't a trap?"

"We do not. We must trust that the reports Darian is giving me are true." She watched the faces of all her commanders around the fire, and could see the worry in their eyes. She knew it was a risky venture, but if they could take back the castle, she knew they could hold it against siege. "Darian has no reason to lie to us. He stands to gain nothing by giving us false information. He is self-serving, loathsome, cruel and vindictive..."

"I see you are talking about me," Darian's voice interrupted from behind her. She didn't notice the look Ceridan was giving her until it was too late. "Oh, not to worry, apologies are not required. I work hard to maintain my reputation. Fear is a strong motivator which allows me to get what I want."

"Fear is no way to rule," Malia said, shifting so that she could see the black wizard.

"Whatever gave you the idea that I wanted to rule? Kings rule. Princes, lords, dukes, and all manner of other titles rule. Wizards make decisions. We advise and influence. Those who fear me are more likely to believe what I say, and the more people who believe what I say, the more credible my decisions, advice and influence are." He took a step forward into the light of the fire and sat down beside Malia. "So tell me, General, why would I not want people to fear me?"

"Respect is much more powerful than fear. Merek held the respect of all the people of Findoor."

"And look where that got him," Darian said with a snide tone to his voice. "No, I think I like my position just the way it is. As for Findoor, I am willing to grant you a limited number of black wizards under my influence. They will help you destroy the last of the defiled on your way to the castle, and inside."

"Such kindness," Malia said, "it does not become you, Darian."

"Do not mistake this gesture for kindness. My King is young and foolish, but I see the value in this. Having undead on our doorstep is a danger to Caldoor. Thus, I have circumvented my King's order so as to ensure the safety of my kingdom."

"Very well. We shall accept your offer, so long as no payment is expected."

"A very wise decision, General." Darian stood abruptly. "I must rest now. I wish you all a safe journey and a prosperous campaign to take back your castle." Without waiting for responses, he walked away from the fire and disappeared into the darkness of night. The group of wizards Darian had brought with him were not resting in the main camp. In fact, Malia couldn't tell where they were resting, as nobody had seen them since the battle ended. They couldn't be far away though, as Darian had paid them a number of visits since the battle ended.

"Why do I feel like we've just gotten in bed with a snake?" Ceridan asked.

"I feel the same," Malia said. "But we must accept what help we can get. Darian's wizards will come in handy. If they can help prevent the death of even one more Findoor soldier, it is worth it to me. After all, their sole task is to seek out and destroy the defiled." The commanders seemed satisfied with that answer. They all agreed that they would head out at first light, and Malia spent the rest of the time at the fire picking away at what was left on her plate. She tried to listen to the stories being told and the songs being sung as they drank wine and ale to pass the night, but her thoughts kept straying back to Seth. She wondered where he was and what he was doing, and if he would once again return to her.

# Chapter 29 - The Wisdom of Arda

Seth appeared on a white sandy beach that stretched to either side of him as far as he could see. He could hear waves crashing in the distance and water lapping at the beach in front of him, and that told him he was in the right place. There was a warm breeze carrying salt water mist into shore that felt refreshing on his skin. One deep breath, and he turned around to see the great Ardan forest towering behind him. "A hundred years and it doesn't look like it's aged a day," he said in awe of the great trees that stretched up as far as he could see. The only way he could tell that it ended at all was from the stars in the murky blackness above.

He stayed on the shore, finding the sounds and smells relaxing, and sat down on the beach. "A hundred years ago, I came here looking for an answer. All I found was more trouble. Maybe my answer was in the right place, but the wrong time." He let out a sigh and watched the stars twinkle in the sky above the Rashean sea. The only time he had ever found peace or serenity was when he was with the Ardans. That was, until Tyriel had found him. He needed some serenity now.

Time went by without much notice from Seth. Stars floated through the sky as he watched the eastern horizon for the first signs of daylight. When the pink glow broke over the sea, he perked up and watched as colors burst around small clouds. The sun rose, and the day began anew with its warm rays lighting up the foliage at the edge of the forest.

Seth stood, stretched, and felt refreshed, even though he hadn't slept. Without waiting any longer, he turned and walked into the forest, being careful not to crush any plants or break any branches from the smaller trees that grew there. Once he was past the border, the foliage let up and the cool dampness of the forest set in. He'd forgotten how quiet and peaceful the inner forest could be, but he enjoyed it as he walked in the direction he thought was right to get him to the Ardan village. That was, if it was even still there. Without Gladius to guide him, he wasn't sure he would be able to find it.

*Listen to the forest,* he thought, remembering the lessons that Gladius had taught him. He took a deep breath and called on the power of earth and time, seeking the way he and Gladius had once walked. The energy combined inside him and spread out before him, showing him what the forest looked like then. Two figures walked through the forest about a hundred paces away. One barely made a sound, walking with confidence, and the other trudged along behind, moving carefully to avoid stepping on anything that might harm his bare feet. As Seth approached, he recognized the pair. The one leading wore blue clothing and had thick black hair. He was young, maybe eighteen years old, and appeared to know the forest very well. "Gladius," Seth said. "I sometimes forget how young you are."

He followed behind the pair, a green misty trail showing him the path until the apparitions faded and the green trail ended at a massive tree. "I remember this," Seth said, not thinking about who might be listening. He reached out and took hold of a rope that was camouflaged against the trunk of the tree and began to climb. Looking up, he saw a familiar sight. Far up in the trees there were pathways stretching from tree to tree and platforms where the little Ardans walked. The village had expanded a significant amount since he was last there. *Of course, it's been a hundred years.*

New platforms and pathways stretched through the trees as far as he could see, but many of the old ones were still in use and in good repair. As he climbed higher, he spotted some of the little feline creatures and could see they had spotted him. He wasn't counting on the element of surprise.

A half dozen Ardans met him at the top of the rope, each with a small spear pointed at him. They allowed Seth to climb onto the platform, but no farther. The largest of the creatures approached Seth and growled something in a language Seth couldn't understand. *Do not make eye contact with one you do not intend to challenge,* Gladius's warning echoed through his mind. "Friends, I mean you no harm," Seth said, raising his hands and lowering his gaze to the platform.

The Ardan warrior may not have understood his words, but he understood the gesture and made a motion with one of his hands. The other five backed off, but kept their weapons at the ready.

"Thank you," Seth said. "I'd like to speak with your chieftain. Can you take me to him?"

He waited for a response from them, but none came. After a few moments, the biggest Ardan circled Seth on the platform and prodded him with the spear to move along a suspended pathway. Seth proceeded and followed the directions of the warrior until they reached the largest tree at what was the center of the village. As he walked, he watched Ardans all around him working and playing. As they noticed him, they stopped what they were doing and stared at him as he went past, only to return to their activities when he was almost out of sight. It was more curiosity that Seth felt than hostility. He was likely the first outsider they had seen in many years, possibly even since he and Gladius had been there a hundred years ago.

The tree before him had a platform around the trunk that spiraled up above the tops of the rest of the trees. His Ardan escort motioned for him to ascend the ramp, and so he did, walking up the path until he reached a large platform that rested above the tree tops. Despite having been there before, the view still took his breath away. Treetops spread out before him as far as he could see and exotic birds flew in and out of them as they went to and from the surrounding sea for food. The sky was clear other than a few tufts of white cloud that drifted by and the sun was up now, making the forest look more like a sea of emeralds.

At the other end of the platform, there was an Ardan sitting and looking out over the forest. "Outsider," the Ardan said, without turning around. "Why do you invade our forest?"

Seth took a step forward. "My name is Seth Alkirk..."

"I didn't ask you your name," the chieftain said. "Why are you here?"

"I'm not really sure, to be honest," Seth said. "I guess I'm just looking for somewhere to hide."

The Ardan chieftain stood up and turned around. His eyes held kindness, but also suspicion. "You are troubled, I can see that. Are you hiding from your troubles, or are you hiding from yourself?"

The thought hadn't occurred to Seth. He'd been so focused on getting himself away from everything, that he didn't think about why. "I don't know what to do. Everybody has all these grand expectations of me."

"Have you considered your own expectations?"

Seth walked to the front edge of the platform and leaned against a wooden railing that appeared to be a part of the platform, like it had been grown that way. He looked out over the forest and heaved a sigh. "I want this to be over."

"Then finish it," the chieftain said, taking a place beside Seth.

"I don't know how. The last time I confronted Grian, he was too powerful for me and my father combined."

"A wise man does not look to others to solve his problems, but instead, looks to himself."

Seth thought about this for a few minutes while watching birds frolic in the trees. Something about what the chieftain said stuck with him. Perhaps because it sounded like an old Earth proverb. *Look to myself, huh?* He opened his mouth to say something else, when another thought occurred to him. *That's it,* he thought, *Look to myself.*

"Thank you, chieftain. You've been very helpful."

Seth walked to the center of the platform, trying to organized his thoughts. He turned around once to say goodbye to the chieftain, but the little creature had already turned away and was meditating again. The only other thing that came to Seth's mind was how he left Malia in the tent. *I don't know what was going on with her, but she deserves more than to be deserted by a jerk like me.*

He focused his mind on the tent in Caldoor where he left her, but also on the time he left. He tried to get as close as possible to that point so that he could avoid as much heartbreak as possible. The power of time and space flowed to him, and he used it to form a protective shell around him for the trip back. The Ardan forest, the platform, the blue sky and birds, all melted away into blackness as he moved himself between dimensions and traveled back along the time line. He reappeared in the tent, though it was dark now.

Beside the cot where Seth had slept was a form in a heap leaning half on the cot, and half on the ground. The mess of blonde hair gave away her identity, and when Seth approached, he could see tear stains on her cheek. "Malia," Seth said quietly, but he didn't want to wake her. He focused his mind, and stopped time, then approached her. "I'm so sorry for leaving you here like this. I should have known you wouldn't betray me like that."

He leaned down and lifted her up off the ground, placing her on the cot so that she would be comfortable. There was a blanket at the end of the cot that he drew up over her because the night was chilly, and then leaned over and kissed her cheek.

"I'm about to do something crazy. I hope you'll understand. It needs to be me, but it also needs to be Galadir. This isn't just your fight or my fight. Grian is threatening all of us. But I know where to look to get the help we need. It's me. It's always been me. I'm going to finish this now."

He stood up and allowed time to resume, then focused his mind on his next destination. With a thought, he disappeared, leaving Malia sleeping peacefully on the cot.

# Chapter 30 - Master and Slave

With the help of Darian's black wizards, Malia led her army back to Findoor Castle without casualty. They encountered few defiled, and those they did encounter appeared to be lost and misdirected. The black wizards made quick work of them, releasing the bodies from their dark magic and destroying the corpses. The weather remained favorable, with only one day sending them a light, cold rain that lasted a few minutes. The rest of the time there were mixed clouds and a cool breeze, but nothing they couldn't handle.

They passed many farmers who were tending to their harvest, as the year was getting on and winter fast approached. Malia learned of the farmer's plight and Grian's request for an abnormally high tithe to the castle. Ceridan assured the farmers that no such tithe would be required and that the standard would be sufficient. He handled most of the political business with grace and kept the remaining citizens of the kingdom happy.

As they approached the castle, Malia found herself smiling for the first time in a long time. The fields around the castle were ill-maintained and very little of the damage done during the battle against Gladius had been repaired. It felt like years since she had left her home behind, but it had been mere months. No guards stood at the gates and no defiled could be seen. In fact, with the exception of the front gates being closed, the whole castle appeared to be business as usual.

"So now what?" Ceridan asked. "We don't just walk up to the front gates and knock, do we?"

"Perhaps," Malia said. "Though I doubt the castle is completely unguarded. The Defiler may be a vile snake, but he is a clever and powerful one. We should use caution on our approach."

Malia led the way, stepping through the grass and weeds on the overgrown hills. The former King had ensured that the hills surrounding the castle were well tended so as to make Findoor Castle as presentable as possible. Grian obviously had no such desires. Many of the farms surrounding the castle had also been abandoned, the crops being allowed to grow wild. Malia didn't blame them. She wouldn't want to live near the center of an undead army either. As it was, the smell of death lingered in the air. That, and the banner that flew over the castle, were the only signs that it continued to be occupied by the black wizard.

With a small group of soldiers and wizards following her, Malia approached the front gates. She instructed Ceridan and the remaining soldiers to wait on the hill for her signal. She had no interest in appearing confrontational if there was no reason to.

The great wood doors in the castle walls were the only thing that had been repaired after the battle and they stood strong, barred from the inside when she checked them. There was a guard's door off to the right of the gates that was made of steel and had a small sliding window in it. She approached the door with caution, one hand on the black steel sword, and the other poised to knock. A tap on the door was all it took and the window slid open, revealing darkness inside.

"Who goes there," an ancient raspy voice asked. The voice had a familiarity to Malia, but she had spent a number of years in the castle and so it may have been somebody she knew occupying the guard house.

"General Malia Corsair of the Findoor Militia," Malia said with confidence. "Open the front gates and allow us to cleanse this castle of evil."

There was a cackle from inside the guard house, and then a hacking sound. A moment later, the voice returned. "Malia. So you survived the battle and the escape. You've done better than I ever dreamed you would. Alas, the Militia is no more. Findoor is finished."

"Nay, it is not true. I lead the Militia still. To whom do I speak? You obviously know me."

"Go back the way you came," the voice said. "There is nothing but death here. Once Lord Grian takes Ducain's Keep, there will be nothing but death everywhere."

"So it is true," Malia said. "Do you truly believe that we will allow him to do that?"

There was another cackle from behind the door. "Do you truly believe you can stop him?"

"There is always hope."

There was a sudden movement in the guard house and a loud thud as the occupant slammed his face against the door with his eye in the slit. Gray flesh surrounded an eyeball that looked about to pop out of its socket. It was red and swollen, and shot with streaks of blood. It stared at Malia with such intensity that she jumped back away from the door and stared at it in horror.

"There is no hope here," the rasping voice said. "There is no force on this world that can stop him. He will take Ducain's, and with the arcane knowledge he gains there, he will rise above all mortals. Death will flow with his every word. People will cower from him, as all the love, and hope, and everything that is good in this world withers away. He seeks the fatespark, and if he finds it, nothing and no one will be truly safe from his might. Darkness will shroud this world and all worlds. Even the mighty Time Weaver will not be able to stop him. Go back the way you came, Malia Corsair. There is nothing but death here."

At the mention of that name, her sword came to life in her hand, growing warm and urging her to draw it. A rage boiled up inside Malia and she stepped forward once more, drawing her courage up. "You will open the gates, or we will tear them from their hinges. I have not come all this way to leave empty-handed. This castle will be ours once more, whether or not you cooperate. You have to the count of three."

The eye in the window pulled away leaving it in darkness once more, and then the window slid shut.

"One," Malia said, backing away from the steel door.

There was a scuffling sound behind the door that sounded as though the guard inside was struggling with the inner door of the guard house.

"Two," Malia shouted, walking over to the great wood gates. She drew the black steel sword and it ignited like the rage inside her. This was her home, and she would not leave it again.

Shouts came from behind the gates, as people screamed and ran. Other sounds, like long dragging steps could be heard. Malia's soldiers readied their weapons and the black wizards raised their hands, each chanting battle incantations.

"Three," Malia screamed, and ran at the gates, channeling all the magical energy she could through her sword. It burst to life, white-hot and she plunged it into the wooden gates. The energy coursed through the wood, burning it from the inside out. Black smoke billowed out from small cracks that formed all the way up the doors. Red lines spread across their surface as Malia continued her assault, allowing the hungry sword to consume all the energy she could give it. With one last thrust into the gates, the wood exploded into a cloud of searing hot embers and flew inward.

A figure standing on the other side of the gates was pummeled by the burning coals. The attack perforated his gray robes and set them aflame, but the figure didn't budge. The smoke concealed the figure's identity, but she could tell it was casting some kind of spell.

When the figure outstretched its arms, a glimmer caught Malia's eye. Gold thread hemmed the gray robe and reflected any light it could catch. "Merek?" she asked, stunned at the wizard's sudden appearance before her.

But it wasn't Merek, or not as she remembered him. This Merek was gaunt and ragged, with gray flesh and eyes that raged wild with power. What hair she could see under his hood was white and matted, and one of his legs was twisted in an awkward way.

"You always were a fast learner," Merek said in his raspy voice. "Now, experience the full fury of Hadra. Alucinatas."

Malia had little time to put up an adequate defense. Merek's appearance shook her to her core, and all she could muster was to lift the black steel sword up before her as a cloud of gray smoke billowed out from her former master.

The smoke struck the black steel sword, which formed a shell around her, but as it traveled past her, she heard screams of agony as her soldiers and wizards were caught in the spell. She looked in time to see their flesh and armor melting away in the smoke exposing muscle tissue, then bone. Their cries continued even after they began to fall to the ground, and only stopped when the remains of their bodies dissolved in the smoke.

It formed a circle around her and Merek, and sank into the ground. There was a rumble beneath her, but before she could set her footing, the entire circle shifted. The Findoor walls collapsed, and large cracks formed on the ground where the smoke had touched. Malia tried to regain her footing, but without warning, the entire circle of ground, with her and Merek on it, lifted into the air, leaving Findoor Castle, the entire kingdom, and her army on the ground below them.

Merek cackled as the sudden rise of the ground beneath their feet forced Malia to the ground. She struggled to her feet, using the black steel sword as a crutch, and then lifted it before her again.

"Now," Merek said. "Now if you destroy me, you'll destroy us both."

The shock of the sudden attack was wearing off, and Malia tried to come up with a strategy to combat Merek. "I thought you were dead. I saw your body."

"You left me behind," Merek said, cackling once more. "And best you did, too. You see, my dear, I've been dead a long time already. But to a powerful enough wizard, death is just a new beginning. Had you taken my physical form when you ran, you and all your soldiers would be dead already."

"Why are you doing this?" Malia asked, trying to stall for time so that she could come up with a plan of attack. The wind whipped past her, and the small island of earth teetered back and forth making it hard to keep her balance. Merek seemed unaffected by the listing of the island.

"Why? Because Grian is making me." He must have seen something in Malia's face, because he continued. "You see, the apprentice returned, and when he did, he found my soul. Apprentice then became master, and master became slave."

The edges of the island began to crumble from the constant wind, and the air grew thin as they continued to rise. Malia could see nothing but clouds around them, and the horizon looked like a blue haze with the night sky above it. Breathing became difficult, which impaired her ability to think. The last thing she could think to do was point the black steel sword at Merek and unleash her own spell in return.

Summoning the power of fire was difficult after the spell she used to burn the gates down, but she managed a meek ball of fire and shot it at Merek. It struck him in the chest and ignited his robes, blowing a chunk of flesh from his chest and exposing ribs. Still, he didn't move, but cackled once more at her.

"Your focus is impeccable, and casting without words is an interesting trick," Merek said. "But you are not powerful enough to destroy me, and you will not regain Findoor unless you do."

"I don't want to destroy you," Malia said. The lack of air made her light headed, and tears stung the back of her eyes, but she held them back, and stood tall, her wild blonde hair fluttering in the wind. "You've always been like a father to me. What has changed?"

"Everything. In order to extend my life, I placed my own soul in a receptacle. Didn't you ever wonder how I lived so long? Grian found the receptacle before my body could regenerate and took control of it, and thus me. That is what has changed, and now you will die. And all of Galadir's hopes and dreams with you. I told you before, there is nothing but death here." He moved his arms so as to hold his hands before him. Gray smoke formed around them and swelled into a tight ball. "Alucinatas," he said once more, sending the smoke toward her on the wind.

Voices surrounded her, louder than she had ever heard before, all screaming. She dropped the black steel sword and tried to cover her ears but it didn't help. The screams intensified until stabbing pain ripped through her head, centered at her ears. She was aware that her own scream had joined the others as she fell to her knees. The island they stood on shifted and sent her sword skittering across the paving stones toward Merek. She saw it sliding and knew if he took the sword, the battle would be over.

With all her strength, she burst forward, throwing herself on the ground chest-plate first and slid toward Merek and the sword. Inches from Merek, she grasped the hilt and swung it, twisting herself on the ground. The blade struck Merek's leg, severing it at the knee, but as he fell, she continued her slide toward the edge of the island. Her free hand was hindered by the gauntlet of her full plate armor, and she couldn't get a grip in time to stop herself. She flew off the edge of the island, and grasped a stone at the last second.

Hanging by one hand, she looked down and saw nothing but clouds beneath her. With her other hand, she lifted the black steel sword and rammed it into the dirt on the side of the island. The blade took over, blazing with fire, and melted the sand around it to fuse it into place. With a second hand hold, Malia tried to pull herself up, but was met by Merek at the edge of the island.

"Let us go for a flight," Merek said with a cackle, as he grabbed her by the neck and pulled her from the side of the island into freefall. The black steel sword broke free with her, now with large, jagged spikes of glass stuck to it. Above her, Malia watched the island of rock, sand and soil break up.

Merek held her by the neck in an iron grip and tried to wrap his remaining leg around her waist. She took the sword and swung it backward, stabbing the dirty glass shards into Merek's body. It was enough to loosen his grip and allowed her to twist.

"Now we play by my rules," Malia said, with fresh anger to fuel her. She forgot about falling and focused on combat. She forgot about who she was fighting. He became yet another faceless sparring partner whom she had defeated many times before. She cleared her mind and grasped the hilt of the black steel sword in both hands, allowing it to take what it wanted from her. The sword blazed to life once more, freeing itself from its glass prison. With one smooth motion, Malia kicked out of Merek's grip, sending her spinning. With each revolution, the sword struck Merek's withered body, slicing through what was left of his flesh, muscle and bones. Each time it struck, the sword glowed brighter, and consumed more power. Merek's body burned from a dozen wounds, and all the while he cackled a hideous laughter that pierced Malia's heart.

Her spin stopped, leaving her falling several feet from Merek's burning, cackling body. His face was twisted into a warped smile with his lips drawn back, and his black, broken teeth exposed. His eyes were hysterical with laughter and rage that would have made a lesser man flee in terror. Bits of his robe and flesh fell around them, and all he could do was cackle and stare at her with those eyes. "We're all going to die," he screamed, and cackled some more.

Malia gathered what was left of her courage. The ground was below her now and coming up fast. She lifted the black steel sword over her head and swung it down in a blaze of fire and heat. It struck the top of Merek's head, slicing down through the middle and dividing him in half. The sound of his cackling didn't stop, even as the remains of his body came apart and exploded with fire, sending bits of him in every direction.

The battle was over for him, but Malia could see Findoor Castle now, and unless she did something quick, it would be over for her too. She focused her mind on the power of air, but nothing would come. Something blocked her ability to draw her other elements. She tried again, and encountered resistance again, managing only a trickle of energy.

There was a burning sensation in her hand, and she realized that her sword was searing hot. Her gauntlet fused to the hilt, which was glowing red with the heat. She tried to shake it off, but it wouldn't budge. Blisters formed on the palm of her hand, sending pain shooting up through her right arm.

Below her, she could see her army, and the castle walls, and the citizens gathered in the square below her. "You are not my master," she said to the sword, that appeared to be jealous of her other gifts.

"You will not interfere with my powers." Through force of will, she closed off the flow of power she fed into the sword. It struggled against her, but her strength endured, and the sword went cold.

Despite the pain in her hand, she tried again to summon the power of air. This time it came to her readily, and when her spell was complete, she called out, "Levitas."

Her downward motion slowed and she came to a stop with only inches between her and the paving stones of the Findoor Castle square.

## Chapter 31 – The Desolation of the Narshuks

A glowing white sphere melted away on the Badlands, revealing two wizards: one in black robes, and one in blue. Gladius took the first step, as he knew where he was going, and led Trysk forward to see what they could do for the remaining Narshuks. He suspected that if they weren't all dead by now, they had to be close. The plague that ravaged their numbers was relentless.

He looked ahead and saw several plumes of black smoke rising in the air. There was a calm on the Badlands that he'd never known before. No wind stirred, and there were no grunts or groans of the meager wildlife that lived there. No birds flew through the sky, and the smoke rose straight up.

"'Tis the calm before a storm," Trysk said behind him, as though he read the blue wizard's mind.

"Are you sure your spell has taken us to the right place?" Gladius asked. "We should hear something, smell something."

"This is the place you pointed to on the map. Perhaps your memory fails you?" Trysk's tone was mocking, and it burned Gladius up, but he couldn't afford to start a fight now.

"Follow me, we'll check out that smoke," Gladius said, and walked away from the black wizard before he lost his temper.

It was a short walk to the source of the smoke, and when Gladius crested the small hill that bordered the north end of the Narshuk encampment, he gasped. The air left his lungs as though drawn from them, and he couldn't believe his eyes.

Before him were all the huts and structures he remembered from before, but there were several large piles of smoldering ashes scattered around the village. The shacks were in disrepair, having

251

been either set on fire by drifting sparks or just left to fall apart, and the central area where they held their rituals was now the home of the largest pile of ash. The whole place was deathly quiet, which sent a chill through Gladius that he didn't like.

"They're gone," Gladius said.

"What do you mean they're gone," Trysk said. He caught up just as Gladius spoke. "There must be some survivors. They've obviously had camp fires burning recently."

"Those aren't camp fires," Gladius said, taking a closer look at the nearest ash pile. It was mostly white and black ash, but there were white fragments as well that had refused to burn. "Pyres. These are funeral pyres."

"Grishtor take you. There's no way that plague could have wiped them all out."

"If there were any survivors, they aren't here. They've moved on." Gladius took a step into the village. "They burned the bodies, and moved on."

"Then we should search for them," Trysk said. "Spread out and find which direction they went. It shouldn't be hard to track them."

Gladius whirled on Trysk, unable to hold his temper any longer. "Don't you understand? They're gone. If they've abandoned this place, they're gone, and they won't be coming back. We're too late. We'll get no help from the Narshuks. Just leave what remains of them in peace."

"You say that like it's our fault," Trysk said.

"It *is* our fault. If we had treated them with the respect they deserved instead of keeping them cooped up like animals. If we had offered them aid when they needed it, instead of coming now. If anyone at Ducain's had seen them as something more than bloodthirsty animals, then maybe they would be here, and ready to help us. But nothing could be farther from the truth. No respect was ever afforded a Narshuk."

"The only thing the Narshuks have ever done is kill. Nothing good has ever come out of the Badlands."

"You still don't understand," Gladius shouted now. Trysk's nonchalant attitude toward the Narshuks grated on his nerves. "We never looked for anything good. Wizards held them down out of fear, and kept them from rising to greatness. It's not lack of potential that is to blame, but our own actions in dealing with them."

"Fine. So what if it was? We can't bring them back. Let us return to Ducain's keep, report what we've found, and get on with the preparations for war. This may be a tragic loss, but Grian isn't going to stop for that. We're needed there."

Gladius stopped and thought for a few moments about anywhere else the Narshuks might be. This was the only camp he knew of, and scouting the entire eastern Badlands for them was not an option.

"Okay," Gladius said. "I'll explain the situation to Serrin."

5

"What do you mean they're all gone?" Serrin asked. "There were thousands of them at one time. Tens of thousands."

"It looks like the plague took most of them. Grian knew what he was doing when he created it." There was a hint of sadness to Gladius's voice that Serrin had never heard before. "It wiped them out quickly. We found funeral pyres in the village, some of which were still smoldering. Wherever the survivors are, they didn't leave long ago. A day perhaps. Still, I think it best if we look at alternate arrangements."

Serrin let out a sigh and looked around at the rest of the council members, including Nadya. "Our neighbors have also declined to help us," Serrin said. "Trade has resumed with Findoor, and they are enjoying the spoils that come with that. They dare not anger the force that controls a large portion of their food supply and we have long been at odds with them anyway. We are on our own then."

"How far away is Grian?" Kenda asked.

"Scouts tell me he is two days out and rides with a vast army of undead. We must assemble all the wizards we can. If Grian takes Ducain's Keep, we are finished. I want every one of you to join me at the entrance to the forbidden zone. We must place additional wards on that library, of every element."

"What about Tyriel?" Trysk asked. "Didn't he say he was once a reaper? Couldn't he summon help from their ranks?"

"I am certain Tyriel will help in our fight, but he is outcast from their ranks and would have no way to contact them. Besides, the Fates are not known for being charitable. They will not interfere in mortal affairs."

"They did once before," Gladius said. "During the Lyecian war, they hunted Krycin."

Trysk snapped his head toward Gladius and narrowed his eyes. "How do you know about that?"

Serrin realized Gladius's mistake too late. He watched, trying to keep his face expressionless, to see what Gladius would come up with.

"How do you know about it?" Gladius said, answering Trysk's question with a question.

"I was in close council with the previous black council wizard, Garrick Trill," Trysk said. "He was alive during the war, and that particular fact was kept secret except among the highest levels of wizards who lived at the time. So I repeat my question: how do you know about that?"

"That's simple," Gladius said with a smile. "Krycin is a dear friend of mine. He told me himself."

Gladius drew a surprised look from everyone in the room.

Trysk stood up and approached Gladius. "You mean to tell me that you know Krycin? You know where he is, and what he is doing? Then contact him, for Galadir's sake."

"I cannot. Even I don't know where Krycin is now, though we were good friends at one time. It has been some time since I've seen any trace of him."

Serrin was inwardly pleased with the cover story that Gladius came up with. It was plausible, and not far-fetched. He raised his hand before the murmur in the council chamber got out of control. "Very well. We are on our own. Assemble all the wizards you can, including the apprentices, and we will march out to meet Grian. We must stop him, at any cost."

All the wizards in the room stood up and filed out except for Nadya, who remained seated. When Serrin saw this, he waited back to see if she was okay. "Are you well?" Serrin asked, approaching her.

"Aye," Nadya said in her strange dessert accent. She made a slow attempt to take to her feet. "Have you ever met Krycin?"

"Yes, a very long time ago."

"When I was at my darkest, and I wasn't sure I could fight anymore, a light pierced through the veil and a hand reach in and drew me back. I think Krycin is still watching over us. I think Krycin is here, on Galadir."

"Perhaps that is so, but I wouldn't count on his help. Seth is right, you know. We must learn to fight our own battles, for the sake of all of Galadir. It's up to us now to defeat Grian."

Nadya's expression darkened a little, but Serrin could tell she was trying to keep up a pleasant demeanor. "I'm afraid. I'm afraid that we will not be strong enough. Grian wiped out the entire previous council, single-handedly. What makes us think we will fare any better?"

"We must, my dear," Serrin said, walking to the door. "We must."

# Chapter 32 – A Game of Chess

General Neil Mathers sat behind his desk in his quiet office shuffling paperwork around. The days had grown long and quiet since Seth had left. What remained was an endless stream of reports and questioning from his superiors. He picked up a large coffee mug and took a sip, allowing the bitter liquid to roll around his mouth before swallowing it.

With a sigh, he placed the cup back down and started organizing the papers, placing various pictures with the right reports and getting ready to present his findings and risk assessments. He still hadn't managed to go on the vacation he had promised his family, and he wasn't sure his wife would ever forgive him for spending so much time at the office. Still, things were starting to settle down, with the exception of Dave and his magic, and Mathers was looking forward to some hard earned time off.

He straightened a stack of papers on his desk and placed them on the corner, moving on to some more pictures. Just as he was starting to figure them out, a gust of air rushed through his office and caught the stack of papers he had just fixed, blowing them off and scattering them across the floor. "Son of a..." Mathers said, looking up at what caused the disturbance. Across from him, standing in the middle of the floor was Seth with a big smile on his face. "You jerk. It'll take me hours to reorganize those."

"Use a paperweight next time," Seth said. There was a gleam in his eyes that Mathers couldn't remember ever seeing in all the times he'd met the mysterious man.

"What do you want, Alkirk?"

"I need information," Seth said. His demeanor changed in an instant and his face was serious again. "About Cy Cooper."

"Who is Cy Cooper?" Mathers asked.

"Tall guy, lanky, dresses in black. Pretty much the scariest man imaginable."

Mathers had a picture in his mind of the man who opened the portal in the parking lot. That had terrified him more than anything in his life. The man had walked into the compound, bypassing all security clearance, stole a dose of the Specter serum, and killed one of his best men.

"By the look on your face, you know who I'm talking about. There was something unusual about him."

"You're damn right there was," Mathers said. "The man was insane."

"No, something other than that. See, he was once a friend of mine. He was also a Lyecian, like me, except his powers had been taken from him. At some point, somebody sent him to earth. I still haven't figured out who." Seth paused and swallowed once. It looked like he was trying to find the right words. "But at some point, Cy got his powers back."

"I can't help you, son," Mathers said. "I only saw your man once, and that was when he opened that portal into your world."

"That's just it," Seth said, his voice raising. "Cy shouldn't have been able to open a rift that big without his powers, and I know he wouldn't have stayed here willingly. What was he doing here on the base?"

"I told you, I can't help you. I'm not sure what you thought you would get from me, but there's nothing I can do." He watched as Seth took a step forward. Mathers placed his fingers over a button hidden under the edge of his desk. It would alert security, and he could be done with this mess.

"Don't fuck with me," Seth said in an angry but controlled voice. His brows lowered as he narrowed his eyes. "Either you gave him something, or he took something, but one way or the other, I'm going to find out. If you won't tell me yourself, I'll tear this base apart brick by brick until I find the answer, and you know I can."

Fear surged through Mathers. He'd hoped Seth would just accept it and leave, but that obviously wouldn't be the case. "Okay. There was a project we worked on just after the first incursion. It was called Specter. It was a serum we could give people to make them like you."

"You son of a bitch," Seth said. "What did you hope to accomplish? Were you trying to create some kind of super soldier?"

"There were obvious military uses for such a serum, but there were also medical reasons. We could have all but eliminated disease. Whole limbs could be regenerated. Lives saved. It could have been one of humanity's crowning achievements, to beat death itself."

"But?" Seth asked.

"But, then the man in black, Cy, attacked and stole it."

"That's what gave him his powers back, then," Seth said. He looked like he was relaxing again.

"There was a problem with it, though. Our test subject appeared successful at first, but later, his entire body combusted and killed several scientists in the process. We haven't tested it since, though our finest minds are continuing their work on it."

"I need it," Seth said. His voice was flat, and serious. Mathers knew that he wasn't going to leave without it.

"You know what I'm going to tell you."

"I know. But I'm taking it anyway. The reason it won't work on humans is because your DNA isn't designed to handle that amount of energy at once. Magical energy can kill you if you're not careful, which is why I spent time with Dave showing him how to control it. I've seen wizards almost killed because they were interrupted while casting a spell." Seth was quiet for a moment, and appeared to be thinking. "There's a storm coming, General. Without that serum, I'm not sure my world will survive it, and I can't guarantee that it won't spill over into this world either."

"I can't give you permission to take it," Mathers said. "We're under a strict security protocol that requires us to heavily guard the serum, which is on the fifth basement floor on the northeast side, locked in a fridge in a safe." He gave Seth a wink, and sat back down behind his desk, ignoring the mess of paper that was beside it. He took out several forms from his desk drawer and began filling them out. When Seth didn't move, he looked up at him. "Well? Go on. I told you, I can't help you."

"Then what are you doing?" Seth asked, looking closer at the forms.

"Filling out a lost or stolen inventory form," Mathers said. "I figure I might as well get a head start."

He looked up in time to see Seth disappear, and sighed when the gust of wind moved through his office again rustled more papers on his desk, leaving them in disarray. "Oh well. Didn't figure I'd get to those tonight anyway."

5

Seth appeared once again in Cedric's chamber in Caldoor Castle, though this time he was in a much better mood. The hour was growing late, and Cedric looked like he was getting ready to go out. He had a lute slung on his back and was dressed in formal attire.

"We have to go, now," Seth said with a sense of urgency in his voice.

"Must we?" Cedric asked, with a smirk. "But I've been invited to play for His Majesty, the King. It's not often an opportunity like that comes up, especially for a brigand like me."

"Yeah, yeah, from rags to riches. Get ready, we have to go."

Cedric peered at him through the ever-present black mask on his face. "What's the hurry?"

"Grian is making a run at Ducain's keep. We need every one we can get." Seth paused, trying not to let the excitement overwhelm him. He continued in a hushed voice. "This is it, Cedric. We're going to finish this."

"Are you so certain that you can?"

"Not me. We. It's going to take a little bit from all of us. The one thing I've learned is that not every battle can be fought by a single person. This is a battle for Galadir, and must be fought by Galadir."

Cedric smiled and clapped him on the shoulder. "That's my boy."

"Where is Mom? I have a present for her."

"I'm not certain. I haven't seen much of her since we arrived. Perhaps check with the servants, they will know where her quarters are."

Seth nodded and led the way out of Cedric's room. After a few minutes of hunting, he found a servant who directed him to his mother's room. Cedric followed close behind, obviously curious about what Seth had brought her. He tapped on the wood door and waited for his mother to answer. When the door opened her expression went from annoyed to a bright smile that warmed Seth's heart to see.

"My goodness, if I'd known you were coming, I would have cleaned up. Come in, Seth," she said. "You as well, Cedric. You are always welcome."

Seth stepped into the small guest room and looked around. Everything was neat and tidy, with a bed that was made, a small table that was clear other than a book that his mom had been reading, and a shelf that was full of books organized in such a way that they looked pleasing to the eye. It was how his mom had always kept things. "Mom, I need your help. It's time to join the battle."

Her smile faded and she paused part way to the table. Looking toward the window she said, "I thought the battle was done. Runners returned saying Caldoor was victorious."

"The battle for Caldoor was won, but Grian is heading for Ducain's Keep. I want you there, by Dad's side."

Her head snapped around and she stared at Seth with eyes full of pain. "I haven't seen your father in over twenty-five years. I'm an old woman now, and he is still a young man. How could I fight?" Tears welled up in her eyes that broke Seth's heart to see. "You go on. I'll only be a hindrance."

"I brought something for you, Mom. Something that will make things right again. You need to be by Dad's side, and he will need you." Seth reached into a small bag he'd been carrying and pulled out a device that looked like a small gun with a glass cylinder attached to it.

"What is it?" She asked.

"It's something the U.S. military brewed up. Something that gave Cy his powers back, and I think it can do the same for you."

She narrowed her eyes at the device, causing the skin at the corners of her eyes to bunch into crow's feet. Seth could see the skepticism on her face, but raised his hand before she could say anything. "Please. We need you."

"Is it safe?"

"For somebody who was once Lyecian, I think so. But not for humans."

The uncertainty faded from her face and she gave Seth a slow nod. "Okay. We'll try it. But if it doesn't work, I don't think I could go to battle without my old powers."

Seth gave her a reassuring smile. "It will work. Lie down, I'm told this is a somewhat painful and violent process. It's going to reactivate certain parts of your DNA that were damaged."

She laid down on the bed and rolled onto her side as Seth guided her. He pulled her graying hair up and out of the way so he could get to the back of her neck, pressed the gun against her skin, and pulled the trigger. The was a hissing sound as the gun discharged, and his mother gasped as the gun injected the Specter serum into her body. When the entire dose was done, Seth pulled the injector from her neck, and was surprised by her sudden scream. Her entire body tensed and curled up on the bed as the serum coursed through her body. Seth watched as her skin tightened and went smooth. Spots that had formed as a result of aging disappeared, and her hair lost all of the gray. A few minutes passed and her shaking changed to trembling, and her breathing returned to a slow, steady pace, but she remained on the bed.

"Well, it didn't kill me," She said, without turning to face Seth.

"It did much better than that." Seth picked up a small hand mirror from her night table and handed it to her.

She rolled over and sat up with her feet on the floor and accepted the mirror. He would have said something more, but the sight of her face took his breath away. The serum took all thirty years that she had gained since he was born from her face and body. She looked young again, exactly the way she looked when Seth met her in the past. She gasped and looked herself over in the mirror, taking in every detail. "How is this possible?"

"They said it was made from my DNA. You should have your powers back."

Seth heard a distinct twang from behind him, like the string of a bow, and watched as his mother snatched an arrow out of the air. She stared at something behind him with a dumbfounded look on her face. Following her gaze, Seth spotted Cedric at the door with a huge grin on his face.

"It would appear as though your serum worked," Cedric said.

The three of them burst out laughing at once, breaking the tension of the situation. When they had all calmed down, Seth looked at the two of them and said, "We have to go now. There's a battle to fight, and a war to win."

"Very well," Catrina said. "I'm as ready as I'll ever be."

"As am I," Cedric said.

"Is Malia still at the Caldoor military camp?" Seth asked, looking at Cedric.

"I'm uncertain, but I believe I heard rumors that the Findoor soldiers were planning an attempt to take back Findoor Castle. Had you not arrived today, I would have set out for there myself."

"Okay. Do you know where Morganath is? We're going to need him too."

"Nobody has heard from him since the attack," Cedric said. "Runners have searched his Caldoor lair and all his usual hiding spots, but nobody can find him."

"Let's get going. I think I know when he is."

"When?" Cedric asked, giving Seth a confused look through his mask. Catrina appeared to share that confusion.

"Yes, when. I think you got the place right, but not the right time. Let's go. I'll worry about Morganath in a few. Ready?"

Both Cedric and Catrina nodded, and Seth focused on his next destination. The three of them disappeared, leaving a void in the room that the air rushed in to fill.

⟆

Seth appeared at the top of the last hill on the road to Findoor, overlooking the castle. Its gates were secured and a small army of soldiers bearing the Findoor crest were just approaching with Malia and her commanders in the lead. They came to a stop and Malia took a small group of wizards and soldiers with her to check out the gates. He watched with interest as the scene played out before him.

Malia approached the guard door and there was an exchange between them. When that appeared to go nowhere, Malia approached the gates and drew her sword. Seth wasn't close enough to hear what was going on, but he could see people over the wall scrambling away from the gates. It surprised him when Malia plunged her sword into the gates and they exploded into the castle. He took a few steps forward when he saw the figure on the other side of the gates.

The figure motioned with its hands and gray smoke flew toward Malia in a cloud. All the soldiers and wizards around Malia vaporized, but she managed to get her sword up in time and used its magic to deflect the spell around her. Seth broke into a run down the hill, but almost tripped over his own feet when a large section of ground lifted up and flew straight up into the air, taking Malia and the figure with it.

"Holy shit," Seth said, watching the chunk of earth fly into the sky and grow smaller by the second. His run slowed as he watched it, but he made it to the hole that was left behind. Ceridan and the rest of the soldiers arrived at about the same time.

"Seth," Ceridan said. "Is there anything you can do?"

"There is," Seth said. "But I won't. I can't interfere with this. It has to happen. Malia must stand on her own."

"She could die up there. If you can save her, you must do so."

Seth shot a glance toward the soldier and narrowed his eyes. "I don't *have* to do anything. She doesn't need saving. This is a battle that must happen, and it will. Now get back, shut up, and wait."

Ceridan looked taken aback by Seth's words, but he did as he was told and backed away from the crater. Seth watched the sky and waited to see what would happen. Moments later, he saw Malia and her shining armor falling from the sky with the other figure not far from her. She lashed out at the figure, spinning in the air and slashing through the thing's body. Her next attack cleaved it in two and sent pieces of its body raining down. She was falling fast and appeared to be having trouble with her magic.

"Come on, babe," Seth said under his breath. "I can't do this for you."

The black steel sword smoked and caused her gauntlet to glow. The look on her face told Seth that she was battling it for control. He gritted his teeth as she approached the ground. At the last second, the sword went dead and she shouted out, "Levitas."

She stopped inches from the ground and hovered in the air, her face frozen in an expression that was mixed between terror and relief. She was alive, and relatively unharmed. Seth watched her lower herself to the ground and get back up on her feet facing Ceridan. He wasn't sure if she had noticed him there, but thought she didn't.

"Is everyone safe?" She asked Ceridan as if nothing had happened.

"We should ask you the same thing," he said back to her. "Those who were clear of that thing's spell were safe. I can't say much for Darian's wizards, most of them were vaporized along with a few of our men. I'm grateful that you are safe."

"Thank you, Ceridan," Malia said and brushed debris from her chest plate. She turned around to survey the area and her eyes met Seth's. "Seth," Malia cried, her face lighting up when she saw him. She ran without regard to those around her or her own safety, scrambling out of the crater. Seth took several steps and met her half way, lifting her into a warm embrace and spinning with her in his arms.

"I saw you fight," Seth said when he put her down. "You were phenomenal."

She paused, her smile fading. "You saw me fight, and you did nothing?"

There was a look in her eyes that Seth had never seen before, and he wasn't sure what to make of it. "That's right. It was a battle you had to fight. One that you had to win on your own. I knew you would never forgive me if I robbed you of that."

Her smile returned and to Seth's surprise, she pressed her lips against his in a slow, passionate kiss. The warmth of her touch and the taste of her kiss made his heart skip a beat, and he hugged her tighter. When their lips parted, he said, "I'm sorry I left you like that. You deserved a chance to explain yourself."

"Do not mention it. The fault is mine," Malia said. "I was..."

Seth placed one finger over her lips while holding her with his other arm. "Don't," he said. "It's okay. I understand."

"Thank you," Malia said, her gray eyes shining with the tears she was holding back.

"Hey, look, we don't have much time. I'm going to clear out all the nasty stuff from the castle, and we're going to hoist Findoor's banner back over the castle, and then you're all going to come with me."

"Where? What is going on?" Malia asked.

Seth let go of her, and said, "Grian is going after Ducain's Keep. If he takes it, we're all done for. There won't be anything I can do to stop him. As it is, it's going to take all of us, and I can't guarantee that we're all coming back. But if we work together, I think we can stop him."

"Who else has joined the battle?"

Seth gave her a sly look and said, "Everyone."

He turned around and walked toward the castle proper, focusing all his will on drawing the power of life to him. He could sense the dark energy of the defiled creatures still present in the castle, and he focused his spell into a wave. Seth raised his hands before him and let the energy go. It flowed away as a massive curtain of white energy that swept across the castle. Each time the wave encountered a defiled creature, the two magics met, and destroyed each other, leaving nothing but a dessicated corpse behind. The guards who were left at the main entrance slumped to the ground, as did every other defiled creature.

Several citizens peeked their heads out from behind closed shutters or stone walls and Seth could hear whispers already. People were talking about him, though what they said was, "Krycin is back, he has returned."

Seth smiled to himself and motioned Malia and the rest of her troops to follow him. He held out his hand and called on the power of earth to produce a large piece of fabric. It was a deep crimson color, and as he walked, the energy coursed through it embroidering a golden crown with a sword through it into the center of the banner.

He raised his hand and pointed at the black banner above the castle, and sent a single ball of fire flying at it. It exploded on impact, consuming Grian's banner and leaving an empty standard waiting for the new banner.

People flowed from their houses and stores once they caught wind of what was happening. Seth held up the banner and called out, "This is your city. Your castle, and your kingdom. Fly your banner high and proud, and take back what is rightfully yours. Never again allow somebody to  control you. Don't ever give up on yourselves. Fight for your kingdom. Fight for Findoor."

Several men took the banner from Seth's hands and walked ahead, entering the castle. Many others cheered and celebrated their newfound freedom. Seth waited and watched the standard high above the castle with Malia standing in silence next to him. Several minutes later, the banner appeared high above the castle, hoisted up on the standard by the two men who had taken it from Seth. At the sight of the banner above the castle, every voice in the castle rang out in unison, in a great cheer to celebrate their victory.

Seth linked his arm into Malia's and led her back toward the gates. "We've got to go. Findoor Castle is ours, but the war is far from over."

"Indeed, you are right. Where are we going?"

"To the eastern Findoor border, to join everyone else. Gather up your troops."

Malia, Seth and Ceridan rounded up every soldier they could and gathered them just outside the front gates of Findoor Castle. Seth focused his mind on drawing raw magical energy and fed it into a transport spell that bloomed above him and covered the small army with a white dome. When it collapsed, the Findoor militia was gone, and the castle's citizens were left to their celebration.

5

Blue crystal lined the walls and floor of the cave that led into Morganath's lair. He was settling on top of a large pile of gold and gems when Seth appeared in the crystal chamber. Despite the intrusion, Morganath got himself comfortable and laid his head down to sleep.

"Not yet, my friend," Seth said.

There was a rumble from the dragon, but nothing more.

"You can't ignore this any more than I can."

"I am tired," Morganath said in a deep rumble of a voice.

"Me too. But we're needed. All of Galadir is needed. If we don't all show up, Grian will take Ducain's Keep, and this world will be lost," Seth said, almost pleading.

Morganath growled and shifted his weight, slid down the pile of gold, planted a foot on an adjacent pile, and got himself comfortable again. "You're meddling with time again," Morganath said. "You know what happened last time."

"I know. But this time I know what I'm doing."

"Are you sure you fully understand the consequences of your actions?"

"I do," Seth said. He looked at Morganath carefully, who now had one eye open, and was watching him, though he feigned disinterest. "You knew, didn't you?"

"Knew what?" The great gold dragon lifted his head now and opened both eyes.

"You knew who I was the moment you saw me, didn't you?"

"Yes," Morganath said. "I knew you were the only one who could cross the barrier. I also knew your father, though his name is lost to me."

"Why didn't you tell me?"

"Would it have made a difference?" Morganath asked. He lifted his great weight up off the pile of gold and took a step toward the entryway.

"I suppose not. I probably wouldn't have believed you anyway."

"The time wasn't right. Now it is, but you appear to have figured it out on your own."

"Are you coming, or what?"

"What if I don't? Have you looked forward to see what the outcome is either way?"

"No. But if you don't come, we'll be one dragon short of a battle, and that would never do."

"I suppose not," Morganath said, with a slight note of humor to his voice.

The great gold dragon walked toward the ledge where Seth stood and placed his neck where Seth could climb on. Once Seth was seated, he said, "Okay, let's go. We've got a wizard to stop."

Seth braced himself as Morganath launched into the air with one great leap and a down stroke of his wings. The thrill of the coming battle was getting Seth's adrenaline rushing in a way he had never felt before. He felt in control, and on top of it. He had a plan, and like a great living chess game, all his pieces were almost in place. He had one last stop to make, but needed to get Morganath in position first.

The pair flew to the back entrance, the one only Morganath could enter through, and escaped into the sunlight. Seth smiled to himself as he leaned forward and said, "Have you ever teleported before?"

There was a rumble underneath him as Morganath let out a growl. "No. I hear it's unpleasant."

"It's the only way to get where we're going."

"Well then, get it over with," Morganath said.

Seth focused on his destination, but held off for a moment. "Be ready to fight. When we emerge, the battle will have already begun."

Without waiting for a response, Seth let his magic flow, surrounding himself and Morganath, and teleporting them away from Caldoor. When they appeared above the eastern Findoor border, soldiers were already engaged with hordes of undead below them. Morganath turned to swoop down on them when Seth disappeared once more, leaving the gold dragon to carry on the battle without him.

# Chapter 33 - The Battle for Ducain's Keep

Serrin led what wizards remained to the eastern Findoor border where they could head off Grian and his army before they crossed into Arvok. His meager defense consisted of no more than a hundred wizards and a small contingent of soldiers to support them. Even some of the more experienced wizards abandoned Ducain's Keep upon hearing their plight, choosing to head south to Astara where they would find solace and resources to continue their research. They had no interest in battle.

Even with this small army, Serrin was thinking up strategies that could give them an edge over Grian. He spoke to the rest of the council as they marched toward the border, trying to keep his voice down so that the others wouldn't hear how distressed he really was. "I can try to keep any wraiths under control, but given the resources Grian has, it's probably all I'll be able to do to keep up with them. Red and white wizards should spread out and take out as many of the defiled as they can. Blue wizards support them with defense and healing spells. Green, gray, black and yellow wizards should support them, and try to carve a path to Grian. Do not engage him directly though. I think our best chance is to attack him from all sides, all at once."

"And if he proves too powerful?" Trysk asked. "Are you ready to give up your life for Ducain's Keep?"

Serrin narrowed his eyes at Trysk, wondering what he was getting at. "I'm ready to give up my life for Galadir. I expect the same from all of you, and everyone here today. The reality is, we're outnumbered, probably out-powered, and some or all of us may not make it through the battle."

"We wouldn't be in such a dire situation if your son had not abandoned us," Trysk said. "He could make quick work of Grian."

"My son is probably wiser than all of us combined, and he's right. Galadir must learn to fight their own battles, without leaning on Seth like a crutch. Are we ready? We're almost at the border."

He looked ahead and saw a black army in the distance moving toward them over the rocky terrain. The area would be smooth plains if it weren't for all the rock that penetrated the surface of the earth. Trees grew short and twisted in what little soil they could find, many of them bearing fruit still, though it was late in the season. The air seemed to chill as Serrin and his army drew closer. He noticed Nadya shiver as they walked and asked, "Are you well enough to do battle, Nadya?"

"Yes, I'm fine," She said, putting on a strong demeanor. "Besides, I owe Grian one."

Serrin caught Gladius giving Nadya a look of admiration as she spoke, but it faded when he saw Serrin looking at him. "Good. I don't expect Grian to follow any sort of battle etiquette."

No sooner had the words escaped his mouth, he heard screams coming from the ends of his lines. The power of air came to him and lifted him up to see what was happening. Each end of their lines were being consumed by clouds of black, non-corporeal creatures. "Wraiths," he said, and flew as quickly as he could to the south end of the army. "White wizards, wraiths to the north," he shouted as he moved.

Five wizards had paid with their lives before Serrin reached the wraiths, and two more died as Serrin launched a powerful ball of white light at them, blasting them away from the army and allowing his wizards time to regroup. There were at least twenty of the hideous creatures shrouded in black smoky robes that trailed away from their bodies. Their facial features were contorted into permanent screams, and they attacked without mercy, moving toward the nearest living things they could lay their hands on.

Serrin called on the power of life once more and sent beams of light down in an area that overlapped both his troops and the wraiths. The beams were harmless to living creatures, and would feel like warm rays of sunlight, but the wraiths were pierced and torn apart by the energy of the spell. Several wizards raised shields of white light before them as more wraiths approached, and Serrin sent another wave of light down at them, destroying all but a few.

There were still screams and shouts coming from the north end of the line, and the white wizards had the south end under control, so Serrin turned around and sped through the air. Attowen was running as fast as his old legs could carry him over the shrubs and rocks that littered the ground. Each time he passed a white wizard, he beckoned them to follow. Fire could be seen going off in bursts at the north end but it was having little effect on the formless creatures.

Serrin dug deep into his reserves and focused white energy into a wall that would separate the largest portion of the remaining wraiths from the wizard army. It erupted from the ground, destroying several wraiths, and causing the rest to shudder and drift away from the shimmering light. Attowen reached the wall and had his wizards launch a volley of white magic spears through the wall at the wraiths. Each time a spear struck one, it let out a horrid screech and dissolved into black mist that withered away into nothing.

The wraiths simply acted as a distraction though, as Serrin realized the remainder of Grian's army was approaching faster than they had expected.

"Regroup," he shouted out over his army. "Ready your spells."

While white wizards dealt with the rest of the wraiths, red wizards approached the front. Serrin also called on what red magic he could muster and prepared to cast. The black army was more massive than Serrin could have imagined, with at least ten thousand strong. His heart sank as he looked down at his meager army.

At the back of the black army was a figure clad in black armor on top of a great war horse. He didn't parade around or wave banners. He didn't shout orders. The black army appeared to know when and where to strike without any orders at all. Instead, the figure on the horse stared straight at Serrin, and he could feel the intense gaze boring through his flesh and into his soul. It was the stare of one who held such immense hatred for another that they would do anything to rid themselves of that person. There was malice in the eyes of his adversary, and Serrin knew that this may very well be the end.

Light blazed at each end of the wizard's line, destroying the last of the wraiths, but they had done their job. Those wizards at the ends of the lines were now skittish and afraid. It also left a large gap at the center of the line with no white magic to reinforce the rest of the wizards. Blue and black wizards were trying to take their place, but they would offer little protection against Grian's defiled soldiers who marched on in silence.

There were no battle cries. The dark army marched forward with the gentle patience of a wave on the ocean, ready to sweep away the wizards who were nothing more than a few grains of sand. With fifty paces between the front lines, Serrin shouted out, "Attack! Incinerate the dark army!"

He let his own spell loose, sending dozens of charged sparks out into the black wave coming toward them. The sparks landed among them and exploded in great balls of fire that consumed everything they touched, and left holes in the army. He readied a second volley as his wizards cast their spells below him.

Waves of fire erupted from the front lines, but of the hundred or so wizards who remained to fight the battle, only fifteen were red wizards, and few others could cast spells of fire. The blaze they created covered no more than a third of the enemy lines, and left many holes for them to shamble through.

The slow wave of defiled soldiers did just that, moving without a word around the blazes and regrouping on the other end. The figure on the warhorse didn't say a word, yet there was a strategy to his attack, and his soldiers moved with the same deadly accuracy as a well-trained army. Serrin launched a second, smaller volley of fire into the army, but couldn't stop them all.

"We need a wall. Form a wall, everyone, in any way you can," Serrin called to his wizards below.

The wizard lines faltered as the dark army drew closer. Less than twenty paces separated them, and some of the lesser casters were already exhausted. The council wizards were focusing on their own spells, and needed time to complete them.

Serrin called on his last reserves, bringing forth a great wall of fire that spread across the enemy lines as far as Serrin could reach. He managed to block their advance momentarily, but the wall still didn't cover the entire front line, and he wasn't sure how long he could hold it up. He lowered himself to the ground, and put everything he had into maintaining and extending the wall. Other casters were coming on now, launching spells of all types into the enemy, but they had barely made a dent in Grian's onslaught.

Several wizards fell from exhaustion, and blue wizards rushed to help them, casting healing spells. The rest of the council wizards were nearby, casting some kind of cooperative spell, and were almost complete, but the dark army approached from both sides now, working their way around Serrin's wall of fire. Several smaller walls appeared on the battlefield, raised to slow down or deter Grian's army.

"There's too many of them," Serrin said to Gladius, the nearest of the council wizards. "We have to fall back."

Gladius gave him a look, but didn't lose track of the spell they were casting. He finished his part, and took a step back. Moments later, the rest of them finished theirs, leaving a glowing, multi-colored egg sitting on the battlefield where their magic had converged.

"We need fire and time to finish this," Gladius said. "Care to have the honor?" His casual approach to the battle left Serrin worried about their fate. Gladius was always a wild card to him, and though Seth may have forgiven him and believed that he had changed, Serrin felt no such thing.

"Very well," Serrin said. He allowed his wall of fire to burn on its own, and focused his energy into the egg, calling on fire and time. The egg was hungry for it, and took hold the moment he engaged it. It lapped up all the energy Serrin could give it and hungered for more. When he had nothing left to give, cracks formed on the surface of it.

"Back off," Gladius said, spreading his arms and pushing his colleagues back.

The cracks spread down the shell of the egg and created a network of fissures that glowed in all colors. The first shards of the shell fell away, and the council wizards all backed up further. Serrin did the same, and watched as a small dragon formed of pure light emerged from the egg and grew. Its wings spread, and it launched itself into the air, growing to the size of a fully grown dragon in seconds.

Gouts of fire shot from its mouth, and a wake of ice fell from it, spreading across the dark army and either freezing or burning them. Its hide was formed of interlocking crystal plates, and it drifted on the wind as agile as a hummingbird, able to stop, hover and turn in the air. It glowed with the power of life, shining down on the battlefield, and attacked with the ferocity of a seasoned warrior with a heart of darkness. Hundreds of the defiled troops were destroyed with each pass across the army, and for the first time, hope filled Serrin's heart, as the dark army faltered.

"Regroup," Serrin said. "Ready your spells."

5

Grian watched the dragon formed of pure magical energy launch into the air. It was the first true display of power he had seen thus far, and looked upon it with admiration. "So, the new council does have some tricks up their sleeves," he said. With a mental command, he ordered his troops to spread out, to reduce the effectiveness of the dragon's attacks. Hundreds of his soldiers were being destroyed because they were crowded together.

The army of soldiers before him were the drones. The distraction as he worked his magic and brought forth the real power. He didn't really care whether they succeeded in destroying the meager defense the council put up. He knew his next attack would finish all but the Time Weaver. With a motion of his hand, he brought forward a small group that had been hidden behind him. "Wait for my signal. When the time is right, wipe them out. That dragon of theirs is an interesting trick, but I can take care of that."

The nearest figure to him spoke in a hollow voice. "Yes, my lord."

Grian urged his horse forward a few steps. It moved with care over the uneven terrain, and had always been a little nervous around the undead creatures, but it responded well, and had been loyal to him despite the beast's obvious fears.

He summoned the power of death within him and projected it into a black spear as he spoke. "Infuscas consceleratai," he said, and launched the spear into the air. It flew without error, striking the crystal dragon in the chest and piercing its black heart. The darkness grew inside of it, and its attacks stopped. Blackness oozed from between its scales and dripped from it. Its wings dissolved, and the power that drove it came unbound. The dragon fell from the sky into Grian's own army and landed with a splash as the rest of its body turned into a black liquid that burst out in every direction.

There was a moment of silence on the battlefield, and Grian imagined the panic the wizards must feel as their greatest spell was defeated so easily. It fueled him and brought a smile to his face. "Go," he said to the hooded figures behind him. "Finish this nonsense so I can claim my library."

Eight of the black hooded figures swept forward, leaving a smoky trail through the crowd of undead. Grian watched as they descended on the position of the seven council members and smiled to himself. "Say goodbye, foolish wizards."

ƪ

The Wizard High Council led the charge against the dwindling forces of the dark army, but as the crystal dragon fell from the sky, Serrin's heart fell as well. More of the wizards were becoming exhausted, and it was getting harder to keep the defiled army at bay. He stopped for a moment and looked around, surveying the battlefield. They had managed to cut Grian's army in half, but racing up through the middle of it were eight dark forms that almost resembled men.

"Ready yourselves," Serrin said. "We've got company."

The words had just left his mouth when he heard Trysk's voice behind him, "Restringuntas."

Attowen, Merisill, Kenda, Nadya and Gladius were all struck by a black bolt from him and fell over, paralyzed. "Trysk," Serrin yelled, and spun to see the black wizard readying another spell. "What are you doing?"

"Taking the winning side," Trysk said. "This battle is done. You've failed, Time Weaver. I've been promised a very lucrative position in Grian's army for what I do today. For ensuring that he wins today, I'll be by his side, learning what he learns, and gaining the power I could have only dreamed of otherwise."

"You're insane," Serrin said. Fear gripped his heart as he saw the eight shadow forms rush into the wizard lines. The first one struck a white wizard, wrapping around the man's body and filling his lungs with the black smoke that trailed it. The wizard's flesh turned black as he let out a strangled scream, that was only cut off when his body fell to dust and his robe settled over the ashes. The shade moved on, killing other wizards in the same fashion, as did the other seven. Their lines faltered, and their numbers dwindled fast as the wizards tried to find a way to defend against such powerful foes.

Serrin snapped his gaze toward Trysk and stared him down with hate in his eyes. "You'll pay for this."

Without warning, both men launched spells at each other. Serrin's was a blast of fire, and Trysk's was a dark ball of energy. The two spells met in between them and exploded in a white hot blaze that sent both men flying backward. Serrin lifted himself up in time to see Merisill's body crumble into black dust. His reflexes took over, and he launched a burst of energy infused with life in a circle out from him. The energy flowed away from him, consuming all the dark energy in the area, and destroying one of the shades in the process. Another shade rushed in and consumed Kenda before he could ready another spell. Her robes settled flat to the ground as the shade rose up to take its next target. Serrin tried to draw energy to him, but was too exhausted, and the magic wouldn't come to him.

There was a sound behind him as Trysk got himself up, but it wasn't what Serrin expected. Trysk let out a startled gasp that made Serrin turn to see what was going on. Lodged in his shoulder was a gleaming arrow that burned his flesh around the wound. Trysk screamed and grasped at the shaft of the arrow, trying to get it out of his shoulder.

Serrin looked up in time to see hundreds of other arrows streaking through the air, piercing the shades and other defiled soldiers and destroying them. Winged creatures of light soared toward him, firing volley after volley of arrows and decimating the front lines of Grian's troops. "The Fioraden," Serrin shouted. "The Fioraden have come to help us. Wizards, fall back and regroup."

He turned to run, and intended to grab Trysk, but the black wizard was nowhere to be found. More fear raced through him, now that he knew how dangerous the black wizard could be and who his loyalties belonged to. He took one more look before he ran to where the rest of the wizards were regrouping, and thought he saw Seth in the sky with the bird creatures. One blink, and the vision was gone. He directed several wizards to help with the remaining paralyzed council members, and ran.

5

The shades had done their job in part, but Grian wasn't happy that some of the wizards remained, and now the Fioraden had joined the battle and were laying waste to his army. He was about to start casting spells when a rumbling sound grew from the south. He looked to see what it might be and saw nothing but a great cloud of dust rushing to the battlefield faster than any human army could run.

"No," Grian said. "It can't be."

As the cloud grew closer, he saw a great army of Narshuks being led by two figures. One was taller than a man, but smaller than a Narshuk, and he knew who it was right away. The other was man-sized, and wore no armor or carried any weapons that he could see. There was a small flash that made him blink, and the man who ran with them was gone. The Narshuks engaged the undead army and tore them to shreds without stopping. The massacre of his troops was more than he could take, and he dismounted his warhorse, walking out onto the battlefield.

"Attack," Grian shouted. "Kill them all."

From behind him, a small army of animated Narshuks advanced, shambling forward. The edge of them engaged the live Narshuk army and the two began tearing at each other with their massive claws. Blood flowed out onto the battlefield as some Narshuks fell to the massive undead beasts. The Fioraden were now swooping down out of the sky, throwing spears and attacking with their swords of light. Grian raised his hands into the air and combined the power of wind, earth and death. Focusing his power through his gauntlets, he let loose a whirlwind onto the battlefield that carried with it black thorns that pierced the Fioraden flesh and armor, bringing a number of them down. The spell moved as Grian willed it, chasing down groups of the winged soldiers and shredding them into clouds of meat and feathers. Blood rained down on the field, and Grian laughed.

He looked to the south where his old commander, Scrag, and the army of Narshuks were tearing apart his undead creatures. Fire and earth came to him and combined in a spell that he unleashed toward them. He lifted one foot and stomped down, sending a shock wave through the ground that built as it traveled and turned into a wave of molten rock. The wave crashed into the Narshuk army, killing some, but many more leaped into the air and cleared the wave. Scrag was amongst them, and despite his old age, ran straight for Grian.

෨

The Narshuks were another pleasant surprise for Serrin. He and his wizards regrouped to the east of the battlefield and none of them had expected Narshuks to show up. Gladius, who had regained mobility, was more surprised than any of them. "I saw their camp. I saw the piles of burnt bodies. They were all gone."

Serrin motioned out to the field, at the Narshuks who were still engaged in battle, and said, "I'm not saying you're wrong, but there they are, fighting for us. Let's thank the gods, and get this battle over with."

"Where are Merisill and Kenda?" Attowen asked.

"Slain. The shades took them," Serrin said, almost choking on his words. "There was nothing I could do. That wretch Trysk is working for Grian. We've been betrayed, but there are still twenty or thirty of us, and now we have two armies backing us up. It's time to confront Grian."

There was a sound, like air rushing away from a position to Serrin's left, and then a familiar voice. "Not yet." Serrin looked to see Seth standing beside him. The rest of the wizards jumped when they saw him. "Wait, just a minute or two more."

Seth motioned to the battlefield, and Serrin looked in time to see Morganath appear in the sky above the battlefield, with Seth on the great gold dragon's neck. "Seth?" Serrin said, and turned to see Seth standing beside him with a grin on his face. When he looked back at Morganath, the other Seth was gone, and Morganath was blasting away at more undead soldiers. Off to the west, where Grian had just come from, a white dome appeared and melted away, revealing more soldiers bearing the Findoor banner. "By the gods," Serrin said, "how have you done this?"

"Just wait for it," Seth said, nodding toward the battlefield.

There was another rush of air next to them, and three more people appeared. Cedric, Catrina and Seth again. Seth disappeared almost immediately, but Cedric and Catrina looked around confused. The sight of Catrina took Serrin's breath away. "My love," he said, and took a step toward her. His heart skipped a beat as their eyes met and he had to force himself not to rush things. She looked younger than he remembered. There was no gray in her hair, and the light in her eyes that he had fallen in love with was back.

"Serrin," she said, though no other words would come.

"I don't know what to say," Serrin said, looking between Seth and Catrina.

"I do," Cedric interjected. "We finish this. Now."

Both Catrina and Serrin looked at Cedric, who was grinning from ear to ear. "Have you no decency?" Catrina said in a mock-offended tone. "It's been twenty-five years since I've seen my love."

"I don't understand," Serrin said. "It's only been weeks for me. How do you look so young if it's been that long?"

"You have our son to thank for that," She said.

"It's time," Seth said, interrupting their reunion. "Now or never, we need to finish this."

## Chapter 34 – A New Betrayer

Tyriel stood guard over the front entrance of Ducain's Keep. His combat skills made him the perfect person to lead the last line of defense. He waited patiently with his scythe drawn for any kind of signal that the battle was won or lost. Several other soldiers around him had long since sat down and pulled out carved stones to play an old soldier's game. They were betting copper pieces, and the youngest of the soldiers was being cleaned out by the others, despite his constant complaints. Tyriel smiled to himself and wondered why he continued to play if he was going to complain about losing.

A crackling sound at the front gate caught his attention. He looked in time to see a black wizard emerge from a small rift and walk toward him on the path. "Ready yourselves," Tyriel called to the soldiers who were so engrossed in their game that they hadn't noticed the black wizard walking their way. They were on their feet in an instant with their swords drawn and ready.

The black wizard pulled his hood back as he approached, and Tyriel breathed a sigh of relief when he saw Trysk's face. "Thank the fates it's only you," Tyriel said. "I thought for a moment it was Grian, and we had lost."

Trysk didn't slow down as he approached, but instead said, "We have lost. It's all over." He raised his hands and shouted, "Obitas nexasa mortai."

Bolts of energy flew from his fingers and struck each of the soldiers and Tyriel in the chest. The soldiers all fell to the ground, dead, but Tyriel felt the magic surround him and try to rend his soul in two. His will was stronger than those around him, and he resisted, though it caused him great pain.

"What are you doing?" he shouted out at Trysk as the wizard prepared another spell. He looked surprised that Tyriel was still standing, but it didn't stop his attacks.

"What nobody else on the council had the strength to do. I'm making way for our new lord and master and if you don't step aside, you'll end up like the rest of your friends here."

Tyriel readied his scythe. "I can't allow this," he said. "You're supposed to be one of us."

"Yeah, well, forgive me for wanting to be on the winning side." Trysk was ten paces away, and still talking as he approached. "All we've done is sit around and talk about what a horrible thing Grian is doing, and how awful it is that he took Findoor, but you know what? I commend him. I commend him on accomplishing a task worthy of the Hall of Heroes. He's achieved more than any of us could have dreamed, and in such a short time. He's worthy of our praise and admiration."

"What about all the people he's killed? All those families who have been torn apart by his ambitions? Does it not matter to you that the moment you outlive your usefulness to him, he will cast you aside? That's what he's done with everyone around him. He won't hesitate to do that with you once you've accomplished what he set out for you to do."

Trysk stopped in front of Tyriel, staring at him eye-to-eye. "We'll see," Trysk said, and shoved his fist toward Tyriel's body.

The motion was faster than Tyriel had expected. He felt the tip of the blade pierce his robe and press against his skin when his physical form vaporized into black smoke, leaving Trysk stumbling forward. Tyriel acted on instinct and whirled with his blade, slashing through Trysk's arm at the wrist. The black wizard's hand fell to the ground, the dagger he held clattering over the stonework. Blood ran from the severed stump left behind, and Trysk screamed as he lifted his arm before him.

Tyriel pulled back his scythe and shook his head. "Do you know why people don't fight death?" he asked, taking a step forward. Trysk backed away from him with terror in his eyes and bumped into the door behind him. "Because you can't win."

He swung the scythe, the motion so natural for him that it was effortless. The tip of the weapon entered Trysk's neck just below his ear, and continued through to the other side, cutting his throat, trachea, and major arteries all at once. Trysk gurgled something as the blood welled up and poured from the mortal wound, and fell to his knees. His remaining hand and his stump grasped at his throat, and he slumped over, spilling blood over the front path of Ducain's Keep. His eyes closed, but he had a smile on his face.

Tyriel's form returned to its solid state, and he stood over the body of the dead wizard. "I'm sorry it had to come to this."

# Chapter 35 – The Last Stand

Malia stood precisely where Grian had stood moments before. She watched the carnage before her, with defiled soldiers being destroyed by the hundreds, and Fioraden and Narshuks fighting together as one unified army. In the center of it all was Grian. An imposing figure shrouded in black robes who launched magic from his fingers like it was a child's game. The black helmet and gauntlets were the only sign that he was armored under his robes, and explained his bulk. She had seen him a number of times while she studied under Merek, and couldn't remember him ever being that big or frightening. The sight of him now struck fear into her heart. This was the man who had stolen her kingdom and laid waste to much of her army. Now was the time to be angry, not afraid.

But Seth was gone again, saying something about other places to be, and she couldn't convince him to stay by her side. For this battle, she would have to rely on the people of her world. The scene before her proved that she was not alone.

"Jax, Ceridan, stay by my sides. Have the rest of the army fan out behind us. We'll sweep the field and destroy anything in our path. Keep the line tight, so we don't miss anything. This will be the last stand of Grian's army of the dead."

"Agreed," Ceridan said.

"My blades are ready for you, General," Jax said, drawing both of his longswords and twirling them once in his hands to limber up his wrists. Malia was still amazed at how natural swords looked when Jax swung them, like extensions of his own arms.

She was about to give the order to attack, when she saw the smaller Narshuk at the front of his lines raise his hand to stop the rest. All the Narshuks bowed low and puffed out their chests, taking in great breaths, and then stood tall as they howled in unison. The sound penetrated the ground, shaking it beneath Malia's feet, and hurt her ears. The effect was more devastating to the defiled soldiers though. In a great wave before them, defiled soldiers disintegrated from the vibration. Fioraden launched themselves into the air to avoid the effect, and Grian raised his arm over his face in an apparent reflex.

When the dust started to settle, Malia saw the lead Narshuk, the one who was smaller than the rest, bolting forward toward Grian.

"Go. Now. Attack," She shouted and drew the black steel sword. Without a backward glance, Malia broke into a run toward Grian. Her sword burst into flames, its hunger fueling her. All she could see was her target, and the Narshuk who was closing in on him as well.

5

After the Narshuks devastating attack, Seth broke into a run and held out his hand. His sword of pure light appeared, sending energy flowing over his body and encasing him in crystal armor. He ran straight for Grian, who had several other attackers closing in on him. There were steps behind him, but he paid little attention to them. Grian was out in the open and within reach.

Above him, Morganath swooped to lay down another line of flames. As he approached Grian's position, Seth watched in horror as the dark wizard reached into the sky and fired a ball of black energy at the golden dragon. The ball struck Morganath in the chest and burst over his hide like a large balloon filled with liquid. It spread over his scales and smoked, causing Morganath to scream with pain and rage. The roar shook the air around Seth, and prompted him to take action.

He focused on Morganath's neck, and called on the power of time and space to take him there. The trip was short, and poorly aimed. He was above Morganath and falling, but the dragon was as well. The black sludge spread across his hide, devouring the dragon alive. Seth let himself fall, calling on the power of water to try and stop Grian's terrible spell. Morganath twisted and clawed at the magic, but it stuck to his claws and wings and only devoured him faster.

Seth used the power of air to accelerate his fall into Morganath and placed his hands on the golden dragon's back. The blue energy flowed into the great dragon, but it was too late, and Seth knew it. He halted his own fall seconds before Morganath slammed into the ground, sending dirt and rocks flying in every direction. Morganath continued to fight the black ooze that consumed him, but it was no use. Seth could see his strength fading fast. He landed in front of Morganath and placed a hand on the dragon's face, with tears welling up in his eyes.

"I can't let you die," Seth said.

Morganath stopped moving. One of his eyes had already been destroyed by the black ooze, but his other looked at Seth. "It's my time." His voice was weak and his breath wheezed in and out. Bones in both of his front legs had shattered when he landed and were bent in awkward ways beneath the dragon's weight. His wings hung limp to either side of him. "Defeat Grian. That's your job."

"I don't know if I can without you. I needed everyone," Seth said. His tears now flowed down his cheeks. The light of his sword dimmed, revealing white steel beneath it. "I needed you."

"I'm glad to have known you, Krycin," Morganath said. His head relaxed against the ground and his body went limp. Seth fell to his knees as the life drained from the great gold dragon.

The sounds of battle continued behind him, but they sounded distant. Slow. Seth focused the power of fire into his hand and let it flow into Morganath. The power ignited within the dragon and consumed his body in seconds, leaving nothing but dust and robbing Grian of a powerful ally.

Seth remained kneeling on the ground as the ashes were taken away on the wind. A cool breeze swept across the battlefield as though the gods themselves had willed it. Morganath's ashes were carried into the west and scattered across all of Findoor.

A voice cut through the grief, one inside Seth's head.

*Young Lyecian, we need you now.* It was the voice of Ferrion, the lord of the Fioraden, and Ferron's grandson. Seth had convinced them to join the battle, and promised that he would support them, but it meant little to him now. *Please,* Ferrion said.

Seth looked up and saw the Fioraden struggling with something else Grian had summoned up. A great black beast made of bits of bone and flesh that had come together in a grotesque humanoid form. It hammered the flying warriors out of the air two or three at a time and didn't appear to care about the constant stream of attacks assaulting it. Every step it took toward the main Fioraden forces drew in more flesh, more bodies, and made it stronger.

*I'm coming,* Seth thought, and stood up. His sword came to life again, shining light out over the field, and Seth took to the air once more toward the beast. He reached the creature and plunged his sword in, carving a great hole in what would be the beast's neck, and as he did, he heard a great roar from behind him, in the direction of Grian.

5

Scrag ran at Grian with all the strength and speed his ancient body would allow. The adrenaline of the battle stole away the aches and pains of his age and made him feel young again. Power surged through him as his feet hit the ground with each step. The only thing he could see was Grian, who still had his arm over his face.

There was a split-second after Grian lowered his arm that Scrag could see the wizard's dark eyes through the slit in the visor of his helm. There was darkness, and power, but nothing like the hate that Scrag had in his. There was also fear. Scrag could smell the fear.

He plowed into Grian at a full charge, latching his powerful claws around Grian's neck and squeezing. The force took Grian off his feet and Scrag lifted him into the air. With his other hand, he swung at Grian's head and knocked the helmet off, revealing Grian's black hair and pale skin. He was so close now, one more hit and this would be done.

Something struck Scrag in the throat, just to the left of his trachea. He felt a blade slice through a vital artery there and his blood flowed. A glance down revealed Grian's booted foot with a blade in the tip of the toe. It was red with blood, and realization hit him. He was finished, but he wasn't going to let Grian have the last laugh.

Scrag looked up at Grian's face to see a smile already spreading. He pounded his fist into Grian's face and sent the wizard flying backwards. Grian rolled across the ground and rose to his feet as easy as any trained warrior could. His face healed, leaving only traces of blood that Scrag had drawn. A step forward brought him into striking range again, and he thrust his fist at Grian's chest, slamming it into the wizard and sending him flying back again.

Dizziness overwhelmed Scrag as blood flowed freely from the hole in his neck, but he continued his pursuit, grabbing Grian by the robes and hauling him to his feet, only to slam his other fist into the dark wizard once again. The black robes gave out and tore away, revealing the armor Grian wore beneath them. Black plate armor protected him. Threads of every color of magic were embedded in the armor and glowed now as Grian summoned magical energy.

"I didn't want to do this to you," Grian said as he approached. Scrag dropped to one knee, the loss of blood robbing him of his strength. "You leave me little choice. Go to sleep now, old friend, and don't ever return."

Grian pressed a hand against Scrag's chest and forced magical energy into the ancient Narshuk's body. Scrag's eyes opened wide and he let out a roar as every nerve in his body lit up in pain. Still, he held onto consciousness, and lashed out once more, striking Grian again in the chest plate and knocking him back.

Scrag fell to the ground, the last of his strength escaping him. He found peace as the cold fingers of death gripped his heart. "Grishtor take you," Scrag said with his last breath, when Grian walked back into view.

"Not today, my old friend. Not today."

꙳

Serrin led the charge from the east with Catrina by his side. Gladius, Cedric, and Nadya followed close behind him. Attowen remained behind to tend to the wounded while they made a last ditch effort to finish the battle once and for all. "We have to strike him together. He may be able to fend off one or two of us, but Malia is approaching fast, and if we don't help her, Grian will make quick work of her."

"Focus on what you're good at," Gladius said. "Use fast, intense attack spells. Don't give him a chance to hit you. Grian can take you out with a single spell."

When Morganath hit the ground, all of the wizards stopped in their tracks and stared. Cedric took a few steps forward and paused. Serrin heard a gasp come from him and knew the sight struck more than just a single nerve. "Grishtor forgive me," Cedric said, taking a few more steps forward.

"Cedric, no," Serrin shouted as the bard walked forward. His words fell on deaf ears.

Cedric lifted a hand to his face and grasped the bottom of his mask. With one smooth motion, he lifted it and tossed it aside. The action startled Serrin and all the others looking on, but before they had the chance to see his face, Cedric doubled over and cried out. His hands hit the ground and he lowered his head, his body writhing and growing before their eyes. His black cloak took on a life of its own and formed into wings and he stepped forward on hands and feet that grew claws. Cedric's neck extended and his flesh turned black and scaly. Seconds later, his size had grown to that of Morganath, and before them was a great black dragon. It let out a roar that shook the air and got Grian's attention.

To the north, there was a great explosion of light as something Grian had summoned exploded, and a cheer rose from the Fioraden in their scratchy, high pitched voices that they seldom used. Serrin flashed a smile at Catrina and nodded. "Now, my love. Now is our chance."

The black dragon that was once Cedric launched itself into the air toward Grian. Rage radiated from the beast, so much so that it startled Grian, taking him off guard. Catrina disappeared and reappeared at the far side of Grian. She launched a ball of fire at the wizard that sent him flying toward the black dragon. At the sudden movement, the black dragon let out another roar and sent a stream of yellow fluid flying at Grian, drenching him in it and prompting screams from the wizard – the first of the battle.

"Go, now. Attack," Serrin said to the others. "Hit him with everything you've got."

As Serrin ran toward the dark wizard, the screams he heard turned into laughter. Smoke rose from Grian's head as the dragon's breath burned away his flesh, but as fast as it could burn away, more skin grew. Grian laughed and turned in a circle to see all the people descending on his position.

"It's no use," Grian said. "You've already lost."

Serrin called on his magic, forming it into a ball of fire and launched it at Grian. It struck the dark wizard and deflected around his armor. It was like hitting him with a small gust of wind that broke around him. Gladius struck him with a ball of ice that shattered on his shoulder. Nadya sent a shower of stones flying at him that bounced off his armor, but did nothing. Catrina blasted him again from behind this time, but her magic was as useless as everyone else's.

With a glance to Gladius, Serrin tried to figure out what to do. Gladius's face held confusion as well, and told him there were no easy answers. "Keep hitting him," Serrin said. "Wear him down."

"That's right," Grian said, laughing. "Wear yourselves down. Exhaust yourselves. It will make it that much sweeter when I kill you."

5

Malia ran toward Grian as fast as she could. The boots pounding the ground behind her told her she was not alone, but she had no intention of stopping. Even at the sight of the black dragon, her heart was too filled with rage to give it any notice. The black steel sword pulsed with the energy that she fed it as she ran – the power of fire that she would use to cleave through his armor and destroy him.

His back was to her when she reached him, and she swung her sword. The built up energy let go, and blasted Grian with flames as the blade struck his shoulder. It was a glancing blow, and did little to the wizard, but left a large gouge in the shoulder of the armor.

"Blast you," Grian said as he spun to meet her. "Ah, Malia. Come to be my bride?"

She didn't wait for him to continue. Malia focused all her strength into a second swing, arcing her sword out to the side and charging the blade. It struck Grian's left arm, slicing through the armor at the wrist, and severing his hand. The hand and gauntlet fell to the ground with a thud, and Grian screamed while cradling the wound. Again his screams turned to laughter though, as the hand regrew in an instant, though the gauntlet was now on the ground.

"Fools. No wizard alive can defeat me," Grian said through his laughter.

The battlefield grew quiet except for the steps of the soldiers behind her. Malia spared a glance and saw Jax approaching, then returned her gaze to Grian. "Perhaps you are right: No wizard can defeat you. But how about a blade slinger? Jax," Malia shouted, but he had arrived beside her already. "Disarm him. Leave him bare, for all the world to see."

The corner of Jax's mouth rose in a slight smile, and he twirled his blades once. "Gladly."

Jax advanced on Grian and whirled his blades, letting the tips of his blades strike Grian's armor. The dark wizard laughed at the display. "What's this? Ordinary blades? No magic?"

There was a strange sound as one of Jax's blades caught something under a plate in Grian's armor. "My blades are my magic."

The graceful warrior launched into a series of attacks that all seemed superficial, each one striking a different part of Grian's body. The wizard tried to protest, and move, but each time he did, Jax would swing a blade near his head and stop him. Malia watched as Jax circled the wizard, hitting him with attack after attack in a whirling storm of swords. The sounds of metal on metal rang out in the air, and Grian laughed at first, but as the attacks continued, the smile left Grian's face. Jax stopped in front of him, his blades motionless, and somebody sent a ball of fire at Grian. It struck, and blasted away the armor from Grian's left arm.

Panic washed over Grian's face as he realized what had happened. More attacks hit him, each one taking a piece of his armor with it. Every element flew from people in a circle around him, and when a great ball of light struck him in the chest and blasted away the chest plate, Malia was the one who smiled.

$$5$$

Seth landed beside Malia so that both of them were standing before the dark wizard who was now kneeling on the ground with pieces of his armor everywhere. The Narshuk and Fioraden armies surrounded the circle of friends who were all there for a singular purpose. Findoor troops stood behind the pair with Ceridan leading them. The black dragon took a step forward, raised a clawed foot, and slammed it into Grian, knocking him to the ground.

There was a moment of silence before Grian groaned and lifted his head. Seth looked down and met his gaze, and saw nothing but hate. "I'll kill you," Grian said, rising up off the ground and lifting his hands toward Seth. The others moved as though they would intervene, but Seth raised a hand to stop them.

"You can't hurt me," Seth said. "You never could."

Grian stood up and shouted, "Adigas Poenai." As he did, he waved his hand at Seth, sending a ball of black energy toward him. Seth stood his ground and infused his crystal armor with the power of life. The spell deflected off his armor and flew into the sky, dissipating into the breeze.

The dark wizard scowled at Seth and launched another spell, yelling the words. "Impuleras."

Again, the spell deflected off Seth's armor, causing no harm.

"Depellendas. Restringuntas. Vimvitas Mortai," Grian said, one after the other, sending three consecutive spells at Seth, each deflecting off his armor and doing nothing. Each time a spell failed, the dark wizards face contorted further with rage. Seth could see that the frustration was causing him to lose focus. "Damn you, Time Weaver," he said, and stepped closer. "Obitas nexasa mortai."

A beam of black energy fired from the palms of his hands and struck Seth in the chest. He focused everything he had on absorbing the energy into the armor. As the energy moved from Grian into the crystal armor, the plates turned black and crumbled. By the time Grian was exhausted, Seth's armor was destroyed, but he was unharmed.

"Enough," Seth said, and swung a fist at Grian. Flames burst over his fist, and he struck the wizard, leaving a burn that blistered and charred the flesh on the left side of his face. Grian took a step back, stunned at the sudden attack. "That's for Malia, one of the bravest warriors Findoor has ever known."

Seth didn't wait for him to recover, but instead swung his other fist, striking him in the chest with another burst of flame. The hit caused Grian to stumble back and cry out. "That's for Findoor."

Confidence welled up inside Seth, and he stepped toward Grian, ready to hit him again. Grian was ready this time and raised his own hands. Both men launched spells at the same time, the energy clashing between them. Seth drew all the energy he could, putting every element into his spell, trying to over-power Grian. The dark wizard appeared to be doing the same, and both maintained shimmering streams of energy that sent sparks and waves of energy out in a circle around them.

Seth became aware that his friends were backing up away from the two of them, but couldn't let his focus stray from the contest between himself and his greatest foe. The streams grew as each of them poured more of themselves into their attacks, and the waves of energy flowing away from them sent rocks and debris away from them as well. Seth focused his eyes on Grian at the other end of the nexus and saw another face behind the dark wizard. It was the face of the old man with the red robes, and he was laughing as Seth weakened from the exertion.

Grian appeared to grow stronger, and took a step closer, focusing his attack and pressing forward. Seth faltered and backed up a step, his attention split between Grian and the old man feeding energy into the dark wizard.

"No," Seth said, and redoubled his effort, pulling everything he could into the attack. All eight elements came to him, and darkness surrounded the two of them as the energy blazed even brighter. Panic washed over Grian's face as the surge was more than he could handle. There was a sudden explosion, and the darkness melted away, along with the image of the old man. Grian flew back and landed on the ground.

Seth walked up to the wizard and lifted his hand, ready to deliver a killing blow. "This is better than you deserve," Seth said, as he moved to strike.

A sudden pain spread through Seth's uplifted arm. A small mark on his arm, like that of an eye, glowed with a gray light – the mark of Hadra. The light grew and the pain intensified until Seth lowered his fist. There was a flash of white light that blinded Seth, and he stumbled back a step. He heard shouts all around him, and became aware of something pressing against his back. When his vision cleared, he saw the sky overhead and he was lying on the ground. He looked at his wrist where the mark had been, but it was gone.

Hands reached down and took hold of Seth's arms to help him up. "Are you well?" He heard Malia ask.

"Yes," Seth said. "I think so."

His eyes focused and he allowed those around him to pull him to his feet. Malia was in front of him, and Serrin and Catrina were to either side of him. "Are you certain? You look deathly pale."

"Yeah. Yeah, I'm fine," he said, trying to look past Malia to the battlefield behind her. "Where is Grian?"

Her face darkened and she looked away. "We did not find his body, though with the amount of magical energy you threw at him, there is no way he could have survived."

"What about his army?" Seth asked, looking around. He could hear cheers rising up from all around him. Howls of delight from Narshuks and the crowing of the Fioraden told him that they were victorious before he heard an answer from those close to him.

"Destroyed," Malia said with relief. She took a step closer to Seth and looked into his eyes. He saw happiness in hers for the first time in a long time. Without saying a word, he leaned toward her and pressed his lips against hers. The warmth of her kiss lifted his spirits, settled his heart, and brought peace to his soul.

When they parted, he looked down at his wrist once more. He hadn't imagined it. The mark of Hadra that signified a debt to be paid to the goddess of shadow was now gone. The debt was settled, though he couldn't figure out how.

# Chapter 36 – Reprisal

"So what are you going to do now?" Cedric asked, peering through his black mask at Malia and Seth who stood next to him at Ceridan's crowning. Findoor Castle was still undergoing repairs, but even the work crews who had continued day and night stopped for the celebration. Ceridan passed the King's Trials on the first attempt, but did so only after Malia had refused, claiming she had no interest in ruling the kingdom she had fought so hard to free. The streets were decorated with banners and streamers, and wizards had placed multi-colored lights over every surface, making the city glitter and glow for their new King who would make his way up the main street and into the castle proper.

Inside the castle was no different, as wizards had worked to clean up and mend tapestries and make repairs so that Ceridan's day would be perfect. The throne room the three companions now stood in was also cleaned and decorated from top to bottom and censers of incense had been burned for days to rid it of the smell of death.

Seth flashed Cedric a smile and said, "I'm not sure. We've been thinking of heading east, to the Arvok Caldera and Alkirk Manor. It needs a lot of work, but it would be a great place to settle down for a while and start a family. Plus there's something I want to look in to there."

"Oh," Cedric said, his voice surprised. "My goodness, I hadn't realized things had gotten so serious between the two of you." He winked at Malia and smiled as her cheeks burned red.

"But of course, Cedric," she said. "Seth and I have not had a moment of peace to enjoy each other's company since he returned."

"Indeed," Cedric said. He looked to the doors of the throne room to see if Ceridan was coming yet. When he saw nobody approaching, and heard no cheers, he turned back to Seth. "My friend, I must ask of you one last favor."

"What is it, Cedric," Seth said. "Anything you want."

"I wish to return to your world." Seth looked at him with one eyebrow raised, and Cedric returned a serious look. "You heard me right. There is somebody there whom I wish to see again. Seeing the two of you together is making me all mushy inside, and so I must answer this call. If nothing else, it will settle my restless heart and give me a chance to gain new stories and songs to bring back to Galadir."

"Does this have something to do with the whole dragon thing?"

"Strictly speaking, I'm not allowed to talk about that. But yes. I gave up who I was to become who I am. I cannot remove the mask, because it hides who I was, in a much grander way than any normal costume could. The mask makes me human."

"So you've been banished for revealing who you were?"

"No," Cedric said, lying. "Well. Yes, perhaps. But only for a short while."

"How long?"

"Oh, only several hundred years," Cedric said with a grin. "In all fairness, I shouldn't have lost my temper like that. 'Tis nothing, really. I'll be back here and cooking up trouble in no time."

"I wish you had told us the truth to begin with," Seth said. "Things could have been different."

"What fun would that be?" Cedric asked, though he didn't expect an answer.

Their conversation was cut short by a burst of cheers that rose from onlookers in the hallway as Ceridan approached. When he walked through the door dressed in full regalia with red jacket, and a long red cloak with the Findoor crest on it, every person cheered him on to take the throne. Cedric remained at the back of the crowd, but Seth and Malia moved to the front and took their place to the left and right of the throne.

Ceridan's steps were calm and measured. His face was serene, with just a hint of a smile on his lips. Cedric thought he looked positively royal as he approached the throne, stepped up onto the platform with Seth and Malia's help, and turned to face the crowd.

Everyone in the room hushed and moved closer to the throne so that they could hear his words. The oath he pledged would be his promise to lead the kingdom to prosperity, and was a tradition of every King who ruled over the kingdom for as long as anyone could remember.

"Friends," Ceridan said, and spread his arms wide. "Join me today as a free people. Join me today in song and story. Never again shall this kingdom fall to tyranny or magic, for the people of this great kingdom have learned to live, love, and fight together in harmony. I cannot promise you that times will always be so happy as they are now, but I will promise you this: With each breath I take, and every measure of my being, I shall lead this kingdom in fairness, bring justice to those who do wrong, reward those who do right, and honor those who have come before us. Together, we will build a better, stronger, and brighter future. Together, we will celebrate our victories, mourn our losses, and learn from our mistakes. Findoor shall forevermore be free."

Ceridan's voice was impassioned and brought strength to those around him. Like a wave flowing through the room, people lifted their heads and shoulders high. Cedric felt himself perk up as he listened, and a single tear came to his eye that he allowed to fall beneath his mask. His heart was split in two as he longed to remain in Findoor.

He turned away from the throne and walked toward the door, leaving the people to celebrate their new King. He had hoped to leave unnoticed, but wading against a tide of people trying to get into the throne room was about as conspicuous as he could get. He managed to find his way to the front entrance of the castle proper, and then things got easier as the crowds thinned and he was able to move faster. When he reached the front gates of the castle, he walked outside onto the field and sat down, waiting for Seth and Malia who would eventually join him.

There was little in the way of comfort from the ground as the recent wars and neglect had destroyed most of the green that once surrounded the castle. The coming winter had claimed the leaves from most of the nearby trees, leaving Cedric no choice but to sit down beneath a barren tree and wait.

To Cedric's surprise, it wasn't long before Seth and Malia arrived. As Seth approached, he said, "I thought you would want to stay for the whole ceremony."

Cedric shook his head. "Nay. I find these occasions dreadfully boring. I thought you two would stay for the entire celebration. I just got comfortable." He patted the dirt to either side of himself and grinned.

"Oh yeah, you look right cozy," Seth said, and smiled back. "Are you ready to go?"

"I don't see how I could be any readier," Cedric said. "It's not like I have much to pack."

There was a feeling inside Cedric he couldn't place. It caused his heart to flutter with anticipation, and excited him. Seth must have noticed something as well, because he said, "Nervous?"

"Nervous. Perhaps," Cedric said. "It's not a feeling my kind is accustomed to."

Malia walked up next to him and offered him a hand to help him up. He accepted it, but when he was on his feet, she didn't release him. "Cedric, you shall do fine. Seth's world is a strange and wondrous place, but I am certain Alex will be happy to help you adjust."

"Suppose she's not interested in seeing me again. Then what do I do?"

"What you've always done," Seth said. "Find a way to survive."

The nervous feeling left his heart and he smiled at Seth and Malia. "I'm ready to go. Be good, you two."

Seth placed a hand on his shoulder and closed his eyes. There was a feeling like his insides were being twisted, but it was brief, and then there was bright sunlight and horseless carriages all around him. Seth was still standing before him, but had let go of his shoulder.

"If you don't mind, perhaps you could give me a hand in finding my bearings," Cedric said.

"I may be able to do you one better," Seth said. He reached into his pocket and pulled out a battered slip of paper with some writing on it. After reading it, he reached out, placed a hand on Cedric's shoulder again, and they teleported a second time.

5

Alex sat in her living room with her feet up after a hard day. She was browsing through some old pictures on her phone, and came across the ones she took of the strange men she encountered a few weeks back. Cedric and Jax. Her life had felt boring since then, when she learned that there was so much more than existed on Earth. Memories like that couldn't be erased by time.

The picture of Cedric made her sigh. She missed his awkward charm and quick wit. He was mysterious, and that alone was enough to keep her interested. He was from another world. Sadness crept over her as she realized that the picture before her was probably the last she would ever see of him.

With a press of a button, she turned off her phone and leaned her head back on the chair to relax. She rested for barely a minute before she heard a strange sound out front of her house. Something told her she needed to check it out.

She got up and rushed to her front window, and caught a glimpse of a dark form walking up her front step. Her heart skipped a beat as the doorbell rang, and she froze for a moment. *Don't be silly,* she thought to herself. *He's gone back to his own world.*

There was a nagging feeling at the back of her mind that she was wrong though. Without another thought, she raced to the door to see who was there. When she opened it, standing on her front porch was a man dressed all in black, who wore a cloak, and a mask over his face. The excitement overwhelmed her, and when she flung open the screen door, she almost knocked him down the steps. "Cedric," she shouted, and ran out to him.

As she threw her arms around him in a hug, he said, "I wasn't sure you would even remember me."

"Of course I remember you. You're the most unusual person I've ever met. I could never forget that. How are you? Oh my god, I have so many questions. What have you been up to? Where is Seth? Did you guys take care of that wizard?"

"Easy now," Cedric said. "I shall explain it to you in good time. For now, I require somewhere to stay. I'm going to be here for a while."

He flashed her a smile as she released him that told her she was in for another adventure. Somehow, that didn't seem like a bad idea.

§

Seth appeared under the tree where he left Malia. She smiled at him as he walked toward her and held her hand out to take his. "So that's it then," Seth said. "Cedric is in L.A. making a new life for himself. With Mom and Dad taking care of the Wizard High Council, I think Galadir is finally safe."

"I heard that Darian is considering taking the black seat on the council, and somebody is coming up from Astara to take the red seat." Malia looked into his eyes and appeared to be thinking deeply on something.

"What's the matter?" Seth asked.

"Well, with everybody else taking care of everything, I am feeling rather useless at the moment."

"No matter what, I will always need you," Seth said and hugged her tight.

"So are you going to whisk us away to Alkirk Manor then?"

"Actually," Seth said, with a serious look on his face, "I thought we'd walk." He released her from his embrace, backed up a step, and then turned toward the east. "There's a whole world out there that I've never seen, and I can't think of anyone else I would rather see it with."

Malia took his hand and the two of them began their long journey into the east, to their new home.

## A Word From The Author

I just want to get this out of the way right now: This is not the end. While Galadir appears to be safe from the clutches of Grian, who knows what vile wizards, monsters, or other dangers might be waiting to be discovered. It's a big world, and The Time Weaver Chronicles was just one of the many adventures to be had.

If you've stayed with me this far, I owe you my sincere gratitude. I do this for you. Every book takes well over six hundred hours to produce, and without your continued readership, I don't think I could do it. So thank you. You are truly one of Knight's Knights.

Writing is often touted as a solitary profession, but I don't think that could be farther from the truth. There are so many people who help and support me on a daily basis, that I couldn't possibly name them all. That said, here is my meager attempt at doing so. I'm truly sorry if I miss anyone.

First, thank you to my wife, whose keen eye seems to catch all of my missing apostrophes, extra hyphens, redundant sentences, and all the other errors that I would otherwise miss. She takes my books from an amateurish mess to a professionally finished manuscript. I couldn't do this without you, Claire.

Nancy, Chris, Brad, Mary, Jacky, Jennifer, Krysa, Melissa, Tim, Dave, Lisa and Terri: You guys are my beta team. You keep things real, and make sure that everyone is acting the way they should be acting, and the story flows the way it should flow. Behind every great author is an even greater beta team, and y'all are the greatest.

In my attempts to raise some money to help with my publishing costs, I ran an IndieGoGo campaign which was less than successful. Still, there were eight wonderful people who pledged their hard-earned money to help with my dream, and I will forever appreciate their kindness. So thank you to my eight wonderful IndieGoGo supporters. I am truly grateful for what you contributed.

Finally, thanks to all of my ABNA, Twitter, FaceBook, G+ and email followers. Y'all make it fun to be online, making me smile, liking my posts, sharing my blogs and just generally being supportive friends. I appreciate every minute you waste online with me.

When all is said and done, my goal is to entertain you, so if you are entertained: mission accomplished. I hope you'll find it in your heart to share my work with your friends, and maybe rave on your FaceBook about how much you love my books. That would be awesome. As an independent author, I truly couldn't do this without your help.

So what's coming next? I hope you'll stick around with me to read The Spell Breaker when it's done. I plan to have it ready for 2015 and it will be the beginning of a whole new trilogy set in Galadir featuring an assassin turned magic-absorbing super-villain. I've been having a great time writing it. After that? Who knows where the winds of Galadir will take us, but I do know this: This is not the end.

For the latest updates from Thomas A. Knight, visit:
http://thomasaknight.com

For additional works by Thomas A. Knight, visit:
http://www.amazon.com/author/thomasaknight